CW00675641

She who is Outside the Universe and Goes Upwards

PAUL LYONS

Published by self published, 2023.

SHE WHO IS OUTSIDE THE UNIVERSE AND GOES UPWARDS

First edition. July 9, 2023.

ISBN: 979-8223333562

Written by PAUL LYONS.

Also by PAUL LYONS

To Kalayani, my Auspicious Kali

'She is the World-Bewilderer. Her lustre is like a strong flash of young lightning; her murmur is sweet as the hum of love-crazed bees. She is beyond the universe, the One who goes upwards...'
Sat-Cakra-Nirupana Tantra

CHAPTER ONE

She burst from a doorway and spat on the footpath, a string of spittle trailing from her lips.

It took me an instant to register how beautiful she was; to notice that the jacket hanging over her shoulders covered a short, pink petticoat; and that all she had on her feet was a pair of Smurf slippers. The day was freezing. The shoppers on Kilburn High Road were all in scarves and woolly hats. My overcoat offered scant protection against the mid-December cold.

The door swung shut behind her and locked itself with a click, shutting her out on the pavement.

A piece of green cardboard, cut into a star shape, with a name scrawled on it in marker pen, was stuck to the intercom. She didn't buzz to be let back in. She stood gagging and glaring at *me*. I was no more than ten feet away from her, at the other end of a narrow aisle between the wire bins of two footpath displays, on one side heaped with shoes and trainers and on the other filled with bottles of detergent and toilet brushes, standing stock still gawking at her.

Her broad lips were moist at the corners where some pimples had been smothered with powder. When she scowled, a dimple, like a surgical incision, stood far out in either cheek. Her body was full and willowy. She was tall for an Asian woman.

I didn't move. It was a struggle to remember where I was going or that I had a meeting to attend.

I was blocking her way, so she pushed leftwards between the pound shop's bins of household merchandise. The wire baskets tilted and scraped as she barged them aside. Bottles of bleach jumped. A pack of washing-up pads fell onto the footpath. She didn't stop to pick it up. As she forced her way across the rows, squeezing between the browsing shoppers, her petticoat snagged on one of the bins.

2

She moved with a supple intensity and angry purposefulness that enthralled me. I found it impossible to move till I knew where she was going, what she wanted.

She grabbed a bottle of Listerine from a display bin. She twisted the cap off, thrust it to her lips, tipped her head back, and filled her mouth with the antiseptic. A blue trickle ran down her chin.

I felt giddy. A stinging heat was threading up my back from the base of my spine, twisting me off-balance.

A man hurried out of the shop. The manager. He'd caught her stealing. He yelled, "Hey! Natalie!"

She ignored him. She jerked her cheeks from side to side, swilling the Listerine round her mouth, and then spat the mouthful under the bin.

I was freezing. The stinging sensation coming up my back was sucking all my body heat from my chest and hands into my spine.

She screwed the lid back on the bottle and, taking the Listerine with her, headed back between the bins towards the door from which she'd emerged.

It opened.

A man stepped out, zipping up his parka. He was heavily built. A white scar on his scalp was visible through his crew cut.

Her voice was shocking.

"Fuck you mother!" She went for the man. People turned and looked. A bin tipped over. J-cloths spilled across the pavement as she rushed at the man. I thought she was going to hit him. "Cut you fuck cock!"

The guy fixed his eyes on the footpath and strode up the aisle between the bins. He pushed past me. His breath smelled of spirits and cigarette smoke. His parka reeked of air freshener. He hurried away up the footpath.

Natalie pressed the intercom buzzer. The speaker clicked and echoed.

I was desperate for her not to go in.

The door unlocked itself. She thrust it open. I glimpsed a hallway. A flight of stairs. She went in, and the door clicked shut behind her.

The stinging in my spine got stronger. I knew that I mustn't think about it. It was just shock, a trapped nerve, a disturbance in my inner ear. It was the cold. I'd come to too abrupt a halt rushing to my meeting. The stinging sensation had nothing to do with what I'd just witnessed. If I didn't ignore it it would overwhelm me. I had a meeting to attend. After the meeting, I was taking my staff and family out to a restaurant. I mustn't let my mind focus on the heat rising up my backbone.

It was no use. As my consciousness entered the burning thread, it grew bright. The stinging turned from heat to light. It became a shining hinge on which the whole of my being was turning towards something I couldn't comprehend. I was frightened I was going to lose my balance. I reached up to grab hold of the awning. Everything to my right—the bins, the bottles of detergent, the pound shop boss staring at me—was heavy and dense. Everything to my left—the shoes, the crowds of shoppers, the awning flapping in the wind—was light and insubstantial.

The stinging brightness was everywhere. The shining hinge was in everything. It was there, still turning, in the detergent bottles. In the heaped shoes. In the glass of the shop window. In the squeal of a bus braking. In the beating of the awning. In the greasy smell off the asphalt.

It became beautiful. The brightness was beautiful because it was a woman. How, or why, it was a woman, I couldn't tell. What woman, I'd no idea. She shone and stung. She was unapproachable.

She wasn't the woman in the pink petticoat. It had nothing to do with Natalie.

I felt a deep joy, more powerful than any happiness I'd ever known. I gazed at transcendence. I stood at the source of things. It was imperative I walk off, up the footpath to my car, get to my meeting, clinch the deal I was in the middle of making, and take my colleagues and family out for a celebratory meal. If I did, transcendence would stay with me. I'd remain in contact with the source. The unapproachable woman would always be there, here, inside me and outside me. If I walked down the aisle of bins, pressed the buzzer, went in the door, looked at Natalie's face again, I'd lose her. If I fucked Natalie, I'd lose everything.

The green star said: ORIENTAL BABE.

I pressed the buzzer. The speaker clicked and echoed.

"Yeah?!"

A woman's voice drowned the squeal of brakes and the hubbub of milling shoppers.

"I..."

"Second floor."

The door unlocked itself. I pushed it open and went in.

The stairs were steep. The carpet had come loose in places.

There were three doors on the second-floor landing. One of the doors stood open, access barred by a security grille.

A big blonde woman looked me up and down through the bars. I was in my business suit. I'd polished my shoes that morning. She unlocked the grille.

"This way."

She led me down a corridor past the open door of a living room. A cigarette smouldered in an ashtray balanced on the arm of a chair. A TV was turned up loud.

"She's just getting ready."

The woman sounded pissed off.

She showed me into a bedroom and then went out, shutting the door behind her.

The room was in deep shadow. A pink lampshade stood on a dressing table. A fan heater roared in the gap between the bed and the wall.

I wondered if I should take my clothes off or wait till Natalie came. I went and stood in front of the fan heater.

The room smelled of air freshener, the same fragrance I'd sniffed on the man's parka as he bolted past me, a sweet heady jasmine. It didn't smother a sour nylon stench from the zebra-striped bedspread with the fresh white towel spread out on it.

I was shivering. It felt chillier here in the bedroom than out on the footpath.

I looked at my watch. My meeting was in Notting Hill Gate. I had ten minutes to get there. A quarter of a million pounds worth of work depended on the presentation I was supposed to be giving.

I heard the springy echo of high heels on laminated floorboards.

The minute she entered the room, everything became simple. I wanted her more than I'd wanted anything in my life.

She looked me up and down, gauging whether I was another psycho. There was a red mark on her chin where the guy in the parka's fingers had forced her mouth open.

She nodded at her cleavage, her petticoat, her legs.

"Okay?" She swayed on her high heels. I smelled beer. She hadn't looked drunk down on the footpath, rampaging between the bins, but she was half cut. "Alright?" I could hear that she didn't speak much English. The ups and downs of an inflected language broke up her syllables, as if there were eggshells cracking in her throat. "Okay?" I realised she wanted me to express approval of her body. She pulled the petticoat over her head. She was breath-taking. Her breasts were taut and full. Her skin was the colour of light honey. Her legs were long and shapely. There were stretch marks above her hips, like water marks on brown satin. The V of her thong cut into her abdomen below a thick, red welt, about four inches long. "Alright?" she asked again, this time with a trace of menace. She was gorgeous, but there were customers for whom a Caesarean scar was unacceptable.

"Yes."

No wonder she was angry. She was stunningly beautiful. She was special. She was meant for a consort for kings and movie stars, but something had gone terribly wrong.

"What you want do?" My mind went blank. "Oral, forty. Sex, fifty. Don do anal. Half hour, eighty. One hour, hundred twenty."

I just wanted to be in the same place where she was.

"An hour." I opened my wallet. I'd brought a thousand pounds with me. After the meeting I was taking my staff and family out for a celebratory meal. I only had fifties. I gave her a hundred and fifty. "Keep the change."

She didn't say thank you.

She pointed at my coat and scarf.

"Take off!"

She rushed out of the room with the money.

I remembered to switch my phone off. I removed my clothes and heaped them on a chair. I pulled off my singlet and stepped out of my underpants.

I looked at the pile of clothes.

They were over-and-done-with. They were already ended—dead. My underpants were real enough, but by the time they reached my eyes they were finished, long gone, in the past.

I told myself it was just the cold, a nerve pinching at the base of my spine, the ringing in my inner ear.

It was the same with the room. The light that brought the pink lampshade and the zebra-striped bedspread to my eyes was the fastest thing there is, but the lampshade and bedspread themselves were so far back in the past, I could see where they'd ended. I heard the fan heater roaring, but it was roaring an eternity ago—in my past, and no one else's. That was the terrible thing. This visible fact— that objects, smells, sounds, even the things I touched, were done with, were physically over— was my fact and mine alone. The room freshener fizzed in my nostrils, a sickening jasmine, but all I could smell was the fact that even the fizzy fragrance was long gone, done-with, odourless. By the time I registered it, even my own body, the thump of blood in my chest, the hammering in my skull, were so in the past, they felt as dead as my heap of clothes. Only the thread of light was alive. The stinging brightness alone was real. And it wasn't just a pinched nerve. It was something far more powerful than a ringing in my inner ear.

I reached down and tried to figure out how to switch the fan heater off.

She was back.

"Okay?"

She undid her bra, stepped out of her thong.

She saw me fussing with the fan heater.

She smiled.

"Cold! Fleezing!"

She stooped supplely, and turned the fan heater up.

She pointed at my socks.

"Okay!"

I took off my watch and placed it on top of the heap of clothes. I was four minutes into my hour.

"What you wan do?"

Having sex was out of the question.

I shrugged.

"Erm. Just talk."

Then I realised I had no clothes on. She thought I was a weirdo. She shrugged.

"Lie down. Do massage. Can talk same same."

I lay on the towel and stared up at the ceiling. A length of disconnected electric cord hung from the plaster above me.

She took a bottle of baby oil from the cupboard beside the bed.

"Over."

I rolled over onto my face.

"What you wan talk about?"

We'd covered the weather. We'd agreed that her body was alright.

Her caesarean scar! She had a child. The welt was still red and raw. Her baby must be very young. How come she was working like this so soon after her operation... perhaps I could ask her... no. The scar embarrassed her. She saw it as a disfigurement. She hated the beautiful water marks on her perfect flanks. Her baby was the last thing on earth she wanted to talk about with a customer.

The bed sank. She climbed above me, placed one knee on either side of me, and landed on my backside.

Her pussy jammed against my coccyx. Her labia were squashed under the weight. She gave off a sharp, dry heat.

She had HIV. That was why she was drunk at three o'clock in the afternoon. She was dying of AIDs. If I had a pimple or an open sore, I'd die as well.

She tipped oil on my back and began to massage. She was sitting on the trapped nerve in my bum.

Her thumbs gouged and slipped. They probed and battered my backbone. It was some sort of osteopathic, 'deep' technique she was too drunk to do properly.

Her pussy jerked backwards and forwards against my coccyx as she worked on me. Her labia spread and moistened. She'd smelled my fear. She knew the reason I was afraid. It turned her on. It made her even angrier. She was slipping around all over my backside.

She forced the heel of her hand into the nape of my neck, overbalanced, and caught me in the ear.

"Sorry."

She rubbed her pussy where the stinging brightness rose from the base of my spine.

"Relax."

Her voice had broken edges and harsh corners.

"Over!"

I did as she ordered.

She glanced at my erection.

"Wan do without?"

"What?"

Our eyes met.

"Fifty pound extra. Do without."

"Without what?"

Her glance shone and stung. She was unapproachable.

"Condom. Fifty extra. Okay?"

"Okay."

She reached backwards and pulled my trousers out of the heap of clothes on the chair. She found my wallet, took out a fifty, opened the drawer of the bedside cupboard, threw the banknote into the drawer, and took out a tube of KY.

She knelt above me and rubbed jelly onto her pussy. The KY glistened in the shaved bristles of her bush.

She grabbed my cock, and brushed lubricant onto the tip with her labia.

"Uh!"

The bristles were prickly.

She dropped onto me like a window with a broken sash cord.

I was separated from my body. Instead of exploding into her, my arousal was flowing backwards, up my spine, away from her.

She jerked around on my cock. She threw her head back and slit her eyes at the ceiling. Her hairclip came loose and knocked against her ear.

"... Yes... yes..."

I wondered if she'd felt the same thing I did—that the room was long gone before it ever reached her eyes. Lying under her, I was miles back in the past, completely dead. Even her own heartbeat and the thoughts in her head came too late to be alive. Only the stinging brightness was real.

Her hair clip fell off as she jerked her body backwards and forwards.

"... Yes... yes..."

She wanted to get it over and done with. So did I. I felt as if my cock had been sprayed with pipe freeze and disconnected.

"... Oh... oh..."

She faked an orgasm. Anger glinted in the caked slits of her eyes. She was dying, and she was taking me with her.

I took the hint. I lifted her with my hips and pretended to climax.

A tremendous pressure gripped my neck and the back of my head.

She jumped off me and rushed to the bedside table. She tore a handful of tissues from a box and grinned at me. She stuffed the tissues into her pussy, as if lavish cum were running down her legs.

She dragged the towel from under me and wrapped it around her.

"Go washing, okay?"

Her eyes were wild. Getting to the bathroom was a matter of life and death. I hadn't ejaculated but she was still scared. She was in the same life-and-death rush as when she'd barged through the bins to the Listerine. I was no different from the man in the parka.

It had lasted seven or eight minutes, and cost me two hundred pounds. I hadn't even climaxed. The pressure gripping my neck and the back of my head was only getting stronger. The stinging sensation at the base of my spine burned its way up my back, vertebra by vertebra. The impulse that had made me walk between the bins and press the buzzer was over. My wanting her more than I'd ever wanted anything in my life was gone. I was back in the here and now, but the here and now was over too. The here and now was an eternity ago. My scalp prickled. I'd had sex with her without a condom. My sexual relationship with my wife was over. I needed to get out the door and get to my meeting. Except my spine was a hinge on which everything was turning towards something incomprehensible. Only the shining thread was real.

She hesitated at the door.

"Come see I again?"

She'd seen a lot of money in my wallet. My clothes were expensive.

I looked around for my trousers. I was as anxious to get out of the room as she was. 'Just talking' hadn't worked. I knew I mustn't answer. I had to say no, I'm not coming to see you again.

I pointed at her belly.

"You've got a child?"

Her hand flew to where the scar was, under the towel.

"Chai. Little girl."

My trousers had fallen on the floor when she took the money. I picked them up.

"Here?"

"Thailand. I Thai."

Her fingers slipped under the towel. The towelling rucked and bobbled. She was rubbing at the welt! Kneading it with her fingernails!

"How old?"

"Four."

It was impossible. It couldn't be true. The scar looked as though it had been stitched up yesterday. She wouldn't stop picking at it under the towel.

"Four?"

She smiled.

"Chai."

The pressure in my head exploded. Pinpoints of light filtered backwards through my skull. Natalie was immaterial. Her pink lipstick vanished into her smile. Her eyeshadow couldn't keep up with the tapering lift of her eyes. The pinpoints of light came from her face and caught in my brain as they went through me, like diamonds in a sieve.

"Who looks after her?"

"I mum."

The doorbell rang. I heard the blonde woman speak through the intercom to someone down on the street. There was a brief interrogation, then a buzz as she released the door catch. Two floors down, the street door closed. The guy was early.

"She name Nok."

"Nok?"

"Nok, same 'bird'."

'Nok, same 'bird'' welled up inside me. It flooded my throat, as if I'd spoken the words myself. Eggshell cracked and spilled in my larynx. It broke my heart. I'd done something irrevocably wrong. I might even pay for it with my life. But as 'Nok, same 'bird'' rose up inside me, I knew that it came from the source of all joy.

I buttoned my shirt.

She refastened the towel.

"You wan see photo?"

"Okay."

She opened the door, checked the corridor, and slipped out, shutting the door behind her.

Footsteps reached the top of the stairs.

I hurried into my shoes.

She came back with a wallet of photos. She sat on the edge of the bed and flicked through the plastic sleeves. She hadn't washed yet. She hadn't had time to go to the bathroom. She was showing me her photographs first.

She held the wallet up at the photo she wanted.

"Nok!"

A small Asian girl in a blue and white school uniform. Her hair cut short, pudding-basin style.

"She goes to school?"

"Room One."

I heard the blonde woman greet the next customer at the grille. There was a jangle of keys. Footsteps passed our bedroom. A door opened further down the corridor. The maid deposited the man in the neighbouring bedroom. The door closed.

"Nok very smart girl."

She bent her head over the snapshot. She smoothed the plastic sleeve with her fingers.

"Nok like eat seven."

"Seven?"

"Eleven."

"Oh. I see."

She smiled. She was the shining hinge on which everything turned. She released the room from its ugliness. She set me free from the horror of what I'd just done. I could get on with my life — go to my meeting, then home to Islington, the restaurant —

as much as the pink lampshade went on with its life, and the day outside went on with its life, and the woman wrapped in the towel, desperate to get to the bathroom, went on with her life, except I was in love with her.

There was a rap on the door. The blonde woman peeked in.

"Oops! Sorry!"

Natalie snapped the wallet shut.

I got the rest of my clothes on.

"Well..."

She stood up. She tucked the towel more tightly around her breasts. She gestured at the neighbouring bedroom.

"One customer. I finish. You wait?"

I put on my watch. My meeting had started twenty minutes ago. There was still time for me to get to the office and make up an excuse for being late.

"Come see man with I?"

For a second, I thought she was talking about the guy waiting in the other bedroom.

"Man?"

We'd booked an early table for our celebratory dinner. The meeting would finish around five thirty or six. Then I was supposed to get back to Islington, pick up my wife and children, and take them on to the restaurant.

Her eyes were grave.

"See man. Is importing."

Her pimp. He'd beat me up and take the money she'd seen in my wallet.

"Now?"

"Mm."

It was as if we'd been together for years.

"Where?"

"Earls Court."

I looked at my watch. It was twenty to four. The traffic would be getting heavy. It would take at least an hour to get to Earls Court. An hour to drive back to Islington. I'd promised to be home by six. If I skipped the meeting, I might just make it.

"How long will it take?"

She shrugged.

"Don know."

She had a right to as much of my time as she liked.

"Maybe he there. Maybe he not. Must wait."

"Okay. What about...?"

I nodded at the next bedroom.

She grinned.

"No be long."

Natalie took me into the living room, introduced me to the blonde woman—Sandra— and rushed off to the bathroom.

"Just a minute, Jim."

Sandra, too, hurried out.

I heard room freshener being sprayed in the bedroom, a door opening—"She's just getting ready"— a glimpse of a grey overcoat going in.

"Oops!"

Sandra pulled the living room door shut.

I heard her deposit the guy in the first bedroom and close the door.

By the time she got back to the living room, she was out of breath.

"Alright, Jim?"

Sandra dropped into an armchair and picked up a mug of tea balanced on the arm next to an ashtray with a fag smouldering in it. A mobile phone and a magazine were balanced on the other arm.

Natalie's heels clicked from the bathroom to the bedroom.

"I'd make you a cuppa, Jim," said Sandra, sipping from her mug, "but she'll only be five minutes."

"Thanks. I'm fine."

Sandra was a handsome woman, fleshy faced, with dark bags under her eyes. She looked to be in her mid-forties. Her yellow beehive ballooned precariously up out of grey roots.

The door opened, Natalie hurried in, handed Sandra a wad of twenties, and rushed back to the bedroom. Sandra put the money in a bum bag strapped around her waist.

The stupidity of what I was doing hit me. I had a good marriage. Melissa and I had always been faithful to one another. She and the children trusted me. Ralph and Meredith would be appalled. That was before I even thought about the possibility of my having HIV.

The TV was switched up loud. Sandra was watching Teletubbies. Tinky Winky, Dipsy, and Noo-noo weren't quite so cute at high volume.

I looked out the window. It was getting dark.

Teletubbies rounded off the afternoon programmes for pre-schoolers. It must be nearly four.

"Natalie's a beautiful girl."

Sandra had a strong northern accent.

"Yes."

"She's new."

She made 'new' sound like 'panting virgin.'

"Just come in. She's Japanese."

Natalie mustn't have had time to tell Sandra that she'd already told me that she was Thai. Maybe 'Japanese' was what the customers preferred to hear, but Natalie had forgotten in her rush.

Four o'clock was too late for me to turn up at the meeting. I had to go straight home. Melissa had taken the afternoon off to get ready for our night out. If I went home now, I could speak to her before the pressure to lie became too great.

The phone on the arm of Sandra's chair rang.

She picked up.

"Hello?" her Newcastle accent turned into a wobbly Oxford plum. "Can I help you?"

She smiled at me as she spoke to the man on the other end of the line.

"Oh, hello, Martin. Look. I'm terribly sorry, Martin," her smile grew conspiratorial, "but I'm afraid Natalie's not here right now. Yes. I know you booked. I'm ever so sorry," she winked at me. "But something's come up."

I was going to be rolled. I was going to get beaten up. Sandra was in on it, too. Natalie was going to take me down to a room in Earls Court, where her pimp was waiting. He'd bash me and steal the rest of my money. They couldn't do it here. It'd upset the punters.

"Yes. I know you booked. Look. I'm really sorry, Martin. She'll be here next Wednesday, alright?"

I wondered how many other men had sat here being winked at, while they waited to go down to Earls Court to see a man. Natalie hadn't mentioned our trip to Earls Court when she'd introduced me to Sandra, yet Sandra was putting Martin off even though he'd booked. Sandra knew that the man in the bedroom was Natalie's last customer. Natalie must have told her about our trip to Earls Court when Natalie left the room to get the photos. It was time to stand up and leave, get out of here quick, while Natalie was still busy.

"That was Martin," said Sandra, putting the phone down.

Teletubbies had finished. A toothy CBBC presenter was introducing the after-school programs. Natalie had been with the customer for nearly twenty minutes.

Missing the meeting was a disaster. I'd only had to turn up, give the presentation, and a quarter of a million pounds' worth of consultancy work was in the bag. Bernard and Pippa would be furious. We were an up and coming company with a growing reputation for cutting edge engineering solutions. We'd been so certain of winning the contract we'd already booked the restaurant.

"The other girls are all jealous of Natalie," said Sandra. "She steals their regulars."

"I bet."

"The customers all want to give Natalie their number."

At least I hadn't made that mistake.

"The boss don't like it when the customers give Natalie their number." I almost heard the 'Oops!' "Natalie thinks it's a hoot, but. The minute they're out the door, she deletes."

I wondered why it was necessary for them to lie—about Natalie deleting customers' numbers, about Natalie's being from Japan. Was Japan somehow more desirable than Thailand? Safer? I wasn't the first man she'd taken down to Earls Court.

Outside the window, the sky was black. The murmur of slow-moving traffic filtered star-wards through a penumbra of streetlamps.

Sandra glanced at her watch.

"Do you want that cup of tea, Jim?"

'Neighbours' had started. There wasn't even time to get to Earls Court and back.

"No, thank you. I'm fine."

I decided to leave. I had to get out of here. Natalie was taking ages in the bedroom. Half past six was the cut off time for my getting home. Melissa knew I'd had a meeting. She knew that the presentation had been scheduled for three thirty and would have been over by five thirty, six at the very latest. If I got back to Islington by six thirty, I wouldn't have to lie to her. I'd be able to walk in, apologise for running late, and whisk them off to the restaurant without going into any explanations, except... then I'd have to make up some story about why I hadn't been at the meeting.

Sitting here was crazy. They were setting me up. They were going to roll me. Natalie's pimp would beat me up and steal my money. There'd be no hiding it from Melissa and the children, if I ended up in hospital. If I made it home at all, that was.

I wanted Natalie so much, it hurt. I'd never wanted anything so much in my life as I wanted her right now. That didn't mean I shouldn't stand up, walk out the door, and never come back.

I got to my feet. If the grille was locked, I'd insist Sandra open it for me.

The stinging brightness was out of control. It had been out of control for almost two full hours. The base of my spine ached. There was a feverish crick where my spine met my neck. The shining thread was growing finer and sharper—and somehow less physical—as it went upwards into my head, as if it were a mind beyond my mind that knew things I didn't know, things that it insisted I see. Those things were everywhere, not just here in this shabby flat. They'd still be there for me to know, out in the darkness and the traffic, in my car, driving back to Islington— a woman shining and stinging, unapproachable— even if I never saw Natalie again.

I heard the bedroom door open. There was a murmur of voices in the hallway. A farewell. Natalie's clashing monosyllables. The man, effusive. A clang as she shut the grille behind him.

The bathroom door opened and closed. I heard the jet of a shower.

I sat down again.

"Perhaps I will have that cuppa."

Natalie came in half an hour later. She'd sensed, in the bedroom, that I was in a hurry, and deliberately taken her time showering.

She was wearing jeans, a white golf shirt, and trainers. She'd washed her hair. Her long black hair hung round her face in a wet tangle. She'd taken her make-up off. Her cheekbones shone. The mark of the man's fingers on her jaw had turned to a child's strawberry. Without powder, the pimples at the corner of her mouth drew her smile back into swampy depths.

"Sorry long time. Must making clean."

She disappeared into the kitchen and came back with two cans of beer.

We drank beer while she brushed her hair. She only brushed it; she didn't dry it. Wind rattled the window. It was freezing outside. She'd catch a chill.

She glanced at Sandra.

"Ring Lee?"

Sandra gave her a worried look.

"Yeah. Better."

Sandra picked up the phone and dialled a number. I realised that Lee must be Natalie's pimp. They were alerting him, telling Lee to get ready.

"Hello? Lee? Yeah. Sorry. Lee, look…"

There were no winks or conspiratorial smiles this time. Lee was not a disappointed customer. Sandra was scared stiff of Lee.

"Look, Lee. Natalie's not feeling well." She held Natalie's eye. "Yeah, Natalie's real sick, Lee." It was the signal that we were on our way. "She can't see the customers looking like this, Lee. I've told her to go home."

Natalie had stopped brushing. She looked as nervous as Sandra. She tried to smile at me but didn't quite manage it.

There'd been a moment's tenderness in the bedroom. She liked me. Perhaps she'd even felt the stinging brightness and knew that nothing else was real, and felt bad about setting me up for her pimp to roll.

I mustn't go with her. I'd make my excuses and leave.

"Will ya send Carla? Or do you want me to close?"

Sandra's bitten fingernails drummed the arm of the chair.

"Okay, Lee. I'll wait." Natalie's eyes were tense. "Yeah. An hour. If Carla's not here in an hour, Lee, I'll close."

It was a signal. The drive to Earls Court would take about an hour.

"Look, Natalie," I said, "I think I'll..."

Natalie wasn't there. There was a noise in the kitchen. The fridge door closing. She came back with four more beers.

"Okay. We go?"

She settled into the seat beside me and opened another can. She had a drink problem.

"BMW!" She noted the Dakota leather upholstery, glanced up at the glass sunroof taking the frozen weight of the night. "Sport Coupe!" She knew upmarket cars. She touched the new leather. "Nice."

I could feel her backpedalling, wondering perhaps if there wasn't more than the eight hundred pounds she'd seen in my wallet to be had if she stuck with me for a while. Her need for money was urgent. A gambling debt? Crack? HIV medication? Lee? She had to get some cash right now, tonight. But she liked my BMW. She knew about cars. She felt at home in this one. Perhaps she liked me, too. We'd talked about Nok. I could feel her wondering if she wouldn't be better off hooking me long-term, getting it together. Except... now it was too late. They'd already rung Earls Court. Lee was expecting us.

We got caught in the rush-hour traffic. There was a jam on Edgware Road, a tailback at the turn onto the Westway. We inched under the overpass and came to a standstill at the junction of Praed Street.

Natalie looked at her watch. I wondered if she was having a struggle with her conscience. She'd felt it, too—diamonds streaming from her face, 'Nok, same 'bird' welling up inside her, her spine a shining hinge on which everything turned.

She opened another beer. She offered it to me.

"Want?"

"Not when I'm driving."

Neon signs climbed the darkness, gaudy clowns on unfooted ladders. Above the stacked chairs in the roped-off pavement restaurants, exploding pineapples and brimming flutes braved the cold in fizzing blues, whites, and golds.

The traffic didn't move.

I was going to be very late getting back to Islington, if I got back at all. Melissa, Meredith, and Ralph were sitting there now, waiting for me. I wouldn't be able to make up some white lie about the meeting running overtime and whisk them off, because Bernard and Pippa would be at the restaurant by now. They'd be furious. They'd tell Melissa that I hadn't turned up at the presentation. The meeting had gone pear shaped. We'd lost a quarter of a million pounds' worth of work. The staff would be there to celebrate, and there'd be nothing to celebrate. I couldn't turn up knocked about, with no money. If I had HIV, there wasn't a lie in the world that would stand up.

Snap!

Another can opening.

"Who's this guy we're going to see?"

"Just man, honey. Is importing."

Her eyes narrowed, cruising the restaurants and locked-up office foyers. She looked tough, with her naked face and wet hair soaking the shoulders of her T-shirt. She was tough, but she still had to steel herself for the coming rendezvous.

"Lee?"

"Vic."

"Not Lee?"

"No. Lee boss. Man is Vic."

"Vic?"

"How you say? 'Vics'?"

She was fidgeting with the hem of her golf shirt. Pulling it up, and tucking it back into the waist of her jeans.

"You want?"

She held out the can.

Her other hand was down inside her jeans, where the caesarean scar was, picking at the welt.

"Want?"

Two policemen were walking up the opposite footpath.

I held the can low. Beer fizzed onto the floor. I took a sip and gave it back to her. Our eyes met, skidded apart.

One of the signs, a neon flower— the casino? a florist?— opened a golden calyx in the darkness.

Natalie knew a place to park on a back street off Earls Court Road. Apparently she'd only been in England a fortnight, but she was already familiar with the area. She led me through dead ends and passageways to a restaurant on the corner of the main drag.

It was a Thai restaurant, the Sawaddee Bee Mai. A life-size Buddha stood in the shoe-box porch, a bouncer refusing the cold admittance with a gilded palm.

I looked at my watch. It was ten past six.

The restaurant was empty. Natalie spoke with a waiter. He nodded, took us to a table, and brought us each a beer.

We drank in silence.

A man was setting up a karaoke player on a tiny stage. The kitchen door swung open and the smell of barbecued chili wafted out.

Some prawn crackers arrived with the next round of beer.

I stood.

"Where you go?"

Her voice was sharp, proprietorial.

"I need to make a call."

Outside, it seemed to have got colder. In the gutter, the wind dismantled a Chinese newspaper.

I rang Melissa. The instant she picked up, before she could speak, I blurted:

"I'm on my way. I'm running late. I..."

"Jim. Where are you?"

I heard the anxiety in her voice. A gust of warmth, a living brilliance, our kitchen, came down the line along with her anxiety.

"I'm on my way."

"Bernard's here. He said you didn't turn up for the meeting."

"Bernard?"

"Jim. What's happened? Bernard says the meeting went badly. Arkwright walked out."

"Look. It's Okay. I'll be with you. Half hour, I'll..."

I pressed disconnect. I hadn't invented a story. Being late wasn't a lie. I hadn't committed myself to deception. When I got home, I could still speak with her. Tell her the truth.

I hurried inside to get my coat.

A man sat at the table with Natalie. He wore a white shirt and black trousers, the same as the waiters wore. He sat listening to what Natalie was telling him. His occasional curt nod to her torrent of Thai wasn't the nod of a man taking an order.

"Jim, this Soom Bon."

He was Asian, about fifty years old, with thinning hair, and a long, hollowed-out face. His face looked as if it hadn't seen the sun in a long while. He glanced up at me, haughty, vacant. Vic, Lee, Soom Bon, he had his choice of names.

He wasn't big enough to give me a shoeing. His thin arms and pigeon chest weren't going to knock me around. He was a blade man. I could see it in his eyes. He was carrying.

"Soom Bon. This Jim...?"

Natalie paused.

I said:

"...Bright."

As soon as I told her, I knew it was a mistake.

"This Jim Bright."

My mobile rang. Melissa. I switched off.

I shook hands with Soom Bon. His fingers were clammy. The sleeves of his shirt were buttoned at the wrist. The whites of his eyes were hepatitis yellow. The guy was a junkie. His sunless complexion said that maybe he'd even done a bit of time recently.

He led us through the kitchen and up some stairs at the back to the second floor.

"Natalie. What's going on?"

She was too tense to answer.

She had a habit. She'd caught HIV from the needle, not a customer. The beer was keeping her going—only just—till her next fix. She shared the spike with Soom Bon. A few minutes more, and she'd be high.

For a clip and roll artist, Soom Bon wasn't doing too well. All the money he took must have gone on drugs.

His tiny room had been turned into a bedsit, with a cooker and a sink in the corner, and a table and one armchair crowded next to his single bed. His eighteen inch TV sat on the table, presumably to save floor space. A row of unframed family photos stood on top of the wall-mounted gas fire, curled up from the heat. Through grubby glass, that shook every time a bus changed gear, a carton of milk kept cool out on the crusty windowsill.

I eased into the armchair, my knees up against his bed. Natalie and Soom Bon sat facing each other on the strip of floor. I wondered if they were going to shoot up.

I was appalled by what I'd just done. Melissa would be out of her mind with worry. Disconnecting on her was unforgivable. Melissa would be trying to ring me right now, as I sat here with my phone turned off.

It was only two paces to the door. Soom Bon was down on the floor, sitting cross-legged. He didn't look too fit. Even if he pulled a knife on me, I might be able to make it out of the room.

Soom Bon reached under the bed. The sleeves of his waiter's shirt tugged at his wrists.

He pulled out a long, flat piece of wood, like an offcut of fence paling, its splintery grain silver with age. The plank had a grid of lines inked on it, with faded drawings in the squares of the grid.

Natalie squeezed my knee.

"Must give two hundred."

She knew there was much more than two hundred in my wallet. She wanted Soom Bon to get a look at my money first.

"Who is this guy?"

"He Vic."

"I thought his name was Soom Bon."

"No. He Vics."

"Vics?"

"How you say...," she frowned, "... a... 'Vics'?"

"A witch?"

She nodded.

The guy was a sorcerer.

I laughed out loud.

She shook her head. She was deadly serious. She was more scared now than she'd been in the flat, while Sandra was talking to Lee. Lee was just her boss. He beat girls up for sloping off with customers, but Soom Bon was even scarier than Lee.

"He can see life before."

"Before what?"

"Re...in... re...in..."

"Reincarnation?"

"Chai."

The two hundred pounds was so that the sorcerer could uncover the secrets of her past lifetimes. She wasn't going to have me beaten up after all. She was just using me to get a free reincarnation reading.

I couldn't make fun of her. Her face was tight with fear. She had 'sex without' for an extra fifty quid. She could handle the man in the parka. Nothing in this life scared her, but her past reincarnations were petrifying.

I took out my wallet and gave Soom Bon four fifties. He tucked them in the pocket of his waiter's shirt.

He blew some dust off his piece of wood. Business had been slow.

It was nearly seven. I wondered how long her former reincarnations were going to take, how many of them there were, the number of different people she'd been stretching back into the past. It had nothing to do with me. Everything is past, even the here and now. Soom Bon's milk carton trembling out on the windowsill was so far back in the past I could see where it had already ended. The light that carried his curling photographs and his greasy TV screen to my eyes was the fastest thing there is, yet his photos and TV screen were already as over and done with as Natalie's former reincarnations. It was ridiculous. Only the thread of light was alive. The stinging brightness alone was real. Buses roared past outside, but the roaring was an eternity ago—in my past, and no one else's. That was the terrible thing. This visible fact—that objects, smells, sounds, even the things I touched, were done with, were physically over—was my fact and mine alone. Even Natalie, sitting cross-legged on the floor, even my own body, the thump of blood in my chest, the hammering in my skull, were over and done with, so far back in the past no reincarnation-reading witch could ever find them.

Soom Bon took a barber's razor from the washstand.

Natalie bent forward. Her hair fell around her face. It had dried dense and crackly in the car.

Soom Bon cut off a length, tied it in a knot, and put it in one of the squares on his board. The knot of hair looked very black and alive against the faded ink.

"Honey!"

I felt an acute reluctance.

She snapped her fingers.

"HONEY!"

"I thought he was doing your lives. Not mine."

"Must do together!"

The razor didn't look too clean. I stared at Soom Bon's jaundiced eyes and hollow cheeks.

I bent forward. The razor touched my scalp somewhere behind my ear. My hair's short and wiry. The blade didn't feel too sharp. He had to scrape to get some hair. He cut me.

"Sorry, sir."

There was a roll of toilet paper on the table. Soom Bon tore off a length and handed it to me.

He ran his finger along the blade, collecting my grey locks on a red fingertip, kneaded my hair into a scut, and placed it on the grid. Sitting on its inked symbol, it looked like a fur ball the dog's sicked up.

I dabbed at my scalp with the toilet tissue. Natalie rubbed my knee.

"Can see you I live before. Two gether!"

We were getting a him-n-her reading.

The witch stared at the board and began to move his lips.

Downstairs, the karaoke started up.

Soom Bon and Natalie spoke Thai. The reading took over an hour.

When we finally made it back to the restaurant, the clock behind the bar said ten past eight.

Beer and food—spring rolls, king prawns, pork sticks in coconut sauce— sat waiting on our table. Natalie had ordered food before we went upstairs.

Green curry and spareribs arrived before we even sat down. The kitchen was in sync with the witch's bedsit.

Boiled eggs in tamarind sauce. Grilled fish, spitting in oil. Tom yum soup on a spirit lamp. Raw beef diced in blood—'*laarp*'— which Natalie tucked into, but warned me not to try.

Her eyes shone.

"Soom Bon say life before, you I love two gether!"

I'd had a feeling he'd say that.

"Life before you I love big *big*!"

Her eyes sparkled. I didn't have the heart to tell her Soom Bon was a con man.

The restaurant had filled up. The smell of beer and wine locked horns with the melted-plastic-pong of singed chili. The karaoke was too loud.

A party of Thai men in business suits had shoved three tables together and were taking it in turns to go up on the tiny stage and belt out Thai pop songs.

A group of Australian tourists—the men in rugby jerseys, the women in ski knits—were crowded in near Natalie and me.

The Aussies were getting into the swing of the karaoke, nodding along and applauding the songs loudly. It was only Earls Court, but they'd stumbled across a native village on their package tour.

A big bloke with peroxide blonde hair and a sunburned face was giving Natalie the eye, as helplessly attracted as I'd been standing on the footpath outside the door with the green star on it. He was young and well built. He was close enough for me to be able to see the confidence of youth sparkle in his blue, troubled eyes.

The boss of the Thai businessmen was up on the stage, the microphone in his hand.

"This song called..." He looked like one of those Asian executives made in the Triads-in-suits mould. "... 'Summer Holiday'!"

The Aussies cheered.

"Cliff Richard!"

"Go for it, sport!"

I'd only ever seen karaokes hunkered in the corner of draughty bars, competing unsuccessfully with the sports screen. This karaoke was rocking.

The little hard nut Thai business guy was going on a summer holiday... His colleagues clapped along to the beat, tough, no-nonsense execs letting their hair down. *The hard nut had no more work for a week or two...* His staff sang along with their boss.

Natalie smiled at the Aussie guy. He turned crimson.

Sir Cliff wobbled to a razor-eyed crescendo, *he was making his dreams come true...*

"He sing good," said Natalie. "Sing English very good!"

For she and you... For... she... and... you...

There was a tumult of applause as the singer sat down.

One of the Thais, in a tan suit, drunker than his colleagues, was grinning at the girlfriend of the Aussie guy who was ogling Natalie.

She looked like a good-natured Aussie girl. She smiled. She was trying hard not to be pissed-off.

Natalie was drinking heavily. She squeezed my knee.

"Life before, you I love two gether, honey!"

I felt desperately lonely.

She took my hand.

"You prince."

"*Eh?*"

I'd been a prince in Old Siam.

"I plincess!"

I wanted to go back upstairs and give Soom Bon a smack.

"You I love two gether. Daddy Mummy say *No!*"

The guy was inventive. Natalie and I had been head-over-heels, but unfortunately our families were deadly enemies. They'd kept us apart. Maybe Soom Bon had read 'Romeo and Juliet' while he was inside.

"You I drown us self."

"*What?*"

Her eyes filled with tears.

"Drown. Two gether."

Natalie and I had made a suicide pact. Holding hands, our clothes weighted with stones, we'd jumped into the Chao Phraya River, Bangkok. For two hundred quid, you got the details.

Her tears turned bleak.

"Make this life you I go bad."

We were being punished in *this* life for taking our lives in our *former* life. She was a prostitute. I was...fucked.

"Now you I love again. Be happy."

Bad things were happening. The way the Aussie guy kept looking at Natalie was getting embarrassing. He couldn't take his eyes off her. He'd zoned out of his friends' conversation completely, and they'd noticed it. You could see that his girlfriend was getting

upset. The drunk Thai guy had noticed that the Aussie's girlfriend
was upset, and he was homing in on her, convinced that his tan
suit and inscrutable leer were making an impact. He lurched onto
the stage and grabbed the microphone. He gave the Aussie guy's
girlfriend a big smile.

"This one Thai song... traditional song... is called..." The smile
was for her, and her alone. "...'You Are More Beautiful Than The
One At Home'..."

Her boyfriend was so busy glancing at Natalie he didn't even
notice. He was giving *me* little glances of helpless envy.

I wanted to shout at him—*Mate! KY jelly and a faked orgasm!*
Natalie squeezed my hand.

"This life you and I love big big. Be very, very happy."

Soom Bon emerged from the kitchen with a tray of desserts on
his shoulder. He was waiting on some tables at the far side of the
restaurant. They required his full attention.

It would have been easier if she'd rolled me. Getting beaten up
by her pimp would have felt better than this. At least, regaining
consciousness in an alley, my wallet gone, my car stolen, I could
have crawled home to Melissa. Apologized to my family. Been
forgiven.

Something bad had happened, back on the footpath, when I
first saw her, and the stinging brightness began. Five hours had
passed, and it still hadn't stopped. The base of my spine was on fire.
The back of my neck hurt. The shining thread cut through my brain
like a wire through rotten cheese. The stinging brightness was a
physical force in my body, but it was outside me, too. It was sucking
my mind out of me as powerfully as it was sucking the reality out of
the crowded restaurant and the din of the karaoke. It was punishing
me for not accepting the glimpse of transcendence it had gifted me
on the footpath. All I'd had to do was turn, and walk off up the
pavement—one step, two, three would have been enough—and get

on with my real life. If I'd made it to the meeting, been home in time to take my family out, the glimpse of transcendence would have stayed with me. I would have stood at the source of things forever. The unapproachable woman would have been mine. Instead, I'd walked between the bins to the door, pressed the buzzer, gone in. And here I was, in a place I didn't want to be, with someone I didn't know, everything outside The Swaddee Bee Mai in pieces.

The Aussie guy was getting so hypnotized I thought he was going to come over and sit with us. Natalie glanced at him, nervously this time. A blush deepened his sunburn.

His girlfriend was up on stage giving 'Hotel California' what for, her Thai admirer singing backing vocals from the floor, doing the twist, jammed between his table and chair.

"This life you I love Number One. Be happy happy."

I called for the bill.

The car was parked in a cul-de-sac of trendy, semidetached cottages, tucked away behind the hotels and towering windows of bed-sitter land.

"Where do you live?"

"Caledonian Road."

I opened the door for her, and she got in. I went around to the driver's side and slid into my seat.

She climbed on top of me and kissed me. Her mouth was cavernous. Her lips covered mine. Her tongue tasted of beer and the blood pudding I'd not been allowed to eat.

Her backside hit the steering wheel as she lifted herself so I could get my hand down the front of her jeans.

She was wearing panties, not the thong. It took me a moment to work my fingertips under the elastic.

My fingers went crazy. They clawed and jabbed. *KY, mate! And a faked orgasm!* Her pussy jerked backwards and forwards, brushing jelly onto my fingertips with brisk, bristly swipes.

Her legs parted. There was no KY. No bristly give. There was no smear of jelly. A sopping wetness clutched my fingers up to my knuckles.

Her jeans were tight. With her hand inside my Y-fronts, I had trouble pushing the denim down below her bum. She wouldn't close her legs so I could get her jeans off.

Taking my fingers out was like dipping them in cold acid. The catch was slippery as I dropped the seat and slid it backwards.

She'd got my Y-fronts around my knees and was hanging onto my cock. I could feel myself beginning to come. So could she. Her pussy rocked above me.

Her knees slid round my kneecaps as she kicked at her jeans.

One of her fingernails dug into the root of my cock, searching. There was no pipe freeze. No disconnection valve.

As her labia found the tip of my cock, her mouth closed over mine. The witch was right. 'Life before you I love big big.' 'You prince. I plincess.' Not that it was true. None of it was real. 'You I drown two gether.' They were just words, but as my tongue tasted them, slithered on their muscular wetness, and raked them from the roof of her mouth, they were all that stood between her and me.

The traffic had thinned. Marylebone Road sped and stalled with the shining ebb and flow of a computer game. The traffic lights versus the taillights. The St Pancras Station clock said ten to midnight.

She stared out at the closed pubs and tower blocks of Caledonian Road.

"Here. Left."

She nodded at a large house that stood on the main road between an alleyway and a supermarket.

There was a sign above the alleyway. Steep steps led from the footpath up to the front door of the house. A piece of wood was nailed across the entrance. One or two of the upstairs windows were lit.

"Up. More."

I pulled further up the road, and parked outside the supermarket. Shelves stacked with fruit and vegetable stood on the footpath. Apples and oranges glimmered under a neon advertisement.

She didn't get out.

"Need money."

I had a couple of hundred left in my wallet. I gave it to her.

She took her phone out of her handbag and made a call.

She spoke rapidly in Thai for a few seconds then rang off. We sat for a while longer, waiting.

It was after midnight but a couple of cars stopped, and the drivers ducked into the shop.

She looked at her watch.

"Must buy some thing."

She got out of the car. I got out too. We went into the superette.

There was a friendly greeting, a man's voice filled with warmth and enthusiasm:

"Hey! Natalie!"

She had a way with shopkeepers.

The guy behind the counter looked about fifty. He had silver hair and a silver moustache. His complexion was olive, but ashen olive, Turkish or possibly Greek.

"Early tonight!"

He liked her.

She ignored him, just like she'd ignored the pound shop boss in Kilburn. I sensed that she liked the guy. She'd liked the pound shop boss too. She had an affectionate way of ignoring people.

She picked up a basket and started throwing things in. I stood waiting by the counter. I felt awkward. Following her up and down the aisles would have been embarrassing, but standing waiting was uncomfortable too. The boss smiled. His smile was condescending.

A young guy appeared through a strip curtain from an open door at the back of the shop.

"Yo! Natalie."

Olive complexion, aquiline features, clean shaven, obviously the older man's son. He looked at me, and said to Natalie:

"You're early!"

A little girl thrust her face out from between his legs. Her dark eyes shone, her gaze following Natalie everywhere.

I sensed that the son didn't like me, but the father was sympathetic.

Natalie's phone rang again. She dumped the basket of shopping on the counter and took out her phone and answered.

"Chai. Mii. Wii natee."

She paid for the shopping with one of my fifty pound notes. Biscuits, a jar of olives, tinned meat, a six pack of Budweisser. The boss packed the items into carrier bags.

She thanked him:

"Korp jai kha, Hassan."

Yes. He was Turkish.

Outside, she kissed me and hurried off down the footpath. There was no 'come see I again?' She was too nervous to discuss hooking up. I felt relieved. It was over.

She passed the steps up to the front door of the house and turned into the alleyway and that was the last I saw of her.

I climbed in my car and drove home.

CHAPTER TWO

There was a free space outside my house, behind Melissa's Audi. It was ten past midnight.

I turned the engine off and sat looking out at my home. There was a light on upstairs, on the third floor, in Ralph's bedroom.

In the tall first floor windows, the curtains were drawn and unlit. There was no one in the living room.

On the ground floor the kitchen shutters were closed, but cracks of light shone between the white, freshly painted panels. Melissa was in the kitchen, on her own, or perhaps with Meredith. Meredith's bedroom was at the back.

We lived in a private street. At this time of night our road was so quiet Melissa must surely have heard my car. It was dark, too, out on the footpath, under the heavy boughs of the plane tree, a long way from the nearest streetlamp. It was hard to say whether the radiance that tinged the darkness was the moon, unseen somewhere, or the glow of the city down the hill towards Kings Cross. It couldn't be this stinging in my spine. The silver thread wasn't real. The brightness most certainly wasn't a woman. It had been going on for over eight hours now. It seemed to be getting even stronger.

I had to tell Melissa the truth. Honesty was imperative. We'd always been truthful with each other. If Natalie had HIV and I'd caught it from her there was no hope. I couldn't even lie and say that I'd taken the risk impulsively, in a moment's madness. I hadn't. If Natalie was HIV positive, her 'fifty pounds extra, do without' was either a callous desperation for money, or a challenge, her crazy 'life before, you I love two gether' daring me to risk everything. And I had. Perhaps the silver thread stinging in my spine, tingeing everything with a radiance that wasn't just the moon or city glow,

its soundless ringing in my ears, was merely the first symptom of
the disease.

The cracks between the shutters and the window frame were
an electric gold colour, stronger than the diaphanous radiance out
here on the street. A lamp in a kitchen asserting that everything,
even the fastest phenomenon there is, is finished before it even
reaches your eyes, is already so far back in the past that all you're
seeing is its ending, the fact that it's over with, even my own body,
the thump of blood in my chest, the hammering in my skull, are so
far back in the past they're as dead as the freshly painted brilliant
white of the shutters.

I sat in the car. I didn't want to get out. I smelled the red
Dakota leather that Natalie had approved of so highly, and looked
at my house.

It had been Melissa's idea to have the kitchen on the ground
floor, taking up the whole of the ground floor of the house, from
the front windows looking out onto the street through to the
French windows at the back and the steps down into the garden. It
had seemed like an odd choice at the time. Our friends all had their
kitchens in the basement of their homes, in homage to the original
'upstairs-downstairs' layout of their Victorian houses. Basement
kitchens feel snug and olde worlde-y. They're the family part of the
house, tucked away below stairs. Greeting visitors, the minute they
walk through the front door, with Poggenphol units and stainless
steel work surfaces, didn't seem right when Melissa first suggested
it, but her choice had turned out to be an inspired one. Kitchens
are more welcoming than living rooms, even state-of-the-art
modernist kitchens like ours. Friends and neighbours dropping in
for a chat liked sitting around our big Nokido kitchen table. It
was more relaxed and informal than trooping downstairs to the
basement or upstairs to the living room, even though the living
room's Berber rungs and Moroccan leather settee were more

comfortable. In summer the kitchen opened out onto the garden. On a weekend you could drink your coffee and read your newspaper of a Sunday morning looking out over spiraea and climbing jasmine and not just a retaining wall. Making the kitchen the first thing a visitor saw coming through the front door had the added benefit of requiring that it be kept neat and tidy. It was a special kitchen. On summer mornings you could listen to the birds in the garden while your coffee brewed whilst simultaneously watching the world go by in the street through the open shutters.

The shutters were closed now, against the cold, strips of light shining through the cracks. Melissa was still up.

Nothing like this had ever happened to me before. Failing to turn up at an important family event, and without even getting in touch, was something that Melissa and I just didn't do. If plans changed or unforeseen events forced a cancellation, we let each other know. The fact that the evening was meant to have been a celebration with my business colleagues made my failure to show up even worse. Melissa was good friends with my partners, Bernard and Pippa. She knew the half dozen people who worked for us. My garbled call from outside the Sawaddee Bee Mai would have made her horribly anxious. My staff and colleagues would have seen her anxiety as she told them I was on my way—only for me not to show up at all! She'd heard, over the phone, how freaked I was. As the evening went on her embarrassment must have turned to torture. If I lied to her now it would only make the torture worse. She'd know at once that I was lying and that something bad had happened during my nine hours' absence. Telling her the truth was going to shock and hurt her, but I had no alternative.

I sat in the car with the lights off and looked up at my house. We'd recently had the front re-painted. The stucco was crisp and bright against the mellow old brickwork. The beads in the fanlight above the front door were delicate as a brilliant white spider's web.

The outside light was on. We'd replaced the treads of the front steps with new Portland stone that seemed to absorb the electric glare in a porous pallor of its own.

For an instant I wondered if the midnight's multi-hued light was coming out of me, whether it wasn't my eyes that were imbuing everything with this indrawn pallor.

I shook my head, and told myself to wake up. Jesus Christ. I had no conscience. The shining hinge upon which everything turned? Transcendence? Standing at the source of things? I was without shame. I was prepared to countenance any derangement rather than face up to what I'd done. It was nine hours now since the stinging brightness had started up in my spine. Whether it was a trapped nerve or an inner ear disturbance or even some sort of psychological shock I'd suffered at the sight of a beautiful woman in a pink petticoat spitting Listerine onto a footpath, I mustn't let Natalie's 'you prince, I plincess' fantasy lure me into lying. 'You I drown us self two gether' was just a pick-up line. 'Make this life you I bad' was merely something she said to hook punters she knew had a bit of money. The same went for 'everything being already over before it reaches your eyes' and 'my body already being back in the past', let alone "Nok' same 'bird'" coming from the source of all joy' or 'pinpoints of light from her head going through me like diamonds through a sieve.' None of it was true. It was all a cop-out. It was worse than a cop-out. I was covering up something horrible that I'd just done with mystical claptrap. I was hiding behind pseudo-spiritual mumbo jumbo so that I wouldn't have to face the sleaziness of my own actions. Transcendence? It was the first step towards a lie, the beginnings of an excuse, a lie to myself as much as to Melissa, at the very best the temptation to put off telling Melissa the truth till later, perhaps the morning, put off the moment with a story, no matter how improbable. Except,

I couldn't think of anything, even the beginning of a story that would work.

I got out of the car and shut the door. The central locking clunked. It was amazing how, just two miles from Kings Cross, the silence could be so deep, almost like the silence at night in the country. It was one of the benefits of living in a private road. The clatter of a late night train, the hum of traffic down on Pentonville Road, were as soothing as the creak of boughs above my head, or a dead leaf scraping in the gutter.

I loved living in this street. It had been a risk buying such a big house when we were so young. Melissa and I had both needed to borrow money from our parents to top up the bank loan for the deposit. Not long out of university, at the beginning of our careers, we could have come unstuck if either of our businesses had failed, but luckily my engineering company and Melissa's design firm had both prospered. We'd got in before the boom in house prices too, and now our house was worth a staggering three million pounds. Not that we'd ever dream of selling it. The children had grown up here. We had nice neighbours and knew all their kids. We were both of us too happy living in this street to even think of selling. The population of the road had remained remarkably stable, in spite of rocketing house prices. It wasn't mere property values that made our street a nice place to live. The houses themselves, the mansard additions, number nineteen's loggia, the general air of upkeep, our friendly residents' association, were worth more than money. Fred Moore, next door, was a banker. The Forsyths, across the road, were lawyers. Jill Wright was in media. Like Melissa and I, they'd built their success on hard work and playing by the rules. Our road had an earned solidity that Shoreditch's glitz and Hampstead's privilege couldn't touch.

I opened the gate.

Melissa and I had argued about the front gate. It jammed on the path, at the lowest point of its arc, before the latch could reach its keep in the pier. It was the house's original gate, cast iron and massively heavy, and had sagged on its pier, had actually pulled the pier that carried it out of plumb, so that its bottom corner ground against the stone of the path and had actually scored an arc into the soft yorkstone, a circular section that grew deeper, and turned into an actual groove, an inch deep and raw against the slab's patina, the closer it came to the footpath. I was the principal in an engineering firm. I knew plenty of subcontractors. Melissa wanted me to get someone to rebuild the pier and rehang the gate, but that circular section of groove delighted me so much, I kept putting it off.

I went up the steps to the front door.

If I told Melissa the truth, if I didn't make up a story, there'd be shock, anger, disgust, but the damage wouldn't be final. There'd be a period of recrimination, our usual intimacy might be affected for a time, even for a long time, perhaps forever, but life would go on. I wouldn't lose anything that I really cherished, not absolutely lose. I'd never see Natalie again, nothing like this afternoon's madness would ever happen again, and things would eventually get back to normal. I'd had a brush with something weird and nasty, but it was over. As long as I wasn't HIV positive I'd had a close shave.

My hand flew to my temple. There was a hairless patch where Som Boon had cut the scut for his fortune telling! I felt the patch of scalp under the porch light. Luckily it was small, no bigger than the tip of my thumb. It was probably less noticeable to look at than it felt under my fingers, a bare patch in my grizzled locks. God. I'd have to tell Melissa about the Sawadee Bee Mai, and Som Boon, too.

I could feel my mind casting round for stories. There were none. None that Melissa would believe. None even that she'd disbelieve, but not question, on the strength of our former trust.

My key was already in the door. It was too late to start inventing stories. When it came to possible reasons for my absence, my mind was a complete blank. If I tried to lie I'd break down halfway through and then things would be even worse. I should have spent the last twenty minutes, driving home from the Caledonian Road, thinking something up. Anything. An accident. A robbery. A shooting. It was stupid not thinking up anything. I'd never see Natalie again. If I'd managed to think up a credible story the afternoon's stupid mistake would have been over and done with in five minutes' time and, if I was lucky, life could go on as normal. Five minutes' awkwardness. A few days' puzzlement, even disbelief, but everything would stay the same.

The key turned in the lock. The heavy front door swung open lightly on its snug hinges. I felt a moment's panic.

The stinging light in my spine was a hallucination. The world turning on a shining hinge was only an illusion. The shining woman coming out of transcendence was a derangement. The idea that everything is already over before it arises, the fact that this crazy idea is physical, that my body's not keeping up with its own vision—it was all madness. It had nothing to do with Natalie. I'd never see Natalie again. It was Natalie that was over. It was fucking her in the car that was finished, not the whole material fabric of my life.

My body was real. The key in my hand was real. The door swinging inwards was real. None of it had ended by the time it reached my eyes. None of it was finished before it touched my hand or sounded in my ears. My life was real, and so was my house, here and now, in the present, at this very instant. My wife, my children, my house, my whole life was with me here and now. Not even the past is past. Only lying could take it away from me.

"What happened to you?"

Melissa was sitting at the kitchen table with a book open, face down, on the glass. Her hair shone salt and pepper blonde in the light from the lamp. The lines around her eyes were drawn tight. She knew something bad had happened, but she hadn't let herself imagine any details.

I stood jingling my keys. I wished like hell that I'd prepared what I was going to say instead of blundering straight in. I should have worked out some prefatory declaration of guilt or apology before I told her the actual details.

"Are you okay?" I saw how worried she'd been. She was angry, but anxiety outweighed her anger. "When you didn't turn up at Carluccio's? And then you rang?"

"Nothing..." I said. "I just..."

The kitchen felt warm and friendly after the cold outside. A friendly brilliance shone down from the lamp suspended above the table. Natalie was unreal. It hadn't happened. All those terrible people—Sandra's Oxford plum. Soom Bon's hepatitis eyes. Lee, and the fear he inspired. They had no substance, none of them, not even Natalie in her petticoat and slippers on the freezing footpath. Pink lipstick vanishing into a smile, 'Nok same 'bird', her body dropping on me like a window with a broken sash cord—none of it was as substantial as this light falling on glass, these kitchen units retreating into dimness, the book on the table, this woman I'd loved for so long.

"What is it, Jim? What's happened?"

"... Jack O'Grady...!" The name came to me out of nowhere. "... You remember Jack...?" The name came to me as unexpectedly as if it had whispered itself in my ear. "... I ran into him... in... Kilburn..." The lines tightened around her eyes. She knew I was lying. "... Taking the car in to be serviced... we had a few drinks..." It didn't matter that she knew I was lying. The lie would become more true as it went along. It had come out of nowhere with the insistence of truth. It would find the part of her that wanted to believe it.

"Drinks? Before a meeting?"

"... You know Jack... He won't take no for an answer..."

It was an inspiration. A horrible one, but still an inspiration. Of all the people we knew, of all the shared acquaintances of our past life together, Jack O'Grady was the only person wild and unconventional enough to make any lie at least partially believable.

She frowned.

"Jack?"

"... He's in trouble... big trouble... he literally dragged me into the pub..."

'Literally was a mistake. 'Literally' was like a flashing red light.

"... They've withheld his passport... There's people looking for him..."

"People?"

She stared at the table. The twisted bronze legs supporting the glass looked unreal. Jack O'Grady, blogger, political activist, conspiracy theorist was perfectly capable of 'literally' dragging friends into pubs. Jack was always in trouble. He was larger-than-life enough to bolster any lie, but even Jack O'Grady was no reason for missing an important business meeting or copping out on a family engagement.

"You didn't ring Bernard."

"... Jack kept pushing drinks on me... by the time I realized I was going to miss the meeting I was hammered... I was so hammered I didn't want to speak to Bernard..."

"Or me?"

She knew it was another woman. I'd been faithful to her for twenty years, but she heard at once that there was a woman involved.

"... Well... I did ring you..."

"Not till nearly seven, Jim." I had no recollection of it being that late. "I was worried sick."

"Yes. I know. I'm sorry..."

"You just blurted out something about coming to the restaurant. Then you never showed up."

I stared at her book. 'The Stone Diaries', face down on the table. I didn't dare look at her.

"Did you go to the restaurant?"

"Of course I did! I had to. Didn't I? It was horrible. Bernard was furious. Pippa was upset. They never signed the contract. No one felt like celebrating. And you weren't there."

"I'm really sorry. I..."

"Why didn't you tell me about Jack when you rang? Where were you?"

"... In this restaurant...and... I told you... I was pissed...I was very pissed... I know you don't like Jack..."

Her mouth tightened.

"I don't dislike him so much that you have to lie about being with him, Jim."

"I know, but..."

I touched her hair. She didn't pull away.

"This is so unlike you, Jim."

"It was Jack," I said. "You know what Jack's like... how he takes people over..."

She didn't believe me, but Jack O'Grady left options, if not of trust, at least of uncertainty, open. Jack's was a name to conjure with. The guy was certainly larger than life. He was so much larger than life I could almost see him. Jack O'Grady was big enough, and wild enough, to carry any story on his cumbersome shoulders. Wild things happened wherever Jack went, much crazier things than getting drunk in a pub and missing a meeting. Melissa loathed him. She'd disliked Jack from the first moment I introduced her to him, back in our university days. She'd never got on with Jack, even when his career was flourishing, and her dislike had turned into a settled loathing when he went off the rails. Jack was perfect. He'd gone off the rails and dropped out of sight completely. We hadn't seen him in over three years now. There was no way she could verify whether my story was true or not.

Melissa looked at me.

"I was so worried, Jim. I kept getting these terrible feelings."

"I'm sorry," I said. "It won't happen again."

At least that wasn't a lie.

She rubbed her eyes.

"What's the matter with Jack? What's his problem this time?"

The ordeal was over. I was safe.

"Oh, nothing. Just the usual. Money problems. Visa problems. The globalist elite's hit men after him..." I tried to grin. "... He's going back to Holland to try and sort things out..."

"What things?"

"Oh... you know... George Soros... the New World Order... the usual..."

I felt like giving Jack a big hug. If he'd suddenly materialized, out of thin air, in our kitchen I would have thrown my arms around him and thanked him for saving my marriage.

I'd known Jack since university. He'd always been pushy and loud and abrasive in his opinions, but we'd got on. With his first class honors degree in politics, Jack had gone into journalism, and initially done well. He'd been a freelance foreign correspondent for APR, and written an influential book on international monetary policy. He was charismatic. He did TV commentating for Fox News and wrote for Breitbart in America. His assertiveness gave his conservatism a teeth-grating edge. For a while he'd been highly respected. He still had followers even now. Jack had only gone off the rails gradually. Women problems. Money. No one knew for sure, but as time went on establishment paedophilia, the 9/11 cover up, the globalist elite's banking monopoly, the Holocaust 'hoax', had filtered into his mainstream reporting, and Jack had gradually become more and more marginalized, and the more marginalized he became, the angrier he'd gotten. I couldn't blame Melissa for not liking him. The last time I saw Jack he'd turned into a rabid conspiracy theorist. He made Alex Jones look considered. He was drinking heavily too. He claimed InfoWars was a front for the Bilderburg Club. He was trying to set up his own more libertarian channel but George Soros, plus the drink, were blocking him every step of the way. Jack O'Grady's coming to mind had been a godsend. It was pretty much the first time I'd thought about Jack in three years, but he'd helped me out. Farfetched stories are the easiest to believe.

Melissa yawned and picked up her book.

"I suppose we should be getting to bed." She looked at me. "I've got a busy day tomorrow."

"Yes," I said. "Me too."

Thank God I hadn't given Natalie my phone number. Sandra had mentioned how customers, the 'other girls' regulars', gave Natalie their phone numbers. 'Natalie thinks it's a hoot, but. The minute they're out the door she deletes.' Luckily the idea hadn't even occurred to me. Natalie didn't have my number. She didn't know where I lived. There was a zero chance of my running into her again. I'd keep well away from Kilburn. I felt a huge sense of relief. I need never see Natalie again.

I'd lied, but it was only a one-off deception, never to be repeated. I could carry on as before. I'd have to invent some excuse—pressure of work, stress—why I didn't want to have sex for as long as it took to have an AIDs test and get the all clear. With this influx of relief I felt less worried about infection than I had out in the car. Finding some excuse why I didn't want to have sex would be easy enough. Melissa and I had a relaxed, companionable sex life. There were often times when both of us were too preoccupied for sex. If the HIV test proved positive all bets were off. I'd just have to deal with that eventuality when it arose.

I switched the kitchen light off, and we climbed the stairs.

"God. You and Jack must have made a night of it," said Melissa. "You look terrible."

I felt terrible. The stinging sensation had turned to a dull, throbbing heat at the base of my spine. The brightness at the back of my head had risen to a cacophonous tingling, that made thinking almost impossible. I'd have to go and see the doctor first thing in the morning. I'd ask him to give me a full check-up as well as arranging for the HIV test. The filament of light travelling up my spine had to have some physical cause that the doctor could diagnose.

I'd not only lied to Melissa, I'd lied to myself, all that bullshit about transcendence, the source of joy, my life turning towards something I couldn't comprehend. It was unpardonable. Having sex with a prostitute was bad enough, but dressing it up in mystical mumbo jumbo was unforgivable. I wasn't the person I'd always thought I was, but at least I'd never succumb to a delusion like that again.

I usually got into the office early, always before eight, often much earlier. The doctor's surgery didn't open till nine. I was a private patient and managed to hassle an early appointment, but still didn't get in to see him till nearly ten.

He looked at me when I told him I wanted an HIV test. I told the doctor I wanted it to be discreet. He took a blood sample and informed me that I wouldn't get the results for another four weeks. I'd braced myself for an immediate yes or no.

The four weeks delay came as a relief. I was already beginning to realize that, like everything else, HIV anxiety fluctuated. Last night there'd been moments when I'd been sweating with dread. This morning I felt as blasé as Natalie, sure that I'd been lucky and that last night's fears had been overblown, caused merely by the stinging sensation at the base of my spine and the hallucination that I had a filament of light travelling up my back.

My symptoms were uncomfortable and disorienting but I was already getting used to them. This bizarre physical discomfort was a bit like worrying about HIV. It came and went. When I was convinced that whatever was happening was wholly physical the discomfort increased and the disorientation became debilitating. When whatever was happening seemed like a form of consciousness and my mind entered the thread of light I felt a sort of euphoria, as if the only thing that mattered any more was this shining hinge on which my whole being was turning.

Euphoria was as inappropriate as dread. I asked the doctor to give me a full check-up, half hoping that he'd find something specific but minor. A trapped nerve, a perforated eardrum, something like that. The doctor examined me, took some more tests, and said that I was in good shape.

The doctor took the blood sample and looked me full in the face. Was I under stress? Did I have any emotional problems? Depression? There were things he could prescribe, anti-depressants, sedatives. I accepted a prescription, determined not to use it. Something told me that medication would only make my disorientation worse.

I couldn't face the office. I drove straight from the doctor's to Kilburn.

I parked the car in the garage where I'd had it serviced yesterday. It was a short walk back to the High Street and the pound store and the shoe store. The bins were already out on the footpath, shoes and trainers on one side, household goods on the other, the bins rocking on their wire legs in the brisk wind.

There was a hamburger restaurant on the other side of the road from the green door. Kilburn High Road was busy this morning. I crossed and went into the restaurant and ordered a coffee, and took it to a table by the window.

It was a weird sort of restaurant. There was something not right about the place, something almost deceptive. At first glance it looked as if it were part of a burger chain, Burger King or Wimpey, but when you looked closer you could see that it wasn't. The restaurant wanted to give the impression it was a chain franchise, when it was really a one man shop. It had the same kind of plastic tables and plastic seats as a Burger King. There were KFC style cream tiles on the floor. Studio engineered pictures of whoppers and sachets of fries covered the walls, but the smell was wrong. The place had a workman's café smell, a greasy spoon stink, stewed tea and tired cooking oil that didn't go with the sculptural chicken nuggets and soft focus shakes. A handkerchief size tapestry of the Blue Mosque hung above a kebab rotisserie half hidden behind the counter.

The coffee was good. It was too good. Not exactly Turkish, but aromatic and real, instead of tongue-scaldingly hot with a photogenic taste. I wasn't sure what I was doing here. I didn't want to think about it.

It was a colder day than yesterday, the wind gustier, ballooning the shoe shop awning that I'd held onto as everything changed. The pound shop man was tidying the items in his footpath bins. They were set out in the same rows as yesterday. The shoe display had attracted a couple of customers. 'Cold. Fleezing.' The fan heater would have its work cut out today. A sudden gust, stronger than the rest, took hold of one of the pound shop's wire baskets, something light, the washing up pads she'd tipped over yesterday, and blew it sideways along the footpath.

The rush hour traffic was beginning to thin out. Between the lumbering buses and the jerky advances of the cars I had a pretty constant view of the green door. No one went in or out. There was a pink curtain in the windows two floors up which must be the living room where I'd sat with Sandra and watched Teletubbies. Perhaps Sandra hadn't opened the curtains because it was such a foul day. She was a woman who'd spent a lot of time in curtained rooms and artificial light. Maybe the flat wasn't open yet. Sandra had been scared of Lee, last night on the phone. Lee was no mere disappointed punter like Martin. Natalie had been nervous too, while Sandra was speaking to Lee. Natalie wasn't afraid to have sex without a condom for an extra fifty pounds, but she was scared stiff of Lee. She'd taken a risk going down to Earls Court with me. It had been a risk for Sandra too. Closing the flat early was something Sandra hadn't undertaken lightly. And today the curtains were drawn and I'd been sitting here for nearly an hour and no one had come in or out of the green door.

I was getting heavy vibes from the restaurant's proprietor. It was lunch time. The place was filling up. I was taking up a whole table and hadn't even ordered a second coffee. The looks the guy was giving me had a pleading urgency along with the dislike. Business wasn't good. Rent was steep on the High Road. The council's business rates were killing him. He'd spent a load of money competing with the Burger King up the road, and no one was deceived. If his café had been a real big-chain franchise he would have been a bored teenager in a cap and apron letting me sit here as long as I liked. I ordered a hamburger and chips. It was surprisingly good.

Across the road a man in a wooly hat walked down the aisle between the bins of shoes and the bins of household merchandise.

He pressed the buzzer, waited a moment and spoke into the intercom. The door opened and he went in. Natalie was there. I didn't know whether to be relieved or appalled.

I finished my burger and ordered some baklava and waited. A middle aged woman with a pram sat down at my table. The table was by the door. There was room for a pram. A quarter of an hour or so later she was joined by a young woman with a load of carrier bags.

Another guy, this one wearing just a polo neck pullover, went down the aisle and was let in the green door. The first man still hadn't come out. The guy in the polo neck would have to wait in the second bedroom where Sandra had put the last customer last night.

I climbed over the young woman's shopping. I squeezed past the pram. I hurried to the counter and paid and plunged out of the restaurant. I ducked across the road and down the aisle between the bins.

The wind was so strong the green star, with ORIENTAL BABE on it, creased and fluttered.

I pressed the buzzer. The speaker clicked and echoed.

"YEAH?!"

"Sandra... It's me... Jim..."

The intercom crackled. I pushed the door but it didn't open.

"... Jim... From yesterday..."

She couldn't have forgotten me.

"Ah. Yeah. Jim..." I waited for the click and the catch to release. "I'm sorry, Jim. Natalie's not here. Natalie don't work here no more."

The intercom went dead.

I walked around the neighbouring streets. I turned off the High Road into a side street, past a church and a playground, then up a busier, winding road towards West Hampstead. I kept walking. I walked fast. Walking helped me think.

'... Natalie don't work here no more...'

I didn't know whether to believe her or not. There'd been trouble last night over Natalie leaving work early. Lee had caught them in their lie about Natalie being sick. '... Don't work here no more...'? Sandra was so abrupt because she was in trouble too. God knows what they'd done to Natalie. Or maybe it was just that customers caught hooking up with girls were banned. Perhaps Natalie was up there working right now, and they just didn't want her to see me again, except... I'd heard how scared of Lee Sandra had been on the phone. Natalie too. There'd been no girl to replace her and they'd had to close the flat. The very feel of the place, the grille on the door, the mobile phone on the arm of Sandra's chair, the smell of room freshener, said that these people were quite capable of knocking girls around. Lee had found out that she'd left work early with a customer. There'd been no girl to replace her and they'd had to close the flat. Fifty pounds for twenty minutes' sex. A hundred and fifty for a VIP hour. It wasn't like closing a shop for a few minutes and putting a BACK LATER sign in the window. There was a lot of money at stake. Natalie wasn't scared of having sex without a condom for an extra fifty pounds, but she'd been as afraid of Lee as Sandra was. Perhaps Lee even forced them to take risks with HIV.

'... I'm sorry, Jim. Natalie's not here...'

The Newcastle accent morphing into an Oxford plum. The hiss of room freshener. Trusting Sandra had been stupid, if Natalie had even trusted Sandra at all. Sandra had helped Natalie lie to Lee, then grassed her up as soon as we were out the door. It was a business in which no one trusted anyone. They were the sort of people used violence to get their way. Lee had physically hurt Natalie. She was locked away somewhere, beaten up. Unless she *was* upstairs now in the third floor bedroom, working. Hurting a girl so that she couldn't work was surely counterproductive. I'd seen the customers going in with my own eyes. Natalie was up there now seeing punters and it was just me who was banned for taking her down to Earls Court.

Half an hour sitting in the living room watching Teletubbies with Sandra, and the paranoia had got to me too, thinking I was going to be robbed, imagining Natalie was taking me down to Earls Court to be clipped and that Sandra would get a cut. Sandra had mentioned that lots of the customers tried to hook up with Natalie. She'd joked about how the customers gave Natalie their phone numbers. 'Natalie thinks it's a hoot, but. The minute they're out the door she deletes.' I was under no obligation to believe any of it, but why hadn't Natalie just asked for my number, if she wanted to see me again? Why hadn't she simply taken my number and arranged to hook up with me some other time, outside working hours, when she wouldn't get into trouble with Lee? Why the stupid trip down to Earls Court to have our fortune told by a junkie? Unless they kept her in some form of confinement, or Natalie hadn't really wanted to see me again, the 'prince and plincess drowning two gether' just drunken talk.

Unless Lee kept his girls in some kind of imprisonment or semi imprisonment. I'd read of such things. There'd be other ways he could punish Natalie besides from beating her up. He probably had people in Thailand. He could threaten her family. He could stop the money she'd told me she was sending back to Thailand. Hurting her was surely counterproductive. A beaten-up face would put the customers off.

Sandra's 'she's new', as if Natalie was a panting virgin and not a tough hooker. Her ridiculous lie about Natalie being Japanese. It wasn't mere sales talk. It wasn't just that Natalie was extremely beautiful, far too attractive to be working in a Kilburn knocking shop. Natalie was worth a lot of money to Lee. That was why Sandra hadn't let me in the door. Lee wasn't about to let the money he'd invested in Natalie be put at risk by her having her hook up with me. In one night I'd spent a ton of money on her. But there were richer men than me. I'd happened to be carrying a lot of cash yesterday, more than I usually carried. It was a coincidence. My nice suit and the thousand pounds in my wallet might have confused Sandra and temporarily thrown Natalie, but when it came down to the sort of money Lee expected to make out of someone as beautiful as Natalie, I was down there with poor old Martin. 'Yes, I know you've booked. I'm ever so sorry. Something's come up.'

It might not even have been Sandra who grassed us up. It was possible that Soom Bon knew Lee and had told Lee about our 'life before' reading. 'You prince. I plincess.' 'Life before you I love big big.' The Sawadee Bee Mai might even belong to Lee, and the waiter had warned his boss that Natalie had bunked off to Earls Court with a Kilburn punter, and not the rich guy she was ultimately intended for. *'I plincess.'* She was. It was a simple statement of truth. Pinpoints of light streaming from her face and catching in my brain like diamonds in a sieve. 'Nok same bird' rising up inside me from the source of all joy. In my world, she was. She was the shining hinge on which everything turned.

I was walking so fast, past yet another church, some workshops, a park, round and back, past the first church, sweat was prickling under my shirt in spite of the freezing day.

I must have walked for nearly an hour before I got back to the door.

I pressed the buzzer.

The speaker crackled.

"Yeah?!"

I made my voice go up high, and tried to put on an accent. What accent it was, I couldn't tell.

"I rang..."

"Second floor!"

The door unlocked itself. I pushed it open and went in.

I took the steps at a run. When I reached the second floor Sandra was coming down the corridor from the living room. I got to the grille before her. The keys were in the lock. I reached through, unlocked the grille and pushed it open.

"Look. Jim..."

I thrust past her.

"Where is she?"

"I toldya, mate..."

Yesterday's chumminess was gone. There'd be no cuppa for me today.

"I need to talk to her."

"... SHE AINT HERE, JIM..."

I barged on down the hallway.

A big black man stepped out of the living room.

"Where you tink you goin', bro?"

He was huge. He completely blocked the corridor. Sandra said:

"This is the guy, Cyril."

I tried to push past him to the bedroom.

"I just want to talk to Natalie..."

"Take it easy, man."

He grabbed me. I'm fairly tall. I'm reasonably well built, but he stopped me dead in my tracks. His hand came down. It felt like a paving slab had closed over my shoulder. There was a signet ring, on his middle finger, with a gold C.

"Just for a minute..."

She was in the bedroom. I didn't care if she was with someone. I needed to talk to her.

"I told ya... Natalie aint here..."

A chubby Asian girl in a red corset poked her head out of the bedroom. She pulled it in again and slammed the door.

"Where is she?"

Cyril was pushing me backwards towards the door.

"Time to go, squire." Cyril spoke quietly. "Don't wanta get hurt, do you?" He gave the impression nothing would please him more than to tear me half. "I don't like people messin' with my girls, bro."

I tried to shrug him off. I held his eye.

"*Your* girls?"

She belonged to me. Not him.

"Get out, Jim," said Sandra. "And don't come back, neither.

I got in my car. I was trembling. I could still feel the weight of Cyril's hand on my shoulder. 'I don't like people messin' with my girls.' It was the way he said 'my'. It scared me.

I headed for the Caledonian Road.

The house she'd gone into last night was on a part of the main drag where, even in the middle of the day, there seemed to be a permanent snarl-up in the traffic.

I pulled into a parking space on the southbound side of the road opposite the house and the little supermarket next door.

I searched in my pockets and found three pound coins. I fed them into the parking ticket machine. *A pound for ten minutes!* I had half an hour. I got back in the car and waited.

The weight of his hand, with its gold C signet ring, like a paving slab closing round my shoulder. I was still shaking. Cyril hadn't needed to hit me. Just his hand on my shoulder was enough to put the fear of God in me. Was that what Lee used to keep his girls in line? Cyril's big hands? Had Cyril used them on Natalie? The chubby girl in the corset had been as scared as me.

In the daylight, the house looked even odder than it had in the dark. It was clearly occupied, and yet the front entrance was blocked off with a piece of wood nailed roughly across the door. It was a tall house, once part of a terrace, but now marooned between Hassan's supermarket and the alleyway. There was a sign above the alleyway advertising a welder's yard out back. At some stage the house's Victorian brickwork had been sand blasted. It was a shade paler than the blackened façade above Hassan's shop. The front steps were preposterous. They were clad in pink paving slabs and steep enough to break your neck on. The piece of wood nailed across the front door announced that the steps were unusable. The entrance was round the side, in the alley, where Natalie had gone in.

If Natalie wasn't at Kilburn she must be here. She was in there now, behind one of the drawn curtains on the upper floors. Beaten up, or just locked up, I had no idea.

A traffic warden strolled down the footpath from the Pentonville direction. He stopped and checked the ticket in my windscreen and wrote something in his book. I looked at my watch. I had seven minutes left.

'I don't like people messin' with my girls.' They weren't Cyril's girls, they were Lee's. Cyril was talking bullshit. It was Lee that Natalie and Sandra had been scared of, and the girl in the red corset too, not Cyril. Cyril was just muscle, Lee's enforcer. He did what Lee told him.

They couldn't have known that I'd go back to the Kilburn flat. Sandra had sounded shocked. They hadn't expected me to show up. Cyril hadn't been there this morning, throwing his weight around, waiting for me. Lee probably had a number of girls working for him, perhaps quite a lot of girls. They lived in the house opposite, in those upstairs rooms. Maybe Cyril had only been at Kilburn this morning as a warning the other girls not to step out of line like Natalie had done. But why? Sandra had given the impression that girls hooking up with customers was quite common. It went with the territory. She'd spoken of the customers 'all giving Natalie their number', as if it were all part of the game. The girls were in the country illegally. Their families were poor. They had no money. Hooking up with an English guy, perhaps even marrying him, was a way out of a bad situation.

I glanced at my watch. My thirty minutes were up. I was parked illegally. The warden was hovering, a hundred meters up the footpath, talking to a stall keeper by the market. I dug in my pocket. Nothing. I didn't have any more change for the machine.

I jumped out of the car and hurried across the road into the supermarket. The older man, Hassan, was there, in the same place behind the counter I'd seen him when Natalie 'must buy some thing.' For an instant, he looked surprised to see me back so soon, but his look of surprise quickly turned to one of amusement. He'd had other guys hanging around for the same reason. He was well aware that the house next door was full of girls working as prostitutes, and that I was a poor chump being led around by his dick.

I gave him a twenty pound note.

"Can you give me some pound coins?" I knew I sounded desperate. "I haven't got any change for the meter."

I grabbed a packet of biscuits off the nearest display. They were thirty p, on special offer.

Hassan counted out my change. A ten pound note, the change out of a pound for the biscuits, and nine pound coins.

I'd got the feeling last night that the supermarket boss was fond of Natalie. She slipped out to buy beer and tins of tuna in his shop. She had a way with shopkeepers. Hassan was the same as the pound shop boss. He'd treated Natalie like royalty.

As I turned to go, a woman came through the strip curtain at the back of the shop. She wore a long skirt and a pink cardigan. She went to the refrigerated display and picked out a two-litre bottle of milk. The little girl I'd seen last night was with her, her big, dark eyes as shiny as when they'd followed Natalie up and down the aisles. Her gaze beguiled me.

"No school today?"

She buried her face in her mother's skirt.

I hurried across the road and pumped all nine pound coins into the machine. A ticket tongued out of the slot. I had another ninety minutes.

I sat in the car and waited.

The little girl's eyes last night devouring Natalie, worshipping her and devouring her... Hassan's courtier's greeting 'Hey! Natalie!' ... his son's frankly possessive 'You're early!'... the supermarket fluorescence... the stinging brightness was everywhere. The thread of light was a woman. How, or why, it was a woman I couldn't tell. She shone and stung. She was unapproachable. She was the source of all joy. No wonder Lee didn't want guys like me hanging around. It was no surprise Cyril wouldn't have people messing with his girls. It should have been easy, to just start the car and drive off, show my face at the office, apologize for yesterday's debacle, get on with my life, but it wasn't. Once you've stood at the source—or sat at the source in a nice car with the heating on—it should be possible to let go of what you've seen, but it isn't. There were other far more important things I should have been doing— apologizing to Bernard and Pippa, sorting out the realtors, driving over to Melissa's office and spending some time with her—things that were far more crucial than sitting in a car, watching Caledonian Road turn luminous, even the billowing awnings and the reek of diesel from the buses and a polystyrene cup skidding down the center lane, turning into a woman's sidelong glance, but moving was impossible. Pulling out of my parking space—I still had twenty minutes left!—and heading for the office was out of the question. Time glittered in her sidelong glance. Space breathed from her lips.

The rhythm of the traffic, the opening hours of the shops, the stall keepers' fight against the cold, were the beating of her heart. All I had to do was sit there, and watch the house, give it time, and I'd know what I wanted to know, what it was more important for me to know than any work schedule or home routine.

Twenty minutes later, a car pulled up outside the house. A grey Mercedes stopped in the middle of the northbound traffic and two men climbed out. The shorter of the two men looked Chinese. The taller was heavily built, Mediterranean looking.

The Chinese man ignored the impatient horns and leant in at the front passenger window and spoke to the driver. The Mercedes pulled away and the two men crossed the footpath and went down the alleyway.

The Mediterranean man was expensively, and conservatively, dressed. Lee saw nothing— not even a beautiful woman—except his own interest. I felt a strange exultation, an uplifting gratitude. Gratitude to the unapproachable woman for showing me this... exultation that my intuition had proved right...

Lee was angry, he'd sent Cyril to the Kilburn flat to frighten the girls, because he was lining up someone far bigger than me for Natalie.

Melissa broke a croissant in half and dipped one end in her coffee.

"You're going in late again today?"

It was already eight o'clock, but the sky was only just beginning to get light. Through the French windows clumps of verbena and drifts of shivering honeysuckle were only just emerging into the dimness.

I popped some more bread into the toaster. Usually I had a takeaway breakfast in the office.

"Yeah. I've got a meeting. Out at Ealing. I don't need to be there till ten." I was still in my dressing gown. Melissa and I only usually breakfasted together on weekends. "I needed that sleep in. I don't know... I was so tired last night..."

Last night Melissa had wanted to make love. At least, I thought she'd wanted to make love. I wasn't really sure.

I'd never realized till now how complicated the preparatory signals were. A glance. A yawn. A touch of her hip as I went to get my pyjamas. A momentary lapse in whatever conversation we happened to be holding. Of course, initiating sex took more of these unspoken signals now than when we first met, but that was a good thing. The step from routine to passion was more formal now because the passion was deeper and more personal. It was a million miles from Natalie's 'What you wan do?' It was still three weeks and six days till I got the results of my HIV test. Backing out of having sex last night had been easy. Melissa hadn't felt offended.

She looked at me.

"Jack rang last night."

"What?!"

"Jack O'Grady. He's back in London. You said."

I stared out the window at the street. My car was parked under the soughing branches of the horse chestnut tree outside our house. I should have made myself get up early and leave for work at my usual time instead of hanging around in the kitchen.

"... Yes... that's right... I know..."

"He said he wanted to catch up." She smiled. "You said you'd already seen him."

"... Yeah... well... I did... but...you know Jack... he's so scatty... he probably meant he just wanted to catch up again..."

The last time I'd seen Jack O'Grady was three years ago. He'd been on a downwards spiral, his conspiracy theories so out of control I'd felt sure I'd never see him again.

"I don't know. He sounded different," said Melissa. "Less manic. More together."

I couldn't believe my ears. What the hell was Jack O'Grady
doing back in London?

"Yeah... well... on the phone maybe... did he say anything
else...?"

"No. Not really."

I didn't have a phone number for Jack. There was no way I
could get in touch with him and tell him not to ring the house. I
felt as if I'd somehow conjured him up.

"Did he leave his number?"

Melissa dipped the other end of her croissant.

"No. He didn't. He just said that he wanted to catch up."

I could feel my grin slipping.

"... Yeah... well... after that last binge of ours... I think I'll give
catching up with Jack a miss..." I looked at my watch. "...I'd best be
off...I have to be in Ealing by ten..."

I got to the Caledonian Road at half past nine and parked
opposite the house. I was on a double yellow line, but I didn't want
to risk getting out and feeding the machine. I'd just have to keep
my eyes open for traffic wardens.

I wished like hell I'd got Natalie's telephone number, or given
her mine. It was strange that she hadn't asked for my number,
or offered hers. We'd shared a reincarnation in old Siam, she a
'plincess', I a 'prince', we'd drowned ourselves in the Phraya River so
we could have a better life this time round, and we hadn't bothered
swapping telephone numbers. It was certainly a bit of an oversight
after paying Soom Bon two hundred quid for the information. On
the other hand, there was the easy-going proprietorship of me and
my life she'd assumed almost immediately after our dismal session
on the zebra-striped bedspread, a sort of giving way fatality, that
perhaps came from her background and culture, a belief that what
would happen would happen of its own accord without any need
to fuss over telephone numbers. Or maybe she'd simply assumed

that, after our spin down to Earls Court, she'd never see me again. In which case, I was crazy sitting here opposite her house waiting for what, I wasn't sure. I needed to forget about her and get on with my life. It was imperative I repair the breakdown in trust with Melissa and sort things out at the office. Seeing her again, even talking to her again, was out of the question. So what was I doing here? I felt like a peeping Tom, looking at the blocked off door, waiting for something to happen in the alleyway that ran down the side of the house. My spine was burning dully. There was a murmuring sound in my ears that wasn't the traffic. Every time my mind strayed near the shining thread of light in my backbone it became a woman, how or why a woman I couldn't tell, just that her brightness shone out of sand-blasted brickwork next to blackened brickwork, out of squealing brakes and flapping awnings and gossamers of petrol fume on the ragged wind, shone out of everything yet was unapproachable. But I wasn't so stupid as to blame mere physical symptoms for the fact that I was doing something wrong. I was jealous. A consuming envy was eating at me. She was special. She was too beautiful for me. She was meant for the consort of princes or movie stars. There was a ladder and I was down near the bottom with the animal in the parka who'd ejaculated in her mouth and poor old Martin, put off with a winking apology, and even Cyril, his big hands merely useful. There were rungs and rungs above me, Lee and the fear he inspired, princes and movie stars, and that special guy, the one who'd sent his accountant, fixer, whatever, the man I'd seen with Lee, Mediterranean looking, in the conservative suit, to line up Natalie for his boss. I stared across the road at the tall house next to the supermarket. I felt sick in my mind.

I sat and waited. The rush hour was over but the snarl-up in the traffic on this stretch of the Caledonian Road seemed never to abate. Even when I'd dropped Natalie back here at midnight, the traffic had been heavy, a slowing down in the stream of vehicles where a rat run down from Islington debouched onto a badly positioned bus stop and drivers double parking to nip into Hassan's supermarket.

Jack O'Grady was in London. It was just a coincidence, a disastrous one, but a coincidence never-the-less. My using him to lie to Melissa and his turning up out of the blue was mere chance. I hadn't conjured him up. It was ridiculous to think that there was a connection between my using Jack to deceive Melissa and his appearing so suddenly, but I couldn't stop a feeling of dread. Melissa hadn't believed my story about a drunken session with Jack in the first place. His ringing and not mentioning it had shaken her trust even more. I hated the bastard. I'd never really liked Jack, even when he was a brilliant, up-and-coming journalist. The guy was pushy. He'd always been overbearing. When he turned into Alex Jones he became unbearable. It was over three years since I'd last seen him. I'd never expected to see him again. It felt almost malicious, his turning up right now.

Pinpoints of light filtered backwards through my skull. They caught in my brain as they went through me, like diamonds in a sieve. The Caledonian Road brightened. A wave of diamonds broke over me. 'Nok, same 'bird' flooded my throat. It welled up from the source of all joy and broke my heart. The Caledonian Road turned on a shining hinge towards something I couldn't comprehend. The unapproachable woman shone out of me. The unapproachable woman came stinging out of my eyes, she came yearning through my skin, beautiful even when she came out as a jam of angry cars and yearned outwards away from me as the nailed-up door of a blank house. Time meshed its gears and blew its horns and inched forwards, but I was still standing on a footpath as a door opened and she burst out, a string of spittle trailing from her lips. Time had passed, was passing, the shining hinge was turning inside everything, taxis, a leaden sky, fruit displayed on a footpath, but nothing was happening. She swigged from the bottle of Listerine and screamed at the guy in the parka, and I was still here, in transcendence, whatever transcendence is, the source of joy, even walking between footpath bins and pressing a buzzer by a green star, ORIENTAL BABE, can't shut out transcendence, obliterate joy.

A bus loomed above me, blocking everything out for half a minute or so. When it pulled away, I saw that a people carrier had stopped on the other side of the road, outside the house.

It was one of those twelve-seater mini buses that have a door at the side that slides open. There were no markings or company name on it.

The people carrier reversed into the alleyway, and parked. An Asian man got out of the driver's seat and lit a cigarette. He strolled out onto the footpath and scanned the passing traffic.

I couldn't see the door in the alleyway into the house, where Natalie had gone in the first night, but after a while a group of women appeared.

They were rugged up against the cold. I craned around in my seat to get a better look. There were about eight or nine girls, all Asian, all young. Puffs of white breath came out of their mouths as they chatted amongst themselves.

One of the women slid the side door of the people carrier open, and climbed in. I was thirty metres away, my view continually interrupted by the traffic, but I could see a pink wooly hat here, a puffa jacket there, a scarf wrapped up high under slanted eyes, black hair cascading from ear muffs. Some of them looked bright eyed and lively, some slow and sleepy. They could have been a party of factory workers being bussed to their shift, or students being picked up for their first lecture.

Natalie was amongst the last into the mini bus. I'd been right about Lee not hurting her. Yes. She was special. She was meant for a consort for princes or movie stars. She was being saved for someone at the very top of the ladder. She was the tallest of the women. She moved with a poise that none of the others possessed. There was no puff of white from her lips, she wasn't joining in the conversation. She was in jeans and trainers and the Gucci jacket she'd worn on our trip down to Earls Court. She was the only one not wearing a beanie or ear muffs. She was vain about how long and lustrous her hair was. The night we went to see Soom Bon she'd braved the freezing night with wet hair.

The Asian man slid the door of the people carrier shut, and walked round to the driver's side and got in. He started the engine and the mini bus swung out into the northbound traffic in the direction of Camden Road and Archway.

It was okay. I was parked facing north on the far side of the road. A gap appeared and I cut across the city-bound traffic and slotted into the northbound flow four cars behind the people carrier.

The going was slow. We went under the railway bridge by Barnsbury Station and passed Pentonville Prison.

The people carrier turned left at Market Road in the direction of Camden Town.

At York Way it turned south again, towards Kings Cross, then took a sudden right under the railway lines and stopped on a corner at the back of the station.

The traffic was less busy here. The people carrier pulled over so suddenly I had to drive past or I would have been seen.

I braked at the junction of Midland Road, twenty meters beyond the mini bus.

I didn't know whether to turn south into the Kings Cross congestion or north towards St Pancras Way. Cars were building up behind me. I needed to turn. I chose north. I went up Midland Road a hundred metres or so and pulled over and waited. If the people carrier turned south I was lost.

It had stopped by a concrete wall between steel pillars. There was a roar of trains overhead. Four of the girls got out and headed in the direction of the station.

A woman met them on the next corner, a white woman, but not Sandra. She accompanied them into the station crowd. None of the girls who'd got out was Natalie. She was still in the mini bus.

I worried that the driver had clocked me craning over my shoulder at them. He pulled up at the junction and turned north, the same way I was pointed. As he drove past he peered up at the girders supporting the railway lines, a mobile phone pressed to his ear.

He dropped two more girls on a corner in Camden Town. They strolled off up the footpath and went into a newsagents. Perhaps the women weren't as closely chaperoned as I'd thought. It was hard to tell.

Down Adelaide Road, heading for Kilburn, I was certain the driver had seen me. I dropped further back and a truck got between us.

The people carrier crossed the main road at the lights at Swiss Cottage and sped off down the hill towards Kilburn. The lights changed red but I managed to get over.

On the corner of Kilburn High Road, at a junction about two hundred metres down from the flat with the green door, he dropped off the chubby girl I'd seen yesterday in the red corset. Natalie wasn't today's ORIENTAL BABE.

There were only three girls left in the back of the mini bus, Natalie one of them.

By now I felt sure the driver was trying to shake me off. He'd definitely seen me. He did a rapid three point turn at the traffic

lights, oblivious to the horns honking at him, and headed back the
way he'd come. Speeding past me, he was still talking on his mobile.
Perhaps to Cyril. Maybe to Lee.

The horns honked even louder at my three point turn in the
middle of queueing traffic. I only just managed to keep sight of
him.

Swiss Cottage. Camden Town. Holloway. By the time we got
to Hackney I was certain I'd been clocked. I no longer cared. I
just needed to know where they were taking her. That was all, just
where. I had no intention of trying to see her again or even talk to
her, I just had to know where she was.

The sign said HACKNEY SAUNA AND MASSAGE.

Shutters, painted black, were drawn down over a low,
single-storey frontage that took up a considerable stretch of
nondescript shopping street. The building looked as if it could have
once been a furniture showroom or a garment sweatshop before its
conversion to a sauna.

There was parking for customers at the back. The people carrier
vanished between the sauna and a workmen's café next door.

"Bloody Arms Fair," I said. "It shouldn't be allowed!" I don't
know why I said it. I'm middle of the road politically. I'm against
the arms trade, but not as vehemently as the words came out. I
carried on, even more vehemently. "Tin pot dictators shopping for
drones and landmines."

"Landmines are banned already, aren't they?" said Melissa.

We were upstairs in our living room relaxing in front of the TV
with a glass of wine.

My mind was in ferment. I couldn't concentrate. Going in to
the office had been out of the question. I'd spent the day driving
around wondering what to do. Every minute that passed, she was
there, behind those black shutters.

The News At Ten was on, an item about the forthcoming Defence and Security Equipment International Fair, to be held at the ExCel Centre in a fortnight's time. The Arms Fair had been in the news a lot. A court case brought against the organizers, Clarion, by Amnesty International had led to the Fair's being postponed from September to mid-December, the marketing of tanks, aircraft and sophisticated weapons systems running almost up to Christmas. There was footage from outside the ExCel Centre, protesters already picketing the Excel Centre's entrance. One banner read 'Santa's Death List'.

Nip down to the shops? Pop in on a neighbour? A walk? I'd just told her that I'd had a hectic day and was tired. I never went for walks of a night anyway. Ten o'clock was too late to drop in on neighbours. We shopped in bulk, every Saturday. We were always well stocked up. We never needed to nip out for a carton of milk or a loaf of bread.

From the floor above I could hear Meredith chatting on her phone. Ralph was over at his girlfriend's.

"Perhaps that's why Jack's in London," said Melissa.

"Jack?"

I'd forgotten all about Jack. HACKNEY SAUNA AND MASSAGE had obliterated even Jack O'Grady.

Melissa smiled.

"The Arms Fair's a bete noir of Jack's, isn't it?"

"Yes... I suppose it is..."

Jack had so many betes noir the Arms Fair was bound to be one of them. The arms companies were leading players in the globalist elite's conspiracy to take over the world. She was right. Jack could well have turned up in London to cover the DSEI Fair for one of his extremist blogs, or even to take part in some protest stunt. Jack was an 'activist'.

"He didn't mention it to you when you met him?"

Melissa still didn't wholly believe my story about running into Jack.

"...Well... yes.... amongst everything else the globalist elite's doing to us... the deep state, Saudi Arabia, the EU..."

I wished I hadn't thought of Jack. If I hadn't been so spaced out getting home from seeing Natalie I could have invented a better story than getting drunk with Jack.

"I thought you said he was going back to Holland."

"... That's what he said.... I don't know, Mel... he's here for the Arms Fair, he isn't here for the Arms Fair. You know Jack. There's no pinning him down..."

I just wished the news would roll on to the next item. The Amnesty International case against Clarion was based on undercover footage showing exhibitors at last year's Fair selling banned stun batons and hand-held electric shock projectile weapons to unvetted buyers. The Defence Secretary, Michael Fallon's, congested face blocked out Big Ben, explaining the strategic necessity of Britain's arms sales to Saudi Arabia. A long haired protester wearing a wooly hat waved a picture of a bombed hospital in Yemen.

It was real. People were suffering. It was as real as this comfortable living room with its polished floor and soothingly vivid furniture, but by the time it reached my eyes and ears it was just a story. In the split second's gap between the screen and my body, ensconced in a Moroccan sofa, all the other stories, Jack's wild theories, Natalie's 'you prince, I plincess', Michael Fallon's evasions, swarmed in a void of lies.

Our long, salmon-pink drapes, drawn against the inclement weather outside, said that stories could be shut out too. Melissa, with her feet tucked up under her and her brown hair auburn in the lamplight, had a knack of dealing with tall tales. She was the opposite of Jack O'Grady for whom the wilder the supposition, the realer it must be. Melissa dealt with the news with wry insight, opposing each item with things she knew and loved, our house, this room, the children, me. The news didn't shake her world in any noticeable way, neither did she need to shut it out as a litany of unwelcome facts. She made things real because she made them her own. She was original, like her home. The kitchen on the ground floor, not in the basement. This expanse of mellow, Victorian pine scattered with Berber rugs and standard lamps. When we were having the house redone I'd assumed we'd simply rip the old floorboards up—they'd been scarred with linoleum glue and patches of damp rot and a hundred and fifty years' worth of nails—and have a new hardwood floor installed. That's what all our friends had done in their houses. But Melissa had wanted something more authentic, and found a retired carpenter, an expert in floors, who knew how to re-fix splintered planks and fill and sand the softwood, till the pine had a warmth and shine teak or iroko could never match.

"Christ!" I put my glass of wine down. "The drawings!"

Melissa frowned.

"What drawings?"

"Rampton Street...phase two..." Rampton Street was one of our sites. My company were consulting engineers for a large hotel rehab. It was conceivable I might need to look at drawings at ten o'clock at night. "... I left them at the office...!"

Her frown tightened.

"It's too late to worry about that now, Jim."

"... I... I promised Bernard I'd run my eye over them for tomorrow..." I leapt up. "... The client needs to make a decision about... I'd better go and get them..."

The sauna's shutters were still down, but yellow light shone through the cracks between the shutters and the painted brickwork. London brickwork is already black, there seemed something grotesque about giving it a coat of black gloss. Only the end shutter had been lifted, where the front door was. Above a damaged awning, HACKNEY SAUNA AND MASSAGE was illuminated by spot-lights.

I parked in the car park behind the building and walked down the alley and crossed to the opposite side of the road.

The sauna's front door was glass, with light shining through from a poky vestibule. The door appeared to be locked. There was a buzzer attached to the jamb. You had to buzz to be let in.

It was a big place, not a one girl flat like Kilburn. This morning they'd dropped three women off here. I felt sick to my stomach. What if she was with someone? I couldn't very well ask for her, and say I'd wait till she was free. I'd never set foot in the place, asking for her might raise suspicions. Cyril had made it clear this morning that I wouldn't be welcome in any of Lee's premises. Sandra's 'and don't come back neither' meant this place as much as the Kilburn flat. Natalie might not even be 'Natalie' here. And what if Cyril was in there now, keeping an eye on 'his' girls, making sure Natalie didn't abscond a second time before Lee lined her up with the Mediterranean guy's boss? There was a churning feeling in my stomach. I'd never been in one of these places in my life. I wasn't sure how they did things. If I didn't see Natalie when I walked in, could I ask for her by name? If Cyril was there I wouldn't escape with a hand on the shoulder and a 'time to go, squire' this time.

It was already ten to eleven. This late at night, it was only a twenty minute drive from home to my office in Notting Hill Gate and twenty minutes back to Islington. I'd left the house at half past ten. If all I was doing was picking up drawings, I needed to be home by half past eleven at the very latest, *with the drawings!* Sometimes Melissa didn't go to bed till late. She'd see me coming in *without the drawings!*

I needed to get to the office as quickly as I could, pick up the drawings—thank God the drawings at least were real—and get back to Islington, make up some excuse about the traffic.

I crossed the road and pressed the buzzer.

Through the glass I could see a second door screened by a strip curtain. The inner door opened, the strip curtain quaked. A black man came out.

For a moment I was sure it was Cyril.

He was tall and skinny. Dreadlocks poked out from under an L.A. Rams baseball cap.

He looked me over through the glass then unlocked the door. "Yeah, mon. Com in."

We sashayed around each other in the cramped space between the two doors. I ducked through the strip curtain.

I had to be in the wrong place. The room was huge. It felt like a betting shop. It was done up like one of those large betting shops where an attempt is made at corporate hospitality. There were sofas and armchairs and coffee tables scattered around. TV screens glimmered around the walls. I half expected to see horses being pushed into starting boxes up on the plasma screens, but instead faces contorted in game show grimaces with the sound switched down. The rap music coming from some tinny speakers somewhere seemed too quiet. It didn't sync with the pictures on the screens.

For a moment I assumed that the black man and I were alone in the room, then I realized that two Asian men were sitting at a sort of cocktail bar in the corner reading newspapers. They looked completely at home. They weren't here for sex.

The room had a sour, steamy smell. It smelled almost as if there was wet rot in the pine cladding. An attempt had been made to smother the pong in air freshener, the same zesty jasmine as in Kilburn, but even stronger. Melissa would smell it on my clothes.

Three girls, two Asian and one Slavic-looking, dressed as nurses, sat on a sofa in the corner talking to a couple of white guys. I'd barged in on some sort of theme night. The nurses' caps looked jaunty, atop cascades of lustrous oriental hair and perched in the East European girl's bleached blonde. The shapely medical bibs were blue pvc, like the aprons in a canning factory. The skirts were extra short showing off almost all of the Asian girl's honey brown legs and the East European girl's pale knees. Their painted eyes surveyed me with disinterest. It was Hospital Night in Hackney Sauna. The two English guys, tattoos bulging from under their T-shirts, were in for a check-up.

None of the three women was Natalie. I'd seen the two Asian girls in the people carrier this morning. The East European girl had a thin, pinched face. Natalie wasn't here.

I wanted to go, but I wasn't sure if the men at the bar would let me. The tall one looked a bit like the guy driving the people carrier.

A voice said:

"How are we this evening, sir?"

For a second I thought it was Sandra. The woman coming to greet me—I was stuck by the door— had the same working class accent morphing into posh as Sandra, except she was short, compact, Chinese—something told me at once that she wasn't Thai— and much older and tougher than Sandra. Hers was a businesswoman's face and not a retired prostitute's. She sounded as if she'd lived in England a long time. She did a much better Oxford plum.

"Let me take that coat for you...?"

"... Jack..."

I didn't want to take my coat off, but the tall Asian guy at the bar was staring at me. He was looking more and more like the driver of the people carrier.

The switched-down music went on and on about West Coast niggaz. The faces on the screens mouthed a rerun of 'I'm A Celebrity, Get Me Out Of Here'.

The woman hung my overcoat up next to the tattooed guys' parkas.

"Would you like a drink, Jack?"

"... Yes... thank you..."

"Beer? Or something stronger? To warm you up?"

"Beer. A beer'll be fine. Thanks."

"Sit down, will you?"

I sat down on a sofa and one of the girls—the skinny one with the wiry hips I'd seen being dropped off with Natalie this morning—came and sat next to me.

"Perhaps Pauline would like something to drink, Jack."

"...Yes... sure... of course... what will you have, Pauline?"

Close-up, Pauline was nice. Her crimson lips were too plump for her narrow face, but she was certainly sexy. Her slim, angular body seemed at home in a faux nurse's uniform. She ordered a whisky and soda.

The manageress took a bottle of Becks out of a fridge by the bar and dropped some ice into a glass. She opened a bottle of soda water and tipped it into a glass and added a dash of whisky from a bottle. She carried my empty glass and bottle of beer, and Pauline's whisky and soda, and placed them on the coffee table.

"That'll be fifteen pounds, please, Jack."

It was cheaper than I expected. I gave her a twenty. I'd brought plenty of money with me.

Pauline poured my beer over the ice cubes. Ice ruins beer, but I refrained from scooping the cubes out of the glass with my fingers.

"Cheers."

Pauline smiled.

"Cheers, Jack."

I got the impression that her English was better than Natalie's. She'd been in the country longer. Maybe Natalie was indeed, as Sandra had said, 'new.'

A door opened at the far end of the room. For a second I thought it was Natalie, coming back from seeing a customer.

A second East European girl came in, peeling off a pair of yellow washing up gloves. She had a congested, angry scowl on her face. She said in an accent that was perhaps Polish or Czech:

"Where's the Fairy Liquid?"

There was still no sign of Natalie. She had to be here. I'd seen her being dropped off this morning with Pauline and the other Asian girl. She had to be somewhere out the back with a customer.

Pauline crossed her legs. Her skirt rode up near her hips. She sipped her drink. At least she didn't see any need to chat, which was a relief.

"So, Jack. Which of these beautiful young ladies do you fancy?"

It was pretty obvious I had to take Pauline, but I was being given the appearance of having a choice.

"Massage sixty five pounds. Sauna an extra fifty..."

The English guys looked like they'd been sitting here all night, but I was being hurried.

"... You can discuss any extra service you might desire with the young lady herself..."

I decided to come out with it and ask for Natalie. I made my mind up to say that I was here for Natalie and that I was prepared to wait.

There was something coiled and feral about Pauline that said she didn't hold back when she was insulted, but I needed to see Natalie. I was desperate to see her face again. Then it hit me...

... I'd been stupid. I was being thoughtless on an unprecedented scale. Natalie was going to get into trouble. This time she was going to get into trouble bigtime. If they found out that I'd turned up here asking for her...

"So. Who's it to be, Jack?"

I smiled brightly at the beautiful young lady, nodded, and she took me out the back.

Pauline ushered me into a cubicle. With the tall massage table and a single chair there was hardly room for the two of us to stand up in.

She unzipped her dress. Her thin shoulders shrugged off the puffy, operating theatre sleeves with a slinkiness that belied her cold manner.

She hung her dress on a hook and unclipped her bra. Her breasts were small and firm. Her hips were even narrower than they'd looked in the nurses' uniform. She kept her panties on, but I could see through the lacy gauze that her mound was clean shaven. Pauline was very sexy. Either she'd been born seductive or her seductiveness was so well practiced it was mechanical, it was impossible to say. I experienced an instinctive distaste, which I could feel being reciprocated.

"What do you want to do?" The same question Natalie had asked me only the grammar was better. "Sex fifty extra. Oral seventy..."

She ran through the same menu of services. She didn't mention 'don do anal.'

"... Erm... just a massage, please... a massage'll be fine..."

She nodded at the table.

"Get on."

I wondered if she was pissed because I'd only ordered a massage. Perhaps I'd insulted her. I was well dressed. I had money. But I'd chosen the cheapest option on the menu. I'd paid the Chinese woman for my massage and the drinks outside. The woman had said I should negotiate any extras with Pauline. The way she'd said it, the customers must be hagglers. Eighty quid for two beers and a massage, maybe they had to be.

"What you want to do?"

She kept her panties on.

I glanced at the ceiling. A CCTV camera looked down at me, a small, cheap one with a coil of flex hanging from it. Of course there was a camera. The cubicle was claustrophobic. It had seen all sorts of madness. There hadn't been any cameras at Kilburn that I'd noticed. Natalie hadn't seemed nervous about showing me her photos. I wondered if the camera was for security, in case a customer got rough, or if they didn't trust the girls to hand over the money for the extra services.

"Oral, forty. Sex, fifty. One hour, one hundred. Don't do anal."

I perched on the edge of the table. It was very high. It squeaked under my weight.

"Look... is it okay if we just talk...?"

Twice in two days! I was turning into a 'just talk' freak.

She looked at me. Now she was openly angry.

"No. Must do something. You time waster?"

She glanced up at the camera and took off her panties. An orchid tattoo, blue and pink, unfurled an inch above her mons.

"...No... it's alright... I'll pay extra..."

Our mutual dislike had already turned into something nastier.

I grabbed my wallet.

She glanced at the ceiling again. If they saw her taking money and not doing anything for it, they might be suspicious.

"What you problem?"

There was more than a note of threat in her voice, not just affronted pride, an arousal as sharp and ungenerous as her snaky hips.

"... Here... a hundred..." I took out two fifties. "... Same as an hour... Look..." She glanced at the camera again, and stuffed the money into a pocket of her uniform. "... You know Natalie...?"

"Wha?!" she spun round. "Wha you say?" Her eyes were wild. "Why you say?" Her scowl was ferocious. "Don't know no Natalie."

"No... Look..." I scrambled in my wallet. "... I saw you... yesterday... in Caledonian Road... with Natalie..."

"Fuck off!" She put her panties back on. "Don't know no girl that name! Who send you?"

She reached for her dress.

"No one sent me."

"You not Jack. You crazy guy come Kilburn make Natalie problem. You name Ja... Ja..."

"Jim," I said. "What problem? Please."

I went to take some more money out of my wallet, but suddenly she was leaning against me, pressing against me, her nipples hot and hard in the tangle of hair on my chest through my shirt.

"Must do."

My wallet jammed against her stomach, between my belly and hers.

"No. Please. Take it. I just want to know..."

She kissed me! Her plump lips plastered my cheek in wet heat! *She was taking my wallet!* My wallet was half in her hands and half in mine, jammed between our bodies, *and she was taking money out! I couldn't tell how much.* She balled the notes up in her fist.

"Where's Natalie?"

Her free hand slipped down to my flies. She rubbed my cock through my pants with a piston-like ferocity, for the camera. It wasn't erect.

"Natalie not here."

"I can see that... where is she?"

"With man." She laughed out loud. "You think you only one?"

"Well... no I..."

She thrust her bottom lip out. It was too plump and juicy for her tiny chin. She unzipped my flies and slipped her hand inside my trousers and groped around.

"She with big man. She with rich man more rich than you."

She found my cock and pretended to pump.

"He very very rich man..." She knew she was hurting me. "...Got Rolex..." She pronounced it 'low-lex'. "...Got man drive he car..."

I tried to shrug.

"So? I don't care. That's up to her."

In a way I felt relieved. I'd been right about Lee lining Natalie up with someone rich and powerful, someone in a sphere that was high above mine. The unapproachable woman hadn't lied, in the car outside the Caledonian Road house. Time glittered in her sidelong glance. Space breathed from her lips. The shining thread was real. The hinge on which everything turned, turned towards something incomprehensible and out of my league.

She unbuckled my belt and pulled down my trousers.

"Give I one hundred I tell you he name."

I realised I still had my wallet in my hand. It gaped open. There was still some money in it.

"I don't want to know his name."

She glanced at the ceiling.

"Must do."

I took off my shirt and singlet and climbed onto the table.

"Trouser off!"

I took my trousers off. I lay face down on the table and felt her fingers instantly dig into my shoulders. She no longer had the money in her hand. Her fingertips raked and gouged. Her nails were far too long to do massage.

"He name Adrian."

Her thumbs found two knots of tension under my shoulder blades and pressed hard.

"So?"

Her fingers were strong and supple. Even with her nails, or nail extensions, whatever, she was a better masseuse than Natalie. The pads of her fingertips worked with a certain relish.

"He not her boyfriend." I didn't believe her. "Give I one hundred I tell you business she he do two gether."

I tried to shrug, but her fingers pinned me to the table.

"That's up to her. That's her business, not mine."

"One hundred and I tell you why Lee don't want you see her."

I shut my eyes. I had to get out of here. I needed to go home and make up some story as to why I'd been away all this time. My suspicions had been right all along. I wasn't the first sucker she'd gone down to Earls Court with. This Adrian character, with the Rolex and chauffeur, had been a prince in old Siam too. Mummy and Daddy had said 'No!' and he'd drowned himself in the Phraya River with her, just like I had. If he was as rich as Pauline said he was, he could no doubt afford to buy Natalie out of whatever financial arrangement she had with Lee and keep her for himself. There had to be an amount of money Lee would accept to let Natalie go.

My wallet was wedged under my stomach, out of sight of the camera. I managed to dig out another two notes. I crumpled them up and slipped them to her.

"Why doesn't he want me to see her?"

"Need more," she said. "Two hundred."

It was pretty obvious why Lee didn't want me to see her. Natalie was meant for a consort for princes and movie stars. The deal had already been done. This Adrian—I felt as if I knew him already—had paid Lee a lot of money to take her away from the

sauna—she wasn't here tonight, she was already gone—and Lee
didn't want me nosing around, messing things up.

I stuffed some more notes into her palm.

"Why?"

"He do business with Lee."

I felt like asking for my money back. I'd guessed that much
already.

"What business?"

"Agency."

"Agency?"

"Adrian has agency. He find big customer. Natalie do special
service for big customer."

Special service? I wanted to tell her it's just sex. Hand relief.
Oral. Sex. Sex without. Anal. One hour VIP. No doubt there were
refinements on the menu, extras for the totally fucked up. But it
was never special, not even then. Pauline knew that as well as I did.
It was only special if there was love.

"What big customer?"

A bleak dreaminess pricked her eyes.

"Very rich man. Like crazy girl."

"Natalie's not crazy."

'Sex without' for an extra fifty pounds. That wasn't crazy, it was
just stupid.

Pauline snorted. Her fingers dug in.

"Natalie?" It was only when she laughed that I felt the depths
of her malice. "Natalie crazy bitch. She think she special. She ba ba
ba boa. She think she number one big boss woman."

Pauline was a nasty piece of work. I wondered if Natalie
loathed Pauline as much as Pauline loathed her.

"She think she angel girl. She say she big Buddha woman. Just
crazy bitch."

Women! I felt like laughing in her face. No man would ever tear into another man with a relish as famished as this.

"Angel girl?"

"Just big nose! Is all!"

"What Buddha woman?"

"She think she special. Gonna get million of million money from big man."

She was right. That pretty much summed it up. Prince and princess. Drowning together in old Siam. A big Buddha woman. An angel girl... it was all about money. When it came to money, there's sphere after dizzying sphere spinning upwards and out of sight forever and ever. The day I saw her in Kilburn, she'd already had this Adrian guy in tow, Rolex man, the chauffeur-driven one, lining her up with someone who had even more Rolexes and chauffeurs than he did. That night in Kilburn, getting into my car, Adrian was already in the bag but she just couldn't help herself. 'BMW!' 'Sport Coupe!' It wasn't beer or heroin that Natalie was addicted to, it was money. Driving down to Earls Court, a can of beer in her hand, her eyes cruising the restaurants and locked-up office foyers, wet hair soaking the shoulders of her T-shirt, picking at her caesarean scar inside her jeans, it was her face naked in the golden explosion of a casino sign that had said it all.

"Roll over."

"No." I didn't want her to see that my cock was getting stiff. She probably knew anyway.

I was a fool. I'd forgotten something fabulously simple. I'd overlooked the blindingly obvious.

Driving down to Earls Court, Natalie steeling herself to meet Soom Bon, me worrying about being rolled, we'd been utterly separate. We'd been the furthest apart of any two human beings in the whole of the city. We'd been even more separate than Pauline and I were now. The thing that was happening to me—the stinging brightness in my spine, the shining hinge on which everything was turning towards something incomprehensible—had been so overwhelming I'd assumed that, in some way or other, in her own way, it was overwhelming Natalie too. I'd assumed—without even putting the assumption into words in case I saw how ridiculous it was—that something so powerful had to be shared. It couldn't be happening just to me, and not to her too. This burning away of the person I really was had begun the instant I first saw her burst from the doorway, so I'd taken it for granted that—in her own way, in her own terms—the same burning away was happening to her too. I'd assumed that some correspondence, unseeable because it was inside her, to the diamonds I'd seen streaming from her face, and to 'Nok same 'bird" welling up inside me, and to the shining hinge turning in everything, had united us, when nothing of the sort had occurred at all. She'd been alone the whole time, and I'd been alone the whole time. The quick fuck in the car after the restaurant had merely confirmed the distance between us. Slithering on her tongue's muscular wetness, raking the roof of her mouth, there'd been far more than just words between her and me.

"Give I hundred more."

"Eh?"

Pauline bent down and whispered in my ear.

"Give I more one hundred."

She was insatiable.

"No. I think I'd better go."

I tried to sit up.

"I tell you where she is."

"It's none of my business."

"I tell you where she go with Adrian."

She was vicious. There was something malign about her. Bad mouthing Natalie wasn't enough for her. Saying nasty things about her friend wasn't satisfying enough. She was hungry for blood. She didn't just want to stab Natalie in the back, she needed to jam the blade in deeper and deeper.

"I don't want to know."

She wanted to get Natalie into even more trouble with Lee than she already was in. She was eaten away with jealousy because Natalie was better than her. Pauline was addled with envy. She wanted me to do something stupid that would screw Natalie up good and proper.

"Give I one hundred more..." Perspiration bedewed the stunning light on her cheekbones. "... I tell you where she go with him tomorrow night."

The restaurant was called 'White's'. It was in a stylish street in Notting Hill Gate, not far from my office— where I still hadn't shown my face.

Pauline had told me nine o'clock. I got there early, and parked opposite. There was no reason why I should believe anything Pauline had told me. If she'd invented the whole thing I was hardly going to go back to Hackney Sauna and ask for a refund of my money. On the other hand, I'd seen Natalie and Pauline getting into the people carrier together. There was a possibility they were friends, even with Pauline's bitchiness, or at least acquaintances, and that Natalie had felt the need to confide her big date to someone.

'White's' was a classy place. I'd been there a couple of times myself entertaining particularly important clients. Melissa didn't like 'White's'. She said the ambience was as ostentatious as the prices.

What I could see of the ambience was a soft glow from tall windows shining through the fronds of frosty Leylandiae shrubs in square, galvanized tubs lined, somewhat militaristically, shoulder to shoulder shielding the restaurant's private stretch of pavement. A doorman in a greatcoat and top hat stood by the entrance, clapping his gloved hands together and breathing out clouds of white air. Melissa was right. 'Ostentatious' was the word.

I felt ill. Whatever was happening, it had nothing to do with Natalie. She and I were two separate animals, in two separate universes. There'd been no diamonds of light streaming for her, no ecstasy welling up, no shining hinge turning towards something incomprehensible. Her mind was on whatever it was her mind was on. I was alone, trapped inside my body with my body's preoccupations, just as she was trapped inside her body with its preoccupations. The thread of light in my spine had nowhere to go, nothing to think. It stung and shone. A numb brightness fanned up the back of my head but refused to turn into thought, let alone understanding. The car's heating was on, switched up high. The sensation that I was freezing was merely an illusion. It had to be an illusion, but my fingers were numb and my feet felt like two blocks of ice. I told myself the cold was psychological, it had nothing to do with the thread of light. The shining woman wasn't drawing the warmth out of my skin. She wasn't focusing my body heat in the relentless blaze in my spine. I was alone with it. It had started on the footpath when Natalie burst from the door, but it had nothing to do with Natalie. And yet the giddiness now was exactly the same as it had been then. Everything to my right—the footpath, a brick wall, a tree beside a gate—was heavy and dense, repelling me. Everything to my left—the road, the Leylandiae, the glow in the restaurant windows—was light and insubstantial, drawing me towards it. The shining hinge was in everything, turning inexorably, endlessly, towards something I'd never comprehend, of which I knew nothing except that it wasn't Natalie. Transcendence? The source of joy? The very thought made me ill. It was fear, pure and simple. I shouldn't even be sitting here.

This was the second night in a row I'd been out late with only a dubious excuse. Melissa was getting more than suspicious. My past loyalty was stopping her from directly confronting me, but she no longer believed my lies. I'd got in from the sauna well after one o'clock. Melissa had gone to bed but she'd been lying awake waiting for me to get back. My fifty minute trip to the office to pick up some drawings had taken nearly four hours. I'd felt her struggling to believe me as I told her that I'd stayed in the office and worked on the drawings there. I'm not a good liar. I'd invented details that had sounded wrong even as they came out of my mouth. Tonight was my second night's going back to the office to work in a row. I was petrified Melissa would ring Bernard and ask him what was going on, and that she'd find out that I was lying.

A couple came out of the restaurant, through the tall glass doors. The commissionaire stepped out into the middle of the road and waved to a taxi down on Westbourne Grove.

The taxi cruised up to the kerb and the couple climbed in. It wasn't Natalie and her date. Adrian. Adrian Whitely. Adrian had a chauffeur. He wore a Rolex. Natalie had boasted about him to Pauline.

The commissionaire glanced at me as he went back to his post. A nice car. I'd been sitting here for half an hour already. He probably thought I was a chauffeur.

The thread of light in my spine had nowhere to go, and nothing to think. It fanned up the back of my head but refused to turn into thought, let alone into understanding, *but it had been right about Lee lining Natalie up with someone big.* The unapproachable woman had whispered the truth the other morning sitting in the car outside the Caledonian Road house when I'd seen Lee and the accountant. Cyril had been at Kilburn, because Lee *had something big lined up for Natalie.* This Adrian character, with his Rolex and his chauffeur, was rich and powerful enough to buy Natalie out of whatever financial arrangement she had with Lee, but even he wasn't the big man, not according to Pauline he wasn't. *'Agency!*

Adrian is agency. He find big customer. Natalie do special service for big customer.' It wasn't just my desperation to see her again that was making me sit here. It wasn't only my wounded pride that she had a man more special than me that kept me sitting here on and on. *'Very rich man. He like crazy girl.'* The thread of light had been right. The unapproachable woman had whispered the truth. And then there were those other things Pauline had said: *'She think she special.' 'She say she angel girl.' 'She think she big Buddha woman.'* We weren't two separate animals, in separate universes. Something real had happened that first time I saw her. Natalie was superstitious, but her 'angel girl' was my shining thread. Her 'big Buddha woman' was my unapproachable source of joy.

A party came out of the restaurant. The commissionaire handed them into a series of chauffeur driven cars.

I looked at my watch. It was ten o'clock already! I laughed out loud.

What a sucker! A hundred quid—plus the two, or more, she'd nicked from my wallet —for a bum steer! There was no Adrian Whitely. There was no such person. Natalie wasn't inside, behind those glowing windows. Pauline's malice was dazzling. She'd sent me on a wild goose chase. I couldn't help admiring her inventiveness. It was almost worth a hundred quid. 'White's'! 'White's' was a famous restaurant. She'd probably read about it in a magazine or heard it mentioned in a food programme on TV. It was an easy name to remember, even for a Thai woman with little English. She'd passed the name on to me for a hundred pounds and the pleasure of having me sit in a freezing car for an hour looking like a complete dill. I deserved everything I got.

A black Mercedes pulled up outside the restaurant. A minute or so later the tall doors opened and the commissionaire bowed a couple out.

For an instant I didn't recognize her. There was something wrong with my eyes. It was Natalie, yet it wasn't Natalie.

She scowled. In the harsh streetlight a dimple like a surgical incision stood far out in either cheek, but the winged cheekbones weren't her cheekbones. The broad lips didn't belong to her.

Like light in slow motion, but quicker than light, the street turned on its shining hinge. She didn't come out of any possible past. Pink nylon petticoat turned to elegant black chiffon. Smurf slippers on a frozen pavement swung sideways into a pair of high heel pumps.

She swayed like one of those celestial musicians you see in Chinese prints. It wasn't just the fact that she was Asian. She towered in the way angels tower. It wasn't merely that her face was geisha pale under the streetlamp. It wasn't just that her body was full and willowy, or that her long slim legs were at home in four inch stilettos. A flaking door with a green star pinned to its jamb turned at the speed of slow motion light to candlelit glass shutting behind her. She stepped out of no past that I knew of, that not a single person on earth knew of, not even she herself, that not even the tapering lift of her eyes could know. 'She think she angel girl.' She was right. 'She say she big Buddha woman.' She was. 'She crazy bitch'. Pauline's envy couldn't touch her. 'She ba ba ba boa'. No malice dared approach her. I was the one who'd been right all along. Natalie was special. She was meant for the consort of kings and movie stars. She was unique, and not just in the way that every individual is unique.

In her heels she was taller than the man she was with. Her hand, where she'd taken his arm, gripped his sleeve, with an easy proprietorship, a little above the elbow. Adrian Whitely was younger than I'd expected, in his mid to late thirties. His suit looked rumpled and ill-fitting next to her well-groomed perfection. He was one of those wealthy men who affect scruffiness.

There was something boyish about his face, a hint of early double chin, next to her ageless beauty.

A chauffeur jumped out of the Mercedes. There was a moment's jockeying between the chauffeur and the commissionaire to open the back door, and she got in. Adrian Whitely climbed in after her.

The street turned on its shining hinge. I felt giddy. There was a slewing sensation, everything to my right, away to the end of the universe, dense and heavy, everything to my left, away to the end of the universe, light and insubstantial, swinging me round, drawing me towards it, towards something I knew right then I would never comprehend. Natalie was where she belonged. On a rich man's arm, transcendent, at the source of joy. She freed me. She demanded nothing, not even desire. I felt a sudden joy, more powerful than any happiness I'd ever known. I could go home, patch things up with Melissa even now, get on with my life, and still remain in contact with the source. The unapproachable woman was here, now, in the car with me. The unapproachable woman, not Natalie, would always be here, now, inside me and outside me. I could go home, make it up to Melissa no matter how long it took, get on with my life, knowing that I'd glimpsed the ultimate

The Mercedes drew away from the kerb. I waited till they reached the corner and turned left onto the main road before I pulled out after them. It was going to be more difficult tailing them in these late night streets than following the people carrier had been in the morning traffic.

The Mercedes crossed the deserted market stalls of Portobello Road and turned left onto Ladbroke Grove. The traffic was a little heavier here. We climbed the hill and descended towards a set of traffic lights. I pulled up directly behind the Mercedes but I had the feeling no one inside the Mercedes clocked me.

The Mercedes turned right onto Holland Park Avenue and then immediately left again into Holland Park itself, a quarter of a mile of mansions descending a gentle slope beneath the branches of overarching plane trees.

The Mercedes stopped halfway down Holland Park. The chauffeur jumped out and held the door open and she and Adrian got out.

They mounted some steps between marble pilasters. A front door opened and they went in.

I parked opposite the house, and switched the engine off and waited in the dark.

A light came on in the first floor windows. The windows were tall and looked out onto a balcony railed in elaborate cast iron. I caught a glimpse of a high ceiling and what looked like the top of a sculpture, before arms, in white shirt sleeves, dragged drapes across. The drapes were heavy, and shut out the light inside.

It was crazy sitting here. It was getting even colder inside the car. I'd switched the heating off. I didn't feel unhappy. There was no torture in sitting here. In fact, I felt quite glad. She'd freed me from something unbearable. I wondered if she'd seen me, parked across from the restaurant. That scowl as she stepped onto the footpath. Perhaps she recognized the BMW, and that was the reason she scowled. Maybe, maybe not. It didn't matter any more. It felt nice just sitting here in the cold, the trunk of a plane tree next to where I was parked, as motionless as a speckled pillar lifting its nave of tall boughs into the streetlight, knitting naked branches and stir-less twigs somewhere high above me.

Headlights turned into the top of the road. They lit my dashboard as they descended.

The car pulled up directly behind me.

Christ! The police! It was crazy sitting here so long in this ultra-wealthy street. The police are pretty much private security when it comes to Holland Park.

A man got out of the car and came walking towards me. I prepared a lame excuse and rolled down my window.

"Get out!"

I recognized Cyril's voice before I made out his face. He was wearing a suit, not the tracksuit and baseball cap I'd seen him in in Kilburn. Tightly plaited corn rows creased the shiny dome of his scalp.

"Get the fuck out of that car!"

I climbed out. He thrust me backwards against the tree. The back of my head banged against the trunk.

"What the fuck you think you're doing here?"

I heard a trace of anxiety in his voice.

I said:

"It's none of your business."

The hand that had grabbed me in Kilburn, like a paving slab closing over my shoulder, caught me above the eye so hard it rattled me against the tree trunk. Lights flashed. There was a moment's blackness.

His voice dropped to a rumble deep in his throat. He didn't want to wake the wealthy sleepers.

"You fuck off out of it. Okay?"

"Okay."

"I don't wanta see your face no more. Okay?"

"Okay."

"Not Kilburn. Not Hackney. Not here. Not nowhere. Okay?"

"Yes."

He pinned me against the tree.

"I see your face again, man, yo dead."

"Let's go upstairs," said Melissa. "You'll be more comfortable upstairs."

Bernard, the elder of my two business partners, stood in the kitchen with a bundle of drawings and papers under his arm looking uncomfortable. He never usually brought work round to our place but things were in such a parlous state at the office he'd turned up after dinner with some matters that needed our immediate attention.

"Yeah. Let's go upstairs," I said.

Our big Nokido kitchen table was better for spreading out architectural drawings and documents on, but it had turned so cold outside the kitchen felt a bit bleak.

Melissa looked at me.

"Wine?"

"Why not."

I was on tenterhooks. I'd spent the day at the office trying to repair some of the damage done by my not showing up at the Arkwright presentation the afternoon I went down to Earls Court with Natalie. The loss we'd suffered was severe. Bernard and my other partner Pippa had been indignant that I'd gone missing for three days. We'd put a lot of time and effort into securing the Arkwright contract and now that it had fallen through we were playing catch up getting new jobs on the books and finding enough work for our staff to do. Bernard and Pippa had been more than indignant. I'd let them down badly. They'd made mutterings about scaling back if I wasn't prepared to give the company my full commitment. I might be the senior partner, but they could still outvote me when it came to policy for the future. I'd promised I wouldn't take my eye off the ball again and now here Bernard was at half past eight in the evening punishing me with some problems that had arisen at Rampton Street.

Melissa uncorked a bottle of red and we trooped upstairs to the warmer colours and softer textures of our first floor living room. Melissa could feel the tension, Bernard's feathers ruffled, my struggle to concentrate. She liked Bernard. We socialized with Bernard and his wife and had taken holidays together with them. Bernard was a worrier. He was ten years older than me and prematurely grey. As a structural engineer he was the bane of architects and their more flamboyant proposals.

He spread out some drawings on our rough-hewn Moroccan coffee table. The drawings curled up at the corner and he weighted them back down with his glass of wine.

"I've got a meeting with Frank Pettigrew first thing tomorrow, Jim, about these phase two drawings. I just wanted to finalize a few things before I see him." They were the drawings I'd lied about the night before last when I went to Hackney. I was terrified Bernard was going to say something that would give me away. "I'm not sure whether we shouldn't pass on phase two altogether..." He looked at me. "... While we're recovering from the Arkwright fiasco..."

He was still angry. 'Fiasco' was not a word Bernard would normally use.

"Well. I don't know..." I said. "Wouldn't that...?"

It was hard to concentrate on what he was proposing. We'd already contracted for phase two of Rampton Street. Pulling out at the last minute would be awkward. Didn't we need as much work as we could get? Or was he thinking about laying people off? Nothing made sense.

Melissa no longer believed my lies about my late night visits to the office, not with the swelling above my left eye where Cyril had punched me. She'd stopped believing me even before I came home with the bruise. If she'd had any doubts that I was lying, my story about stumbling on the stairs and hitting my head had convinced her. She didn't believe a single thing I was telling her, but she was giving me time. She was waiting for me to come clean and tell the truth off my own bat. Love was struggling to overcome concern. She was restraining her need to interrogate me so that I could stay the man she loved and take this last opportunity she was giving me to be honest.

"Jim?"

"... Yeah, but... if we pass on phase two they might hand the whole thing over to Hansons..."

"Yes, but..."

"Are these the drawings that you went to get?" said Melissa. "The other night?"

"No," I said. "That was other ones."

"I don't know, Jim," said Bernard. "Perhaps we ought to scale back."

Bernard didn't give me away. He was so worried about Rampton Street he hadn't even noticed. I was glad he was here. The three of us were old friends. It felt almost convivial, Bernard, Melissa and I sitting with a glass of wine in the warm glow of the standard lamps, a freezing wind rattling the branches of the horse chestnut tree beyond the richly coloured curtains. I relaxed a little. Melissa couldn't interrogate me as long as Bernard was here.

"Perhaps we should ring Pippa..." I took my cellphone out of my pocket. "... See what Pippa says..."

"I know what Pippa thinks already." There was a trace of impatience in Bernard's voice. "She wants to pass on phase two."

"Well, then..." I said.

I put my phone down on top of the drawings.

I decided that when the questions came I'd face them head on. Tonight. Tomorrow. When concern overcame love and the interrogations started, I'd brazen it out. It didn't matter how absurd I was going to look or sound. I didn't care how incredulous in her heart Melissa was going to be. I'd stand by my stories for as long as it took, till this nightmare was over. I'd never see Natalie again. It was finished. It had never even really started. She'd freed me. She shone and stung, here in my spine. She was unapproachable and that was the way I intended to keep it from now on in. I'd get on with my life knowing that I'd stood, at least for an instant, at the source of joy.

Brazening it out with Melissa wouldn't, deep down, be dishonest. Standing by my stories, even if Melissa didn't believe them, wouldn't be lying. It was easy. I'd never see Natalie again. It was over. It had never really started in the first place. She was off with Adrian Whiteley and his Rolex and chauffeur and the 'big man' he was lining up for her. She was meant for a consort for kings and movie stars. That was what I'd seen last night as she came out of the restaurant. *She think she big Buddha woman'. 'She say she angel girl'.* She was right. It was no less than the truth. She was destined for big things. With his chauffeur and his house in Holland Park and his staff to draw his curtains for him, Adrian Whitely was wealthy in a way I would never be. And there were men even wealthier than him. It was as simple as that. It was all about money. *'BMW!' 'Sport coupe!'* Driving down to Earls Court to see a sorcerer. It wasn't beer or heroin Natalie was addicted to, it was money, and she had every right to demand money. It was true. She was an angel girl. A big Buddha woman. She was special. She was too special for me.

I topped up Bernard's wine.

"... Up to you, Bernard... Your call..."

I was still getting over my confrontation with Cyril. My eye stung like buggery. Driving back to Islington after he hit me, I'd felt concussed. When I got back, Melissa had been in bed but still awake. I'd felt so shaken, making any sense at all about how I'd come by a cut forehead and swollen eye had been impossible. It wasn't just the blow, how hard he'd hit me. Cyril was scary. 'I see yo face again, man, yo dead.' They weren't empty words. It wouldn't have surprised me to learn that Cyril had actually killed people. I'd been stupid answering him back, telling 'it's none of your business.' It was very much his business. The anxiety I'd imagined I'd heard in his voice, for *his* girls, was all in my head. The guy didn't know what anxiety was. I hadn't been doing any harm, sitting in my car outside Adrian Whitely's house. There'd been nothing for Cyril, or even Lee, to worry about in my following Natalie back to Holland Park. Adrian Whitely no doubt had his own security arrangements. A man as wealthy as that would have his own staff to see off unwanted snoopers. Cyril worked for Lee, not Adrian Whitely. Yet he'd turned up within twenty minutes of my parking outside the house. He'd turned up pumped and angry. Someone had got in touch with Lee and told Lee that I'd followed Natalie back to Holland Park. It could only have been Natalie. That scowl on the footpath. The way she dipped her head as she climbed into the Mercedes. She'd seen me parked across the road as she and Adrian came out of the restaurant. Natalie had told Adrian, Adrian had got hold of Lee and Lee had sent Cyril to scare me off. Something big was going down and they were edgy. Pauline was right. *'Get big customer.' 'Do special service.' 'Gone get big man give she million of million money.'*

Bernard sat back in the settee.

"You should get that eye seen to, Jim. It looks nasty."

"That's what I told him," said Melissa.

"Nah," I said. "It's nothing."

In fact, the bruise hurt like hell. The swelling above my eye felt hot. My eye had closed up. There was a cut by my temple where the capital 'C' of Cyril's signet ring had punctured the skin.

I grinned.

"A dab of Dettol and a bit of TLC. That's all it needs."

My phone rang.

My glockenspiel ring tone vibrated my cell phone across the blue and white shapes on the Xerox-d drawing.

"Ah! That'll be Pippa..." I said, and picked up.

"Jim...?!"

I jammed the phone hard against my ear—they'd hear it was a woman's voice, the broken eggshells in her throat—and jumped to my feet. I strode to the window.

"... Jack?"

It was the first name that came to mind.

"Jim...?!"

Her voice was frantic.

"...What's the matter, Jack?..."

It was too late to pretend it was Pippa. I couldn't pretend it was Pippa, I'd be seeing Pippa at work in the morning.

"Come see I?"

"... What's the matter...?... what's wrong...?"

Melissa's glance flinched. Bernard looked away.

I put my hand over the screen and said to Bernard:

"... Jack... Jack O'Grady... an old mate of mine... he's... he's in trouble...*What*...?" I said into the phone.

"Come see I Hackney?"

"Now?"

"Chai! Is importing!"

She was breathless, berserk.

"What's the matter?"

"Can't say! You come!"

The line went dead.

"That was Jack," I said. "Jack O'Grady... He's back in town... an ex journalist... conspiracy theorist really..." I tried to smile. If I stopped smiling, Melissa would confront me. "... I had a drink with him the other day... used to be a top journalist... conspiracy theory, man!... it's done his head in..."

I looked at Melissa. Her forehead knit.

"... Jack's in a lot of trouble. I've got to go..."

Except for the one on the end, the shutters were still down. It looked as if the shutters were kept permanently closed. Strips of yellow light shone through the cracks. HACKNEY SAUNA AND MASSAGE hung above the footpath, sporadically spot-lit. The punters must get off on chiaroscuro.

I parked round the back, SAUNA CUSTOMERS ONLY. I was a customer, so that was okay then.

I rang the buzzer and the black guy opened the door.

"Yeah, mon. Come on in."

It was impossible to tell if 'come on in' had modulated from cool into a greeting.

The place felt smaller than I remembered, less like a betting shop and more like the foyer of a small hotel.

The same two Chinese men sat at the cocktail counter with a younger Chinese man who, from the way he stared at the girls, was a customer.

There were no nurse's outfits. The two Thai girls I'd seen the other night were there, in standard sexy gear. The East European girl had on a pair of hot pants tonight. Pauline was chatting with a young white guy, stroking his muscular Polynesian sleeve. It looked as if Hackney was well stocked with tattoo parlours.

Pauline didn't look in my direction.

The place was busier tonight. There was no sign of Natalie.

"Beer, Jack?"

For a second I didn't realise that the manageress was talking to me. She'd remembered my name!

"... Erm... yes... thank you..."

I took my overcoat off.

"Here, darling," said the manageress. "I'll hang that up for you."

"It's okay." I sat down with my coat in my lap. "I'll hold onto it."

I glanced around the room. One of the guys at the cocktail counter, the one I imagined was the people carrier driver, looked at me.

Natalie definitely wasn't here.

She'd set me up. I was becoming a nuisance. I was in for more than a smack in the face tonight.

My beer arrived. I grinned at the manageress. Seven pounds fifty for a 500 ml bottle of Budweiser. There was something charmingly upfront about it.

"You do Thai fight? *Leally?*! You been *Pattaya*?"

The tip of Pauline's orchid unfurled its pink and blue sepal from her hot pants. Leally? Pattaya? I got the impression she was dumbing down her English for the white lad's sake. She was perched on the arm of his sofa, her perfect nails communing with his tattooed elbow.

She glanced at me. The night before last I'd given her four hundred pounds. She was debating whether to dump the young guy and come and perch on the arm of my chair instead. She kept glancing at me but she wasn't smiling. No. She was better off where she was. I was about to get a kicking.

I realised what had happened. Pauline had grassed me up to Natalie. She'd told Natalie about me being here the other night. That was why Natalie had insisted I come to the sauna tonight. I was more than just a nuisance. I was becoming a threat to her scene with Adrian Whiteley. When I went out the back with one of the girls I was going to get the kicking of a lifetime.

I glanced at the door into the vestibule. It stood ajar, but the glass door beyond the strip curtain was locked. Standing up and asking to be let out was not an option.

"So," said the manageress. "Who do you fancy, Jack?"

None of the girls offered to come and sit next to me.

The east European girl I'd seen in the washing up gloves the other night was now intent on her phone. The Thai girls chatted with each other and with the tattooed guy.

"Well, Jack?"

"Erm..."

There was still no sign of Natalie. I'd been here ten minutes already. If she was out the back with a customer, they were taking their time.

No. She wasn't out the back. She'd set me up. She wasn't even here. Cyril was, in a cubicle out the back.

The room felt smaller than before. It was as if a ghastly social function were being held.

The buzzer buzzed. The black guy pushed through the strip curtain. I heard the front door open. Cyril. They'd contacted Cyril.

Natalie rushed in. Her face was shiny from the cold.

She strode across the room. She didn't look at me. She dumped a Nisa carrier bag crammed with shopping on the cocktail counter.

"Fleezing!" The Chinese customer stared at her. "Very cold!"

She took a packet of cigarettes out of the carrier bag and jammed it in the pocket of her puffa jacket. From the jacket's short hem all the way down to her glass-heeled stilettoes her legs were bare. Her knees looked cold.

She rooted round in the carrier bag and produced a box of Mister Kipling date slices, a quart of Hague, an unbranded bag of fortune cookies and a six-pack of Stella.

She unzipped her puffa jacket, her fingers impatient with the zip. She resented having been made so helplessly alluring. She shrugged the jacket off. It was like watching a cocoon unzip and a never-before-seen loveliness slip out and shake its unbelievable wings.

She opened a beer and climbed onto the remaining stool at the cocktail counter. She rubbed some warmth into her knees.

"Don like cold," she told the tattooed lad.

She still didn't look at me. On the phone she'd sounded frantic. Now she was businesslike, chatty. Over the phone, I'd got the impression that she was scared stiff, that she was in some sort of danger. Now here she was, running errands to the shops and smiling at the customers. I'd already made the mistake of thinking that she was being held prisoner in the Caledonian Road house, when, in fact, she'd been out last night dining at 'White's', and now she was popping out to the shops for supplies, and charming the pants off the tattooed guy. If she'd really been as frightened as she'd sounded over the phone, if her terror had been real, she would have run away when they sent her to the shops. She would have gone to the police, gone anywhere but back here, even in her hot pants and bikini top, never mind the cold.

"Well, Jack?"

I jumped to my feet before the young guy could move in, and nodded at Natalie.

She took me into a cubicle. With the tall massage table and the chair there was hardly room for the two of us to stand up in.

Her voice was shrill.

"You fuck Pauline?!" For a second I didn't understand. She was screaming at me. "You do with her?!" Her hand wandered to the scar on her belly. The welt was even rawer than the day I first saw her. "Pauline say you do fuck with her!"

She was shouting so loud they must surely be able to hear outside.

"Natalie!"

I tried to put some authority into my voice. I'd just watched her walk out of a restaurant on a man's arm. I'd sat in my car and seen her go into his house with him, the light come on in the upstairs window.

Her eyes were bleak and hard.

"You do sex with her I kill you!"

She meant it!

"Of course I didn't have sex with her. Stop it."

I grabbed her by both shoulders. She was shaking. It was unbearable the way her shoulders shook.

"She bitch. She bad girl. I fuck kill her!"

I held her against me.

"We only talked."

It wasn't a hundred percent true but she was scaring me.

She pressed against me. Her breasts felt furious under her bikini top. Her hot pants ground against my flies, her belly rubbed against my belly, rubbing the hated scar away.

"We only talked. Okay? I was looking for you."

She looked at me.

"Yes?"

"I promise."

"I sorry. I stupid girl."

She still didn't quite believe me.

We kissed. Her tongue remembered my tongue, quick and muscular, searching for words, for stories about princes and princesses. She pulled back.

"Wha! What you do you eye?"

Her fingers were hot on my face. Her nails picked at the cut, opening it, making it sting again.

"Sit down! I look!"

I climbed up onto the table. It squeaked under my weight.

"How you do?"

She kissed my eye. Her tongue found the place on my forehead where Cyril's signet ring had cut me.

"What happen?"

She'd seen me last night. That scowl as she came out of the restaurant, she'd seen me at once, the dip of her head climbing into

Adrian's Mercedes, she knew I was sitting on the other side of the road in my car. She knew I'd followed her back to Adrian Whitely's house.

"What you do?"

"Look. Natalie..."

She knew Cyril had caught me outside the house. She knew perfectly well that Cyril had hit me. It was her who'd alerted Lee that I was there.

"I get cream. TLC."

The door slammed. She was gone. I sat on the table and waited for Cyril to come.

She came back with a bottle of Dettol and a packet of cotton wool and a roll of elastoplast. She soaked a handful of cotton wool in the yellow antiseptic and dabbed at the wound. It was Hospital Night after all.

"Must clean. Can not dirty."

"Ow!"

She rubbed the Dettol into the bruise too hard. She was as clumsy at first aid as she was at massage.

"Can not dirty. Get in fection."

Her English was limited, but she knew 'infection.'

"Natalie..."

"Must careful, honey. Can not give hurting. Danger."

She unpeeled some Elastoplast. She didn't have any scissors. She bit the plaster and tore off a jagged length. She flattened it over the wound.

"I love you, Jim."

I didn't know what to say. I couldn't speak. My hands filled with an exquisite softness like I'd never touched before. She kissed my forehead, my eyes, my hair. Her shoulders turned to knuckles, her fingers struggling behind her back with a fastener.

The table squeaked.

I held her close with every ounce of strength I had in me. If a hair's breadth came between us I'd end up in free fall, I'd drop down the abyss that separated us.

"No! Don't!"

Her bikini top fell on the floor.

"Natalie!"

The crown of her head bobbed miles below me, her hair tumbling around her face.

"Stop it!"

She was on her knees. She was kneeling before me. *She was unlacing my shoes.* I felt my foot lift, like a hoof about to kick. She pulled off my shoe, peeled off my sock and stooped. I ran my fingers through her hair. I tried to lift her by the rich warmth of her scalp. I was scared she was going to kiss my feet.

My trousers tumbled around my ankles. She pulled my underpants down.

"Natalie..."

I hadn't come here for sex. My cock was so stiff it hurt.

Her tongue closed over my glans like a door shutting out the world. We were in a room made of breath, her tongue a sweet nothing turning me to a sigh.

"Natalie..."

Melissa and I didn't do oral much. On the few occasions we did, it was somehow shy and quick, not all consuming.

They weren't her lips, they were Pauline's, plump and greedy, it was Pauline's tiny chin pumping and gnawing, *we were even in the same cubicle as I'd been in with Pauline.* Her breasts wet up and down in time to her mouth's slavering. Below her spine's shining freefall the back of her hot pants moue-d above the crease of her arse.

I slid off the table and got my cock out of her mouth. I didn't want to cum in her mouth. I grabbed her by her armpits and lifted her onto the table and pushed her down onto her back. This wasn't me. I was a gentle lover. I didn't manhandle women. She was already pulling her pants down as her head banged on the skimpy massage padding.

I stalled above her, trying to hold onto my orgasm. She arched her back. Her hips lifted to take me. She was so wet it tore my heart open as I impaled her. A leg went around me. A foot landed in my back. Eggshells were cracking in the back of her throat, words I couldn't understand, waves warm as egg yoke, came surging up her body and broke over me. She was climaxing even before I'd even fucked her properly.

I rammed my cock into her again and again, hurrying to catch up, wanting to let go, meet her, except... nothing happened. I wasn't going over the brink with her. I wasn't reaching climax. I couldn't cum. Cumming was a million miles away. I was cold and alone. I was completely on my own.

The unapproachable woman shone and stung. She approached. We were one. The brightness was unbearable. I was freezing cold. My spine was a frozen hinge that hurt as it turned. She lifted me out of my body towards her inexorable eyes.

Natalie moaned. Her nails raked my back. Her body lifted towards me again. Her bottom was slippery and I couldn't even cum.

CHAPTER THREE

"You upset Bernard last night," said Melissa. "Running off like that." She was furious. She'd reached the end of her patience. "First you don't show up for the Arkwright presentation. Now this."

It wasn't Bernard she was upset about.

"... Yeah... well..." I said. "... I'll give Bernard a ring and apologise... Jack's in trouble... big trouble... Jack's suicidal... I wouldn't have run off like that except I was worried Jack might do something stupid..."

She didn't believe a word I was saying. I couldn't even pretend to believe what I was saying myself. It wasn't a matter of believing or not believing. As long as I kept putting one detail after another out there into the empty space between us, it didn't matter how unreal the lies sounded, they put off the recriminations for another minute or two.

"... When I got to his house he was drinking heavily... he was drunk..."

"House? Where's he living?"

"... Hotel... down at Earls Court... he's staying in a hotel..."

Melissa strode to the French windows. She stood looking out at the garden. The sun had come out. Her shoulders lifted, taking a deep breath. This was it.

"Do you think we can risk the garden?"

The change of subject was so abrupt I felt sure the moment of rupture had come. She was holding back from accusing me because the pain was too sharp.

"... Maybe... why not...?"

"It's still very cold."

Ralph's twenty-first felt like a gift from heaven. It came like the sunlight breaking out on the garden, like a lie holding off the unforgivable. Ralph's party was due to start in a matter of hours.

110

There was frost on the honeysuckle but if the sun stayed out we could risk drinks in the garden. I was spared a little longer. There were things that needed finalizing even more urgently than the truth.

I'd got back from Hackney at two a.m., late enough for Melissa to be asleep. It had been a busy morning, and in a few hours' time we were having people over to celebrate my son's birthday. Accusations and recriminations were out of the question. Excuses and confessions weren't an option. It was Ralph's twenty-first. No matter how terrible either I or Melissa felt, we couldn't let things get out of hand on Ralph's big day. I had another seven or eight hours to bolster up my story, and stop the dreadful from happening.

"I'll do a fondue. They're good if it's cold."

She looked at me.

"What time did you get back last night?"

"... One... two... I'm not sure..."

"I didn't think you liked Jack all that much."

It was true. Jack and I were mates at university, we'd kept in touch when he was an overseas correspondent, but I'd never really liked him much as a person. Jack had a bullish insistence on always being in the right at every moment on every issue. Even when he was a respected journalist, there'd never been any room for even a moment's disagreement with his point of view. Jack forced his opinions on you in a way that had become more and more unlikeably dogmatic the deeper he'd descended into the paranoid realms of conspiracy theory.

"... I know, but... he was really freaked..."

I'd been stupid snatching at Jack for my lies. Melissa had stopped believing me the minute Jack had rung the other morning.

"Who's that?" Ralph came drifting into the kitchen. "I didn't think you knew any really freaky people, Dad."

It was good to see him. Tousled hair, sleepy eyes, still in his dressing gown, Ralph could get things back to seeming normalcy with one wry smile.

"I was young once too," I said. "Don't you know any freaky people?"

Ralph was in his third year at medical school, majoring in psychiatry. Melissa and I had hoped that he'd choose surgery. Psychiatry felt a bit 'freaky' for someone as straightforward as Ralph, but my son had developed a certain dashing urbanity over the last year or so that would possibly suit psychiatry well. One could picture him charming mental patients and psychiatric conferences alike with his frank good nature.

"That friend of yours? What's his name? Jack?"

Both Ralph and his sister Meredith were now familiar with my Jack O'Grady story.

"Yes." I made a face. "Nine eleven. The holocaust hoax. Pimlico paedophiles."

"Meredith rang," said Melissa. "She's going to be late."

Ralph shrugged.

"Oh well. Never mind."

Ralph hadn't particularly wanted a big party. He hadn't particularly wanted a party at all. I'd got the impression, when we first mooted the idea, that he'd much rather have spent his birthday with his girlfriend. Her parents had a place in the country that Ralph was fond of. He hadn't been keen on the party idea at first, but had warmed to it once he saw how much Melissa and I wanted it.

"Paedophiles! Nine eleven!" said Melissa. "It's absurd!"

"I know…" I grinned. "… I told you Jack was freaked…"

It was the sort of party I like best, neither too formal nor too frenetic, what, in days gone by, might have been called an 'at home', about twenty of Ralph's student friends upstairs in the living room playing music, and a similar number of our friends, neighbours and work colleagues down in the kitchen exchanging news and gossip.

The weather was still cold. The sun shone, but it was certainly too chilly to think about going outside for drinks. The kitchen was crowded and noisy, our guests happy to admire the frost-tinged beauty of the garden through the French windows.

Bernard and his wife were there, and Pippa with her toddler. We didn't talk business. The three of us had known each other long enough not to have to talk shop, even with things at work being so tense right now. Bernard didn't mention my absconding in the middle of last night's conference.

Four o'clock came, and Meredith still hadn't arrived. She was coming down from Durham, but had rung to say that her train was delayed. My daughter was in first year at Durham University, swept up in the pre-Christmas freshman whirl, but fond enough of her brother to take the ten hour round trip down to London for his twenty-first.

She'd already rung twice to say she was running late. I'd offered to pick her up from the station but she could hear how busy we were and had insisted she'd come up from Kings Cross on the bus.

I made a fondue. Fondue is my one culinary accomplishment. I felt a bit embarrassed about the way it always ended up being my big party piece.

Ralph and Jemima came down from the living room to fetch some more champagne and snacks for the guests upstairs.

Ralph showed off his new watch to neighbours and uncles who'd known him since he was a baby. Those of them who hadn't seen him for a while were struck by how handsome Ralph had become. Ralph's childhood interest in people had turned into an infectious charm that seemed almost wasted on his somewhat horsey girlfriend, though he and Jemima seemed to be fond of each other.

"No. No. Landmines have been banned since nineteen ninety seven. They don't sell 'em any more!"

"The Princess of Wales campaigned against landmines," Norman Braithwaite, chair of our residents' association, comfortably informed us.

"It's got nothing to do with bloody landmines." Melissa's brother Tony was getting hot under the collar. A stringy man in his early fifties and a staunch Tory, Tony was offended by the anti-Arms Fair protesters' long hair. "Load of bloody trouble makers."

"That's Greenpeace, not anarchists."

"They don't sell landmines! Landmines have been banned since nineteen ninety seven!"

"Yes, but what about the Yemen?" Norman's a bit of a wooly socialist. "The Saudis bombing the Yemen... and that chap in Indonesia..."

Melissa's brother bristled.

"It's business, Norman. It's good for the economy. Somebody's got to pay for all these scroungers on benefits. We didn't used to balk at a few dictators when Britain was great."

"Yes, but..."

The hubbub in the kitchen was convivial enough to encompass even party political differences.

Melissa came up to me. She looked at her watch.

"Should we have the cake? Meredith's still not here."

"I don't know... she said she'd be here by four..."

"The Sandersons need to go soon."

"Okay. Let's have the cake."

A few words about a cake, it felt like the best conversation we'd had in days. The party was a success and we'd done it together. Days like this were the most precious thing there is, animal warmth, two dozen friendly bodies crowded into a kitchen, shutting out the cold. It was more than mere cold that this company kept at bay.

It kept out sordid thoughts and despicable intentions. It shut out sleaze and nightmare. The shared warmth in the kitchen was lit by a shared intelligence, a mutual understanding passed from face to face, from smile to smile, that kept out even the unapproachable woman and what I'd done last night. I'd never see Natalie again. I'd wait till I'd had the HIV test, been given the all clear, and pick up the frayed threads of my real life, and this time I'd never let go of my real life again.

"Cake! Cake everybody!"

A throng of footsteps came clumping down the stairs. The kitchen filled up even more. Everybody squeezed in. Someone switched the light off. It was pitch black outside now and the kitchen was plunged in an appropriate darkness.

"... Happy birthday to you...!" For a slim, sometimes nervy woman Melissa had a surprisingly strong singing voice. "... Happy birthday to you...!"

Everybody was singing.

The cake was magnificent. In the darkness the tiers of cream and jelly and chocolate glistened in the heat from the twenty one candles. Melissa placed the cake on the table.

"... Happy birthday, dear Ralph..."

Both the young voices and the older voices grew in confidence, lifted in chorus.

"... Happy birthday to you!"

There were a few hip hip hoorays from the older guests. Ralph blew out the candles. His face shone in the light of the guttering flames. There was a cheer and the light came on.

Ralph picked up the knife. With the meticulousness he'd been blessed with since he was a child, he made sure he found the dead center of the cake before the tip of the knife touched the cream.

The front door bell rang.

"Meredith!"

"Meredith's here!"

"Wait, Ralph. Wait." Everybody was smiling. "Wait for your sister."

"That's what I call timing!"

"What a stroke of luck!"

"Open the door, somebody. Quick. Quick."

I heard the front door open, and Melissa's voice:

"Jack...!... goodness me!.... Jack O'Grady!"

From the moment he entered the room, it was clear Jack wasn't well. His face was red and bloated. His overcoat hung open and some flabby paunch pushed through his shirt buttons, yet he was sweating. A glandular sheen glazed his eyes. They were the eyes of a diver coming up out of deep water, struggling with the bends. He was with a woman. The woman looked even more freaked out than Jack.

"Sorry... Sorry everybody... Didn't mean to butt in on you, Melissa..." He grinned at me. "... Apologies, Jim... didn't realise you were having a..." He saw the cake, the knife in Ralph's hand. "... Hi, Ralph... sorry, mate... it's your birthday... happy birthday, son... sorry to crash in on you all like this..."

"It's fine, Jack. It's quite alright," said Melissa. "It's nice to see you. Jim said he ran into you the other night."

"The other night?" Jack looked perplexed. "... No... we just flew in this morning..."

"But Jim said..." Melissa glanced at me. "...You and he, you had a drink together, when was it? Tuesday, Jim?"

I couldn't look at her.

"Tuesday?" said Jack. "No... we've been in Singapore... this is Sylvia..." Sylvia didn't smile. "... No... we just flew in this morning..."

"Jim?"

I shrugged. Everybody was looking at me.

"Jeez. Look. I'm sorry, Melissa..." Even Jack, in his paranoia, had picked up how angry Melissa was. "... I should have rung first..."

"What is it, Mum?" said Ralph.

"... I shouldn't have just turned up out of the blue like this..." said Jack. Melissa was trembling. "... Except... there's something big going down..." There was always something big going down in Jack's life. "... I need to speak to Jim..."

"Jim?"

She had a napkin in her hand, twisting the Christmassy paper between her fingers.

"Nothing," I said. "It's just... I'll explain later..."

"What's going on, Dad?"

I'd thought Ralph hadn't paid much attention to my comings and goings. The knife was still in his hand, but he'd forgotten all about his birthday.

"Nothing," I said. "Nothing's 'going on'..."

There was nothing to connect any of this to Natalie. There was no evidence that it was a woman. If I had had an affair—which I hadn't—it would have been with someone in the office, a social acquaintance. There was no way any of our guests could have connected my lying to Melissa with my sleeping with a prostitute. I still had time to make it right, it was just that now wasn't the moment. There was no space left to work out what to do. There were things I could say that would stop this from happening but I couldn't think what they were.

I looked at Jack.

"What did you need to speak to me about?"

Jack looked round at the puzzled faces.

"...Well... Not now, mate... you're busy...it's not all that important..."

"No, mate. What is it?"

"... No... really... I'll catch you later..."

I turned to Melissa. It wasn't fair, her wanting to drag me over the coals in front of all these people.

"Look. I won't be long. I'll just... talk to Jack..."

I headed for the door.

"... No. Really, mate... it's alright..."

"I'll be right back, everybody!"

I was almost shouting as I grabbed my coat.

Jack wanted money. He'd turned up unannounced because he was in urgent need of cash. A lot of cash. He had some sort of problem and it was major. He'd lost my phone number so he'd come straight to the house from the airport to ask for two thousand pounds. I hadn't seen him for three years. We weren't what you would call close friends. There were a dozen people in London who knew Jack better than me—he'd always had his 'supporters' and his 'contacts'—but I was the one he'd turned to when he was in trouble. If I hadn't felt so wretched I might have been flattered.

We sat at a table by the window in a bar in Kings Cross, around the corner from the hotel where Jack and Sylvia were staying, watching the crowds on the narrow footpath rush towards the station entrance in nervy, tail-lit blackness.

"I had to get out of Singapore, Jim. I'm in deep shit. They've stopped my bank account."

Jack's permanent five o'clock shadow had grown silvery since I last saw him. He was now pretty much completely bald, but he was one of those strong-jawed bald men who don't need to shave away the last pathetic wisps to look menacing.

It felt strangely secure, sitting here with him and Sylvia, watching the crowds hurry past, with my life going down the pan. I'd forgotten how overwhelming Jack could be, how he swept you along. I knew that it was a false sense of security his mania was giving me. I fully understood that the minute I stepped out onto the footpath this cocooned feeling would drain away like quicksand under my feet, but I wasn't angry with him for turning up at my door unannounced. I'd conjured him up myself, with my lies to Melissa.

"They tried to stop Jack coming into *his own* country!" said Sylvia. "Held him at Heathrow for six hours. A British citizen! They tried to cobble together some phony excuse for not letting him in."

Sylvia had an American accent. She was a tall, raw-boned woman, attractive in a ravaged sort of way. Jack always had some girl or other in tow, mothering his latest crusade.

He rubbed his mouth.

"They don't want me in London, Jim. For the next few weeks." He shared an initiatic smile with Sylvia. "Not till the Arms Fair's over."

It was always hard to pin down who the 'they' were in Jack's world picture—the globalist elite, the Saudis, the Washington neocons, the Russian oligarchs—it was always just 'they.'

Jack needed the two thousand pounds to send to someone he knew in Singapore who was in trouble with the police. There were people, Jack's 'sources', in trouble with the police all over the world.

"Anyway..." he swirled the remainder of his beer round in the bottom of his glass. "... Thanks for the money, Jim..."

"No problem."

"... I'll give it back to you as soon as possible..."

I wasn't going to hold my breath. In fact, I felt a pleasant sense of irresponsibility at not having to care whether he paid me back or not.

It was time to shake hands, wish him good luck, and go home and speak to Melissa, confess about Natalie.

Jack looked at me.

"... Sorry I crashed Ralph's party like that, Jim..." It was a struggle for Jack to concentrate on anything other than 'they' and his battle with 'them', but he was making the effort. "... I never even wished him happy birthday..."

"It's okay," I said. "It's nice to see you again, Jack."

It was, too. Jack's tales of shady arms deals and the satanic doings of the elite dwarfed my domestic problems. At this very moment, there were thousands of people being killed all around the world, even as we sat here stretching out a half of beer. It put going home and speaking to Melissa into perspective.

"... Melissa looked upset..."

"No, no. Melissa's fine."

"Did I put my foot in it? Say something I shouldn't have?"

"No. No, Jack. Not at all..."

I'd given Jack his money. I probably wouldn't see him again for another three years. There was no need to go into the gory details.

I stared out at the rushing pedestrians streaming by, heads down against the cold.

"I used you, Jack."

For the first time since we'd been sitting here, Jack looked nonplussed.

"Used me...?"

"... To lie to her... Melissa... about something... well, actually...about a woman... I've been seeing a woman..."

I was confessing! To a man I hardly knew, and didn't much like. I should have been back home, confessing to my wife, and I was pouring it all out to Jack O'Grady in a Kings Cross pub!

Jack stared at me.

"You? A woman?" He looked genuinely surprised. "... I thought you and Melissa were... you know... solid..."

"We are... were..."

I felt as if I'd let him down. Hard-living Jack O'Grady, wandering the world from hotspot to hotspot, waging war with systemic evil, and somehow or other, even at a three years' distance, I'd been a bulwark against chaos for him, a little bit of security.

"Well... I'm sure you can patch it up..."

"Yeah. Maybe."

I'd already given him the two thousand—I was carrying a lot of money these days—there was no reason for us to sit here any longer. I needed to get up and go home and make a clean breast of it with Melissa.

I looked at him.

"The Arms Fair?"

Jack rubbed his eyes.

"Yeah. The ExCel Centre."

"They postponed it till December?"

He grinned at Sylvia.

"Yep. I told you. Something major's going down." Something major was always going down with Jack. "The Saudis'll be there. King Salman's boys." He spoke as if he knew King Salman personally. "Shopping for ISIS."

"With American money!" said Sylvia. "Thanks, Hillary!"

I felt out of my depth.

"I thought Trump had stopped all that."

"Trump? No way. Trump's in the Saudi's pockets too."

Sylvia laughed at me. She shook her head at my naiveté and laughed out loud. She had big front teeth, like a horse.

"Why do you think he hasn't said a peep about Yemen?"

I needed to be home, with Melissa, telling the truth about things that mattered, not discussing Trump and ISIS and King Salman as if it was last night's episode of East Enders.

"No, man," said Jack. "There's something big going down."

It was sad to see Jack so obsessed. His war with the 'fake news' had unsettled his wits. His 'something big' always had to be bigger than any bombshell the media could come up with. According to the newspapers the Arms Fair had been postponed due a lawsuit brought against the organisers by Amnesty International, but in Jack's world the postponement had to have a far more sinister motive than that.

"The big boys are coming to town," said Sylvia. She looked like a Manson Family hippy who'd never outgrown her moment in the limelight.

"Big boys?"

"That's right," said Jack. "You've heard of Pizzagate?"

"No."

Jack explained something about paedophiles and a pizza restaurant in New York that Hillary Clinton used and the New World Order. I didn't understand.

"Although these guys aren't paedos. They're ladies men."

"They take it out on women," said Sylvia.

"Take what out on women?"

Instead of answering my question Jack posed a question:

"These people profit off death and destruction, Jim..."

"They're brutal dictators," said Sylvia. "Some of the most brutal dictators around. They'll do anything for power."

"... Tens of thousands of innocent civilians killed by these weapons they're stocking up on..."

"It's pure evil."

"... How do you think they do it?"

I had no answer.

"You have to be lacking in human feeling, Jim," said Sylvia. "Inured to evil."

"They hold these parties," said Jack."

"Parties?"

I was lost. There's nothing wrong with parties. I'd just come from the warmth and conviviality of my son's twenty first.

"*Sex* parties," said Sylvia. "Being as how they're *men*, of course."

"Right."

"It's more than sex," Jack corrected her. He held my eye. "You know the illuminati?"

"Not personally."

My joke fell on deaf ears.

"They're bound by an oath of secrecy." I wasn't sure who he was talking about, the arms dealers or the brutal dictators. "They consolidate their secrecy with the things they do at these parties."

"Women get hurt," said Sylvia. "A few have died. It's all part of the fun."

Jack sipped his half of John Smith's.

"It's the old illuminati tie. They're bound together by the crimes they commit..."

"At these parties."

"... It's how evil works, Jim."

I pitied him. Back in the day, when he'd been a mainstream journalist, before his articles in the Times and the Independent dried up, and Reuters dropped him, Jack had been an articulate and charismatic man. He'd campaigned against the arms trade with an idealist's vigour, unthreatened by the things he attacked. But something had gone wrong. Jack hadn't merely aged, he'd grown coarse and stiff in his mind. It was there in his face, in the set of his unshaven jaw and the shininess of his eyes. The international arms trade had got to him. Too close a proximity to evil had sucked the objectivity out of him. His daily struggle with the forces of evil had not only ruined his career, it had clearly brought him to the brink of clinical paranoia. The globalist elite, the illuminati, the military industrial complex, whatever, they'd turned Jack from a truth-sayer into a fantasist. Facts no longer needed checking. Facts were, in fact, beyond checking. If you can imagine it to be true, it's true. The deepest truth colludes with the deepest lie. My summoning Jack up out of nowhere with a deception proved it.

"Lockheed Martin. Boeing. Northrop Grumman. BAE. Raytheon. They'll all be there."

"Where?"

I wasn't following.

"London. The Arms Fair. In a fortnight."

I stared out at the bustling pavement, the torrent of travelers pouring from the trains mixing with the early Saturday night streams of local pleasure seekers while the blackness took hold. I wanted to tell Jack and Sylvia that everything begins from inside your body, NATO, the Clintons, war, everything. No matter how separate and lonely your body feels, this is where it all starts, in the small of your back, at the base of your spine, a stinging and burning, an unapproachable woman shining and burning, and coming out through your eyes, out into everything. Even the London Arms Fair comes through you from beyond. Even Hillary, even ISIS, are an eruption out of transcendence. If they're not you'll end up sitting in a bar staring out at the onrush of darkness forever. The comfort of discussing evil will shut you out of your real life for good and all.

"Something big's going down?"

"It certainly is." There was a relish in Jack's voice. He rubbed his hands together like a man sitting down to a juicy steak. "You bet there's something big going down."

"That's why they didn't want to let Jack into the country," said Sylvia. "Not till the Fair's over."

"You wouldn't believe the amount of people they get turning up. Or the kind of people either."

"Sixteen hundred exhibitors from fifty four different countries!"

"And that's just the regular dealers. The ones the government vets."

"Vets? That's a joke. The big boys don't get vetted. Or their customers. The big boys fly in under the radar. And the government talks about compliance? Regulations?"

"Well... I suppose that's inevitable..." I said. "... Where there's money involved..."

"Top brass from all the Third World juntas, Jim." Jack was in his element. "Some of the most brutal dictators around. Our own corrupt politicians. It's party time for the globalist elite and their international hit men, Jim. And boy, do they know how to party!"

Christ! He was back onto his sex party!

"... Well... yes... I'd best be going..."

I finished my beer. It tasted terrible. We'd been sitting so long my Stella had gone flat.

"Sick evil fucking fuckers!"

I was suddenly very tired. I felt cold and alone. My eyes hurt. Their fantasies no longer shut out the night.

Jack shook his head.

"People who have unbridled power do unbridled things, Jim. It's a turn on holding someone's life in the palm of your hand."

I stared out at the people scurrying to clubs and bars and their homes in the brutal cold. The travelers had caught their trains. It was mainly pleasure seekers now, out there in the neon darkness. I was angry with Jack. I no longer felt sorry for him. He'd ruined Ralph's party, and fucked me over in the process.

Sylvia leant in close. I caught a whiff of perspiration under what smelled like patchouli.

"The last Fair. A girl ended up dead. No one even knows about it."

I pushed my chair back and stood up.

"... Yeah... well..." I said. "... I'd best be getting home."

I looked down at the pair of them, huddled over their dingy table. They were pathetic. The proximity of evil? Evil sucking the objectivity out of you? It had nothing to do with evil. There's no such thing. There's plenty of pain and misery. There's a lot of injustice in the world, but if you try and pretend it's a conspiracy, them against us, you end up like Jack, huddled over a half of Stella in Kings Cross, no money, visa problems and a paranoid girlfriend, at home with evil, the grand conspiracy a Fantasy Land sex party.

"... So... well... good luck with everything..."

It was time to go home and tell Melissa the truth.

Her reaction stunned me. I'd expected shock, anger, tears but I wasn't prepared for how immediately proactive Melissa became. Shock and anger were a call to action. There were tears. Her pain was obvious, but it galvanized her.

"How much money have you given this woman?" Money was the least of our problems. "How much, Jim?"

I shrugged.

"I'm not sure."

She whipped out her phone, logged into our account and checked my withdrawals. With the money I'd spent on Natalie and Pauline and the two thousand I'd given Jack it came to quite a lot.

"How could you?"

I realized that money was a way of saying things that were too threatening to say any other way. Bringing up money was a way of minimizing my treachery but it still stung. Melissa was too fine and proud a woman to be yelling at me about money.

"I'm not letting you do it Jim. I'll ring the bank. I'll block the account."

I was speechless.

"Okay. That's fine. If you want."

"A prostitute? You've been sleeping with a prostitute?" The fact that Natalie was a prostitute seemed to have shocked her even more than if I'd slept with someone from our social circle, a friend's wife, a woman at work. "I hope you took precautions."

"Erm..."

"Jesus, Jim!"

"I haven't... you know... with you... since it started..."

Natalie was gone. 'It' was over. 'It' had never even 'started.'

"Have you had a check-up?"

"Yes... well...I've got to wait.... three weeks I'll know..."

She bit her lip. Her chin trembled.

"Three and a half thousand pounds! In less than a week! She's certainly got her hooks into you!"

I didn't have the heart to tell her about Jack's two thousand. It didn't really weigh in the balance.

"It's not like that."

"No?! What's it like then?"

I didn't answer.

"Three and a half thousand pounds, it must be pretty good!"

"What?"

When it came to money, I'd been stupid. Melissa and I both had personal accounts, but the bulk of our money was in the joint account we used for the mortgage and standing orders. My personal account was pretty much empty. I was so used to making day to day withdrawals from our joint account, I hadn't bothered to top up my personal account since putting down the deposit for the BMW. All my last week's withdrawals, including the two thousand I'd just given Jack, had been from our shared account. Last week had been so hectic I hadn't even got round to covering the initial thousand for the firm's meal from the company account. I felt a spasm of anger that she had me thinking about money instead of discussing anything serious.

"IT. Sex. It must be pretty good!"

"It's not just sex."

"What's her name?"

"Natalie."

"She's English?"

"No. Thai."

"Oh that's great! Thai! She's an illegal."

I shrugged.

"I don't know. I'm not sure."

It baffled me, in fact it was starting to anger me, this harping on about money and her insistence on Natalie's being a prostitute, and Thai, as if being Thai was a crime. Melissa wasn't racist. She was an intelligent, liberal person, with an intelligent, liberal person's sympathy for women trafficked into prostitution. It wasn't as if Natalie was from our own social circle, someone I could have a real relationship with. She was a victim, an object of pity, not the Scarlet Woman from some Victorian Social Improvement pamphlet.

"Well..." her voice quivered. "... What are you going to do?"

"What do you mean what am I going to do?"

"Are you going to stop seeing her?"

It wasn't a threat. She was maybe even throwing me a lifeline. I stared at the French windows and the darkened garden beyond.

"I don't know."

"Promise me you'll stop seeing her."

It was going to take a long time to rebuild trust, if we could rebuild it at all. We might never be as close as we'd formerly been, but if I promised to never see Natalie again there was a chance Melissa would believe me. This whole thing would have been an aberration, a fucked-up middle aged man's sexual lapse, sleazy but, in the end, forgivable. Natalie would be merely the object of male lechery, a victim, a thing of pity, forgettable. She wouldn't shine and sting. She wouldn't be the unapproachable woman out in the darkness making everything new and beautiful. There was no such thing.

"I'm sorry," I said. "I can't promise that."

Next day, at work, I popped out at lunchtime to get some cash from the ATM. Our joint account blocked me. Melissa had meant what she'd said. She'd frozen our joint account.

I had to withdraw the cash from my personal account. I was down to five hundred pounds already. I rang Jack and asked when he could give me my two thousand back. He promised to do his best.

For the first time since I was a teenager, I had money problems.

Melissa didn't ask me to leave. It would almost have been easier if I'd been able to clear out for a week or two, and stay with a friend, while we tried to sort things out, but I had so little money clearing out wasn't feasible. It was coming up for Christmas. Most of my friends had families. The ones who didn't have families were away, or celebrating in style. I couldn't land on them with my problems and no cash.

I moved out of our bedroom into the upstairs guest room.

Ralph and Meredith were all for booting me out.

"You bastard!" My son was shouting at me! "How could you do this to Mum?"

His urbanity vanished. His therapeutic cool collapsed. He was an angry fourteen-year-old again, yelling at his father.

"Mum's in bits!"

I could hear how much he loved Melissa.

"You're despicable!"

He sounded like a pubertal Jordan Peterson.

"Why don't you just piss off! Go away!"

He was my son. I'd given twenty years of my life to him, rearing him and loving him, I wasn't about to take my marching orders from Ralph.

Meredith was even more vehement.

"You're horrible, Dad. You're a sexist pig. You abuse women."

I was an abuser of women. All women. Melissa, Natalie, Meredith, it made no difference. Women were my victims. Like all first year students, Meredith was a feminist. I was a man. I was behaving in character.

"I don't know how you can go on staying in this house, Dad. I think you should leave."

It was my house, and she was my daughter. I let her rant. I could see how upset she was.

I don't know what I would have done if Melissa had asked me to leave. Ralph was right. Melissa was in bits. Meredith was right too. I'd abused my wife. But you don't chuck twenty years of marriage away in ten minutes. I knew Melissa hoped this wasn't the end. I hoped so too. She hadn't asked me to leave because she couldn't believe that there'd been anything real between Natalie and me. Melissa was waiting for me to change my mind and promise to break it off with Natalie. There wasn't even anything to break off. But in the meantime, while we all waited, I moved upstairs to the guest bedroom in the attic.

It was a tiny box room on the fourth floor with a single bed, a shelfful of books on the wall, and a view, at night, through a Velux skylight, of stars swimming in the milky glow of central London. I moved a few things in and bunkered down.

I kept out of the house as much as possible. I left for work in the dark before anybody was up, and came home late, after dinner, when Melissa, Meredith and Ralph were watching TV in the living room. I seemed to live on the stairs, grabbing some food in the kitchen when the kitchen was empty, creeping past the sound of the TV in the living room and up to my attic bunker. I only ever seemed to be there in the dark. I got fond of the view of the night sky through the ceiling. At the very top of the Velux's double glazed rectangle of blackness there were one or two stars that I particularly loved. They gleamed and coruscated, like pinpoints of frost, above the murk of the city night glow.

I also grew fond of the bookshelf in my new room. None of the twenty or so books on it were things I'd ever actually choose to read myself, but I liked to lie on the bed and look up at them because they were a link with the past, they formed a sort of chronicle of the people who'd stayed with us over the years. I realized what a sociable family we'd been. We'd certainly had a lot of guests. The books were all the ones that our guests had left behind, that there hadn't been room for in their suitcases when they packed to leave, or that they'd read and hadn't wanted to keep. *Beloved*, bequeathed by one of Melissa's university friends. *The Worst Witch*, abandoned by a school friend of Meredith's after a sleepover. *Assegai* and *Bravo Two Zero* donated by Melissa's dad. *The AA Guide to England and Northern Ireland*, discarded by my father, over from Australia with Mum for the motoring holiday of a lifetime. Melissa had informed my father of my delinquency, and he was now no longer speaking to me. *Freedom From The Known*, *The End Of Time* and *The Serpent Power*. For a while I couldn't remember who had left those three behind, before it hit me— Jack! Jack O'Grady had stayed with us, many years ago, with a crazy hippy girl, one of Sylvia's predecessors. It was strange how Jack, whose focus was entirely political, seemed to attract women who were into Eastern religion. I guessed the link was the occult, the Tantric 'Left Hand Path'—from the look of the three books— to the evil fucking fucker's satanic sex parties.

I took down *Freedom From The Known* and skimmed a few pages.

'When the brain discovers something new, a new function is born; a new organism comes into being. We must challenge the brain itself, to find out whether it has the capacity, the energy, the drive, the intention, to break down this continuity of the past, so that, in the

act of ending, the brain cells themselves undergo a change, a transformation.'

No wonder Jack's girlfriends were so spaced out. They were reinventing their brains, with the aid of drugs, no doubt, Jack's paranoia adding a political dimension to the craziness.

Sleep was out of the question. I had a look at *The End Of Time*.

It was by an odd-ball physicist, Julian Barbour, who maintained that, on the quantum mechanical level, time is an illusion imposed on space by—I felt ill—an inadequate neural set-up.

I put *The End Of Time* back on the shelf. There's enough madness in the world without appealing to quantum space to back it up.

The Serpent Power was the worst of the lot. It was a study of some occult sect that specialized in sexual sublimation. A force called Kundalini could be aroused during sex, when 'ejaculation is inhibited and a syncope occurs', for God's sake!

'...She is the sleeping Kundalini, the World Bewilderer, fine as the fibre of the lotus-stalk. Her lustre is strong as a flash of young lightning. Her murmur is sweet as the hum of love-crazed bees. She is the One Who Goes Upwards, and is beyond the universe, and is consciousness itself...'

I put the book aside. It made me ill just thinking about it. Maybe that was all Jack's problem was— sex, pure and simple. His 'satanic sex party' and his 'evil fucking fuckers' were nothing but sex sublimated into politics. Jack directed his orgasm force towards the New World Order instead of up 'the fibre fine as a lotus stalk.' No wonder the guy was paranoid. It was hardly a surprise he hooked up with these occult chicks. The more I thought about it, the more certain I became. Yes. Sitting over our dismal halves of Stella in that dreary Kings Cross bar, Jack's relish was more than just a man's sitting down to a juicy steak. He, with his 'people who have unbridled power do unbridled things', and Sylvia, with her 'the big

boys fly in under the radar'— they were pretty much copulating in
the bar room window.

Almost a week passed and I didn't hear from Natalie.
Something told me not to go back to the sauna looking for her. I'd
given her my number that night in Hackney, but the days went by
and she didn't ring. Natalie hadn't given me her number. I hung on
in the guest bedroom. Perhaps it was over. Lee's deal with Adrian
Whitely's contact was going ahead. Her frantic call had only been a
moment's uncertainty. She liked me, but now bigger wheels were in
motion. Perhaps if I waited it out long enough things might even
get better with Melissa and the kids.

I was working long hours, trying to sort out the mess I'd made
losing the firm the Arkwright contract. Things were tense in the
office. Pippa wasn't speaking to me. Bernard was angry, and only
talked to me when he really had to. They blamed me for the
problems we were having and knew those problems were caused
by my sleeping with a prostitute. My lying to Melissa about the
Rampton Street drawings had, in some way that I couldn't
understand, catapulted us into taking on the phase two
consultancy when things were already upside down, and now
Rampton Street was in difficulties too.

I kept myself to myself. I spent us much time out of the house
as possible. I made sure I got to work in the dark of a morning,
and left well after dark at night so as to arrive home after Melissa
and the kids had eaten and were upstairs camped in the living room
watching TV.

A week went by.

I was at work, staying late.

It was nearly nine. The cupola of the Coronet Cinema, a dim,
faux-Byzantine excrescence girdled in decrepit neon, fazed the
darkness outside my office window.

This late, it was safe to go home, make my furtive ascent to the attic in the lull between dinner and bedtime.

I'd already eaten. Dawdling to rustle up something in my state of the art kitchen was out of the question.

If I made it up to the box bedroom without running into Melissa or Meredith or Ralph I might even have enough concentration left to give *Freedom From The Known* another go.

My car was parked round the back. Our firm had worked on the mews development where our offices were located and we had half a dozen spaces in the private car-park, six whole bays that were worth their weight in gold in these warden-infested streets.

The car-park was poorly lit. It wasn't a worry. A tall, steel automatically operated security gate, to which only residents and people from our offices had the remote control, blocked off the Victorian arch out into the street.

I was parked at the far end of a row of empty spaces. As I opened the door of my BMW and was about to climb in I heard a footstep behind me. A hand closed over my shoulder.

"Get in, Jim. I wanta talk to you."

"Alright."

I had no alternative but to do what he said.

Cyril went round to the other side of the car and climbed into the front passenger seat. The upholstery squeaked under his weight.

"This is stupid," I said. "Anything happens to me..."

He twisted the rear view mirror towards his face and looked for something— a spot? A nick? It was impossible to see in the half light—on his cheekbone.

"Put the heating on."

I started the engine and turned the heating on.

"I need to talk to you, Jim."

He was big and heavily built. If I jumped out quickly enough I might possibly out-run him. Except the security gate was shut and the stairs back into the building were double locked.

"What about?"

Cyril rubbed his eyes.

"Lee don't like people messin' with his girls."

"I thought they were *your* girls."

He looked at me.

"Whatever."

Natalie said that Cyril was 'security'. 'Security' was another unexpected word, like 'infection', to turn up in her vocabulary.

"You were a bit slow the other night," I said. "Ten minutes? A man can do anything in ten minutes."

Cyril grinned.

"You wanta try me?"

"Not me. I wasn't talking about me."

My girls? He was sleeping with Natalie. Getting it on with *his* girls went with the territory. Cyril was the reason Natalie hadn't rung. He was sitting in my car to make sure I got the message.

"Knock them around, do you? Your girls?"

"Ey?"

The upholstery creaked. Corn rows glistened, drawn tight on the gleam of his scalp.

"Look, Jim. You don't have to like me. And I don't have to like you, alright?"

"Alright."

"I'm gonna talk to you. Okay?"

"Okay."

"I shouldn't be tellin' you this. Natalie's stopped workin'. Lee's particularly adamant Natalie don't see no one no more."

"Where is she?"

"Caledonian Road. You been there. She aint allowed to go out, but." He grinned. "Not even to Hassan's next door or nothin'."

I looked at him.

"Is she alright. They haven't...?"

"No. She's fine. She's just..."

"Have you...?"

Just because he slept with her didn't mean he didn't knock her about.

"Fuck you, Jim!" For a second he thought about hitting me. I didn't care whether he did or he didn't. "Fuck off, man." Even his eyes were pumped. "I'm security. I look after the girls on out visits. Lee's got his own guys, Chinese, do the heavy stuff."

It seemed like a pretty fine distinction.

"*They've*...?"

"No. Nothin' like that. They're keepin' a close eye on her, is all. They've taken her phone. That's what I wanted to talk to you about..." My heart began to beat. Cyril rubbed his fingers across his mouth. "... Natalie seems to like you..." My heart started beating faster. "... She aint said nothing to you, has she...?"

"To me? About what?"

"This Arms Fair thing."

"*Ey*?"

"...I've asked her, but she won't say nothin'... I thought she might've... you know... she likes you..."

It was true. I'd glimpsed transcendence. I'd stood at the source of joy. I was still standing there. She liked me.

"What Arms Fair thing?"

Cyril lifted his face to the mirror again, searched for some imperfection. He was a handsome man. He took good care of himself.

"You won't tell Lee?"

I laughed out loud.

"How could I do that?"

Cyril laughed too. He cocked his head, an honest man savouring an absurdity.

"Yeah... well...you know this Arms Fair thing's goin' down in a coupla weeks?"

"Yes."

"... Word is..." He leant towards me. "... Lee's arrangin' somethin' with some geezers comin' over for the Fair... Lee's arrangin' some girls for 'em... Natalie aint said nothin' to you about it has she...?"

"A party?"

Cyril's face brightened.

"She's told you?"

"No... no... nothing like that... it's just... you know..."

My head was spinning too much to bring up Jack. Explaining about Jack and the New World Order and Sylvia's evil fucking fuckers was beyond me.

Cyril looked at me suspiciously.

"Yeah, well. No one's sayin' nothin'. That's what worries me." His anxiety sounded real. "When the girls keep quiet about somethin' it generally means it's somethin' heavy."

"Natalie never mentioned anything to me."

"Yeah, well. Thai birds are all paranoid. I got the impression, but, she trusts you..."

I shouldn't have been feeling this sudden rush of joy. Flooding over Jack's paranoia and past Cyril's gangland know-how ecstasy felt more like delirium.

Cyril stared out at the wall directly in front of the car.

"Geezer hurts my girls, he's dead." I believed him. I could feel it. He was taking a risk even talking to me. "You know that house in Holland Park?" He chuckled. "Where I saw you the other night?"

"How could I forget?"

"That Adrian Whitely geezer..." Cyril grimaced. "... He's a cunt. I don't like the way he's takin' Natalie out in particular, to 'is fancy restaurants."

"In particular?"

"Yeah. It don't feel right."

"Well..." I felt my face go hot. "... She is... you know... a knockout..."

I felt like a prurient adolescent, the way he looked at me.

"This 'big Buddha woman' trip of hers. She's an 'angel' or some fucking thing."

I couldn't help smiling.

"Yes. I know."

"Word is she's got a bee in her bonnet about this Adrian Whitely guy, n these geezers he's linin' up for 'is party. She won't say nothin' to me, but."

I felt like grabbing the big hand resting on his knee and shaking it. The gold C that had cut my eye glinted in his signet ring.

"Maybe they're something from her 'life before.'"

Cyril laughed out loud.

"... Yeah... when she was a plincess..."

He reached up and twisted the rear view mirror back to something near its original position.

"... Well... if you hear from her... if she says anythin'..."

"How? Lee's keeping an eye on her. He's taken her phone."

Cyril took his mobile out.

"... She'll find some way... she's a big Buddha woman... n..." He chuckled. "... She likes you, man..." We exchanged numbers. "Give us a bell if your hear anythin', eh?"

Cyril opened his door and was gone.

It was nearly ten before I got home.

The light was on on the first floor in the living room windows. Melissa and the kids would be up there watching TV.

Meredith had stayed in London. She'd taken time off from university to be with her mother.

Ralph had given up the opportunity of a winter break at his girlfriend's house in the country.

They'd be up there camped in the living room, listening for my footsteps as I came in, ignoring me when I passed the living room door on my way upstairs. The arrangement suited me fine. I didn't feel like talking to anyone anyway.

I slipped my key into the front door and opened it as quietly as I could.

Melissa was sitting in the kitchen.

As usual, by this time of night, the table was cleared, the washing up done, and the plates and glasses put away in the cupboards. The kitchen felt bleak.

"Jim. We've got to talk." I sat down. "This is killing me."

Laminate and stainless steel reflected in the blackness beyond the French windows.

"Maybe I should move out," I said. "It isn't working like this."

"Yes. Perhaps you should." The lines around her eyes were tight and shiny. "Have you thought about what I said? About seeing David?"

David was a doctor acquaintance of ours. He'd given up his GP practice to set up as a psychotherapist.

"Yeah. Maybe."

"You look terrible. David might be able to help."

If I looked terrible, I certainly didn't feel it. My heart was still skipping to Cyril's 'she likes you, man.' He'd said it twice.

"Why don't you talk to David? He's very good."

David was a nice guy, but, as far as I could see, his patients were mainly the neurotic children of our friends.

"I'm not sick."

"No one's saying you are. It's just... if you and I can't discuss it, maybe talking to David will help."

I was aware that since the stinging started in my spine I'd been looking stressed. Since the unapproachable woman began shining in my spine, my face had grown thinner. But that was just lack of sleep. It was the overtime I was doing at work. The world was turning on a shining hinge towards something incomprehensible. It was bound to feel a bit uncomfortable.

She began to cry.

"This thing's important to me, Melissa. I'm not letting David diagnose it out of existence."

"What thing?"

"I don't know," I said, and headed for the stairs.

I shut the door and lay down on the bed. A spray of stars shone in the top right hand corner of the skylight. I took *The End Of Time* down from the shelf and opened it.

The physicist was called Julian Barbour. For such radical material, he had a cosy prose style. He certainly knew his quantum mechanics. Maybe he was right. Time's an illusion imposed on space by an inadequate neural set-up. It was what I'd felt in the bedroom in Kilburn when Natalie switched up the fan heater. I only perceive what is already finished. Things end faster than the speed of light, yet I remain awake.

I put *The End Of Time* back, and took down *Freedom From The Known*. It was by some Indian guy.

'When the brain discovers something new, a new function is born; a new organism comes into being. We must challenge the brain itself, to find out whether it has the capacity, the energy, the drive, the intention, to break down this continuity of the past, so that, in the act of ending, the brain cells themselves undergo a change, a transformation.'

It sounded sick. More than just neurotic. Crazy. A suitable case for David. But maybe the guy had a point. It was clearly the inadequate neural set-up he was on about. That bit felt right.

I put *Freedom From The Known* back and took down *The Serpent Power*.

'*...Her lustre is strong as a flash of young lightning. Her murmur is sweet as the hum of love-crazed bees. She is the One Who Goes Upwards, and is beyond the universe, and is consciousness itself...*'

I should have stuck to Andy McNab.

The next day I went down to Kings Cross, looking for Jack and Sylvia.

They weren't at their hotel. They hadn't checked out, the manager told me, they simply weren't there.

When would they back? He didn't know. Days? Hours? They hadn't said.

It was a bed and breakfast hotel, but it didn't seem to have any dining area. A flight of stairs led straight up from the cubby-hole reception desk by the front door. If the rooms upstairs were as cramped as the downstairs hallway, it wasn't the sort of place you could spread out and relax in. In fact, after five minutes questioning the manager I was starting to feel claustrophobic myself. I could understand Jack and Sylvia staying out.

I wondered if they were down at the ExCel Centre helping prepare for the Arms Fair protests. But that wasn't Jack's style. Jack was a behind-the-scenes man, an infiltrator and string-puller. Picketing and placard waving weren't his thing. He and Sylvia could be anywhere in England, conducting clandestine meetings with their contacts, or they might simply be roaming the streets and stretching out halves in dingy bars till it was time to go to bed.

Had they said where they were going? The manager shrugged. He was an expansive Lebanese man, but some of Jack's paranoia seemed to have rubbed off on him.

For a moment, sitting in my car with Cyril, Cyril's 'arrangin' somethin' with some geezers comin' over for the Fair' had battened onto Jack's 'they hold these parties, it's how evil works, Jim...' But that was ridiculous. Jack was just a helpless conspiracy theorist. Jack had lost the plot years ago. His 'something big's going down' had nothing to do with Natalie or '*my* girls'. Cyril was a realist. He wasn't into fantasy like Jack. Even I knew that business deals involve favours and that sometimes the favours are girls, especially in the Third World countries where a lot of the Arms Fair customers came from. I'd seen it myself, on business trips, paunchy, middle-aged executives with gorgeous girls on their arm, oblivious of how pathetic they looked. That was what Cyril was talking about, it was what Lee was arrangin' with Adrian Whitely. It was grotesque. It was banal but it was hardly 'evil', not in the way Jack used the word. Lee's sleazy businessmen, even if they were arms dealers, were hardly the 'pure evil' of bombed hospitals in Yemen and children maimed by landmines. Evil's not a conspiracy. If you go down that path you're heading for the supernatural. You're one step away from believing in the Devil.

I left my card and asked the manager to ask Jack to ring me when he got in. He took the card, but I didn't hold out much hope of hearing from Jack again.

It was nine days now, since I'd last spoken to Natalie, at the sauna. She'd said she'd ring, but nine days had gone by and I still hadn't heard from her. Cyril had said that Lee had taken her phone, but I wasn't sure if I believed his story about Natalie being kept prisoner in the Caledonian Road. I wasn't sure what I believed.

Perhaps it was simply over. Maybe our brief fling had petered out. She'd found someone else, and it was pretty obvious who that someone else was: a ten million pound house in Holland Park, a chauffeur driven Merc, uniformed staff to draw his curtains. Adrian Whitely was richer than me, and that was all there was to it. Cyril's stories about Natalie being denied a phone, shut up in the Caledonian Road, Lee 'keeping an eye on her', were just that, stories. Why he'd bothered to jump me in the carpark and tell me a pack of lies was beyond me. Perhaps in their world, Cyril's as well as Natalie's, lying is compulsory. Cyril with his imprisonment fairytales, Natalie's 'prince, princess' story. They lived in a world of constantly shifting deceptions, especially Natalie with the untruths, even the kind ones, she must have to be perpetually telling men. She'd probably lost track of what was true and what wasn't a long time ago. She was up there with Julian Barbour, 'time is an illusion', and Krishnamurti 'when the brain discovers something new, a new function is born' and, worst of all, 'She Who Goes Upwards', the 'World-Bewilderer.'

I liked Cyril. He was a thug. He no doubt got up to some pretty nasty stuff, but his affection for Natalie had been obvious. Natalie was lucky to be one of *his* girls. Cyril was an okay guy, but the lies and paranoia had got to him too. Natalie wasn't a prisoner in the Caledonian Road. She was probably at this very moment relaxing in a first floor living room in Holland Park. She'd failed to ring me, not because Lee had taken her phone, but because she no longer had any need of me. She didn't want to talk to me. It was over.

On the way back to the car I passed the bar where I'd sat with Jack and Sylvia, on Ralph's birthday, discussing the Arms Fair and the globalist elite. The table by the window was occupied by a young couple rugged up against the cold, rucksacks and suitcases piled by their chairs.

It was time to go home and say sorry to Melissa, and really mean it, and promise her I'd never see Natalie again.

I decided to go down to Earls Court first, and talk to Soom Bon.

It was still early evening when I walked into the Sawaddee Bee Mai.

The restaurant was empty. A waitress was setting out napkin dispensers. The melted plastic smell of barbecued chili came from the kitchen, but there was no one eating.

I pushed through the door to the kitchen and went up the stairs. No one tried to stop me.

Soom Bon's room was on the third floor.

I knocked on his door.

There was a muffled exclamation from inside.

"Mii arai?"

I realized that I didn't even know whether Soom Bon spoke English or not. The time I'd visited with Natalie the conversation had all been in Thai, with Natalie translating for me. Then again, if Soom Bon waited on table downstairs he had to speak a little English.

The door didn't open. I knocked again.

"Baep diaao!"

This time the exclamation was less muffled. Perhaps he was in bed. At five o'clock in the afternoon. Maybe he was with a woman.

I knocked again. The door finally opened.

Soom Bon was in his pyjamas.

I'd forgotten how unnaturally pale his face was for an Asian. Not exactly pale. Sunless. Jaundiced. The pallor of a man who'd read a Thai comic book version of *Romeo And Juliet* in a prison library.

He didn't remember me, but neither did he seem fazed by seeing a farang— Natalie called Europeans 'farangs'— standing at his door in this all Asian establishment.

I stretched out my hand:

"Do you have the night off?"

His handshake felt clammy. His wrist was limp. The night I'd visited with Natalie he'd been spaced out, but still on the ball enough to read our fortunes and serve desserts downstairs

afterwards. This evening his hand trembled, his grip was rubbery.
There was no way he could wait on table tonight.

He grinned. He'd finally remembered me.

"You want reading?"

I didn't know what I wanted.

"Well... if you're not busy."

The room was sweltering. The gas fire was on full blast. I
squeezed into his armchair. The armchair was too close to the fire,
but there was no way I was sitting on his bed.

It was crazy standing unmounted photos along the top of a gas
fire. The snapshots curled and cringed away from the heat. Family
groups. Children. Dogs. A house on stilts. Temples. I nodded at the
teenager in the orange robe.

"You were a monk?"

"Chai."

Even with the shaved scalp and confident eyes, the young monk
in the photo was clearly Soom Bon.

He reached under the bed and pulled out his plank.

"What you want me read?"

I realized that there was some sort of 'vics's menu, different
prices for different readings, but I was fucked if I was here for a
reading.

"Natalie."

He drifted away.

"Who?"

He'd forgotten her.

"Natalie. I came here with Natalie. Before."

His eyes focused.

"Oh...chai, chai... Nam Huan."

"Nam Huan?"

"Natalie Thai name. She Nam Huan."

I wanted to ask him what it meant.

He held my eye.

"Two hundred."

I saw that I could haggle. The guy was desperate.

I was getting low on money myself, but I took out my wallet and gave him two hundred. I instantly felt stupid. I was about to get an even bigger load of bullshit than last time.

He stared at the grid of squares and the inked symbols on the plank's silvery grain. He looked round for his razor on the washstand.

"No.... no.... I just..." I waved the board away. "... I just want...you said... last time I was here... that Natalie was a princess... in her life before... and that I was..." I blushed. "... A prince... and that we were in love... and..."

My face burned.

His eyes clouded over. He was having trouble remembering.

"... We drowned ourselves..."

I felt ridiculous.

He nodded.

"Chai, chai..."

Soom Bon stared at the board and began to move his lips.

"... No... NO!... You said... last time... that Natalie was a 'big Buddha woman'... you called her an 'angel girl'..."

I couldn't remember if it was Soom Bon who'd said that about Natalie, or if Natalie had said it about herself.

Outside a bus changed gear. The whole room rattled. One of his photographs toppled off the gas fire, got trapped an instant in the grille against the flames, and dropped onto the carpet. He pushed the board away and said:

"... Chai chai..." Soom Bon smiled benignly. "... Nam Huan be a... she be a... in Thai we say she be 'arhat'..."

"Arhat?"

"... Arhat... no come back... after this one life she don't come back no more..." A desolate feeling swept over me. Spittle webbed the corners of his mouth. "... After this one life she don have no more lives..." He grinned. He was getting into his stride, the prison library coming back to him. "... In Thai we say 'arhat'... say 'she deserving'... 'she worth'...?"

"Worthy?"

"Chai. Chai. She worth-ee... we say she be no returner..." He was pulling out all the stops. "... Go heaven, don come back no more..."

"I thought she was supposed to be a princess."

"... Chai chai..." His eyelids dropped. He started to nod. "... life before... Nam Huan from big family... she 'arhat' woman... be princess... no come back..."

He was getting mixed up. He was confusing his reincarnation story from my last visit with gibberish from his time as a monk.

"... Nam Huan angel girl this time... this time she big Buddha woman... no come back..."

"Okay. Thanks."

I stood up. It was time to go.

I stooped and picked up the fallen photograph. It was the one of Soom Bon as a young monk, radiating happiness and serenity. I put it back in its place on top of the gas fire.

He'd ripped me off again.

"If Natalie's an 'arhat'," I said. I tried not to sound pissed off. The poor guy was in a bad way. "If she's so deserving and so worthy, how come she's getting such a rough deal *this* life, shut up in the Caledonian Road? Working for Lee?"

He stopped nodding. His smile turned confidential.

"... Give I one hundred more... I say you..." He glanced at the door. "... I must not say you... but I say..."

He was worse than Pauline.

Until I could get my joint account sorted out I was down to my last seven or eight hundred.

"Say me what?"

He held his hand out. I gave him two fifties.

He folded them up and slipped them into the breast pocket of his pyjamas.

"... Natalie have sister..."

It was like feeding money into a story telling machine.

"Sister?"

He nodded in the direction of West Kensington.

"... Back home... back Thailand... Natalie have sister... beautiful same she... man he kill sister Natalie... man rape she, kill she... angel girl don forget... big Buddha woman she never forgive... one day Natalie kill he back... "

He should never have been a monk. He oughtn't to be waiting on tables. He should have been a screen writer for soap operas. Those Jackie Chan movies with the unbelievable plots that only a comic genius like Jackie Chan can redeem.

"... Big man sell gun... kill sister Natalie...one day Natalie find he... soon Natalie kill he..."

"What man? Sells guns?" I looked at him. "An arms dealer?"

Soom Bon stared back at me. The words were unknown to him.

"He killed Natalie's sister?"

Soom Bon shrugged. He looked yearningly towards his bed. He couldn't remember. The information had come to him from halfway between a hundred pounds and a heavy sleep.

My phone rang.

"Jim?"

Natalie's voice was frantic. Soom Bon nodded at my phone.

"Come get I?"

"What?"

"Come house. Leave car."

"Eh?"

"Wait Hassan. Come get I. Please. Quick."

The line went dead.

By the time I got to the Caledonian Road it was starting to get dark. The permanent snarl-up in the traffic outside the house was taking on a rush hour irritability, baffled headlights and glaring spurts of red.

I guessed that 'leave car' meant I was supposed to park somewhere off the main road, not right outside the house.

I turned west into a hinterland of warehouse cul-de-sacs and council estates. A white van pulled out of a thirty minute loading bay and I grabbed the space.

I walked back to the main road.

Perhaps that was the thing about reality. In reality, nothing connects. Apparent links between any one piece of information and any other piece of information are an illusion... Jack's *sick evil fucking fuckers'*... Cyril's *'bee in her bonnet about Adrian Whiteley n this geezer he's linin' her up with'*... Soom Bon and his *'Nam huan is a non-returner, she deserve, she worthy'*...it was like the glare of the rush hour traffic. It had a direction, but in and of themselves, the headlights and taillights were all lost. Soom Bon said that Natalie had a sister and that Natalie's sister was killed by a man who sells guns, but that didn't make sense either. In the limited number of things Natalie had told me about herself, her family had figured prominently. She'd spoken about her mother and father's farm. She'd told me about Nok's father, a customer in Bangkok she'd shacked up with for a while. She'd shown me her photos of Nok the first time I saw her, yet I'd never heard her mention a sister, not even once.

Hassan's display of fruit and vegetables stood out on the footpath as usual, soaking up the fumes and the sign's fluorescence, insisting on a bleak freshness. It was colder out here than in the freezers inside.

Inside, the shop smelled of figs and mildewed cardboard.

The woman I'd seen the last time I was here was behind the counter, in the same pink cardigan.

She ignored me. She knew I wasn't here to purchase anything.

At the back of the shop, the strip curtain parted and Hassan's son came out.

He was carrying a suitcase. The suitcase got caught for an instant in the tangle of multi-coloured plastic.

Natalie was directly behind him, saying something into a cell phone.

"Mai. Mai. Mai dai. Mai roo waa. Mai dai."

The phone had a shiny brown sleeve, like flock wallpaper. It wasn't the one I'd seen her use the night I first came here.

The little girl looked up at her with wide, awestruck eyes. Natalie was too busy on the phone to notice her. Hassan followed them in a glare of TV light from the back room.

I realized how close together the rows of shelves were. The suitcase banged down the narrow aisle. A tin of sardines dropped on the floor and rolled across the dirty lino and under the shelf opposite.

When he reached the space in front of the counter Hassan's son put the suitcase down in front of me. Neither he nor his wife would look at me.

Natalie gave me a brief, tense smile, and carried on with her phone conversation.

"Chai. Chai. Baawk mai dai. Nung Yao mai roo waa."

Her tone was businesslike, an executive too busy for greetings, or, from the way the little girl's eyes drank her in, a princess in flight.

We all stood in a group front of the counter waiting for Natalie to finish her conversation.

"Mai. Mai. Mai dai."

She looked pale. Too pale. Her face was white with talcum powder. She'd dusted her cheeks and chin and forehead with talc, as you might a child's after a bath.

She tousled the little girl's hair and looked at me.

"We go."

She was wearing a pair of jeans and the puffa jacket she'd worn in the sauna and down to Earls Court. There was a smear of rust, and what looked like axle grease, on the arm. One of the nylon puffs was torn. It spouted white stuffing.

The door pinged. Everyone jumped. A customer came in.

"Thank you, Hassan."

She hugged the old man.

Hassan dived over to the liquor display and reached down a bottle of champagne. He gave it to her.

I picked up the suitcase. It was big but lighter than it had looked when Hassan's son humped it along the aisle. There were some airline stickers on the side. Thai Air. Emirates. Garuda. She hadn't even removed the luggage tag from around the handle.

"Thank you, Haluk."

Hassan's son didn't smile.

"Thank you, Elif."

His wife smiled politely.

We were out the door.

"This way."

We headed Northwards up the footpath, away from the house. It meant a longer walk round to the car but someone might have been looking down from the windows of the house.

The suitcase was cumbersome on the crowded footpath. I found the retractable handle, pulled it out and set the suitcase on its frail wheels.

We turned into an alley cutting back towards the housing estate. The suitcase bounced and twisted on the cobble stones.

In the car she looked at me.

"Where we go?"

It was a good question.

I drove east.

Holloway. Stoke Newington. Lea Valley.

The rush hour traffic was slow. There was a bottleneck on Lea Bridge Road at the turnoff to Orient Way. A tailback of homebound brake lights winked impatiently in the darkness.

"Go hotel?"

For a moment, the way she said it, I wondered if she'd expected me to take her home to my house. She knew I was married, but perhaps she was used to set-ups— possibly Hassan's, or Haluk's—with second wives. Except that was impossible. Lee would find her at my place. If, that is, Lee would come after her, if she was running away from Lee at all.

I nodded at the smear of rust.

"Your jacket's torn."

She grinned.

"Must go on roof. Jacket break... how you say...on...?"

She made a hammering motion.

"A nail?"

"Jacket break on nail."

She'd climbed out of a back window of the house, and across a roof into Hassan's building. There was grease on the knees of her jeans too. The phone with the flock wallpaper sleeve was one that Hassan had given to her.

I wanted to ask her about her sister being killed by an arms dealer, if that was what 'man sell gun' in fact meant. Soom Bon had called her 'worthy', 'she who deserves', a 'no returner.' I wanted to ask her what Soom Bon had meant by calling her an 'arhat'. It sounded like some technical term in Buddhist belief. I'd come across 'arhat' in that book Jack's crazy ex-girlfriend had left in the guest bedroom, *The Serpent Power*. There were a million and one things I wanted to ask her, but she was too tense and withdrawn to question. Perhaps her sister was a painful subject, if there'd ever been a sister. I couldn't question her anyway. I didn't want her to know I'd been to see Soom Bon. She'd think I'd been checking up on her.

I didn't have much money left. If we stayed in a hotel, it wasn't going to be the Ritz. Perhaps she was used to expensive hotels.

She'd certainly looked at home walking out of 'Whites' on Adrian Whitely's arm. She'd spent nights in Holland Park.

I wondered why, if she wanted to run away from Lee, she hadn't rung Adrian Whitely. Adrian Whitely was far better placed to help her escape than I was. If, that is— in spite of her torn jacket— escaping was what she was actually doing.

She nodded at the struts and C-beams of skeletal tubing.

"Play game?"

"Yes. The Olympic Stadium."

Skirting the stadium and Stratford station I saw a Holiday Inn and checked in there.

I hadn't stayed in a Holiday Inn since my late teens, backpacking round Europe during my university holidays.

The room was clean. The window overlooked Romford Road, it didn't give out on a concrete wall or anything, but I still felt claustrophobic.

Natalie put her suitcase on the luggage stand and took out a bathroom bag and went into the poky bathroom and locked the door. I realized I didn't have any toilet stuff of my own.

She came out of the bathroom and switched on the TV and put the bottle of champagne Hassan had given her in the tiny fridge. She hung our coats in the wardrobe, and more of her own clothes from the suitcase, another pair of jeans, some skirts and blouses, on the wooden hangers chained to the rail. She was used to hotel rooms, Spartan as well as five star. Modular bathrooms and franchise décor didn't faze her.

She smiled at me and took a flat package, clumsily wrapped in silver paper with a pink bonbon on it, from the outside compartment of her suitcase.

"Ey?"

She laughed and tossed the package on the bed.

"Is nothing. Haluk give."

"Haluk?"

"Son Hassan."

Whatever the package contained, it was flat and very light, almost weightless. I guessed it was a present from the little girl, a drawing or a good luck card that Hassan's granddaughter had made for her and wrapped up with childish magnificence. Hassan and his family were fond of Natalie. Given Lee's violence and the fact that a lot of money was at stake, the shopkeeper had taken a risk helping her escape across the roof, if that was actually what had happened.

She slid onto the bed and picked up the remote control and surfed TV channels.

She'd washed the talcum powder off her face. I wondered if she'd put it on to protect her skin against the cold, out on the roof. Her cheekbones shone like white honey. She was immaterial. I was too tense to keep up with the tapering lift of her eyes. The pressure in my head exploded. Only the shining thread was real. Pinpoints of light filtered backwards through my skull and caught in my brain as they went through me, like diamonds in a sieve.

"How you eye?"

"Okay."

The swelling where Cyril hit me had gone down, the cut had healed up.

"What's going on, Natalie?"

"What you say 'on'?"

"Lee? Cyril? This Adrian guy?"

"Why you say?"

It was none of my business. I was stuck in a Holiday Inn in Stratford, not sure what I was supposed to do next, but the details weren't my concern.

"What's happening?"

"Nothing." She kept surfing the TV channels. "Nothing happen."

"Don't be ridiculous!" I didn't care if she understood my English or not. "Cyril said there's something going on with the Arms Fair. Cyril said that Adrian Whitely's lining you up with some men. A man."

She laughed and climbed off the bed.

"Cyril crazy man. Cyril don know what he say." She opened the fridge and took the champagne out. "Must happy, Jim."

I didn't feel happy.

"What was Cyril on about?"

"Must drinking champagne Hassan."

She handed me the bottle. I unfastened the wire, and popped the cork.

"Ai-ee!" Champagne fizzed and went streaming down the neck of the bottle. "Glass!" She grabbed two glasses off the tea tray. I filled them. "Must drinking!"

I raised my glass. A toast felt stupid.

"To..."

Natalie clinked her glass against mine.

"... You I love two gether!"

The champagne wasn't a brand I recognized, but it tasted okay. Hassan had given us the best bottle in his display.

I tried to open the window. It only opened a crack, just a few inches' gap at the top. The traffic noise came up very loud.

Natalie refilled our glasses.

"Why you talk Cyril?"

"I didn't talk to Cyril. He talked to me."

I explained how Cyril waylaid me in my car. I told her that Cyril was worried about her. I described how Cyril had asked me if I knew what was going on with her and Adrian Whitely.

"Cyril ba ba ba boa. He thinking too much. Adrian just customer."

We kissed.

Her tongue freed me from words. Our tongues remembered things our minds had long forgotten. The blood sharpness of laarp. That first kiss in the car. A prince and princess sharing one breath as they went under. Her tongue a salamander drowning in fire.

"I sorry, Jim... cannot do homework..."

"Homework?"

"...Sex... have period... cannot..."

I realized my hands were cupped around her bottom. Yes. I could feel the weightless contour of a sanitary pad.

I shrugged.

"It's okay. It's alright."

In fact, I felt relieved. Maybe Cyril had got the wrong end of the stick. Perhaps Cyril had got it completely upside down. Lee wasn't keeping her prisoner in the Caledonian Road at all. All that had happened was, it was her time of month, she'd had to stop working for a week. Adrian Whitely was fastidious when it came to menstrual blood. The climb across the roof was just a crazy story. She'd left the house by the alleyway door and simply hung out in Hassan's back room till I got there. After she'd hung out with me for a few days and her period was over she'd go back to work. She'd torn her jacket somewhere else.

"... Three days, Jim... two may be... can fuck good..."

"It's alright. It's not important."

She slipped her hand between my legs and rubbed my cock through my trousers.

"*Is* importing. Must happy."

I had an erection. My cock ached so bad it hurt.

I wondered if that was what had started this burning stinging in my spine, in the bedroom in Kilburn— being aroused, going over the brink, but not ejaculating, faking an orgasm to match her faked orgasm. That was why my head had exploded and the pinpoints of light had gone through me. Maybe that was all I'd seen out on the footpath— not an unapproachable woman shining and stinging, but only a baffled orgasm.

"Cyril said Lee took your phone and kept you in the house because of this man at the Arms Fair."

She put her arms around my neck.

"Cyril don know nothing."

"Cyril said Adrian Whitely is arranging something for this guy. That's why Lee took your phone and kept you prisoner."

She pressed against me.

"How you say 'plis...on...er'?"

"Lock up. Prison. Gaol."

She laughed out loud.

"I no gaol!" Eggshells of merriment cracked in her throat. The idea was hilarious. "Lee don lock I gaol!"

She stopped dead...

... Oops...!

... Her grand entrance from the back of Hassan's shop... Haluk humping her suitcase between the shelves... 'Wait Hassan. Come get I. Please. Quick'...her jacket torn and grease stained...

"... Lee... just take I phone... don wan I talking you..." She was making it up as she went along. "... Lee try stop you take I... cannot...!" Her jeans were tight. They pressed against my flies. The sanitary towel rubbed against my erection. "... I no finish contract..."

"Contract?"

A sudden weight oppressed me.

'Contract'?

With her limited vocabulary, 'contract' wasn't a word she should know, like 'infection' and 'security.'

"Chai laaeo. I do contract with Lee..."

"What contract?"

"... Must give he back... I... I... how you say... oh...?"

"Owe?"

"Chai. Owe. Lee bring I England... must give he back..."

She owed Lee money.

"How much?"

"Lot."

"How much?"

She shrugged.

"Twenty five..."

"Thousand?"

"Chai...I sorry I don say you be fore..."

She explained how the system worked. Lee smuggled the girls into England. He had expenses. Air tickets. Bribes. Lots of Backhanders. Accommodation in the Caledonian Road. His expenses came to around ten thousand pounds per girl. To cover his costs and make a profit, the girls had to pay him back twenty five thousand pounds, working in his flats or saunas. It usually took a girl six months to pay off her contract. As Sandra had said, Natalie was 'new'. She'd only just arrived in the country. She'd only been working for Lee for a couple of weeks when I saw her on the footpath in Kilburn. She'd worked off some of the money, but she still owed Lee twenty thousand pounds. If I wanted to take her I'd need to front up with the money.

"Lee scary I no pay he... Lee scary I run way with you, no pay contract... take I phone... he send Cyril scary you..." Cyril'd 'scary-d' me alright that night in Holland Park. Cyril's story about the Arms Fair and the 'big man' at the Arms Fair was just to scary me some more. It had worked. I was scary-d. Lee was scary-d. Cyril was scary-d. Everyone was fucking scary-d. "... I climb on roof..." She knew her story didn't make sense. "... I run way from house..." She was making it up as she went along. She'd never been a prisoner. She hadn't run away at all. She was mine. I now owed Lee twenty five thousand pounds. "... I run way cause I love you, honey..." She kissed my throat. She pressed her body against mine. "...I love you very big..."

"Yes. I love you too."

I was running low on money. The Holiday Inn was cheap. I'd only booked one night. My bank account was down to seven or eight hundred. I only had a couple of hundred in cash on me. I had an overdraft facility. I could dip into petty cash at the office until I sorted things out with Melissa. Even raising twenty thousand pounds wouldn't be too big a problem. I had more than adequate collateral to get a loan with. The weight I felt was more than just money.

"Soom Bon said the Arms Fair guy killed your sister."

"Wha?!"

"Soom Bon said..."

She let go of me.

"Wha you say?" For a second I thought she was going to hit me. "Why you talk Soom Bon?!"

"He said you had a sister, and that this arms dealer guy killed her."

Her eyes were wild.

"Soom Bon idiot man... why you go see...?"

"I'm just saying what he told me. You had a sister..."

She laughed out loud.

"...She friend, honey... she just friend... she no sister...Thai people have friend say she 'sister'...same same 'honey'..." Perhaps I'd got the wrong end of the stick. Except her voice was frantic. Her eyes were wild. "... Thai people have friend say she 'sister'..." Maybe I hadn't understood what Soom Bon was saying. It was a Thai thing. Your female friend was your 'sister'. Your male friend was your 'brother.' Any older person was 'uncle.' I'd even heard her call that 'bitch', Pauline, her 'sister'. "... Just friend, honey... she die Bangkok... police don say how she die..." Except, she was frantic to convince me. "... Is nothing honey... must happy... you I must love two gether ..."

She sounded as desperate as I felt. 'You I love together' was the most farfetched story of all.

We'd only been here an hour and it already felt like a lifetime.

"Haluk's daughter gave you a present!"

"Wha?"

I pointed at the package on the bed.

"The little girl in Hassan's shop. She gave you a present?"

Her face flushed.

"... Chai... mai chai..."

... *Yes... no...*

"Aren't you going to open it?"

Suddenly she was giggling, like a little girl caught stealing her mother's lipstick.

"... Chai... chai..."

The stickytape holding the bonbon had come unstuck. The clutch of pink ribbon flopped around as she picked the present up. The silver paper bulged. She slipped her fingernail under the fastenings and slit the package open.

"What is it?"

Eggshells crackled in her throat. Her eyes brimmed. She elbowed tears from her eyes.

"Haluk he crazy man!"

The gift wasn't from the little girl at all.

"Haluk baba ba boa."

It was from the little girl's father, Hassan's son.

She lifted it by its pink ribbons out of the wrapping. For a moment I thought it was a piece of pink tissue paper, or maybe two or three layers of pink tissue paper, each layer so transparent you could still see through it when the layers fizzed together. It wasn't paper. It was nylon, gathered into crimson flounces at the bodice.

"Ey?"

Diamonds of hilarity winked in the skin around her eyes.

"Haluk think I like."

"Was he...?"

"Mai chai! Mai chai! No customer..." The laughter took hold. She doubled up. "...He just think... he just think... *I like*!"

She held the negligee against her chest. Gauzy. Flouncy. See-thru. It was fucked up. It was something a paedophile might give his daughter for Christmas.

I shook my head. I couldn't stop laughing either.

"Haluk has a very strange idea of... of..."

I cracked up. Haluk had a very strange idea of... I didn't know of what... women's fashion...?... women's hearts...?... women's patience...?... his doe-eyed wife's patience behind the till...?

The pinpoints of hilarity turned to tears in her eyes. Her shoulders jumped around so badly she could hardly speak.

"... Haluk... he crazy man... but he... *good heart!*"

"Yeah. Right."

She grinned.

"I try?"

"Yes. Go on."

She pulled her T-shirt over her head and peeled off her jeans.

"Don look."

She turned her back on me and took her panties off. In the crotch of her panties the sanitary towel was stiff with blood.

She slipped the negligee over her head and straightened the straps on her shoulders. She turned round.

"It's hideous."

The nylon was so diaphanous that even through three layers I could see her caesarean scar above her mons like a shadowy grin through the fizzy pink.

She wiggled her bottom.

"I super model... chai?... I sexy girl...?"

"Chai."

She flounced to the door and back, catwalk style, the curves of her bottom swinging the nylon from side to side.

"... You wan fuck I...?"

She slipped her nipples from the rose bud flounces and licked them till they were engorged. She had a good sense of humour. I'd never realized.

"Yes. But..."

"Wan?"

"But..."

She swung backwards against me. An angel swayed backwards into my arms. A celestial musician strummed my cock with her arse.

"Wan do?"

I grinned and kissed the pink string on her shoulder.

"I thought you said you don't do anal."

Her shoulder blades wriggled against my chest. She lifted the negligee over her head.

"Only say for customer."

I felt privileged but confused.

"Yeah, but..."

"Have bleeding do pussy cannot. Bad luck!"

I tried to unbuckle my belt and pull my trousers down, but she kept rubbing her arse against my crotch. The connection was too precarious to risk a break.

I managed to get my pants off and my underpants down.

I folded my hands around her belly. I pulled her hard against my cock.

I felt a dry prickle where her caesarean scar was. She grabbed my hand and dragged it away. I'd encroached on her privacy. Touching the scar was an invasion of privacy worse than fucking her arse.

"Moment! Wait!"

She disappeared into the bathroom. She came back with a bottle of baby oil.

"Look... Natalie..."

She knelt on the bed and cocked her bottom in the air and poured baby oil down the crack of her arse. The oil ran between her cheeks, over the furled lips of her pussy and dripped onto the bedspread. She lifted her backside higher. The oil puddled in her ring.

"...Natalie..."

I'd never done anal.

She worked the oil into her ring with her fingertip. I straddled her and she guided the tip of my cock into the space she'd made.

It was too small. She was far too tight. Her bottom was way too shapely. Her bum was too perfectly made for this to be happening. It was where the stinging brightness was. It was where the shining thread began. Her coccyx jerked liked a cracked knuckle. She gripped my cock with her ring. Small muscular clasps squeezed the tip of my cock, showing me where the woman who shone and stung was, the unapproachable one inside her burning towards the surface, towards my tailbone yearning for her tailbone, two points of light fusing into one brightness, brightness rising upwards outside us like the candescence up a hurricane lamp, towards the source of all joy.

As I thrust into her, the slither of baby oil turned to a tube of sandpaper, bucking backwards at me as I thrust deeper and shot my emptiness into her emptiness.

CHAPTER FOUR

It was the first night I'd spent away from home like this.

In the morning I booked another two nights then went to the office and got the accountant to pay my next month's salary early, into my personal account not my joint account with Melissa. Advancing my salary wasn't a problem. I was the senior partner in the firm. I had bonuses and other lump sum payments pending on top of my ten thousand pounds monthly salary. That was the immediate cash flow issue sorted.

I realized that Natalie couldn't stay at the Holiday Inn. I'd have to find her somewhere to live. It would mean renting a flat, but even that wasn't a problem. Ten thousand was plenty for deposits and rental in advance and any other expenses setting up a second home might require.

I'd find somewhere for her to live but she'd have to live on her own. I had no intention of moving out of Islington. Islington was my home, even if I was only camping in the guest bedroom. Ralph and Meredith were still based at home, even if Meredith was currently in halls of residence at Durham University. There was no way I could sell the house, or even broach the subject with Melissa, even if I'd wanted to. The tension at home was intolerable, but they were still my family. Perhaps, in time, we'd all get used to the new situation.

Natalie's mention of her 'contract' was more immediately worrying. I wasn't at all sure that such contracts even existed, even as undocumented money she might owe Lee. I was aware that Lee might have his own ways of enforcing his contracts, but I also had a lurking suspicion I couldn't shake that her imprisonment and escape from the Caledonian Road might have been staged for my benefit, and that her 'contract' might be a means of getting money out of me for her own purposes. I was in love with her. I wanted her more badly than I'd ever wanted anything in my life, but that didn't mean I one hundred percent trusted her. Still, Stratford was a long way from the Caledonian Road. If Lee was looking for her, it was unlikely he'd be able to find her if I rented somewhere in a quiet part of the East End.

I'd been lucky with the timing of my visit. It was Pippa's day off and Bernard was out of the office. If either of them had been there questions might have been asked about what I was doing transferring money. I might even have met some resistance. They both knew about my problems at home. They were firmly on Melissa's side. Bernard was still angry about my dashing off the night he came over to talk about Rampton Street's phase two.

I went through a few drawings while I waited for the accountant to transfer the money.

"Where's Bernard?"

The accountant looked at me. He only worked for us part time, but he liked to act as if he was an integral part of the outfit.

"Rampton Street. There's a problem with the groundworks."

We'd taken on the Rampton Street phase two work against Pippa's advice. I couldn't remember coming to a decision one way or the other, but Bernard and Pippa were now blaming me for pushing ahead with phase two so soon after the Arkwright debacle.

"Yeah. Well..." I didn't want to think about it. "I'll look over the survey at home."

"You're not going down?"

He was the accountant, the engineering side of the business had nothing to do with him.

"No. I've got to get home. Something's come up."

"I think Bernard expected you to go down."

Even the accountant was getting uppity.

"I've got the groundworks on my computer. I'll have a look at it at home."

Standing in an excavation with Bernard scowling at me wasn't going to sort anything out. Besides... the groundworks were stage *one*, not stage two. They were even on my back about stage one now.

It was eleven o'clock before I pulled up outside my house. Melissa's car was gone. Melissa was at work. Ralph's motorbike wasn't parked on the kerb. Ralph was at the university, in his room in Gower Street, working on his thesis.

I opened the front door and heard music. Meredith was upstairs in her room. It was the middle of term, but Meredith had stayed on in London after Ralph's birthday party, to be with her mother.

I overcame the urge to tiptoe as I went up the stairs. God. What was happening to me? This was my house. She was my daughter. There was no need to act as if I was a burglar or something.

On the second floor, Meredith's bedroom door was closed. It stayed closed as I walked past. I felt relieved. I didn't have time for one of Meredith's tantrums. I'd only come to pick up a change of clothes and my pyjamas and my bathroom stuff to take back to Stratford.

It was stuffy up in the box bedroom. Even in this cold weather the tiny guest room felt overheated, the whole house's central heating trapped under the roof, with a wintry sun toasting the Velux skylight from above.

I packed a few things in a hold-all and zipped my laptop into its travel bag. I could have a look at the drawings when I got back to Stratford.

No. The drawings were important. There were some decisions only I could make. I needed to pass my thoughts on to Bernard as soon as possible. I'd promised the accountant I'd look at them when I got home. Working in the Holiday Inn with the TV on and Natalie channel surfing wasn't an option.

I took my laptop out of its travel bag and sat down on the bed and switched it on.

My laptop was on factory settings. Someone had scrubbed my computer. My work. My email account. My internet banking details. My downloads. My documents. Everything, the Rampton Street drawings included.

I stormed down the stairs. I banged on Meredith's door. I pushed it open.

"What's happened to my computer?"

Ralph and Melissa were angry with me, but only Meredith could have done something as vindictive as this.

She grinned.

"You've abused my mother. I've abused your computer."

"Oh fuck off with that shit!" She saw 'abusers' everywhere she looked. "You've scrubbed my work!"

She was curled up on the bed with her phone.

"You hurt Mum!"

All the years I'd spent carrying her on my shoulders and reading books with her and helping her with her homework, and she thought she had the right to deliberately take me down.

"My work, Meredith! I need it for my work!"

"It's only a computer, Dad. Mum's a person."

She was triumphant. It was like talking to a two-year-old. Meredith had never been easy-going like Ralph. Right now she looked small and compact and waspish. Where Ralph had a certain analytical coolness, even when he was angry, Meredith's anger always ended up magnified out of all proportion.

"I'm a person too. Alright?! I'm your father!"

Nineteen years of love and nurture don't go up the spout just because you do something a nineteen-year-old feminist doesn't approve of. You can't scrub the past like you scrub work off a computer.

"I feel sorry for that poor woman. I really do, Dad."

"Oh Jesus, Meredith. Give it a rest!"

"She's your victim, just like Mum is. You prey on her too."

I could hear the conversations she and her mother had been having, Melissa spilling all the gory details.

"I promise you, Meredith. She's okay. Alright?" She was a big Buddha woman, a princess in old Siam, not some complacent victim for Meredith to trot out every time she felt peevish. "She doesn't need your pity. She doesn't want it. Okay?"

When she was little Meredith had been a passionate protector of helpless animals. Hamsters. Gerbils. Cats. Dogs. She'd mothered them with heart-warming intensity. Now it was rape victims and prostitutes.

"This isn't like you, Meredith. It's so petty. So vindictive."

"I don't know why you keep hanging around like this, Dad. Why don't you piss off back to your girlfriend!"

She was a distraught child. I was her father. All I had to do was promise never to see Natalie again, for Meredith's sake, if not Melissa's, and it would all be over. Melissa and I had always been happy together. We weren't like those parents who don't get along but stay together for their children's sake. Doing the right thing by your child is even more important than not hurting the woman you love.

"Shit, Meredith."

I pissed off back to my girlfriend.

I didn't go straight to Stratford. I took the opposite direction to Stratford and headed west through Camden Town then up the Finchley Road. At the top of the hill I turned down West End Lane and parked outside the Fortune Green Cemetery.

It was over a year since I'd been here. Nicholas's grave was in the north eastern corner of the cemetery between the Bianchi monument and the tap.

Eighteen years ago, the tap had worried me. There'd been an underground leak in the pipe somewhere, and the ground around the tap was permanently wet. Today it was hard and brittle.

The grave was well kept, though without the colour and tidiness of some of the better attended graves. The rose bushes had been clipped back hard. A philadelphus that had got out of control had been removed. Melissa came periodically with clippers and rubbish bags.

Our son's headstone had been carved by a sculptor friend whom we'd later lost touch with. The over-delicate Gothic script had blurred in a few places.

'Praise for the singing,
Praise for the morning,
Praise for them springing,
Fresh from the world.'

How gauche the words looked on the weathered stone, but you're emotional when you've just lost a three-year-old child. You believe that you'll never forget a single thing about him.

We'd been helping a friend move house and Nicholas had run out behind the van our friend had hired and was killed by a faulty back door swinging open as the van drove away.

It had been more than emotion, or even shock, those first few months after the funeral. The freshly dug clay had a sewage-y smell that had dismayed me. The spring fizz in the April air had sprung 'fresh from the world.' Melissa had felt it too, she'd felt it keenly enough to put it into words: Nicholas was still here. He was no longer a tiny sweet three-year-old body. He'd had to become as big as the earth itself to do it, but we could feel him. He was still here. He'd done it for us. He'd stayed to comfort us. He'd become everything there is so that we could know that he was still alive, and even nearer than he'd been before.

It was just the shock still kicking in. But that was what I'd felt, standing on this very spot on a perfect April morning. The sensation had been powerful, even though it had faded within a few days and reality had reasserted itself.

Being thoughtful people, readers of books, Melissa and I had both tried to hang onto our Nicholas-outside-time-and-space moment. We'd brought up the curved nature of space and quantum time from the usual pop science paperbacks. We'd discussed Gaia and earth consciousness with a desperate intensity, but in the long run none of it had helped. Our son was gone.

Natalie was waiting for me when I got back to our room. So was Pauline.

"Pauline come see I, honey!"

Pauline stood at the window blowing cigarette smoke out at the Romford Road through the narrow aperture the building regulations allowed.

"I ringing Pauline. She come see I!"

Not long ago Natalie had been screaming that Pauline was a bitch, she was going to kill her.

Pauline gave me a blank smile and an off-the-shelf hello. There was no sign that a week ago her fingers had been digging into my bum while she grassed Natalie up.

Pauline was dressed to kill. Maybe she'd paid off her contract and was no longer a prisoner at the Caledonian Road and was allowed to spend nights she wasn't in Hackney out clubbing. Her skin-tight white slacks looked expensive. Each leg had *windows*—there was no other word for the rectangles of see-thru plastic in the skin-hugging cotton—climbing the smooth honey of her narrow thighs. Silver sequins on her white T-shirt spelled HOT across her flat chest. Her poisonously sexy vibe made the outfit look pretty good.

"I lonely, honey. Ringing Pauline."

I realized that, even in the few hours I'd been away, that was one of the things I'd been worrying about, Natalie getting lonely on her own in the hotel room. She was used to being amongst people. Solitude was not in her DNA.

"Pauline Frank go lala."

"Frank?"

"She boyfriend."

"Right."

It wasn't just the fact that a few days ago they'd been mortal enemies that didn't make sense. If Natalie really was running away from Lee, then Pauline oughtn't to be here. If Natalie was as scared of Lee as she said she was, asking Pauline to pop over ought to have been the last thing on her mind. There was no one, not a single person on God's earth, I felt sure, who'd trust Pauline as far as they could throw her. She'd tell Lee where Natalie was 'hiding' the minute she got back to the Caledonian Road.

I decided to ask her to leave.

There was a knock at the door. Pauline ignored it.

Natalie jumped up and ran to the door.

She let in a thin, grey man of about forty. He was wearing a London Transport uniform. Pants. Jacket. Shirt. Tie. Badge. The ticket inspector's hat. He was carrying a bottle of Johnny Walker in a presentation box.

He looked at me and said:

"Sprung bleeding overtime on me." I didn't know what to say. "Weren't like I hadn't just done ten hours straight, was it?" He kissed Natalie's cheek and handed her the whiskey. "Anyway. Sorry I'm late." I glanced at Natalie. *Late?* "A bloody kip would've been nice." He did look tired. In fact he looked exhausted. "That's flippin' management for you."

His face was a drained, whey-grey colour.

He took his hat off and looked around for somewhere to put it down. He placed his hat it on top of Natalie's suitcase.

"Hello, love."

Pauline offered him her cheek. He kissed it, and she went back to jetting smoke out the window. He grimaced. "Frank..."

I held out my hand.

"Jim."

We shook hands. There was only one chair. Frank took it and I sat on the bed.

I wondered if I should go home and speak to Meredith. I'd been wrong to flare up at her. Wiping my computer was nasty. Destroying my work was completely puerile, but I did have back-ups for the really important stuff she'd deleted. At times Meredith and I had had a prickly relationship, but we'd always been able to talk. I admired her impulsiveness and her willingness to act on her principles. I'd forgotten how young and idealistic she was. I should have sat down and talked to her instead of rearing up. In fact, the sparky way Meredith stood up for abused women and victims of male oppression was impressive. If I'd managed to explain my feelings for Natalie to her, and what Natalie was really like, my daughter might have seen that, far from being a victim, 'that poor woman' was as strong and sparky as she was.

Pauline finished her cigarette. She flicked the butt end out onto the traffic roaring below and came and stood over Frank. She looked him up and down.

"Why you no change?"

"I told you. They sprang bleeding overtime on me."

"Cannot go out wear uniform." I glanced at Natalie. *Out?* "Uniform not handsome."

Frank grinned at me.

"She's used to four star generals."

"They don let you in!"

I tried to catch Natalie's eye. *In?* Natalie ignored me. She'd already opened the whiskey. She was looking around the room, our pair of glasses set up on the table.

"Only two glass."

Pauline perched on Frank's knee.

"Holiday Inn. Charlie Cheap. Never have nothing."

Frank dug me in the ribs.

"They're used to the Hilton."

"Fuck off," said Pauline. "Why you say?"

I wondered if I was Charlie Cheap.

Natalie was pouring the other two whiskies into the pair of teacups.

I raised my cup to Frank.

"Nice drop."

It was, too. I felt raw and lonely. The burn of the Johnny Walker went down well.

Meredith was wrong saying these women were victims. Looking at Pauline curled up in Frank's lap it was hard to say who was the victim and who was the oppressor. Pauline could fold up like a coiled pythoness. The hungry windows in her slacks and her HOT flat chest were swallowing Frank whole, in his London Underground uniform, digesting him in a gulp and spitting out the wedding ring that stroked her bony hip. If I'd stayed and had it out with my daughter I might have been able to explain to her that, yes, perhaps there was an inner cost to pay, even a terrible price, in selfishness and viciousness, but the snake skin, the devouring surface, isn't merely in men's minds. It's not just a glittering exterior that men lay on women to abuse them. It's in the air, everywhere, between any two people. It was here, in this room, shining and stinging, separate and other.

There was a knock on the door.

Natalie jumped up and showed another couple in. We were gathering for a night out. I looked at her.

"Natalie. We can't. What if Lee..."

"Jim, this Gigi. Gigi, this Jim."

It was the chubby girl in the red corset I'd seen in the Kilburn flat, poking her head out of the bedroom the day I met Cyril.

"Sawaddee ka, loong."

Gigi had a relaxed, natural smile. She was wearing a classy chiffon cocktail frock. It suited her very well. I liked her as much as I disliked Pauline.

"This Ravindra."

Gigi's boyfriend was a dapper Indian man. He looked to be well into his sixties.

We sat around drinking Frank's whisky. The room felt crowded. There were no more cups or glasses, so Natalie and I shared a cup, Gigi and Ravindra shared a cup, and Pauline and Frank, as the suppliers of the whisky, had a glass each.

The party soon split up into men and women.

Pauline climbed out of Frank's lap and joined Gigi and Natalie on the bed, chattering in Thai. Ravindra and I perched on the edge of the bed closest to Frank's armchair and made desultory conversation.

Frank nodded at the girls.

"Like a flock of bleeding parakeets."

He was right. There was something preternaturally flamboyant about the women, laughing and gossiping in their broken eggshell tongue, their animosities and difficulties submerged in a village-y camaraderie, while we three men sat stiff and grey discussing football and the economy, tip toeing around Brexit.

Ravindra was an accountant. He ran an accountancy business in Ilford that also dealt in immigration problems and visa applications. He was a tubby little man in glasses, with silver hair and a gold tooth. He made pronouncements. He proffered advice unasked. He had a paternal self-assurance that didn't sit quite right with the classy young prostitute on his arm. Perhaps being Asian Ravindra understood Thai women better than Frank and I did, but I had a feeling there was a grim old amma back in Ilford running things. Ravindra was soon giving Frank and I advise on how to handle Thai women. The trick was to be firm, especially when it came to money.

The subject of the girls' contracts came up.

"Running away is madness, Jim." Ravindra seemed to know all about Natalie's escape from the Caledonian Road. "Lee's a reasonable man."

He advised me to take Natalie straight back to the Caledonian Road, now, tonight. Lee would be angry, but there'd be no violence. Lee had a busy period coming up and he needed Natalie to work. She could work her contract off quickly, in a couple of months, then leave the Caledonian Road if she wanted to.

Ravindra wasn't so much tubby as dumpy. There were dark, puffy bags under his eyes. I wondered if his lack of charm gave him a head start when it came to handling women. The authority with which he spoke was not based on anything as precarious as personal attractiveness.

He looked around at the cramped room, the unpleasing décor, Romford Road outside the window.

"Natalie can't stay here, Jim."

"I realise that."

"I've got a house. Natalie can live there when she's worked off her contract. She doesn't have to stay at the Caledonian Road."

Ravindra owned a number of houses, in Plaistow and West Ham. He rented out rooms to girls who'd paid off their contracts. The rent was steep for Plaistow, but he was taking a risk letting to illegals.

"The thing is, Jim, you have to take Natalie back to Lee's right now."

His businesslike tone rang false. The fact that he knew so much about Natalie and me made me nervous. Ravindra was a bullshitter, but if he knew as much about Lee, and Lee's business, as he claimed he'd certainly grass me and Natalie up. If, that is, there was anything to grass up, and Natalie's escape wasn't just a scam, that Javindra was in on too.

"A woman likes to know where she stands, Jim." I wondered if he was threatening me. "Thai girls like to be with other Thai girls."

Gigi wasn't his girlfriend at all. She was his second wife. She managed his house in Plaistow as well as working part time at Kilburn to help with the family budget. I liked her. Life with Javindra can't have been much fun, but Gigi seemed to have a lively sense of humour. She'd make a droll comment and have the three of them collapsed on the bed in stitches.

"You've got to be firm with them, Frank." For a second I thought Javindra was going to pull the girls up on their hysteria. "You need to put your foot down with Pauline."

Frank wasn't listening. His shoulders rose and fell. His head had sunk onto his chest. He'd nodded off.

Ravindra explained Frank's situation to me.

Frank wasn't firm enough. He was in the process of losing everything. Money. Family. Home. Frank was in as much trouble with his wife and children as I was. I felt a chill run though me.

Frank failed to control Pauline. He gave Pauline a great deal of money but didn't use the money he gave her to keep her in line. Pauline still hadn't worked off her contract. She was greedy. She spent money on clothes and clubs. Her financial demands were swingeing. On his London Underground wages Frank couldn't keep up and had had to come to terms with her needing a second boyfriend, a Cypriot builder in Shepherds Bush, with whom he shared her. The builder didn't give Pauline as much money as Frank did, but he looked good in club gear. Frank worked all the overtime he could get, but he was still losing everything, his wife, his children, his house, for the occasional bleak little party like this and the thrill of having a girl with windows in her slacks perched a moment on his knee.

Gigi cracked a joke. The parakeets shrilled, Frank no longer heard. He snored tranquilly.

Javindra smiled.

"He doesn't put his foot down."

When the whisky was finished we woke Frank, and went out to eat. Frank had come straight from work by public transport, so he and Pauline came in my car.

Ravindra and Gigi went in Ravindra's Honda. It was only a Civic, a 2012 Civic at that, not a patch on my BMW. I felt drunk and slightly crazed.

We ate in a large, busy Chinese restaurant in Hornchurch. The restaurant served some sort of noodles the women were keen to eat.

I drank a lot of beer and tried to relax, but Ravindra's advice, that Natalie ought to go straight back to the Caledonian Road, was doing my head in. If Natalie really had escaped from the Caledonian Road, we shouldn't even be sitting here. If she truly was running away from Lee, then we ought to have stayed put in the hotel, or even moved on somewhere else before Pauline or Ravindra could tell Lee where we were. It was quite possible that her flight had been staged for my benefit, and yet Ravindra kept warning me that Lee would come after us. I should take Natalie back to the Caledonian Road before something dreadful happened. Lee was reasonable, but he could become violent very easily. Cyril had said the same thing, that Natalie was a prisoner in the Caledonian Road house. She hadn't paid off her contract. Lee would be more than angry. He was lining her up with some guy from the Arms Fair and she'd gone missing. And yet here we were, eating noodles and drinking beer in Hornchurch, on our way to some club in Romford.

Natalie had changed into the black cocktail dress she'd worn to White's the night I saw her with Adrian Whiteley.

She had a way of maintaining eye contact, and touch contact too. A smile. A hand on my knee. A look. A wordless intimacy amid the hubbub of the restaurant and the tensions rife in our ill-assorted group. It felt more convivial than the most engaging conversation.

Frank's face was ashen. Ravindra and I had withdrawn into prickly silence. The girls chattered on. It was ten o'clock before Natalie called for the bill. Apparently I was paying.

The club was called ATIK. It was a huge, sprawling place bathed in pink and purple light on the outside and pounding darkness inside.

An advertisement said that on non-house nights they held boxing matches on the main dance floor.

The doorman was nearly as big as Cyril. He didn't want to let Frank in. Frank's London Transport uniform didn't meet the dress code. It was only because it was a week night and we were with three flamboyantly sexy girls that Frank, Javindra and I got in at all.

My own night was going badly enough, but Frank's was like a runaway train down an insomniac tunnel— a twelve hour shift at Baker Street, two hours drinking in the hotel, three at the restaurant, God alone knew how long we were going to be in the club, sex with Pauline at some stage— and he was on early tomorrow.

The lighting out on the dance floor was impenetrable. Frank, Javindra and I sat at a railing above the arena looking down at the girls as they danced in black static, pink and purple riptides tugging at their ankles.

There was only a small crowd. There was nowhere to escape from the music.

Everybody seemed pissed off that it wasn't house night. There was a meat market vibe but it was coming more from the staff than the customers. Pauline and Gigi looked as if they knew the place. I wondered if they came here to pick up guys their own age on their nights off.

"The Dancing Queens," said Frank.

He was no longer making sense.

The music was at the far end of a bleak universe from ABBA. But Frank was right, that was what the three Thai girls were. They were regal. They ruled the dance floor, Pauline in particular. They gave the robotic beat courtly syncopations. It was tiring just watching them. They danced as a threesome. It wasn't the sort of dancing you needed to have partners for. Guys cut in and out of the girls' exotic swaying, on tangents of their own. Occasionally the three of them were picked up and carried along in a crowd surge

"They're relaxing," said Ravindra. "They're not here to score." A hunk was homing in on Gigi. "After a hard day's work, sex is the last thing on their minds."

"Dunno about that," said Frank.

I decided to get up and dance. I'm not a great dancer and I was drunk, but anything was better than sitting here listening to this. Frank was okay, but Javindra was a total prick.

She saw me coming and stepped out of the melee. Her beauty hit me full on. She was the loveliest thing in the meat market, but no hunks cut between us, no dudes moved in on her. She stepped beyond all eyes but mine.

My neck hurt. There was a stinging sensation in my spine. I felt freezing cold except for the sharp heat in the small of my back. Bodies jostled and surged, but the unapproachable woman stayed unapproachable. I was drunk. Natalie wasn't all that great a dancer.

She was self-conscious in a way I never would have expected, not wholly connected, as Pauline was, to the heart-stopping swaying of her hips or the unmistakable pumping of her pussy under the chic chiffon.

We danced face to face, without touching. She seemed as unsure as I was whether what we were doing was even dancing at all. Pinpoints of light were streaming from her face and catching in my brain, in my brain and mine alone, like diamonds in a sieve as they went through me.

Yes. Natalie was self-conscious. Her shoulders lifted and missed the beat. My feet couldn't find a rhythm at all, just a piston's pounding turning to a heartbeat. The unapproachable woman shone and stung. She cast a sideways glance at Natalie and me, just Natalie and I, lost in the uproar of her heart. Jack's girlfriend's book called her 'She Who Is Outside The Universe And Goes Upwards.' The Serpent Power was right. No other name could touch her.

Somewhere in the darkness Pauline and Gigi flitted through pink and purple puddles, a fat girl danced with the handbag at her feet. It was okay to be afraid. The world is always turning on a shining hinge, on a stinging thread in your spine, towards something incomprehensible, towards something which you can only fear.

Natalie smiled and I heard 'Nok same bird'. 'Nok same bird' welled up inside me. It flooded my throat. Eggshell cracked and spilled in my larynx. I'd done something irrevocably wrong. I was doing something irrevocably wrong, but as 'Nok same bird' rose up inside me I knew that it came from the source of all joy.

I danced on a frozen footpath, between bins of footpath merchandise, in a sidelong glance, in a glimpse of transcendence, knowing that if I walked off up the footpath and never came back this transcendence would stay with me, I'd remain in contact with the source.

Natalie dipped and swayed, a celestial musician in the pink and purple harmonics. She towered, the way angels tower. Her face was geisha static above Pattaya break beats. The runaway train hurtled down an insomniac tunnel, but the ashen fuck, somewhere up ahead, would never catch her. Perhaps it was just the drink. Maybe it was just the meat market that never closes. You don't need to talk or dance or even score to sway with the Buddha woman. Sorry, *big* Buddha woman. Everything was suddenly okay. My life wasn't going down the gurgler at all. Everything started here in my body, dizzying to this machine beat. I was transcendence itself. I was the source of joy. Natalie wasn't a threat. She'd come to free me from time and space, from my own body if need be. I hadn't walked down an aisle between wire bins of shoes and household merchandise and rung a bell with a green star next to it. How could I have? I was everything, bins, shoes, washing up pads, the lot. I was the green star and the buzzer. I was ORIENTAL BABE. I was Natalie. Fucking her meant less than the smell of room freshener or the blast of a fan heater. Loving her was mere body warmth being sucked away into this stinging and this burning. Only the shining thread was real, and Natalie knew it as well as I did. We were one. She was the left side of my body and I was the right. I was the right side of her body and she was the left. No wonder dancing was so hard. She made everything light and insubstantial. I made everything dense and heavy. But it didn't matter, as long as we were inside the thread, as long as the shining hinge was still turning towards the incomprehensible, which wasn't incomprehensible at all, because I was It and she was It. Even Gigi was inside me. Even Pauline and her snake hips jagging at the ragged edges of my light which wasn't pink and purple at all. It was transcendent light. It saw everything, and lit nothing. It brought the past back to life, a fan heater and a smell of air freshener throwing off their gravestone lids and stepping forth redeemed. It brought the future back to life and redeemed its peculiar brand of death. There was no need to stand beside a dead child's grave and grasp at him. This truth is so great, it doesn't need renegade physicists to explain it. This truth is so momentous it doesn't require a fucked up guru to put it into words. The Serpent Power? I was It, dancing on Her tail, 'She Who Is Outside The Universe, And Goes Upwards'.

I didn't take Natalie back to the Caledonian Road to face Lee, as Javindra had suggested. Natalie didn't want to go back to the Caledonian Road. She was adamant that talking to Lee was a bad idea. Lee was a bad man. He'd hurt her, after what she'd done. Lee would make sure she never ran away again.

"Want stay with you, honey." She didn't want to stay with Gigi in Plaistow either. "Don like Javindra." We were agreed on that one. "Go Plaistow Lee find I easy." I was frightened that Javindra had already spoken to Lee,

We checked out of the Holiday Inn that morning. I needed to find somewhere for her to stay.

We looked at rooms in shared houses.

The respectable landlords seemed suspicious, the dodgy ones seemed dodgy.

We inspected a few studio flats, but they were even more cramped than the Holiday Inn. A couple of days and Natalie'd be climbing up the walls.

I hadn't sorted out my joint account yet. Melissa was still blocking my withdrawals. She'd also started talking about divorce proceedings, before I could even get at my share of our savings.

I'd already taken a month's salary in advance. I was spending so little time in the office, asking for a second month in advance was out of the question.

It was frustrating having a large amount of money, half of which was rightfully mine, and being unable to gain access to it.

I ended up renting a house, a small, two-bedroom terrace house in Stratford.

At nine hundred a month, the rent was cheap enough for a furnished place, but with the deposit and a month's rent in advance and some extras—rice steamer, woks and chopping blocks, a DVD player, a proper shower—moving in swallowed up the bulk of my available money.

The house was brand new. We were its first tenants. It was one of three new-builds constructed to the same scale as the Victorian two up/two down terrace houses it abutted.

The rooms felt raw and unlived in. You could smell the mastic curing around the bathtub, and the glue still setting beneath the linoleum tiles. The furniture was Spartan, flat-pack beds and a Homebase sofa. The front door opened straight into the living room.

As soon as Natalie moved in, I realized that claustrophobia wasn't her problem, so much as solitude. I was still spending half my time at Islington, hoping to sort things out with my family. I was away a lot, but every time I opened the front door at Stratford I could feel how much Natalie wasn't used to being on her own. In fact, she hated it. The Caledonian Road house had been oppressive, but at least there'd been other girls there. Even just one night at the Holiday Inn she'd had a visit from Pauline and Gigi. Pauline and Gigi immediately popped in to the new place, so did some other girls of Lee's, which made me nervous of our whereabouts being discovered, but there were still long stretches of the day when Natalie was left on her own. Even at Kilburn there'd been Sandra and her friend the pound shop boss. Every time I kissed her to drive back to Islington I sensed that back in the village where she came from there'd always been people around, she'd never been so alone.

A few days after we moved in she said:

"Have house. Mum Nok come see I?"

"Yeah. Okay. Great."

I jumped at the idea. There was the second bedroom for her mother and daughter to stay in. Having them visit would be a huge help to Natalie, and it would be a pleasure for me to meet her family. Natalie came from such a different culture, from a way of life that was so obscured by the way she lived in London, it would be nice to get to know her mother and Nok. They could come on tourist visas. There'd be no immigration problems to worry about.

On the other hand, that meant two airfares, plus money for entertainment and shopping, on top of what I was giving Natalie for housekeeping. I was going to have to raise some more cash.

I rang Jack O'Grady and asked for my loan back. Luckily, Jack answered his phone.

"Sure, Jim. I'll be straight over."

I was taken aback. I'd half expected him to be up North somewhere, or even out of the country. I only just managed to give him the Stratford address, and warn him not to go to Islington, before he rang off.

It meant dropping what I was doing and ducking off work again. Jack sounded as if he was in a rush. I high tailed it over to Stratford, half presuming he'd fobbed me off again, not really expecting to see him.

When I opened the front door, Jack was sitting in the living room. Sylvia was out in the kitchen with Natalie.

"Hey, Jim! There you are! At last!" He asked me for some more money. "Just another thousand, mate. Till Friday."

He needed another thousand pounds so urgently that, in the forty five minutes since our phone conversation, he'd forgotten all about returning the two thousand.

One of his contacts had been picked up by the police, in Jakarta. Jack needed the money to pay a lawyer.

Something bad had happened to Jack since I'd last seen him. Something had tipped him over the edge. Jack was finally cracking up.

He leapt up from the sofa and shook my hand, as if we were long lost brothers. He hugged me. He paced the room.

I hadn't seen him for three years, we'd only spent an hour together in a Kings Cross bar, but suddenly I was the only person in the world who understood what was going on. Sylvia and me.

Sylvia came in from the kitchen with a plate of spring rolls. She looked at me.

Her gaze was religious. Sylvia believed in the global capitalist conspiracy as lugubriously as any spinster at the communion rail believes in hell. Jack had it too— faith, ravening belief, a creed. A creed is a more basic animal need than food or shelter.

I told Jack I couldn't give him any money. He barely heard me. I was here, that was all that counted. I was a fellow believer, someone he could commune with.

"They're closing in, Jim. The Arms Fair. It's the big one. I told you. They'll stop at nothing."

I tried to calm him:

"There's no *them*, Jack...no plot... it's just... *people*..."

I felt a desperate need to argue the toss, even if I wasn't making sense. I'd changed too, between my last seeing Jack and now. Something had altered in me too, without my knowing.

Sitting and listening to Jack's madness was no longer an option. I knew that what I said was right. Human nature was the problem, not the globalist elite... not even human nature, just the simple fact that we inhabit separate bodies, that it's hard to care about what our skin can't touch and our eyes can't see. It's difficult to imagine the suffering of others when they're thousands of miles away and come from a different background. I knew I was right, but putting it into words was impossible.

"You're right, Jim! That's exactly it! *People*! These people are psychopaths. They'll stop at nothing!"

He kept bringing it back to individuals. He insisted that the 'someone' whose name his Jakarta contact had given him—Jack wouldn't tell me the name—was alone responsible for the Yemen, Iraq, Libya, Afghanistan, Syria, everything. It wasn't human nature, people in general, that caused all the suffering, it was a name, a name that Jack had and that no one else knew. He was medieval. Jack believed in the Devil. He had a list of devils, called the New World Order, that were hell bent on taking over the world, led by some guy somewhere—only Jack knew— who was Satan himself. Satan was on his way to the Arms Fair.

Natalie came in with some beer and a plate of piping-hot dumplings. Jack grabbed one and stuffed it in his mouth.

"Thanks, Natalie."

It was the first time they'd ever met, but Jack addressed Natalie as if they'd known each other all their lives.

He grabbed dumpling after dumpling off the plate. He stuffed them steaming hot into his mouth as he talked. He hadn't been eating properly.

"These people are twisted, Jim," said Sylvia. "They're sick." I wondered if she meant me. Sylvia didn't approve of my standing up to Jack. It had nothing to do with my not giving him money. People who disagreed with Jack were evil.

"I know, but..."

Natalie said:

"Bad people dumb."

Even Jack stopped talking.

Sylvia stared.

I was taken aback. I hadn't imagined that Natalie could possibly have been following the tirade of English.

"Buddha say. Bad people dumb."

It was the first time I'd ever heard her mention Buddha directly. All the 'angel girl' and 'big Buddha woman' stuff I'd heard from other people. From Pauline. From Soom Bon. From Cyril. I'd got the impression that the Buddhist religion, per se, didn't really interest Natalie. I'd assumed that she only believed in the superstitious side of it, the prince and princess drowning themselves in their life before, the fortune telling and sorcery side of Buddhism, not the doctrine itself, whatever that was. It was a teaching I knew almost nothing about, but I guessed that what she meant was that people who did evil things weren't in and of themselves evil, they merely did wrong out of ignorance. I had a feeling that that was what the Buddha had said in his doctrine—that there was no such thing as intrinsic evil, there was just a failure to understand reality.

Natalie laughed out loud.

"Buddha talk shit."

It shocked me, not so much her contradicting the Buddha—if she had indeed contradicted the Buddha—but the vehemence with which she said it. She couldn't have been following the ins and outs of Jack's paranoia, there was no way she could have kept up with his personal war with the New World Order, and yet she'd come down on the same side as Jack!

I protested:

"... No...!... we're all trapped... it's just that we're all... trapped in an economic system..." 'Economic system' was way too weak, but I couldn't think of an alternative. "... That leads to evil things, but none of us, in and of ourselves is evil...as individuals..." That didn't sound right either. "... It's just that we're helpless..."

"*System*?" Sylvia's voice was vibrant. "It's a machine, Jim. It's a death machine, not a 'system'!"

There seemed to be times when Sylvia took over Jack's train of thought, seamlessly, without faltering, while Jack descended into the depths and wrestled with George Soros personally.

I looked at Natalie.

She scared me. She scared me more than Jack did. Jack's paranoia was pathetic. Jack was merely a deluded man acting out his hang-ups on the biggest stage he could find. 'Buddha say shit' was different. She was topping up Jack's beer, she'd moved on, but her vehemence hung on in the room, in the air, in a freezing brightness, between us, dancing face to face in blue and purple riptides, on a frozen footpath. I believed Soom Bon's story of a murdered sister and the big Buddha woman's revenge as little as I believed his prince and princess and their dip in the Phraya River, but something was wrong. The unapproachable woman shone and stung. In this freezing brightness, the unapproachable woman was approaching. She cast a sideways glance at Natalie and me, at Natalie and me alone. Her brightness lit everything and saw nothing. It brought the past back to life right here, right now. It brought the future back to life, with its peculiar brand of death. Jack's hippy girlfriend's book called her Kundalini. The Serpent Power. She Who Is Outside The Universe And Goes Upwards. I'd got it wrong. I hadn't seen what was staring me in the face. Standing at the source is stupid. Dancing at the source is even crazier. My logic had deserted me. There can only be one source, and it's the source of evil as well as joy.

Jack surfaced:

"You sure you can't raise that thousand, Jim? It's a matter of life and death."

"... No... I'm sorry..." I could feel Natalie listening hard. We were talking about money. "... Maybe when I free up some funds... I've got a bit of a cash flow problem right now..."

I looked at Jack.

Jack wasn't listening. He was on his phone, talking to someone, urgently, impetuously, in a manic code of his own. They were talking about the Arms Fair but the details were way over my head.

Jack had already forgiven me. He was back on his hobby horse, riding hard, tilting at the Globalist Elite.

Nights when I was back in Islington I worried about Natalie being alone in the house in Stratford. She hated being on her own. She seemed to spend most of her time sleeping. She drank a lot, without seeming to be particularly addicted to alcohol, even when she drank on her own. She was glad she was no longer being bussed to the sauna. She was relieved not to have to work anymore, but neither did she behave like someone who'd just been freed from captivity.

Lying in my single bed in the box room looking up at the stars and the city night glow through the Velux window, I kept thinking about 'bad people dumb' and 'Buddha say shit.' It still upset me. She'd said it with so much vehemence, with a sort of gloating malice. She was glad the bad people were dumb, and there was one in particular who was bad and dumb. Buddha talked shit because the bad man's ignorance wasn't going to save him. His dumbness wasn't going to let him off the bad thing, the very worst thing, he'd done.

It disturbed me so much, I'd spoken to her about it. Or at least, I'd tried. She refused point blank to talk about the dead 'sister' Soom Bon had told me about. There was no such person. The murdered sister was just a fantasy of Soom Bon's. 'Soom Bon dreaming, honey.' But if that was the case, why did she accept Soom Bon's other 'dreamings' so whole heartedly? She believed Soom Bon could see back into the past. She believed he could see into the future. She believed in Soom Bon's clairvoyance with a childlike gullibility, except when it came to her 'sister.'

Nights alone in the box room, the stinging in my spine got out of control. The singing in my ears turned from background tinnitus to a presence in its own right, a presence in *her* own right. The vibration that touched my tympanum was female. The unapproachable woman whispered like bees in a meadow heady with pollen. There were moments when being spaced out—I was hell of a spaced out—turned to a sort of clarity, without there being anything to clarify.

I grinned at the skylight with a malice of my own. I ought to buy a plank and ink some squares and symbols on it and do spirit readings, two hundred quid a pop.

I couldn't sleep. I was dead tired, but every time I was about to drop off dread seized me. The dread went on and on, except for moments when it took on a funky beat, and I smiled up at the night sky and heard a ganja-rich voice strutting his dread in Babylon.

I couldn't sleep, so I tried to read.

Bravo Two Zero stalled on the second or third sentence. I kept missing something the words were trying to tell me, and had to go back over them again and again.

The AA Guide to England and Northern Ireland had some nice pictures, but the lochs and thatched cottages turned claustrophobic on me.

Jack's hippy girlfriend's books were the most accessible. The words went on and off in my head like Christmas lights at Westfields Shopping City. For a paragraph or two they'd illuminate something real, before flicking back to darkness.

'*Time is an illusion foisted on the brain by the configuration of space.*'

Soom Bon knew all about that.

I shut *The End Of Time* and tried *Freedom From The Known*.

'*When the brain discovers something new...*'

Exactly. Jack's New World Order.

I shut *Freedom From The Known* and had a look at *The Serpent Power*.

'...*She is the sleeping Kundalini, fine as the fibre of the lotus-stalk...*' I could feel Natalie, alone in Stratford, in front of the TV, cracking another beer, surfing from channel to channel. '... *Her lustre is strong as a flash of young lightning. Her murmur is sweet as the hum of love-crazed bees...*'

Yes. I'd seen Her on the dance floor at ATIK.

Nights were mad, but the days were liveable. They fell into a routine of their own. Less and less time at the office, and more spent driving between Islington and Stratford. While I clung onto Islington for dear life, with only the occasional confrontation on the stairs or accusatory conversation in the kitchen to shake me off, Stratford took on a magnetic ordinariness that quickly became more comfortable than the tension at home. Natalie cooked lunch for me, prawn soup and red curry if she was up, MacDonalds and Pizza Express if she was down. I suggested trips out to Mill Hill for a pub lunch, or to White Water for shopping, but she preferred flopping around the house in her pyjamas, drinking beer in front of the TV and making love upstairs. It was a long time since she'd shacked up with a customer. The last couple of years had been hard, working in Dubai and Hong Kong, and now she was recuperating in this state of humdrum suspension. It felt as if she was waiting for something, passing the time till the thing she was waiting for happened, more than she was hiding from Lee. If Lee was angry with her and wanted to fetch her back to the Caledonian Road, he'd now had ample opportunity to track her down, and nothing had happened. Her friends, including Pauline and Gigi, popped in and out, any one of them capable of grassing her up to the boss, and there was still no sign of Lee. A couple of times the front doorbell rang while we were making love, rang insistently, followed by a demanding call on Natalie's phone and I had to get dressed and go downstairs and make embarrassed conversation with some bright-eyed Thai girl.

If Natalie was in a state of suspension, drifting from day to day, waiting for a twist of lustrous black hair on an inked paling to speak, I floated along in my own state of suspension, waiting on God knows what. Melissa didn't bring up the subject of divorce again when she accosted me on the stairs, but I had a feeling she was taking steps behind my back. Access to our joint account remained blocked. When I asked her to trust me and let me draw out some money she grew indignant. It felt unfair. The money was mine as much as it was hers, in fact I'd contributed considerably more to our joint account than she had. It felt more than unfair, but when I contacted our bank I was told that Melissa was taking steps to close the account. Had I not received the appropriate letters? Hadn't I read the bank's email notifications? At least, until I did something about it, the money was frozen for Melissa as well as me, hanging in its own state of suspension.

When I was in Islington I avoided running into Melissa on the stairs as much as I possibly could. My flights up to the box bedroom grew more and more furtive. Melissa had lost weight. There was a nerviness I'd never seen in her before. Her face was grey and haggard. In Stratford on the other hand, Natalie grew, if anything, even more beautiful. The long vacant days suited her. Stretched out across the pillow, her hair grew even more lustrous. Her skin felt even softer and warmer under a sloppy old pair of pyjamas. Her foot was even shapelier in the Smurf slippers than in the high heels she'd swayed out of White's on Adrian Whiteley's arm in.

I liked the Stratford house. After Islington's spacious first floor living room, it felt convivial watching TV with pedestrians passing directly outside the window. If the passers-bye were talking loudly you caught snatches of their conversations, head down into the wind and sleet while we sat snug inside, the central heating switched up to Bangkok temperatures.

It was the lunchtime re-run of Neighbours. There was a knock at the door.

Natalie jumped up. She put down her glass and stepped over to the front door.

"Pauline coming."

A blast of freezing air blew into the room as she opened the door. She'd just come out of the shower. Her hair was wet. She was wrapped in a towel.

"Wha?!"

A man's voice said something. The broken eggshells sounded sharper than Thai.

"Arai-eee?"

"Hi, babe," said Cyril, over Lee's shoulder.

Lee shoved Natalie backwards into the room. He looked younger than the bullet-headed little guy I'd seen through the traffic on the Caledonian Road. He slapped Natalie across the mouth.

"Hey!"

I didn't even get out of my seat. A big hand closed round my shoulder.

"Take it easy, man."

I didn't like the way Cyril was looking at me.

Natalie had blood on her lip. Lee'd caught her with the back of his hand, with the gold ring crusted with diamond chips he wore. He started yelling at her. It wasn't Thai he was screaming at her but Natalie was nodding her head.

"Chai. Chai."

She seemed to understand him.

Cyril grinned.

"So you're Natalie's boyfriend." He leered at Natalie wrapped in the towel. "Lucky man."

Lee showed Natalie the back of his hand again. She stepped backwards and knocked into the coffee table. A bottle of beer went over. Lee wouldn't stop yelling at her.

Cyril laughed.

"Not a happy bunny. You've been stupid, Jim." He didn't know me. He'd forgotten that we'd ever spoken. "Very very stupid."

I should have listened to Javindra. It was obvious Lee was going to track us down eventually. It felt strange it had taken him so long. Cyril stood close above me, knee to knee. I tried to get to my feet.

"Take it easy, bro." I was in for a beating this time.

Lee was still yelling at Natalie. The guy wouldn't stop.

Natalie answered him back. The defiance in her voice scared me.

Cyril laughed.

"She's telling Lee she loves you."

Cyril put on a little girlie voice.

"Jim I love two gether big big."

I didn't believe him. He was laughing at me. He didn't speak Thai.

Natalie raised her voice. Her eyes flashed.

Cyril chuckled.

"Jim look after I number one good. She's standing up for you, Jim."

"Fuck off."

Natalie snapped her fingers at me.

"Honey!" There were red marks on her cheek. "Must give money! Lee want twenty-two grand."

"Ey?!"

"No pay contract. Must give now."

Cyril laughed out loud.

"Getting a girl into England don't come cheap, mate."

"Twenty two thousand? I can't raise twenty-two thousand... just like that."

"Gonna have to, bro."

Lee strode to the window and stood staring at the passers-bye. His shoulders rose and fell.

"I sorry, honey." Natalie's eyes were wild. "I no pay contract." There was a smear of blood on the corner of her lips. "You got money, honey. Can do."

Cyril's face was ashen. He rubbed his mouth.

"I admire your bottle, Jim. Thinking you can run out on us. Most guys wait till they've worked off their contract."

Natalie was crying.

"I sorry, honey. I scary I say you bout money, you don love I no more."

I wondered whether it might not be better if they took her back to the Caledonian Road. The nightmare would be over.

Natalie's eyes were red. She rubbed a smear of snot away with her wrist.

"Please, Jim."

Lee nodded at Cyril.

Cyril smoothed his dreads down and readjusted his baseball cap.

"Twenty two grand, Jim. You've got a week."

I awoke in the dark.

In the window, a street-lit blind that had slipped its runner let in a tangent of orange light.

Nicks of shadow flecked the woodchip.

There was a smell of new mattress, the shop odour of stiff pillow slips. A radiator crackled inches from my head.

Natalie was asleep. Her naked bum nestled in my crotch. Her hair was in my face, her leg flung backwards across my knee.

It had been light when we'd made love. I'd meant to get back to Islington by nine.

My hand was cupped between her legs, fingers bent, palm arched, a hand trapping a wasp. I sensed, from the way they ached, that my fingertips hadn't moved from the prickly warmth above her pussy for a long time.

She hadn't shaved. The bristles on her mound breathed in and out between quick and fingernail, the heel of my hand anchored in the warm give of her stomach.

Somewhere below my palm, her caesarean scar refused to be touched.

I had no idea what time it was. It felt late. A clock ticked just behind my head, but I knew that if I turned to look at it, I'd wake her. I didn't want to wake her.

Somewhere in the nightmare arrangements of my home life, I'd promised to always get back to Islington by nine.

The prickle of her bush turned to a speck of rubbery skin. Her clitoris felt miles down, below the folded softness, unreachable, tiny, a grain of sand stuck on a bony resistance.

I knew that, in her own way, she too felt the stinging brightness. She too, in some prince and princess dream she was having, saw the shining thread of something that was unapproachable, yet everywhere.

The twenty-two thousand no longer mattered.

As she breathed out, my fingertip rose on the peak of her pussy. The speck of rubbery skin pressed against my fingertip, working itself moist, wetting my fingertip, trapping it in finer and finer folds of slipperiness. The grain of sand slid sideways and vanished on a bony push.

She drew in a long, waking breath and spread her legs wider. A hardness gathered, grew heavier, touchable, a callous under my fingertip.

A foot landed on my knee. She gripped my cock with her bum, squeezing my erection with small clasps of her arse muscles, showing me where the stinging brightness was, inside her body, burning towards the surface.

My finger slipped on her clitoris and slid down a spasm of wetness. It was time to fuck. It was time to roll face-to-face and screw. There was no alternative.

As I fingered her wet lips my palm grazed the scar. In the dark the welt felt bigger and rawer than it looked in the light. She'd been picking at it. She'd been fiddling with it worse than usual lately. Four years, and it felt as if it had only just been stitched.

She reached behind her and touched my cock. I could tell from the way she held it that she was some way from waking up.

She guided it towards her ring. I drew away from her. She was coaxing the tip of my cock towards the place where the stinging brightness was, where the shining thread began, where the woman who shone and stung was, inside her body, burning towards the surface, my tailbone yearning for her tailbone, two points of light fusing into the one brightness, rising like the candescence up a hurricane lamp, towards the source of all joy, that turns into emptiness every time.

I pushed her hand away. Her body floated backwards into me, warm and heavy, her bottom undulating in its own tide, faster and faster as my finger found her clitoris again, her whole weight weltering on a speck of slithering stillness.

She cried out as she came.

My semen spattering up her spine didn't wake her.

It was difficult raising Lee's twenty two thousand pounds.

Melissa refused to even discuss releasing funds from our joint account. When I argued that half the money was mine she said that it wasn't. She was already talking to a lawyer.

Getting another salary advance from my company should have been easy, but it wasn't. I'd been slack and irresponsible at work, I'd taken my eye off the ball, and Bernard and Pippa were justifiably angry. No matter how urgent finding Lee's twenty two thousand pounds was, I couldn't look my partners in the eye and ask for it. I needed much more than another month's salary anyway.

I found a company in the back pages of the Sun that would lend me forty thousand pounds with some property deeds as collateral. I couldn't raise the money on my Islington house as it was in both our names, mine and Melissa's, but my company owned, and let out, a small office facility in Clerkenwell where we'd begun trading before we moved to the larger premises in Notting Hill Gate. It was my name and Bernard's that were on the deeds. I forged his signature and provided enough paperwork for the loan sharks to give me the amount I needed. The interest was exorbitant. I'd have to repay the first instalment out of the loan money itself till my next salary check came due.

My house was worth well over three million pounds. If it came to selling it, my half share would end up at around a million and a half at a conservative estimate. I had a stake in the assets of my company that came to nearly as much again.

I felt bad going behind Bernard and Pippa's backs, but I had plenty of money coming to me, enough to make up any temporary shortfalls.

I signed the loan agreement. It was going to take five days for the money to reach my bank.

As well as the rice steamer, Natalie had bought a mortar and pestle for mashing chili.

She ate a lot of fish with chili sauce. I got used to the molten plastic smell of chili being singed. Natalie barbecued the chilis on a skewer over the hotplate on the stove. I had to disconnect the smoke alarm in the kitchen.

I visited her at odd hours, but often ate dinner at Stratford rather than grabbing a takeaway to take back to Islington.

We ate in the living room on the coffee table in front of the TV on, listening for a knock on the door. I was worried that Lee would come back.

"You don want give so big money is okay. I go back working."

"No. It's alright."

"I go back working, still love two gether."

"The money'll be through soon."

She knew that I still wasn't wholly convinced that her flight from the Caledonian Road hadn't been staged for my benefit and that Lee's visit, even when he'd hit her, wasn't just part of a plan to extract money from me. Javindra had explained how the contracts worked and I believed her when she said she'd only been in England a short time, but a week to come up with twenty two grand seemed a bit much. Why the rush? Did they know I couldn't stand the idea of her going back to Kilburn or putting on that plastic nurse's uniform in Hackney and were using it to extort the money from me? Natalie seemed to have got over the shock of Lee's visit pretty quickly. There was still a cut in the corner of her mouth where Lee had caught her with his glitzy ring but she didn't seem nervous of Lee or Cyril coming back.

She topped up my beer.

"Cyril say true. I lucky Lee don hit I bad. Only slapping."

"Mm."

I didn't want to talk about it.

"Cyril good man."

"Yeah?"

I wasn't so sure. Cyril scared me. He'd been happy to stand and watch while Lee slapped one of *his* girls around. I had a feeling Cyril's loyalties were with Lee not Natalie. Cyril had sounded genuinely concerned about the Arms Fair party when he'd cornered me in my car at work. I'd got the impression he was sincerely anxious to know who Adrian Whitley's punter was, but he may only have been making enquiries on Lee's behalf. On the other hand, Natalie's liking for him seemed to be whole hearted.

"Cyril say Thai."

"So I noticed."

'Jim I love two gether big big.'

"Cyril working long time with Thai girl. Say Thai good."

I spooned some more green curry onto my rice. Natalie didn't eat her rice with a spoon. She rolled it into a ball and dipped it in the sauce with her fingers.

She liked to sit on the floor when she ate, cross legged in front of the coffee table, while I leaned down from the sofa.

Behind her, the floor was covered with photographs. They were the photographs of Nok and her family she'd shown me in the flat in Kilburn the first time I saw her. She'd taken them out of the wallet's plastic sleeves and laid them out in rows on the carpet. I wondered if any of the photos—there were some pretty faces amongst them—was the sister who'd supposedly been raped and murdered.

"Why didn't Lee take you back to the Caledonian Road?"

She shrugged.

"Don know. You say you pay money."

"Yeah, but... he was angry... but he still let you stay here."

There was something she wasn't telling me. There were lots of things she wasn't telling me. I didn't mind. My background was just as perplexing to her as hers was to me. Soom Bon's story about the murdered sister and the big Buddha woman's vengeance was simply part of a world I didn't understand.

"Who's Adrian Whitely?"

She looked at me.

"Just customer, Jim. I finish with he. You pay contract I no must see he no more."

I wondered why, if Adrian Whitely was just a customer, he hadn't paid off her contract and taken her to live in Holland Park. He was clearly in a better position to look after her than I was.

She studied my face.

"You okay, Jim?"

"Yeah. I'm fine."

"Do sex, not happy."

"I'm alright."

"I! *I* not happy!" Her voice was strident. "Do sex, water come I mouth. Water come I eyes. Can not see. Can not breathing."

Her vehemence shocked me.

"That's just Soom Bon."

Perhaps being overwhelmed by water, the fear that the witch had planted in her mind, was her way of dealing with the stinging brightness that was overwhelming me.

"Do sex, water come up. I let go you hand. Can not see you face. You gone."

It was pretty much how I felt too, after we'd made love.

"I guess I'm not into anal."

"Why you laugh I?"

Living on her own was driving her crazy. She cooked and cleaned but, except for me, or when friends dropped in, there was no one here to admire her spic and span house or appreciate her cooking. She wasn't eating much herself. She was drinking more than she was eating. A lot of the time, when I couldn't get away from work or had to make it back to Islington early, her curries went into the bin uneaten.

The photos were getting out of control. They were everywhere, neat lines of them, but taking over the carpet, marshalled in rows between the coffee table and the TV. You had to be careful where you walked. Nok's doll face and pudding basin haircut. Her mother's tanned cheeks creased by the sun. Her father a tall man— she got her height from her Dad—up to his waist in water. Banana leaves. Dogs. Nine inch nails in a coconut tree. A man in a business suit I guessed was Nok's father, the Shell executive Natalie had shacked up with in Bangkok. Children swimming in inner tubes in a river. Buddha radiating a web of string. She kept moving the prints around, changing the photos' positions in the lines, it was more as if she was reading Tarot cards than enjoying pictures of home.

"Honey..."

She dipped a ball of rice in the curry. Her fingernails came up flecked with specks of chili, like red glitter.

"Yes?"

"... You know you say Nok Mum can come see I...?"

"Yes."

"...When money come... after pay contract..." she hesitated, "... You buy ticket?... Nok, Mum, come see I?"

She certainly knew how to take the wind out of your sails. She was aware I was having trouble raising the money for her contract. Being treated as if I was Mister Rich Guy wasn't really what I wanted. On the other hand, there'd be plenty left over from the forty thousand after I'd paid Lee, even with the next interest instalment.

"Yes. Okay... good idea... I'd like to meet Nok. And your mum."

"Can stay here."

"Yes. Of course."

There was the unused bedroom her mother and daughter could stay in.

"Uncle too?"

"*Uncle?*"

I knew Thai families were close, but surely that didn't mean the relatives could pile in too.

"Mum, Nok, scary fly they self. Uncle come with."

Her mother was a forty-five-year-old woman. Surely she could fly on her own, with the little girl. They didn't need chaperoning.

I didn't want to pay for her bloody uncle too. I guessed that her mother might be an uneducated country woman, who'd never been outside Thailand. Natalie had told me that her mother couldn't read or write. But her mum had got used to the idea of her daughter working overseas and sending money home quick enough. Surely she wasn't such an innocent she couldn't get onto an aeroplane by herself. I'd have to pay for an extra air fare if the uncle came too.

"...Well... yes... I suppose so..."

The loan money hadn't even arrived yet. The next interest instalment was going to eat into the eighteen thousand pounds I'd have left after I paid off the twenty two thousand for Natalie's contract. Three air tickets, money to live on, shopping, I was looking at another five thousand pound chunk out of my leftover cash. I wasn't used to being anxious about money.

"... Yes. Alright... I suppose so...your mum and Nok can sleep in the front bedroom. Your uncle will have to sleep down here on the sofa."

"Cannot!"

"Eh?"

"Don need!" She clapped her hands and laughed like a little girl. "He sleep temple!"

"Temple?"

"Uncle stay Wat Leytonstone. He big monk."

The money from the loan company came through, the first interest payment already deducted—a thirty seven thousand pound electronic transfer into my personal account.

Lee wanted cash.

Natalie waited in the car while I went into the bank.

It took half an hour for the teller to approve the withdrawal with the manager.

They put the twenty-two thousand pounds into two envelopes and squeezed a fat rubber band around the pair of them.

The envelopes were bulky. I had trouble stuffing them into my inside pocket of my coat. The money knocked against my chest as I returned to the car.

Natalie was dressed up.

She'd put on a pair of strapless stilettos with glass heels, a black miniskirt, and an off-the-shoulder top. The afternoon had turned cold. The car's heating was switched way up.

We drove down to Soho.

"Lee not Thai," she said irrelevantly for the hundredth time. "He Chinese."

Lee's being Chinese somehow made him more dangerous.

Pleats of oyster-grey silk hung from her nipples to an inch above her skirt. I could feel her fingers itching to dig under her waistband and pick at her scar, but the skirt was too tight. This morning the welt had been bleeding.

The underground car park in Shaftsbury Avenue was full.

We drove around for a while. I finally found a space in a vacant lot behind a cinema, manned by a twitchy teenager with teeth missing.

It was dark by the time we walked back to the lights of China Town. Natalie's heels clicked like splinters of ice on the pavement.

A smoker standing outside the Lord Derby with a pint in his hand looked her up and down and whistled a white cloud.

I was about to hand over twenty-two thousand pounds to a man I didn't know and didn't trust. If, after I gave him the money, Lee took Natalie straight back to the Caledonian Road, there'd be nothing I could do about it.

I'd never seen Natalie so nervous. She brushed at her skirt. She tugged her top. Her nails fluttered at her belly. Her phobia with the scar was out of control.

She seemed too on edge for my suspicions about her setting me up to be correct.

It all depended on Cyril. I felt sure that Cyril would be there when we met Lee. If Cyril's anxiety about Natalie and the man at the Arms Fair was real then Lee would certainly take Natalie back to the Caledonian Road. If Lee started slapping Natalie about again, would Cyril intervene? Lee was his boss. Cyril hadn't intervened when Lee hit Natalie when they dropped in on us in Stratford. If Lee got rough, would Cyril step in? What would I do?

We walked down a passageway off Merde Street.

Natalie nodded at an entrance.

"Here."

We went in. I pulled open an upholstered door that said: PRIVATE. MEMBERS ONLY.

There was a small lobby with a marble floor and a carriage lamp suspended on a brass rod from the ceiling. Music floated up from the basement.

A girl sat in a booth between two flights of stairs, one leading down and the other leading up. She gave us a hostile look as we took the stairs up.

A door opened. We walked into a flat. It was a bit like the Kilburn flat, except the floorboards were real oak, not laminate.

A woman led us into the living room. Lee and a younger Chinese man sat on a sofa, eating at a coffee table. Cyril was standing by the window with his back to us.

Cyril turned and glanced at Natalie as if he couldn't quite place her. There was no, "Hi, babe."

Natalie took off her coat and draped it over a chair.

Lee and the young Chinese man ignored us. They were bent forward over the coffee table eating out of tinfoil containers.

The muscles jerked in Lee's throat and jaw. He ate like a man digesting a pair of secateurs.

We sat down. Natalie crossed her legs.

The sexy clothes were a mistake. She sensed it, too. She must have wanted to come across as powerful and business-like. She didn't. Her naked shoulders and long legs looked vulnerable, almost innocent. The 'new girl' the VIPs favoured.

Lee glanced up from his chow mein. A woman who can sleep with fifteen men a day and still be innocent was worth much more than twenty-two grand.

He went back to his noodles. He'd already made up his mind. He'd take the money and send Natalie back to the Caledonian Road. I'd get a beating for the inconvenience I'd caused him.

Natalie and Lee began to talk. Natalie talked quietly, quickly. Lee interrupted with abrupt shakes of his head.

Cyril sat down in an armchair. He leaned back comfortably and studied Natalie's legs. With her legs crossed, the skirt rode up near her split. For a second I thought she was going to reach under the waistband and finger her scar.

I wondered if she'd slept with Cyril. He surveyed the oyster grey pleats with a proprietorial cool. She didn't have a bra on underneath.

Natalie was talking fast. She seemed to be speaking a mixture of Thai and Chinese. Lee continued to shake his head.

"Honey! Please!" She snapped her fingers. "Money! Give!"

I took the envelopes out of my coat pocket and handed them to her.

Natalie put the envelopes on the coffee table next to the food containers. Neither of the Chinese men looked at them.

Natalie pushed the envelopes between the containers. Lee shook his head.

The younger Chinese man picked up the envelopes, slit them open with his fingernail, and counted the money.

Lee began shouting at Natalie. I could hear him deliberately, cold-bloodedly, working himself up. A fortnight. The customers. The other girls. The flat closing early.

Natalie nodded agreement. He was going to hit her.

I checked the distance to the door.

Cyril got up and stretched.

I tried to catch Natalie's eye.

She was nodding, head down: Okay! Alright! Yes! Okay! Okay!

I'd been at enough meetings to hear, even in Thai and Chinese, that she was giving ground, making a concession. She was promising Lee something.

"Chai. Chai."

Lee stopped shouting. His hand trembled as he picked up his fork. We'd spoiled his dinner.

Natalie grabbed her coat.

"Honey!" Her voice broke. "Come! I free! Go pub!"

I stood up and buttoned my coat.

Cyril stood up too.

"Sounds like a good idea, man. Think I'll join youz."

We sat in a bar off Marshal Street. It was six o'clock. We'd got in early enough to grab a table by the wall, before the after-work rush-hour arrived, but now the place was packed.

Standing-room-only drinkers crushed in around us, raucous, shoulder-to-shoulder. Screens glimmered above the sea of heads. Speakers thudded out un-placeable music.

We sat with our backs to the wall on a bench at a table that inched towards us as the press of bodies got heavier.

Natalie wasn't talking. Her rush of exhilaration in Lee's apartment— 'Honey! Come! I free! Go pub!'— had morphed into an oblivious disregard for everyone and everything. She was drinking Peroni. The only thing that seemed to interest her was getting drunk.

Cyril and I made conversation.

"No, bro. I told you. I'm security." Cyril rubbed his eyes. "Strictly security."

"Security?"

I wondered why he'd joined us. He made me nervous. I had a feeling Lee'd told him to keep an eye on us, find out something that Natalie wasn't telling him. Cyril was likeable, Natalie seemed pleased that he'd accompanied us, but he'd stood and watched while Lee hit her.

"Drive the girls on out visits. Wait for 'em while they're inside with the punter. Make sure they're alright."

"Right."

It was the same distinction he'd made sitting in my car, between 'security' and the more unpleasant forms of discipline Lee left to his Chinese staff. It was a fine distinction, but it seemed important to him.

"I look after my girls, bro."

"Mm."

'Out visits' were when the girls went to see customers at hotels and private addresses. Cyril was supposed to drive them there and back, and hang around in case there was trouble.

There'd been no sign of Cyril hanging around outside White's or hanging around outside Adrian Whitely's house in Holland Park. Not until I showed up. Adrian Whitely was above surveillance. Cyril hadn't been making sure Natalie was alright that night, not until someone rang and told him I was there.

"I look after my girls, bro." I didn't have to like him, as I long as I understood how he felt about his girls. "They got my number on their phones. Guy gets rough, I'm in there, man." Cyril had broken down front doors and smashed his way into hotel rooms. He seemed to enjoy his work. "I'm in there 'fore the cunt gets goin.'"

"Yeah, but..." It didn't sound much like security to me. What degree of harm could a drunk or a psychopath do before Cyril got there?

"Geezer hurts my girls, bro, he's dead."

'Security' was one of the words, like 'infection' and 'immigration' I hadn't expected Natalie to know. She used it with a solemn affection. I looked at her. She was miles away.

Natalie had no doubt been on out visits with Cyril. She must have his number in her phone. I wondered if she ever called him, nights she got lonely in Stratford.

She sat unspeaking, drinking steadily, gazing at the backsides, shoulders, and faces packed around us in the overheated room. She wasn't cut off at all. I'd been wrong. She hadn't retreated into her shell. Far from being oblivious, she was aware of everything that was going on around her in the crowded, noisy room. Cyril and I were the ones who were oblivious.

I wished Cyril wasn't here. She was sitting on the other side of him, looking cold and tense. I wanted to lean across him and hug her. Squeeze her tight. She hadn't lied to me about the contract. Lee hadn't stitched me up. I'd paid the money and now she was free.

The table kept inching towards us, the backs of legs in suit pants, jostling thighs pushing the table into us.

She'd been more frightened than she'd let on, back in Lee's apartment. The meeting had been an even bigger risk than I'd realized. She'd damaged something inside her, confronting the boss. She'd made a concession. I'd heard it as they argued. She'd come to some agreement with Lee, or else we both would have both ended up getting a beating. She'd been hurt, and now she was repairing the hurt with a hypnotized absorption in every laugh, greeting, thud of the speakers and slop of spilled beer, every shout, order, preen and guffaw, every glimmering screen and clink of change and thudding syncopation, every gust as the door opened and shadow out on the footpath, a bus slicing through a street light, a hypnotized absorption that took in everything, stars, winds, continents, nebulae if only she could get this one thing straight in her head.

Perhaps it was just the upwards slant of her eyes, a glance that was both sideways and full on, a gap on either side of her field of vision where she did her real looking. The girls' hairdos. A bloke's back pocket. A meaty hand on a slight shoulder. A laugh so neighing it was visible. Whiffs of sweat, wine, deodorant. The Peroni fizzing in her throat. She didn't miss a thing, not even the stars and continents. She wasn't really focussing. She gazed through the gaps on either side of her field of vision where everything really comes from. She seemed mesmerised, but she wasn't. She was getting steadily drunker, but the gaps on either side of her field of vision were turning so fine and piercing they were stopping her from keeling over, or even nodding off. She was surveying the pub through such fine apertures it felt as if the whole universe might get inside her.

Cyril nudged me.

"Watchin' out for Immigration."

Maybe he was right. She dreaded being sent back to Thailand. The way she was staring, she could well have been searching the crowd for Immigration officers, planning escape routes if an Immigration officer stepped forward to grab her.

"Coupla the girls got picked up in Hackney last week." Cyril seemed to relish handing out snippets of sex-trade gossip. "Fightin'.

Pullin' each others hair out, they was. Scratchin'. Everthing. Thai bird and an Albanian bird. Deadly mixture, bro." For a big bruiser, Cyril had a certain charm. I could see that there was something about him that would make the girls feel safe in dangerous situations. "Fightin' over a customer. Punter freaked. Called the cops." He chuckled. "Girls' feet never touched the ground. Stuck 'em on the first plane back to Bangkok. 'N wherever it is in Albania." Cyril's eyes were bloodshot—too many nights sitting in his car outside hotels and private residences—but he had a swashbuckling smile. He was likeable enough. Except, he worked for Lee. The room was hot. The noise was deafening. I felt a bit drunk myself. The meeting had stressed me out more than I'd realised. "Thai girls..."

The table lurched. Beer jumped out of my glass.

A group of young guys, five or six of them, horsing around, tight up against our table, were staging some sort of mock wrestling match.

The table jolted again. Natalie's glass rocked. The table juddered her knee—she'd crossed her legs— back into her belly. She didn't seem to notice. She stared as if the jolt had come from the far end of the cosmos.

Cyril leaned forward.

"Excuse me, bro."

A couple of the guys spun round, their agro no longer mock.

Cyril didn't speak. He nodded at the table.

They picked it up as gently as a firm of specialist removalists with a Mappin and Webb drop-leaf, and shifted it out into open territory.

"You work for Lee?"

Cyril shrugged.

"Yeah. It's better than the door."

I wondered if 'the door' was slang for some other gang he'd worked for, before Lee.

"Doorman. Bouncer. You know the Starlight, Ilford?"

"No."

"Pickin' out the crazies in the queue. Breakin' up fights. That sorta thing. It's easy work. Lee pays better, but." It didn't sound all that easy to me. An eight hour shift, standing at a door, patrolling a dance floor full of drunks and druggies waiting for a fight to break out. It couldn't be very relaxing, even for a guy as big as Cyril. "Yeah. There's cunts think they're tough." He grinned. "You have to mash a geezer's face every now and then. The trick is knowin' when a fight's gonna happen before it happens, like. Then it's easy."

We both looked at Natalie. Cyril had noticed her drunken absorption too.

Skin. I told myself. It was just skin. But it was hers, and nobody else's. Moist and shiny in the heat, with its own salt perfume. Face, shoulders, cleavage, arms. The cocked print of her knee. A depth of leg. Just skin, but it knew every crease, dent, and curve of who she was, like a lover's hands. It was only skin, but it saw more than her fixed, glazed, drunken eyes. Her skin saw what a lover's hands couldn't. Her mind had slipped out through her eyes and covered her whole body. Her skin saw everything. Her skin made everything vast and equal: me, Cyril, her silk top, her miniskirt, the table; the legs, backsides, and faces in front of us; the laughter, the smell of spilt beer and wet carpet; the shrieking hinge on the door to the toilets; and her, the beating of her heart.

Cyril came back with another round. He smiled down at her.

"Away with the fairies."

He topped up Natalie's glass for her.

"She aint told you nothin' about these geezers at the Arm's Fair has she?"

"No. She gets angry if I even ask her."

We both looked at her. She wasn't listening. She was absorbed, engrossed. Even if she had been listening she wouldn't have been able to follow our English all that well.

"That's what I'm sayin'," said Cyril. "Girls keep somethin' quiet like this, it's somethin' heavy."

"I don't think she's seen Adrian Whitely again, not since she ran away from the Caledonian Road." I sounded like the junior law enforcement officer in an action adventure film. Perhaps I was. "I could be wrong, but."

"He's a sick cunt."

"Adrian Whitely?"

He hadn't looked too sick to me, coming out of White's with a gorgeous chick on his arm, the two of them chauffeured back to his mansion in Holland Park.

"Yeah."

"In what way?"

"Dunno. The girls just say he's into sick sort of stuff."

"Sick?"

"They won't say. Maybe he can't get it up, and takes it out on them. A sadist, like."

"...Eh?... I don't think I've seen any..." I glanced at Natalie. "... You know..."

"No. Neither have I. I dunno. His chauffeur always picks them up." We glanced at Natalie. It was as if she wasn't there. It was as if the room and the crowd and the music and the conversation she was staring at had replaced her." If he's linin' her up for someone higher up maybe he isn't allowed to... you know..."

"He sees other girls besides Natalie?"

"Yeah. But Natalie's 'is favourite." Cyril's eyes sparkled. "Maybe she does the business for him."

The sparkle was affectionate.

"Talking to Lee just now..." I said. "... I got the impression she promised Lee something. Came to him some sort of agreement with him... I don't know... I could be wrong. I don't speak Thai, or Chinese, I just..."

"Yeah," Cyril grinned. "That's why you didn't go home in an ambulance, Jim. Natalie promised Lee she'd keep seeing Adrian Whitely."

"... Oh... right..."

"Lee was very angry about her running away." I was wondering who would have put me in the ambulance if Natalie hadn't come to an understanding with the boss, Lee, the young Chinese guy, or Cyril. "They didn't go into detail. They knew I know Thai. I got the impression Lee weren't forcing her or nothing. It was Natalie who was into it."

"Maybe she likes Adrian," I said. "Even if he is, you know..." I felt ill. "... Adrian's loaded."

Cyril shrugged.

"Yeah. Maybe. He's loaded alright. The girls like punters can't do the business. It's easier work. Until they turn nasty."

"... No. I mean, maybe she *wants* to hook up with one of the men Adrian's lining up for her at the Arms Fair..."

I wondered if I should tell him Soom Bon's story about her sister.

"Yeah. Well. There's big money for her if she does it."

"No... I mean... You know Soom Bon...?"

"Yeah. I know Soom Bon. The hopped up seer."

"I know, but... you remember you told me Natalie had a bee in her bonnet about the guy Adrian Whitely's lining her up with at the Arms Fair...?"

"Yeah. I remember."

I told him Soom Bon's story about the 'big man sell gun' who killed Natalie's 'sister.'

Cyril rubbed his mouth.

"'Sister' can mean anything in Thai, Jim. It can be their worst enemy if they're havin' a drink. It don't necessarily mean blood or nothin'."

"Yes, but whenever I ask her about her sister she clams up. She gets even angrier than when I ask her about Adrian... You said she's got a bee in her bonnet. Maybe it's this Arms Fair guy."

Cyril grimaced.

"I dunno, Jim... maybe, but... Soom Bon?... some of them ex monks go into the 'vics' business, they're total fruit cakes..."

"See man?"

She hadn't spoken for so long, her voice was startling.

"What man?"

"Man over there."

She nodded at a young bloke in jeans and a pink golf shirt pressed against the far wall, holding his pint up near his shoulder because of the press, chatting to a girl.

"He police man."

"What?"

"He cop."

She was paranoid.

Cyril and I both glanced at the guy. There was no way of telling whether he was a policeman or not. It was all in her head. The bloke in the golf shirt had a certain bouncy machismo. An assertive chat-up style with his girl. He could have been a cop. Or a taxi driver. Or an insurance broker. It was impossible to say.

"That he wife."

Natalie nodded, not at the girl the 'cop' was chatting to, but across, on the other side of the room, at a fat woman in a business suit sitting with a group of office workers.

Cyril grinned at me.

She was in Fantasyland.

"He wife cheating he."

"Oh yeah?"

The fat woman and her friends from the office had taken over three tables and shoved them together, forming their own little island of noise in the ruckus of the room.

"He wife sleeping with Arab man."

She ducked her head, and nodded at the middle-aged Pakistani man with the care-worn face—he looked like an exhausted sales rep, or maybe a teacher— who sat opposite the fat woman, chatting sociably.

"Police man wife selling drug with Arab man."

I wanted to reach over and squeeze her in my arms. I loved her. I wanted her to be mine and no one else's. I needed to look after her. She'd been sitting there for over an hour, while Cyril and I chatted, casting these English drinkers in a private soap opera in her head.

The Arab drug dealer (the Pakistani sales rep) was using the policeman's wife (the fat woman) to front his takeover of a drug cartel (an office boy in a tight suit, a peroxide blonde receptionist, and a janitor in a raincoat). The grey-haired janitor (the cartel's security) had just clocked the policeman tailing the gang. The cop (the guy in the pink polo shirt) had been suspended from the case by his senior officer (absent) but was tailing the gang (chatting to the girl) hell-bent on vengeance.

"Police guy got knife."

Cyril's glance sparkled. He raised his eyebrows. The girls were all a bit paranoid.

I looked at my watch. It was nearly nine.

"We'd better make a move."

"Yeah. Me too, man. The old lady don't sleep too good till I get back."

I hadn't pictured Cyril as having a wife. I realized he was older than he looked. Cyril appeared to be in his late twenties, but he must have been closer to forty. The work her did, his old lady must have missed a lot of sleep.

Natalie put on her coat. Cyril shoved our table further out into the forest of legs, and helped her with the arms.

"Excuse me. Thanks. Do you mind?"

I was in the lead. It was difficult pushing through the mass of bodies towards the door.

As I reached the door, I heard a scream somewhere behind me. For an instant, I thought it was Natalie. The scream was followed by raised voices, yells, hysteria.

I glanced back.

The crowd tided towards the bar.

A table went over. Glasses smashed on the floor.

The young bloke in the pink golf shirt was tangled up in the fallen table. He was holding a blade to the Pakistani man's throat.

The office boy, the receptionist and the grey-haired janitor were on the floor.

The fat woman was leaning backwards against a shelf of Toby jugs with blood coming out of her mouth.

Outside, the air was raw. We hurried up the footpath in silence.

I wanted to say something. Talk about what had just happened. Put it into words. I needed to hold a discussion, find answers to urgent questions: at what point does protracted observation become psychic insight? Is there any difference?

"Fuck me," said Cyril. "She shoulda worked on the door."

Natalie flopped onto the bed, her knees up, her legs spread, a pillow under her backside.

Her skirt and thong were folded neatly on the chair, the skirt stowed to the size of a face flannel, the thong more obscene folded

up than when she'd had it on, the top's pleats spread out over the
back of the chair like a tiny silk accordion.

"No talk, honey."

My cock swung around awkwardly in front of me. I ached to
ram it into her, keep ramming till I exploded.

"What did you promise Lee?"

"Nothing."

She parted her labia with the fingers of both hands, the moist
cleft glistening. A crimson nail circled her clitoris like a lacquered
shield.

"Cyril said you arranged something with Lee."

"Cyril say wrong. He don talk Thai properly." Her bum lifted.
"I love you, honey. I promise I never go working no more." She was
lying. She swung her knees above her head. "Please."

'Please' wasn't a word she ever used. It wasn't a plea now. She
just didn't want me to feel like an idiot, handing over twenty two
thousand pounds and she was still on Lee's books.

I spread the cheeks of her arse. Skin. Just skin. Hers, and
nobody else's. It knew every crease, dent, and crevice of who she
was. Her mind slipped out through her eyes and covered her whole
body. The stretch of pale honey below her vagina. The blue-brown
ring tightening around her anus. Her skin saw everything. It made
everything vast and equal, a tangent of orange night, the radiator's
crackle, the smell of new mattress, a stiff cock, the beating of her
heart.

I touched her coccyx with the tip of my tongue. I shut my
eyes. When skin sees, the body disappears. Skin sees everything and
nothing.

She let me feel her weight, pressing the crease of her bum down
the length of my tongue. There was a sharp, latrinal taste.

"Yes…"

She'd seen much more than a jealous cop and his wife in the pub. She'd done something far more magical than foresee a fight.

"Down little bit."

I tongued the softness under her tail. Something melted at the base of my spine.

"...Yes.... there..."

For a moment, I thought she was going to ask me: 'You wan do anal?'

I slid my tongue from her tail up to her pussy, luxuriously, lavishly, like I was licking a pungent ice cream.

I couldn't wait. I had to fuck her now.

"... Down more..."

I had hold of both her ankles. I shoved them above her head. 'Down' was up. My tongue flowed up silky wetness and stung on something sharp.

Her fingernail refused to budge. The manicured shield circled her clitoris in a world of its own.

"... No...."

With the tip of my tongue, I found the place she wanted. The very tip of my tongue hovered in her wetness, not too deep, like a hummingbird pecking a flower.

"... Yes..."

A couple of vertebra up, the back of my spine turned molten.

She took hold of my hair with both hands and carted my head up—she didn't want my lips anywhere near her scar— and dumped my mouth on her belly.

I didn't want to kiss her navel. I forced my head down and licked the hated welt.

"No!"

It felt bigger and rougher under my tongue than it looked to the eye. I examined it with my lips. I plastered stitch welts and inflamed tissue with the flat of my tongue. It's you. It's yours. It's all I want.

An acid heat filled my stomach. I was drunker than I thought. I'd licked something noxious off her anus. The helpless candescence in my spine flared up as high as my heart.

She had hold of my cock, forcing it away from her pussy. My cock, and her fist, swung around in mid-air, banging against the inside of her thigh.

She rubbed the tip of my cock on her clitoris. My urethra slithered on a lemon pip of slippery hardness.

I pressed her nipple against the back of my teeth. My jaw ached with the effort not to bite her. She moaned a gabble of Thai. I'd hit on the place she liked.

Her collar bone, her throat, her mouth. It was skin. Just skin; she had no body. The candescence had taken it.

I didn't want to come. I didn't want to let go. I didn't know where she was. My eyes were open, but her skin was an endless darkness. It saw everything. It made everything vast and equal. I was a jabbering stranger in a pub, a table, legs, backsides, faces, laughter, the smell of spilt beer and wet carpet, the shrieking hinge of the door to the toilets—and I was her. I was the beating of her heart.

Our eyes met. We gazed and saw nothing.

Her hips lifted. I felt her fingernail move. Something small and hard inserted itself into the slit of my urethra and began to thrust.

I felt myself beginning to come. I couldn't. Her clitoris plugged the slit, sharp as a piece of grit kicking inside me. There was a stinging pressure, as the kick flowed backwards into my spine like the backwash of a wave.

As she dropped out, and I came over her hips, between her legs, something gripped my chest from behind, through my spine. Natalie's fingernails were clawing my back, but it wasn't her hands that gripped me. It was her heart. My arms were around her, crushing her, trying to make her stop, let go of her hold on my chest. I wanted to hurt her, but my arms had turned to light; they were being devoured, from the fingertips to the shoulder by the candescence. As my cock pumped semen into thin air, I felt her struggle to throw me, as I struggled to throw her, two wrestlers pinned down by a pounding stillness.

CHAPTER FIVE

We waited in the crowd by the Arrivals gate. I could feel her excitement and, underneath her excitement, a tension I couldn't quite understand. Her daughter was arriving. She was looking forward to seeing her mother. She should have been happy, but she was tense and on edge.

She kept glancing around at the crowd behind us.

"Uncle say thank you..." For the hundredth time, she told me how grateful her uncle, the monk, was for my buying his ticket.

"It's okay. Don't worry."

I hadn't made a fuss about the extra money. She was carrying on as if I was a penny-pinching scrooge unable to enjoy a moment's generosity.

She was wearing a pin-stripe trouser suit and a silk blouse with a wide collar. The outfit seemed too formal for meeting family off a plane.

It was only a little over a month since she'd last seen her Mum and Nok. I understood that their parting, five weeks ago, must have been fraught, the family not sure when they'd see Natalie again, their farewells at Suvarnabhumi International in Bangkok overshadowed by Natalie's forged passport, Lee's connection drilling her on the arrangements for getting through Immigration at Heathrow. It must have been distressing, but now her mother and daughter were coming for a prolonged stay. She had to be pleased, but instead she was uptight.

"Give ticket for monk is good luck."

I wondered if she was nervous because we stood out, a middle-aged man and a beautiful young Asian woman.

"Buddha give you I big luck."

For the hundredth time, she glanced at the guard patrolling the Arrivals Area. If she looked at the guy's walkie-talkie and

223

submachine gun much more, he was going to come over and question us.

Then it hit me.

"This is where you came through?"

She nodded.

"Chai."

No wonder she was on edge. A month ago, she'd walked between these same screens, on the other side of this railing, metres from safety, terrified of being stopped.

"It must have been tough."

She shrugged.

"Was okay."

She wasn't as blasé about it as she was pretending.

"I say passport man I have English husband waiting I." She smiled. "I say passport man I husband live West Ham." Her smile wobbled. "I see them on TV. West Ham play Manchester. I say West Ham, passport man let I through."

"Must have been a Hammers supporter."

She shrugged.

"Don know."

Her eyes flicked from the guard back to the gate.

A flight from India was coming through. An old man with a box of mangoes tied to his suitcase walked out between the screens.

"Girl with I say she student. Police come. Send she back."

No wonder she was nervous.

At last, some of the arriving crowd began to look as if it might have come off Thai Air 2QF. A party of baseball-capped teenagers chattering in what sounded like Thai. Some sunburned Aussies. The flight had started out from Sydney.

An orange robe. A bare shoulder lugging a battered suitcase.

Natalie nearly jumped out of her skin.

A small, wizened monk walked through the gate. He stopped
dead in the middle of the gangway, scanning the waiting throng,
blocking trolleys and the crowds of passengers. He looked lost. He
rooted around in his shoulder bag and took out his phone.

"Not he," she whispered. "Not uncle."

There was no mistaking when the family finally did come
through. A small, black-haired child in a frilly dress leapt from the
front of a trolley heaped with luggage, dashed across the walkway,
hurled herself under the railing, and grabbed Natalie's knees.

"Mair! Mair!"

Natalie held the little girl at arms' length and yelled at her. She
seemed to be scolding the child for some chocolate she'd got on her
dress.

"Sokrabrok!"

She licked her finger and rubbed at the stain. The chocolate got
darker. Nok kicked and wriggled.

She was a beautiful child. She was as beautiful as her mother.
Nok had Natalie's steep forehead and winged cheekbones,
and—determined to escape the dry cleaning—Natalie's frown.

Natalie scowled.

"Sawaddee Daddy Jim!"

'Daddy' knocked me sideways. It was too soon for 'Daddy.'

The child looked up at me. She was suddenly too shy to speak.

"Sawaddee por!"

Nok pressed her palms together and gave me a nervous wai.

"Hello, Nok," I mumbled. "Welcome to England."

I gave her the present I'd bought her, a pop-up book of English
nursery rhymes.

Her big, brown eyes gazed at the jolly wrapping paper. It took
seconds for her to feel brave enough to take the present out of my
hands.

Facially, Nok was the spitting image of Natalie, but she had a reserved, slightly guarded expression, a self-conscious poise as she studied the gift, that was nothing at all like Natalie.

I wai-d Natalie's mother.

"Sawaddee khrap. Sabaidee mai?"

Natalie's mother was a handsome woman. Her tanned face was much browner than Natalie's, and deeply seamed from exposure to the sun. The fingers clutching her handbag were gnarled and calloused. She wore a flouncy floral blouse that didn't go with her work-toughened body.

Natalie's mother wai-d me awkwardly. She was flustered. Their trolley was blocking the walkway.

A blaze of orange appeared beside her.

This monk wasn't small or wizened. Natalie's uncle didn't look the slightest bit lost. He was as self-possessed as the other monk had been nervous. Even the saffron of his robe seemed more vivid. There wasn't a trace of jet lag in his bright, penetrating eyes.

He smiled down at Nok, beamed at Natalie.

"Jim. This Pra."

I knew that 'pra' was an honorific. 'Pra' was the title of respect with which one addresses a monk, but I forgot to wai him.

It wasn't just Nok's reserve that convinced me, or her self-conscious poise, a poise that somehow resembled the man's. It was the way Pra looked down at the child, the way he smiled at Natalie. He gazed at the two of them with more than an uncle's tenderness. I saw it instantly. Pra was Nok's father.

"I sorry." We filtered into the London-bound traffic. "I stupid."

"It's okay. I understand."

"I think you don see."

Nok looked much more like Natalie than she looked like Pra. Her physical resemblance to the monk—a delicacy around the mouth, a tightness of the chin—was slight. It hadn't even been his affectionate glance at his daughter that had made me realize. It was something I sensed in the man's heart, a feeling I'd known myself, when Ralph and Meredith were little: 'This child is part of me.' And the way he smiled at Natalie— I'd felt the same with Melissa: 'This woman and I are inextricably linked.'

"I sorry I say you lie."

"Please. It's alright."

"I love you, Jim. Cannot tell lies."

I was stuck in the outside lane, crawling along behind a truck. The lorry's taillights were flashing, but it refused to pull over onto the hard shoulder.

Natalie's mother, Pra, and Nok were in the backseat. None of them spoke English, but I still felt awkward talking in front of them like this.

"I think you be angry because he Nok daddy. I think you don love I no more."

"Don't be silly."

Nok was sitting in her grandmother's lap, watching wide-eyed as her grandma pointed out a jumbo jet coming in to land. Natalie's mother knew what we were talking about. She felt as awkward as I did.

"Pra I love same brother sister. Not same you I love. Man woman."

"Please. It's alright."

Pra gazed out at the flat Hounslow landscape.

"Only do one time."

"Natalie, it's none of my business." That sounded hurt and resentful. I had no right to feel either. "Nok's lovely. I'm so pleased to meet her!"

"I stupid. I think you don see."

It was six thirty. The evening traffic was heavy. I cut into the middle lane.

"Natalie. Look. You're a beautiful woman. You're a good person. Of course there'll be someone else who loves you."

"Cannot! He monk!"

She tried to sound indignant, but she knew as well as I did that the tenderness the monk hadn't been able to hide was for her as much as for Nok.

"I've got. You know. People I love too."

I meant what I was saying, but the truth was that, meeting her as a prostitute, seeing the way she worked, I hadn't imagined her loving, or being loved, by anyone else till twenty minutes ago.

"My wife. My children. My family. I can't just turn my back on them any more than you can turn your back on your... family. I don't want to."

I felt as bleak as the roadside landscape. I had turned my back on my family. I'd pushed aside twenty years of married life. Camping in the guest room, hanging on for the occasional tense meal together, clinging to Melissa, Meredith, and Ralph had been more destructive than simply walking out the door. I had a past, the same as Natalie did. What I said was true. Of course, I loved my wife. I couldn't stop loving someone I'd known for twenty years. The happiness, however, was irretrievable.

"Just love same brother sister."

If it was true, she was lucky. If she and Pra had a loving friendship, it was more than Melissa and I had now.

"Only do one time!" she wailed. "I get baby!"

"It's alright! It doesn't matter!"

I didn't want to think about it. One time. A thousand times. It wasn't important. It was only sex—the thing for which I'd destroyed my family.

"Why's he here?"

I knew the answer already.

"He come working temple. Is all."

"Really?"

"Don angry, honey. I promise I don't say lie no more. Pra come working, is all. He new boss Leytonstone Temple."

Maybe it was true. Pra might well be taking over the running of the London temple, but that wasn't the real reason he was here.

"Couldn't the temple buy him a ticket?"

An embarrassed silence came from the backseat. They knew we were arguing. All three of them, even Nok, had a pretty good idea what we were arguing about.

I dropped Natalie, her mother, and Nok at the house in Stratford, then drove Pra to Leytonstone Temple. It wasn't far. It ought to have taken ten minutes, but a water main had burst on Romford Road.

Pra sat in the back seat. He didn't speak English, and I didn't speak Thai. Neither of us made any attempt at conversation.

He'd heard Natalie and me arguing. Now that he and I were alone together, I hoped he didn't interpret my silence as resentment. He was an impressive man. I didn't need to speak to him to know that he possessed a certain authority. His silence wasn't ungracious. Pra kept the distance befitting a 'holy person', as Natalie called the monks.

Only one lane of the road was open. A workman with a walkie-talkie and a STOP/GO sign on a pole alternated the east- and westbound traffic.

Pra stared out at Romford Road.

Rundown Victorian houses. A length of terrace converted into a bed-and-breakfast hotel. The big detached house with fairy lights over the porch that was a mosque.

He wasn't just here to work at the Leytonstone Temple. It seemed a bit of a coincidence that he'd turned up so soon after I'd paid off Natalie's contract.

We reached the place where the water main had burst. Half the road was flooded. Maintenance trucks stood around. A tar kettle smoked and stank. Men up to their waists in a trench worked under arc lamps. Water, pumped from the excavation, squished under my tyres as we inched past.

Pra gazed out at the roadworks.

I wondered if he disliked me, if he'd taken me for a frequenter of prostitutes and withdrawn in distaste.

Questions welled up inside me, slow and heavy as the bubbles in the tar kettle.

How long had he known Natalie?

Nok was four. That meant he'd known Natalie for at least five years. Probably longer.

Did Nok realise Pra was her father?

Nok had picked up the embarrassment in the car driving back from the airport, but she called him 'loong', 'uncle'. Not 'por', 'daddy'. She'd been instructed to call me 'Daddy'.

If Natalie had been working at the time Nok was conceived—and they only 'do one time', as she said— how could Natalie tell that Pra was Nok's father? She'd have slept with other men. Why hadn't she been on the pill? I'd always assumed that Nok's father was someone Natalie had lived with.

Had Pra been a monk when he got her pregnant? Or a customer?

We crossed Wanstead Flats. A stream of taillights stitched depths of scrubby darkness together. In the dappled ebb and flow, Pra's face was imperturbable.

Nok's father had presence. He looked to be about the same age as me, perhaps a few years younger. The bare brown shoulder emerging from the folds of his orange robe was muscular. The dark shadow on his closely shaved head said he'd sacrificed a full head of virile black hair. I could readily believe he was a senior monk, senior enough to take over the running of the Leytonstone Temple. He'd clearly been in the sangha much longer than five years. I knew that monks were afforded a high status in Thailand, on a par with royalty, but the man's presence was more than just the aura of social position. He had an inner presence, in fact an authority that only be called spiritual—without any of the charismatic jive that's taken for 'spiritual' in the West. The fact that he'd fathered a child whilst in the sangha, or maybe escaped from fatherhood into the sangha, in no way lessened the dignity that he possessed. When it came to spiritual status he put me on a par with Jack's hippy girlfriend—a Poona suicide—and her crazy books. Natalie's ex could even have been a vipassana master and achieved the insight into the True Nature Of Reality that Soom Bon had aimed for but failed to reach.

My sat nav took me into a hinterland of suburban streets on the western side of the common.

Asian corner shops. A boarded-up pub. A stranded liquor store. A bus route on a street too narrow for buses.

We stopped at a small terrace house. For a second, I wondered if I'd punched in the wrong address.

We were parked outside a house, not a temple. It looked exactly like all the other houses in the terrace, a small two-up-two-down place.

The downstairs bay window was in darkness, the curtains drawn. A lit ceiling shone above net curtains in an upstairs window. There was a garage annexe on one side.

A prickle of frost had already whitened the stainless steel beads of the block and render front wall. The night had turned freezing.

Above the garage annexe, there was a sign, with gold lettering: *WAT BUDDHADHARMA.*

Pra opened his door.

"Kop koon khrap."

"You're welcome."

I wai-d him, and felt a momentary antagonism when he didn't wai me back. Of course he didn't. Monks don't wai, not even royalty, they only wai the Buddha.

Realizing how cold it was, Pra pulled the robe up around his bare shoulder.

He had a tattoo on his bicep.

It surprised me that a monk should have a tattoo. The tattoo looked as if it had been done a long time ago, long before he joined the sangha. The ink had faded. The blue outline had leached into his sleek brown muscle. It was crudely drawn. In fact, the tattoo looked home-made. It was a device I was familiar with, but couldn't place... the head of a bull with elongated horns...

Yes. That was where I'd seen it... on a can of Red Bull.

I woke with a start, with a feeling that I'd slept much longer than I should have.

I was in Islington, not Stratford.

Outside, it was still dark, the window in the grip of a wintry blackness that felt hours away from dawn.

The bedside clock read five forty five! It was late! I always left for work at five! I should have been up, dressed, and out of the house three-quarters of an hour ago!

I needed to use the toilet. The urgency to piss had woken me up, thank God.

Ours was a big house. We had three bathrooms. The largest was directly below me, on the third floor, where Ralph and Meredith's bedrooms were. I risked waking my son and daughter, if I used that one.

There was an en suite bathroom attached to the master bedroom on the second floor, where Melissa was now asleep. Going in there was out of the question.

At the bottom of the house, in the basement, there was a small shower room, which we only used when we were out in the garden.

I climbed into my suit, found my bathroom bag, picked up *The Serpent Power*—I was still picking my way through Arthur Avalon's thicket of Tantric terminology—and crept down the stairs.

The basement shower room had missed out when we had the house refurbished a couple of years previously. The basement shower room may even have missed out on the refurbishment before that. The olive-green shower stall, the beach-pebble splashboard and the triangular mirror on the under-stairs cupboard were 70's style.

There was no time to shower. I shaved as quickly as I could, brushed my teeth, gathered my belongings, and crept back up the stairs.

Melissa was standing outside the kitchen door.

"I need to talk."

I stopped myself from looking at my watch.

"Yes, of course."

She switched the light on. We went into the kitchen and sat down at our new table.

"I don't know how much more of this I can take, Jim."

She was in her dressing gown, clutching the collar at her throat to keep the cold out. She'd lost weight. Even her hands looked thinner.

"Where were you last night? You didn't get back till after midnight."

I'd taken Natalie, her mum, and Nok to a Thai restaurant. Natalie and I had made love afterwards, hurriedly and miserably. Pra's being in London had come between us.

"You're spending more and more time with her."

This was it. Melissa wanted a divorce.

"Is she beautiful?"

Not as beautiful as you, I wanted to blurt.

"Yes."

"How old is she?"

"Twenty-six."

Melissa had aged in the last month. She looked five years older than she did four weeks ago.

"What's her name?"

"Nam Huan," I said.

Melissa's fingers twisted the collar of her dressing gown. Her hands were those of an old woman.

"I thought I knew you, Jim."

"I thought I knew myself."

Her face was pale and tight.

"There was nothing wrong. Was there? Between you and me?"

"No. Nothing at all."

Her voice grew brittle.

"We've got to do something, Jim. It can't go on like this."

We'd always been honest with each other. If I told her I'd never see Natalie again, I'd have to do it. It would have been a destructive and expensive six weeks, but it'd be over.

Pra was here now, Nok's father, the man Natalie had known for five years, more. I hardly knew Natalie myself. We had no shared language. We could barely speak to each other. Pra and Nok, Natalie's real life, were here now.

"What's the matter with you, Jim? You look freaked out of your head."

She glanced down at my book—*The Serpent Power* by Arthur Avalon—on the green oilcloth, next to my bathroom bag.

The Subtle Body. Irreducible Consciousness. Freedom From The Known. The End Of Time. If I said I was having a nervous breakdown, she'd forgive me.

"Nothing's the matter," I said. "I'm fine."

I picked up my stuff and headed for the office.

We were having trouble at Rampton Street. The Rampton Street site was part of a major development in the City Of London, near London Wall. Taking on phase two of the project would have stretched our resources at the best of times, but with the setback my firm had suffered after losing the Arkwright job, the day I first saw Natalie, we were struggling to keep up. We'd hired extra staff to cope with the workload, but the freelancers we'd brought in weren't as efficient as the people we'd laid off after the Arkwright debacle.

The developer, Kingsmead Holdings, were in financial difficulties themselves, and their lawyers were looking to shift losses sideways onto the builders and consultants, and we, as consulting engineers, were a major target. I'd taken my eye off the ball. In the upheaval Natalie had caused in my life, I'd failed to properly supervise the contract negotiations and had signed up for deadlines that we couldn't meet that had swingeing penalty clauses.

Bernard and Pippa were barely speaking to me. They'd gone beyond recriminations and emergency meetings and were grimly soldiering on, attempting to renegotiate with Kingsmead Holdings. They were so angry with my pushing ahead with phase two, and so judgmental of the way I was treating Melissa, I had the feeling they were keeping me in the dark over crucial decisions.

Things were so unpleasant in the office and my conversation with Melissa had upset me so much I decided to give work a miss.

It was still early. The morning rush hour was only just starting up.

Natalie had mentioned us taking her mother and Nok to see Big Ben, so I headed for Stratford.

I was getting used to the drive from Islington to Stratford. In fact, the roads were turning into a sort of pilgrim's way. A rat run spiraling back on itself. A set of traffic lights permanently caught between red and green.

I was immersing myself in the books Jack's hippy girlfriend had left in the guest bedroom. Today it was *The Serpent Power*'s turn, but I was battling my way through *The End Of Time* and *Freedom From The Known* as well. I'd never read books in this way before, knowing they held secrets vital to my existence. The secrets weren't the three books' actual theses—theses required too much concentration, particularly the physicist's stuff about the wave function and quantum mechanics—but in the odd phrase that would leap out at me, or an occasional insight spinning off at a tangent, and the odd phrase would become a stretch of footpath, and the occasional insight would become an arcade of shops on the way from Islington to Stratford, the beaten track a pilgrim's path as much as it was a drive to my girlfriend's door.

Places are more important than events. Places are the nodes in the web of events that hold the chaos of random moments together. Places shine, like these pinpoints of acid sunlight burning through the leaden morning clouds.

A pub in Newington Green raised its footpath trapdoor for an early morning delivery. Down in the cellar someone was throwing crates of empties up onto the pavement. The fact that 'She Who Is Outside The Universe' *goes upwards* was unbearable.

A place *is* an event. Any spot on the surface of the earth is a 'copulation of the Manifest with the Unmanifest' as Arthur Avalon, translating the Sat-Cakra-Nirupana Tantra, puts it. None of it need be true, but it was nicer than having to think about load bearing walls and first fixing schedules.

In Lea Bridge Road, at the clump of willow trees by the white lock keeper's cottage on the canal, I drove through a moment of water logged timber and steaming dung a hundred years ago, stored up just for me in chilly ground behind a railing. Julian Barbour's assertion that time is an illusion created by a place's, any place's, constant collapsing out of probability into being was poignantly tangible, certainly more tangible than wiring specifications and certification schedules.

I was anxious to get to Stratford, but the pilgrim's way kept holding me back. At the junction of Lea Bridge Road and Orient Way, the unknowable-ness of the 'known' rose up in a stretch of traffic islands and warehouse courtyards. That everything is constantly new, even on a dull winter's morning, revealed itself in galvanised pedestrian barriers where no one walked. Whether unknowableness involved 'the brain discovering something new, a new function being born' was not as obvious. Whether it meant 'freedom' was less and less likely.

It was still only half past seven, but when I got to Stratford, everyone was up. The house was encouragingly alive with activity.

Nok was in the living room in her pyjamas playing a computer game on the TV. My pop-up nursery rhymes had been trumped by Angry Birds.

Natalie's mother was in the kitchen, washing up. Back home in the village she was used to waking at four in the morning to get the day's rice cooking on an open fire.

Natalie's Mum was a couple of years younger than me, but the flouncy blouses she favoured, and her floral skirt, were what, in London, only elderly ladies would have worn. She had Natalie's high cheekbones and full, broad lips, but they were masked by a net of deep, tanned wrinkles.

We hovered around one another, unable to make conversation.

I could tell Natalie's mother felt awkward about Pra's being here. She was embarrassed that Natalie was spending so much time with Pra, but her embarrassment had an edge of defiance to it, too. She'd had a hard life. She was a tough woman. The lines in her face were from more than just heavy work in the sun. The set of her jaw wasn't mere patience. Natalie said that going off to work as a prostitute had been her decision, made off her own bat when she was sixteen, not her mother's. But I wondered if this was true.

I retreated to the living room to try out the little Thai I'd learned on Nok.

I pointed at the Angry Birds zapping one another.

"Len geem mai?"

It was a huge effort for her to drag her eyes away from the screen, but she forced herself, and gave me a stunning smile that said she hadn't understood me.

I pressed on. I pointed at her T-shirt.

"Suuai!"

She was wearing a pretty yellow T-shirt with sunflowers on it, and SUMMER SMILE in glittery letters. She certainly looked suuai.

Natalie came down the stairs.

"Poot 'thank you, Daddy'!"

Separation had given her an abrupt way of addressing her daughter. She was still in her pyjamas too.

Nok clammed up. Natalie raised her voice:

"'Thank you, Daddy'!"

Nok stared at the carpet. She was tongue tied. She was only four years old. It seemed a bit early to be forcing her to speak English.

"POOT 'THANK YOU, DADDY'!"

"It's alright, honey. She doesn't have to say it if she doesn't want to."

Nok called Pra 'loong', uncle. She didn't seem to know that Pra was her father. I felt awkward being lumbered with 'Daddy', remembering the tenderness and pride with which the monk had looked at his daughter.

"She go school! She know how say!"

"It's alright. It's not a problem."

We got ready to go out. Nok switched off her game. Natalie's mother appeared with her handbag.

"I tired, honey. You do. Okay?"

"Eh?"

She kissed me.

"I very tired. Need sleeping more. You take Mum Nok go see London, mai?"

She gave Nok and her mother some instructions, and headed back up the stairs.

"Natalie?"

"No sleeping last night, honey. You see London better more than I."

We drove straight into the rush hour.

In Stratford High Street we ran into the Bow Lane tailback and got held up at some traffic lights by a roundabout with a sculpture made of bent steel girders painted different colours. The lights changed half a dozen times before we made it past the station.

Nok and her grandmother sat in the back seat, getting a bird's eye view of a genuine London traffic jam. Bow Lane didn't interest them. Apparently the traffic jams are even more spectacular in Bangkok.

I'd rung Natalie twice last night. Her phone had been switched off both times. Natalie never switched off her phone, not ever. I'd assumed, or at least hoped, that last night she'd been busy with her mother and Nok. Now I knew why she'd blocked my calls.

Nine o'clock was a crazy time to go sightseeing. It took two hours to fight our way down to Westminster Bridge. When we finally got there, there was nowhere to park.

Nok didn't seem interested in Big Ben. I drove over the bridge and found a multi-storey car park by the Shell Centre. By the time we got back to the river Nok was getting fractious. I bought her an ice cream.

Natalie's mother looked lost. Her grim mouth and bleak expression conveyed anxiety more than any interest in London. She knew that Natalie had spent the night with Pra, and she was worried about the effect this was having on me. They'd obviously flown over thinking they could keep Natalie and Pra's relationship secret but love had got the better of discretion.

I couldn't tell what effect Natalie's spending the night with Pra was having on me. I'd been impressed by Pra. He was Nok's father. I was glad that Natalie had a stable relationship in her life, and that prostitution hadn't destroyed her ability to form a lasting bond. Pra's being a monk would make it awkward, but I got the impression that the Buddhist sangha was more tolerant than the Church when it came to sex. Perhaps Pra planned to leave the temple.

It was lucky that Natalie's Mum didn't speak English and I didn't speak Thai. We didn't have to talk about it.

There was a long queue for the London Eye, but Nok brightened up once we got in our capsule and were finally slowly rising above the Festival Hall and the Oxo tower. She was a lovely little girl. She seemed to be gripped more by the slow motion rise of the floor and our gradually increasing height above the ground than by any of the sights I tried to point out to her. She'd probably never heard of St Paul's Cathedral or Tower Bridge. She took in London with a rapt solemnity, not because it interested her, but because it was part of an initiation which she was undergoing, and which she knew she was undergoing, and which she knew she was ready for. She already had two take-offs and two landings in a jet aeroplane under her belt, and now this silently rocking ascent. She was used to farms and village life, but London didn't faze her. She took things in her stride. She was as adept at living as she was with her thumbs and Angry Birds, going up level after level. New things didn't frighten her.

I could feel Nok bracing herself for a new life. She'd been instructed to call Pra 'loong', but she must know the monk was her father. She was too bright-eyed, her gaze was too open, not to see the love and tenderness with which the big man in the orange robe looked at her. It was impossible not to delight in her good luck and admire her courage. She knelt on the bench solemnly, her nose pressed to the glass, taking possession of the future as surely as she took possession of London spreading out beneath her. Nok deserved every bit of luck she could get. She'd seen very little of Natalie during her four years on earth. Natalie's Mum and Dad had brought her up while Natalie worked— in Bangkok the first six months of Nok's life, Natalie making brief trips up to Chiang Rai to see her daughter, then in Hong Kong and Dubai, before the brief trip back to Bangkok for her flight to London. Nok probably hadn't seen much of Pra either, if he was as high up in the sangha as Natalie said, and busy with temple business. London lay stretched out below, drab and freezing cold, the Thames a grey welt, Highgate hunched in shrouds of mist, Shooters Hill rain-blackened, Nok's property more than mine or anyone else's, like the future.

It was pretty clear what would happen. As soon as Pra's visa extension, to work at the temple, came through, he'd leave the sangha and set up home with Natalie and Nok here in London. There were better opportunities for them in England than in Thailand. Pra was a capable, intelligent man. He'd have contacts in the London Thai community to help him get a job or set up a business. Natalie would stop working and take care of Nok. I sensed— 'sokapbrok!' at the airport, the way Natalie had sloped out of today's expedition— that there was a certain nervous distance between her and Nok. Of course there was. They'd spent so little time together. Once she'd set up home with Pra in London Natalie could get to know her daughter better. Her insistence that

Nok call me 'daddy'—there'd been a nervous distance in that too—was just her way of soothing my hurt feelings at being replaced, and to guarantee my continued financial support till she and Pra were on their feet. Once Pra was established, he'd find a way of sorting out Natalie's immigration status.

Watching Nok firmly braced against the vast distance under her feet, as we reached the top of our revolution, I realised that the child had given me one last chance of making things good with Melissa, and renewing my damaged relationship with Ralph and Meredith. It was a gift that only a child could give. There was nothing more precious than family. Ralph and Meredith had once been sturdy four-year-olds like Nok, their faces pressed against the future. It's children who make the world new, not a lurid transcendence festering in sexual novelty.

The last few weeks had been a descent into an unspeakable shallowness. The madam at Hackney Sauna and her 'cheers, Jack', Pauline in the cubicle, 'must do', Cyril and *his* girls, Jack and the globalist elite and the 'sick, fucking, evil fucking stuff they're into'. Evil isn't profound. Evil's not some deep secret only an expert in conspiracy can see into. It isn't Jack's Devil. Or Natalie's Arms Fair man. Evil is the surrender to shallowness. It's sacrificing the simple— family, children, trust—to the trite. The last few weeks had been a nightmare, but now the nightmare was over.

Nok pressing her face to the glass, Pra turning up out of the blue, Natalie's spending the night with him... I realized that I'd been given a final opportunity, a moment's grace, to get my life back on track. Repairing the damage that the last four weeks had done would take a long time. Completely repairing the damage I'd done to my marriage and my family might be impossible, but Melissa had offered me a last chance, the morning I was late for work. 'There was nothing wrong. Was there? Between you and me?' The question had been the assertion of something simple and real. Our relationship had always been a good one. What she'd said was right: 'We've got to do something, Jim. It can't go on like this.'

After the Eye, we had lunch at a café on the South Bank and then went on a boat trip down the river to Greenwich. Nok fell asleep. I could feel that Natalie's mother was having trouble coping with the cold, even in the glassed-in section of the boat. She kept nodding off. It was seven before I dropped them back at Stratford. Natalie wasn't there. She'd already left to see Pra.

I decided to wait at Stratford till she came back so that I could have a talk with her.

Nok and her mother went to bed. I sat downstairs in front of the TV trying to put the things I wanted to say to her into English she'd be able to understand. I was glad she'd decided to make a proper family with Pra and Nok. It was the best thing for her daughter and it gave me the chance to try and repair the damage I'd done to my family. I had no idea what the procedure was for a monk leaving the sangha and marrying, but it was clear that she was deeply attached to Pra. He was an impressive, capable man. That much had been obvious from a single meeting. The sangha is much more tolerant than the Church. Men enter and leave the temple pretty much to fit in with the needs of their family. Natalie had even told me how a man can become a monk for just a week, to attain merit, or get a bit of good luck with a pressing problem. I'd seen photos of young boys having their heads shaved to be monks over their school holidays. Thai Buddhism was flexible. Pra had taken over the running of Leytonstone Temple, but he wouldn't be at Wat Buddharama tonight. He and Natalie were probably staying at a hotel somewhere while Pra sorted out his visa situation and the formalities of a 'big monk' disrobing.

I sat thinking it all through. I wanted to convey to her the relief I felt that it was over. She knew that I was a family man. She'd sensed that I loved my wife and children, and the hurt I was doing to myself with this rupture. I'd keep paying for the house till she and Pra were settled. They could even take over the rent if they wanted to stay here. I had a feeling that Natalie had her heart set on staying in England. It would take a long time and a lot of money to sort out Natalie's visa status, but once I'd made my peace with Melissa and got access to my money again I'd be able to help. They'd find a school for Nok. Nok would do well at school. She was a sturdy little thing, emotionally as well as physically. She'd pick up the language quickly and probably end up outdoing the English kids in the playground.

The relief of returning to a normal life grew stronger and stronger the longer I sat thinking about it. Conjuring up a future for Natalie was reinstating my own future. Pra's turning up in London had saved me from something terrible. I'd said and done some dreadful things to Melissa, but I knew she'd forgive me. I could almost feel the weight of the twenty years Melissa and I had spent together here in this bleak Stratford living room, as if all the minutes of my life with my family were gathered into the here and now and were substantial enough to lift me out of this visible shallowness back into depth and substance.

The clock ticked. The programmes flicked by. The stinging sensation in my spine got more and more acute. The thread of light silvered the room in its own kind of TV shine. My eyelids were stiff, they felt like they were made of lead, yet the light got stronger. It illuminated nothing but itself. It was the shallowest thing of all.

Eleven came and went. Natalie still wasn't back. She was spending the night with Pra. I resisted the temptation to climb the stairs, fall into bed and spend the night in Stratford. If I was going to get my real life back I was going to have to start out immediately. I could talk to Natalie tomorrow, or whenever I next saw her.

It was more urgent that I get back to Islington. If Melissa was still awake I could apologise there and then for what I'd said this morning. Melissa was right. Things couldn't go on like this. I needed to tell her that I'd made my decision.

When I got back to Islington, there was a letter waiting for me on the kitchen table. I took it upstairs to my room and opened it.

There were two separate letters inside the envelope. One was a petition for divorce, with an Acceptance Of Service form for me to sign.

The other was a note from Melissa. She'd been reluctant to go ahead with filing an application for divorce and hoped that we might still avoid a separation, but since the grounds for divorce were adultery and a petition on the grounds of adultery needs to be filed within six months of her, the petitioner's, becoming aware of the adultery, her solicitors had advised her to file now. Natalie would not be named in the petition. Melissa didn't want to cause visa problems for Natalie, but evidence of my adultery would be provided, if challenged, by Ralph and Meredith, to whom I'd spoken about my affair. Since the Islington house was my children's principal residence, as well as hers, Melissa understood that I would understand that the house would not be sold and that she would continue to live here. Any negotiations about equity in the house or division of our shared assets should wait until we had decided what both of us wished for from the current situation. Melissa was prepared to release funds to me from our joint account, but only by cheque signed by both of us, not ATM withdrawals. She hoped that the present application might ultimately prove unnecessary and that we'd eventually come to an amicable arrangement without it.

The divorce petition was a fifteen page document from the court, with boxes to be filled in regarding the substance of the adultery charge, financial statements, property adjustment orders, secured provision orders and costs.

I signed the Acceptance Of Service form, and put the filing for divorce aside to look through later. I wasn't daunted by the legal jargon, but I didn't feel like dealing with it right now.

I opened *The Serpent Power* and went back to the chapter I'd been reading, on Embodied Consciousness. Energy Centres. Mantras. Cosmic Cycles. It made much more sense.

Around eight o'clock the next evening I went back to Stratford.

I'd left for work early without seeing Melissa or speaking to her during the day. The divorce petition had come as a shock, especially with Melissa's accompanying generosity. The impact of the legal filing put lesser issues into perspective. Melissa and I would sort things out. Melissa still wanted to sort things out. We'd talk. Make arrangements. I could finally sincerely promise her that I'd break it off with Natalie, now that Pra had shown up. The document said I had six weeks before anything dreadful happened.

I'd spent the day thinking over what I wanted to say to Natalie, about Pra, Nok, and the future, that I wished them well. I was glad Nok was finally going to have a family. I'd help them in any way I could.

I paused at the front door, my key in the lock.

Directly behind the front door, the living room was in pandemonium. Laughter and shouted conversation vibrated the flimsy panelling. Thumping music shook the imitation Tudor fanlight.

I hesitated on the doorstep. Perhaps it would be better if I just went straight back to Islington. The coming conversation with Melissa was urgent. I'd put her through enough already without any more delay.

I thought I caught a snatch of Pauline's voice. The door was ridiculously lightweight for the front door to a house.

The house was brand new, but its raw yellow brickwork was already showing signs of wear and tear. The skinny pillar by the footpath had lost its capping. A lump of masonry, with the wrought-iron gate still attached, leaned against the gas meter.

I needed to talk to Natalie.

I turned the key, pushed the door and it banged against something directly inside. There was only just room to squeeze in.

"Sawwadee ka!"

"Sawwadee khrap!"

"Loong Jim!"

The living room was packed.

The coffee table leant on its end in the bay window crushing the slats of the venetian blinds. The sofa had been pushed back against the door to make room for a load of plastic mats spread out on the floor. The mats were crowded with people sitting cross-legged, eating, drinking, and preparing food. The music was deafening.

"Welcome!"

"Happy happy!"

"Uncle!"

Gigi and Pauline were there with a number of other girls, the dark-skinned one who'd got out of the people carrier in Camden Town, the delicate girl I'd seen in Hackney in a nurse's uniform.

I stood half in and half out, wedged between the door and the back of the sofa looking down on the heads of the people lodged in the three-seater.

A blue rinse perm the size of a fireman's helmet swivelled and an elderly Thai woman glared up at me.

Gigi rushed to introduce us.

"Jim. This Missus Leepatwat."

"Koon mair, thii khuue Loong Jim."

Mrs Leepatawat's face was as rigid as her hairdo. She didn't like me.

"Jim. This Mister Leepatawat."

A small, elderly Thai man raised his glass from the far side of the room, where he sat talking to Frank and Javindra.

I could see through the doorway into the kitchen that the kitchen was as crowded as the living room. A fat woman had picked Nok up and was bouncing her on her hip, a drink in her other hand. Natalie's mother was trying to open the fridge. It was hard to tell whether the people jammed around the microwave were cooking or partying, or both. There were too many people for such a small house.

The only one who wasn't there was Natalie.

The music was ear-splitting.

'BOOM thii rak BOOM thii rak BOOM BOOM BOOM...'

I knew 'thii rak'. Natalie called me 'thii rak'.

Darling.

'BOOM, darling. BOOM, darling. BOOM BOOM BOOM...'

The living room floor was so jammed with people sitting cross-legged, and so littered with bottles and bowls and saucepans there was no room to dance, but Pauline was on her feet anyway, her painted toenails anchored between tureens and glasses, shaking her booty from the ankles upwards. She danced better than Beyoncé.

'BOOM thii rak BOOM thii rak BOOM BOOM BOOM...'

A beer appeared in my hand. Gigi introduced me to more people. The dark-skinned girl was Amy, the delicate one was Carla. Their steep Asian faces were heavily made up. They looked as if they'd just come from work.

"Where's Natalie?"

Gigi did a double take.

"Natalie go buy beer." She wasn't a good liar. "I ring. See."

She grabbed her phone and thumbed a number.

I'd been trying to get hold of Natalie all day myself. Every time I rang, her phone had been switched off. This time she answered—if, that is, the voice on the other end of the line was hers. It sounded like a woman.

There was a brief exchange in Thai. On Gigi's end the words were more a warning than a query.

I wondered if Natalie had a second phone.

Gigi rang off.

"Natalie buy beer. She coming now."

I needed to go. I shouldn't even be here. There were important things I had to attend to, things that urgently needed sorting out. I'd had the divorce papers for nearly twenty four hours and I still hadn't looked at them, not properly, let alone returned them to the court or to wherever I was supposed to register my response to Melissa's petition. I needed to speak to Melissa first, before I answered the application. We could surely sort things out without going through the whole messy business of separation and a division of assets. Hopefully there wouldn't need to be a separation at all.

I decided to give it another ten minutes.

The last thing I felt like doing was talking to Frank and Javindra, but the hubbub of Thai was so overwhelming that that was what I ended up doing.

Javindra immediately started lecturing me.

"I told you you should have taken Natalie back to the Caledonian Road, Jim." His nose was out of joint because I hadn't heeded the advice he'd given me in the Holiday Inn. It upset him that I'd not returned Natalie to her rightful owner, Lee, and let her work off her contract like other punters did. I'd broken some unstated rule of the sex industry code of conduct by paying her contract off myself, in full. "Twenty two thousand pounds..." He gestured at the din and chaos. "... And now look where you are!"

I should have been in Plaistow, paying him two hundred pounds a week for a box bedroom. It disturbed me that Javindra knew the exact amount I'd given Lee.

"Twenty two grand?" Frank's eyes were glazed with exhaustion. "You're crazy, mate." Frank wasn't wearing his London Transport uniform tonight. He was in a Tottenham football shirt with 9 KANE on the back. "She's probably got a couple of other mugs 'paying off her contract' too." He put 'paying off her contract' in air quotes. Frank sounded less philosophical and more bitter than the night we went to ATIK. I wondered if he'd reached some sort of crisis with Pauline. His stoicism over the Cypriot builder was no longer keeping out the hurt. "Thai birds, Jim. All they think about is money."

Frank pissed me off nearly as much as Javindra. I didn't tell him that Natalie wasn't a bitch like Pauline. Natalie wasn't a complacent doormat like Gigi either, happy with second wife status to a sleazebag accountant. Natalie had a proper relationship, with a man from her own culture and background, someone who was respected in the Thai world.

Javindra grinned.

"Frank never puts his foot down." He nodded at Pauline, dancing amongst the bowls and bottles. "Pauline's got a new guy. A Russian helicopter salesman."

I felt myself stiffen.

"Eh?"

"Yeah. A bigshot helicopter salesman. At the Arms Fair."

"It's opened?"

I hadn't been following the news these last few days.

"Opened yesterday," said Javindra. "Frank won't be seeing much of Pauline this week."

"Fuck off," said Frank. He sounded wretched.

Javindra smiled.

"You could have saved yourself twenty two grand, Jim."

I looked at him.

"In what way, Javindra?"

He shrugged.

"Natalie'll be earning so much money this week she could have paid the contract off herself by Friday."

I said:

"Natalie's stopped working."

I didn't tell him about Pra. It was none of Javindra's business.

He laughed out loud.

"That's what they all say. These helicopter salesmen types are big spenders, Jim. Natalie'll be a rich girl by this time next week."

"Probably blow it in a fucking week too," said Frank.

I didn't disabuse them. Frank was a dope. Javindra was in with Lee. They lived in a world where the lies and back-stabbings spiraled down into murky depths where something as simple as love was invisible. My feelings for Natalie were none of their business. Natalie and Pra were none of their business either.

I looked at my watch. It was after nine. Ten minutes? That was half an hour ago. Buy beer? I wondered what the next excuse would be. Natalie wasn't going to show. It was time to stand up and go home. There were things I urgently needed to sort out back in Islington.

A scrabble of arms and legs clambered into my lap. A hot breath, smelling of Coca Cola, blew in my face.

"Daddy!"

Frank smiled desolately.

"You've won a heart there, Jim."

Nok was humping the Winnie The Pooh toy Natalie's mother had bought her in Hamley's. The big plastic thing was some sort of educational toy, a Roll n Learn Tree Playset, to teacher her English so Natalie wouldn't have to bother. It was a bit bulky for a four-year-old. She'd already lost the plastic balls that rolled between the pair of plastic trees when the music played and the A J Milne animals popped their heads out and spoke.

Nok got herself comfortable on my lap.

"Duu, duu, Daddy! Chan dai!"

She pressed a button and Winnie the Pooh clunked out of a tree and said 'I like honey' with an American accent.

"I rike lun ee!" shouted Nok.

She was a lovely little girl, bright-eyed and unspoiled.

"Eye Ore! Eye Ore! Tham Eye Ore, Daddy!"

I was the Eye Ore specialist.

I pressed Eye Ore's button and sang along with the donkey:

"Hu-lloooooorrrrr, Poooh."

Nok dissolved in fits of laughter.

"HU-LLOOOOOORRRRR, POOH!"

She'd had a hard time. Natalie never there. Not knowing who her father was. At least Nok would be happy soon. She was enjoying the party too. She liked being the centre of attention with all these exotic ladies and London Thai bigwigs.

"Who's the old lady?"

"Mrs Leepatawat?" said Javindra. "She's a big cheese in the East London Thai community. She and her husband, that guy over there..." He nodded at the small Thai man in glasses. "... They own a couple of restaurants and a shop in Plaistow. They're big donators to the temple."

"The one in Leytonstone?"

"Yeah. Wat Leytonstone."

I wondered if that was why Mrs Leepatawat looked so grim. She had a cast-iron smile, and it wasn't a happy one. She was angry that Pra was leaving the temple for Natalie. Perhaps Pra's disrobing for a prostitute brought disgrace upon the temple. The social wing of the sangha was less tolerant than its founder. I had a feeling that

Mrs Leepatawat was here to put pressure on Natalie. She and her husband were waiting for Natalie to get back so they could start in on her with the full weight of the Thai community behind them. Perhaps that was why Natalie wasn't here. I was stupid hanging on, waiting for the ruckus. The old woman wasn't too pleased with me either, as the one who'd paid off Natalie's contract so she could run away with Pra.

The way she scowled, Mrs Leepatawat most definitely wasn't impressed with Pauline's dancing.

Pauline knew how to move. The 'thii raks' were riding the 'BOOMS' and the 'BOOMS' were grinding the 'thii raks', but not in Frank's direction. Out in the middle of the floor, shimmying above the tureens and whiskey bottles, Pauline was fucking a Russian helicopter salesman.

Someone topped up my beer. Natalie still hadn't appeared. It was crazy hanging on for her, but I couldn't go make myself go.

It was only a fifteen minute drive from the temple in a taxi. Unless she and Pra were in a hotel in another part of London. Gigi had rung her over an hour ago. If the brief exchange had been with Natalie at all, that is. She was certainly taking a long time to buy some beer.

There was a deadline before which I had to respond to Melissa's divorce papers, otherwise Melissa could proceed, but the deadline was some way off yet. Six weeks. I hadn't even looked at the papers properly. The whole thing seemed too crazy. Divorce was absurd. Even a temporary separation was extreme. The filings alleged adultery, but that was all over now. Once I'd spoken to Melissa we could at least come to some sort of arrangement, even if we couldn't patch things up entirely. Sleeping in the guest bedroom was a nightmare, but it was better than a complete break. I knew that, in her heart, Melissa didn't want a complete break. All I'd needed to do was speak to her this morning instead of leaving for work early again, and now I'd be late home and she'd be camped in the living room with Meredith and Ralf.

I decided to get up and leave. I needed to do it right now. I was a bit drunk, but not so drunk that I couldn't tell Melissa that it was over with Natalie and I wanted to try and make things better.

There was a knock at the front door. Javindra said:

"Hey! Look who's here!"

I searched for Natalie. Amy was opening the front door for Cyril. Cyril's bulky form was pushing past Mrs Leepatawat's sofa, followed by a tall teenage boy.

I'd forgotten!

I was meeting Cyril here tonight, with his son, Leon. I'd completely forgotten! It was pure accident that I was here at all.

The boy was carrying an armload of books. I'd said I'd help Leon with his maths! Cyril's son was preparing for his maths GCSE. I'd promised Cyril that I'd look through some algebra tests with him. I hadn't known, when I made the arrangement—neither had Cyril to judge by his scowl— that there'd be a party here tonight and the house packed with rowdy Thais.

Cyril shoved the sofa to one side and squeezed in.

His eyes were bloodshot. He grinned down at Mrs Leepatawat. He knew her.

"Evening, maam."

Mrs Leepatawat jumped to her feet and stalked off into the kitchen. She didn't like blacks.

Cyril made Leon sit down in her place on the sofa.

The boy was slim and willowy, there was nothing at all of Cyril's muscly bulk. Leon seemed reserved, next to Cyril's expansive rumbustiousness. There were no dreads or studs.

Cyril glanced at Pauline.

"Okay, beautiful?" He winked at me. "Lettin' her hair down after all them tanks n helicopters." He grinned at Frank. "Don't worry, mate. It's only a week."

He asked the woman who'd been sitting beside Mrs Leepatawat to move, and I picked my way across the floor and sat down next to Leon.

"Say thank you to Uncle Jim, Leon."

The boy thanked me. He was sixteen, preparing for his GCSEs. He seemed studious and shy, but in a poised sort of way. I wondered if he knew that all these sexy girls were prostitutes, and that his father smashed down doors and crashed hotel rooms looking after them.

"Leon got 'is test next week."

Leon opened his books and showed me some quadratic equations he was having trouble with.

The music was deafening. It had changed to a lachrymose love song. Someone had turned the volume up. The maudlin chanteuse was even louder than BOOM thii rak. The beat was Death Metal slow but Pauline was still dancing, winding her butt round the tranced rhythm, still hypnotically hot.

"Leon like football better than he like math," said Cyril, with a trace of menace. "Maths's 'is weak ting."

We ran through a few univariates. If math was Leon's weak thing, he was destined to play for England. He was a clever kid. The equations he was having trouble with were the same ones Ralph had had trouble with at the same age, and Ralph ended up with an A star in maths. Leon was bound to do well in his exams. Cyril was putting him through a pricey private school.

With the beer I'd drunk, and the music and hubbub of conversation, it was hard to concentrate on the equations.

Over by the door, Gigi and Amy were putting their coats on, getting ready to leave. I glanced across at Javindra. His pompous smile had gone tight at the corners.

I felt a warm pressure against my leg. It was Carla. She wasn't on duty tonight. Carla had squeezed into the sofa next to me. The sofa was small, a skimpy three-seater. It was a tight fit.

Carla leaned across me and frowned at the book open on Leon's knees. Her hand dug into the cushion under my thigh.

"Wiicha kan-it-dtah-saat! Dichan chawp!"

Apparently she liked maths. She was interested in Leon's quadratic equations. Or maybe it was Leon she was interested in.

Carla was even slimmer than Pauline, but her body had a softness and delicacy that was the opposite of Pauline's snaky angularity. She tucked her feet up under her. It was like feeling a newborn foal, its legs folded beneath it, pressing warmly against my shoulder.

"Since a can be any number except zero..."

She leant across me. Carla was definitely more interested in Leon than quadratic equations. She didn't look much older than him.

"...x is the unknown..."

"Same you wan know?"

"Yes. That's right."

I didn't mind teaching Carla too. She had a lovely, innocent openness. Her attractiveness was magnetic, but Leon ignored it. His father hovered menacingly.

"... And a, b, and c are the constants..."

"Same you don want know?"

She was as bright as Leon. Leon finally gave her a smile.

"... So if you know the square root of this side of the equation..."

Carla leaned across me. Her long, shiny black hair skimmed the open page.

I could feel Cyril, ex doorman of the 'Starlight', Ilford, keeping a close eye on her. Leon was going to get an A star in his maths GCSE or there'd be hell to pay.

A key jiggled in the front door. The door banged into the back of the sofa. I felt a blast of cold air on the back of my head.

"Ee-eeeee!"

A hand thrust down from above and grabbed Carla's hair. Natalie's fingers clutched a handful of Carla's hair and jerked her head backwards. Her high-pitched scream was terrible.

"Ee-eeeeeee dam!"

Carla tugged her head free and jumped up.

Natalie came round the corner of the sofa and went for her. She was yelling things at Carla.

Carla blazed a few words back, but Natalie's anger was too much for her. Carla turned tail and fled into the kitchen.

"Natalie! Stop it!"

Natalie headed for the kitchen, after Carla.

"You mine! She cannot take!"

Mrs Leepatwat appeared in the kitchen door. For a moment I thought Natalie was going to go for the old woman too.

"She cannot touching!"

She had two bands of white string tied round her wrists, one on each wrist.

"Chill, Natalie," said Cyril, pissed off at the interruption. "Jim's helpin' Leon with 'is maths."

The state Natalie was in, there'd be no more equations today.

The white string round her wrists was for good luck. When someone wished to bless you they tied white string around your wrists. The monks tied string around devotees' wrists at the temple.

Natalie was still shouting. She grabbed my arm.

An African man carrying a box of Budweiser had followed her into the room. He looked lost.

Cyril raised his voice:

"Take it easy, babe. You've got it wrong." He grinned at me. "Thai birds, bro." Natalie pulled me to my feet. She was dragging me towards the stairs. "Can hold their drink. But they're murder on the sniff."

The bedroom was as bleak as the day we moved in. Brilliant white woodchip. The light shade too small to screen the bulb. A flat-pack wardrobe. The brand new blind still off its runner, its beaded pull hanging down like a skimpy white rosary.

Natalie stared at me. Her eyes were blank.

"I sorry. I see she touch you. I think she do bad."

She'd just come from the temple. She'd just come from seeing Pra, she had no right to think 'bad' about anything.

She threw her handbag on the bed and paced up and down. The room was stifling. Someone had turned the heating up high. Sweat beaded her upper lip, but she didn't take her winter coat off.

"Fleezing."

She didn't even unzip the coat, or undo the collar where it was clipped high around her throat.

"Natalie. It's too hot in here."

"I crazy girl."

If she was high on cocaine, the 'sniff' was having a bad effect on her. Her anger downstairs had been out of all proportion to what she'd seen.

I wondered if she really had been doing coke. She didn't even look drunk. Pra was a monk. He didn't use drugs. Not even alcohol, not even when he was about to leave the temple.

She was stoned, but it wasn't coke. Her skin gave off a sweet, fruity smell, faint but pungent, that I couldn't place.

I wondered if she'd had a fight with Pra, if things had been said that were driving her out of her mind.

"I sorry."

"It's alright."

"I love you, Jim. Don wan no girl take you."

She had no right to say it. She loved Pra, not me. She'd just come from seeing him. She had no right to talk about girls touching me.

"You I love two gether, Jim."

"Look, Natalie..."

She plonked down next to me on the bed, still in her coat. The heat was suffocating, but she'd forgotten to take it off.

"Have bad time life before. This life must happy."

Drowning in the Phraya River was the last thing I felt like talking about.

She massaged my leg. Hectically. Frantically. Palms burning my trousers. All ten fingers probing. All ten fingernails raking.

It was a type of massage I was getting used to. I'd seen Gigi massage Javindra's leg in the same way. Even Pauline massaged Frank's leg, in its London Transport trousers, like this. An osteopathic squeeze on the upper thigh then a bulldozing pressure knee-wards. The bar girl squeeze. The barstool-to-barstool massage while negotiations are ongoing. Usually it felt intimately impersonal, tonight it was just crazy.

I nodded at the string round her wrists.

"You've been to the temple?"

She looked at the string as if it was the first time she'd seen it.

"Mai chai. Do I self."

Something bad had happened between her and Pra. The lie was childlike in its transparency. String tying is a transaction, string tying is a blessing offered by one person to another. There's no such thing as 'do I self.'

I wondered if Pra had changed his mind about leaving the temple. Abandoning the sangha after decades as a monk had proven too much of a wrench. Pra had got cold feet. He'd come to England to be with her, but now that he was faced with the consequences of his decision he'd pulled back from the brink. He'd put her in an impossible position, wanting to keep on seeing her, but at the same time wanting to stay at the temple. He was a spiritual man. He'd followed a spiritual calling. He loved Natalie, but he loved the sangha more. There were the social pressures too, Mrs Leepatawat and the East London Thai community downstairs leaning on him. Pra had gone back on his promise. No wonder she was distraught.

"Too hot!" She'd finally remembered she had her coat on. At long last she was taking it off. I felt a crazy relief as she unbuttoned the high collar. "Cannot breathing!"

She unzipped the coat at the front and threw it on the bed. I stopped breathing myself.

Perhaps she had been a princess in old Siam. Maybe she had once been a royal maiden attendant upon the King.

She looked stunning. She was wearing a traditional Thai costume, a red, ankle-length sheath rich with silver and gold embroidery, the strapless bodice encrusted with filigree brocade, a regal sash draping her bare shoulder, held in place by a belt of gilt medallions.

It was a dress that princesses wore. I'd seen photos of the Queen of Thailand in a similar sheath, and royal dancers in the temple in Bangkok. It was a dress to be worn on ceremonial occasions. I'd seen a photo of a similar style gown... in a wedding photo. It was a wedding dress!

Natalie was dressed for her marriage, and she'd come back crazy. She'd come back so distraught Cyril had assumed she was high on cocaine!

She was dragging gold necklaces over her head, through a ruined bouffant. Her wrists were stacked with bangles. I hadn't even registered that her hair was done up, the beehive collapsing as she tugged dangling charms and gold leaves out of it.

"Natalie. What's the matter?"

"Hot. Cannot breathing."

She unzipped the sheath at the back.

"I'll turn the heating down."

The thermostat was over by the door. I stood up. She grabbed my arm.

"No, Jim. Don. Don leave I."

"I'm not leaving. I'm."

"Wan do sex?"

Her smile was terrible.

She was pulling the sheath down round her hips. She was fighting with the stiff embroidery. It was a silver and gold stitched straitjacket. Something popped at the back and the bodice dragged her bra down over her belly. The sash got jammed under the medallions. Her breasts were wet and slippery. Her belly was bathed in sweat. She was a frantic butterfly, furled and glistening, trapped in its flamboyant cocoon.

"Fuck I, Jim."

The belt snapped. Medallions pattered on the carpet. She rammed the sheath down round her knees. It took her panties with it.

"Natalie. What's wrong?"

"Nothing wrong."

The welt on her stomach was shocking. It was bleeding. She'd been picking at it so badly the caesarean scar was more like a knife wound than something a doctor had done.

She folded herself around me, covering the hated wound, not embracing me. Her leg went up over my hip. Her breasts ground against my shirt. Her mouth closed over mine. We kissed. It shouldn't have felt good, but it did.

She ran her fingers through my hair. She unbuttoned my shirt. She took my pants off. I couldn't keep up with her nakedness. Her skin saw too much.

"Cold, Jim. Hold I."

Even with my clothes off I was suffocating. I sat on the edge of the bed completely lost. She climbed on top of me. A hand searched for my cock. It shouldn't have been stiff, but it was. She dropped onto me like a window with a broken sash cord, her arms round my neck as kissed me, her legs round my waist, her slippery depths rocking me like a stiff, awkward child.

My hands closed round her butt. Her bottom was wet, with perspiration or arousal I couldn't tell. Her shoulders were still shivering.

"I love you, Jim." I didn't know what to say. "Fuck I."

I couldn't. My body was rigid. The thread of light shone. It stung the base of my spine. I couldn't move. Her pussy rocked and squelched on my cock. The room was too hot. I wasn't breathing any more.

I felt blood from the welt smearing my belly.

"I big Buddha woman." Cyril was wrong. She wasn't stoned. She was something far worse than stoned. "You big Buddha man."

She rocked faster and faster, lubricating herself on my cock. Her eyes were empty. She was seeing with her skin.

"I angel woman. You angel man."

I didn't feel like an angel man. Bugger 'big Buddha man' too. I was a shining, stinging speck of nothingness, a pinpoint of need in a vast emptiness. Fuck 'angel man'. All I wanted was for her to hurry up and come.

"You. I. Twin two gether good good."

She sank her teeth into my shoulder. I could feel her struggling not to bite too hard, and failing. The nails combing my back suddenly dug in.

"Ow!"

I stared at the string round her wrists. A single loop of white string on either wrist, expertly knotted.

"Do I self!" She was lying. Of course Pra had tied the string. Even fingers as supple as hers couldn't have wound the string one-handed and tied such a secure knot. "I say you! Do I self!"

The whole point of tying string is that it's a blessing, a good luck charm, a ritual that one person performs upon another. 'Do I self' was blasphemous.

"You I twin two gether!" 'Together'? We were about as twinned two gether as a pair of lizards entwined in a hypnotized arabesque on a wall. "You I high class. Can do two gether!"

She lurched across me, her pussy clutching my cock, masturbating in my lap, and rooted around in her handbag.

She took out a ball of white string.

I felt like laughing. *I* was getting the string treatment now. It was my turn to be blessed. She was going to tie the string round my wrists, to go with the string Pra had tied around her wrists!

"Natalie. I..." She laughed out loud. "No!"

She was winding the string round her throat!

"Natalie! NO!" She lifted her hair at the back and got the string tight around her windpipe. "Stop it!"

Her eyes were a viscid haze. She wound the string around her throat a second, a third time.

"Just joking, honey." She wrapped the string around her throat a fourth time, pulled it tight and knotted it. "You prince. I princess. Chai?" She reached, and looped the string around my throat! "Mummy Daddy say no! You I drown our self two gether."

I tore at the skein of string. She wasn't joking. She was rehearsing unspeakable sex acts.

"Natalie don't!"

Her arms were around my neck, festooning my throat in string. The string round her throat tugged so tight the skin turned pale where it dug in. She started to choke.

"Just funny, Jim. Just making joke."

I tore at the string. I couldn't breathe. The stupid game was exciting her. She kissed me again and again, her pussy jerking on my cock, her butt lifting and jerking trying to come.

"He... don know ... I... I big Buddha woman..."

"He?"

"... He don know you big Buddha man..."

"Who?"

She was incoherent. Gargling sounds were coming out of her throat.

Surely 'he' was Pra.

"... Yes... yes... come on... fuck I..."

She'd tied the string so tightly round her Adam's apple I couldn't get my fingers under it. I was choking her. I forced my fingers under the ligature, choking her more.

"Natalie! Don't be stupid!"

I got my fingernails under the string. Her face turned red. Her body jerked. The knot slipped and the tangle of string came loose.

Her head flopped forward.

"Just joking, honey... just bit fun..."

She flowed into my arms. Waves of slippery warmth streamed up her back under my hands. She cried out something in Thai. Her bottom lifted, kicking on my cock. She was trembling so much it felt less like an orgasm than a spasm of fear.

I couldn't respond. I felt nothing. Swaddled in wet heat, my cock had been sprayed with pipe freeze and disconnected. I was as scared as she was.

CHAPTER SIX

Javindra was right. The Arms Fair had started. I half expected to hear from Jack again, or perhaps even see Jack on TV outside the ExCel Centre amongst the protesters being hauled away by police. At times the protests grew violent. Demonstrators in Halloween masks lay down in the road outside the Centre. Police horses broke up picket lines. A vicar joined the anarchists going under the hooves. News coverage of the protests outside alternated with shots of the ExCel Centre's vast interior, photogenic jets and missiles suspended outside time, politicians giving interviews in front of tanks.

'He' was Pra. 'He don know I big Buddha woman' was merely some row she'd had with Pra. The crazy thing with the string around her neck was just revenge on Pra. They'd had a fight. 'He' had nothing to do with Soom Bon's junkie fantasies or Jack's 'sick fucking evil fucking cunts'.

Javindra was also right about Lee's girls being busy. Pauline, Gigi, Carla and Amy were all seeing Arms Fair delegates, their normal Hackney or Kilburn routine out the window in a heady round of snatched luncheons, expensive trysts and late night parties militated by the punters' busy schedules. Lee's connection with the Arms Fair scene through Adrian Whitely was paying dividends. When the girls weren't with their customers, they often popped into Stratford, even if Natalie wasn't there, so I saw a lot of Frank and Javindra too. Javindra was more uptight than usual, Frank was even more miserable. Pauline boasted about her Russian and how much money he was spending on her. Gigi, Carla and Amy were more reticent, but they were all getting bigger tips than they ever got in Hackney or Kilburn.

Javindra— his spite was almost pathological— insisted that Natalie had an Arms Fair customer too. I didn't bother to disabuse

him. Whatever his arrangement with Gigi was, or his familiarity
with the sex trade, it had left him incapable of entertaining the
notion of anything so simple as loyalty or love. I'd seen Natalie's
wedding dress, the stunning Thai wedding sheath she'd gone to
the temple in and come home in such a terrible state. No wonder
she'd been distraught, all those necklaces and bangles, tearing at
the golden ornaments in her hair, no wonder she'd done that crazy
sex thing with the string, not even telling her mother or Nok of
her marriage, her mother and Nok not even being there at the
temple, leaving her mother and daughter at the party to be scowled
at by Mrs Leepatawat, and instead of the ceremony there'd had an
argument and Pra had backed out at the last minute!

Not even Cyril knew about Natalie's relationship with the
monk. Cyril spoke Thai, but no one had told him that Nok was
Pra's daughter. Cyril was still under the illusion that Pra was
Natalie's uncle, and that he'd travelled to England merely to take
over at the Leytonstone temple. Cyril, for all his Thai know-how,
had swallowed the story about Pra coming on the same flight as
Natalie's mother and daughter as a mere chaperone for nervous
females. Even Cyril, with all his 'geezer hurts my girls, he's dead',
didn't know what was going on.

Cyril loved his girls. He kept as close an eye on them as
humanly possible, but when they went to see their Arms Fair
customers they went on their own. They were picked up in
chauffeur driven cars and dropped back in taxis. Cyril wasn't
allowed to even take them to their rendezvous let alone wait
outside in case there were problems. These were wealthy, powerful
men, politicians and arms trade insiders. They didn't want to be
tailed by a dreadlocked ex-doorman. That week Cyril was on a
short fuse. On the couple of occasions I saw him at Stratford, the
big man was abrupt and edgy. Being shut out of the Arms Fair
setup upset him. He kept as close an eye on Pauline, Gigi, Amy

and Carla as he could, from a distance. He still seemed to believe, as he had on the night he'd interrogated me in my car, that Lee was lining up a 'big man' for Natalie through Adrian Whitely, and that Natalie had some bee in her bonnet about Adrian's 'big man'. Cyril's protective instinct had its erotic side. Natalie's relationship with Pra had slipped under his radar completely.

I still felt unsettled by the night with the string. Maybe Pra wasn't quite the impressive spiritual presence I'd driven home from Heathrow. He had his wild side too. There was his Red Bull tattoo, maybe just a teenage aberration, but still evidence that Pra had had a life before the sangha. Natalie certainly had her wild side, sex without a condom for an extra tenner. She'd had her wild side back then, in Bangkok, working as a prostitute and not using contraceptives. It was hard to pin her down that week. She was in and out. I hardly got a chance to sit her down and talk to her about what had happened after the party. It was over and done with. She hardly remembered. She had more important things on her mind. Throttling herself with blessing string was just a bit of fun. A joke, honey. Lovers' horseplay, why was I so uptight? I was uptight because we'd been fucking at the time, not very efficiently or lovingly, but technically having sex. I couldn't tell how she'd managed to keep breathing. She'd choked me. I'd nearly passed out. What would have happened if we'd both passed out? It wasn't funny. What was even less funny was her determination to lie about it now. She'd been angry. I'd never seen such fury in my life. Her rage was even more frightening than her crazy sex games. She'd come back from the temple berserk. I could understand that she'd felt hurt and slighted, but her love had turned to an almost insane level of hatred. 'He don know I big Buddha woman.' She was as crazy as Jack. Her 'he' was as mad as Jack's Devil, as 'these people and the sick, fucking, evil fucking, stuff they're into'.

On consideration, it wasn't really a surprise that Jack never showed up in the TV footage of the Arms Fair protests. Jack was probably in Jakarta or Nicaragua by now, ahead of the game, his work in London done. The death machine moves fast. The Globalist Elite don't let the grass grow under their feet. Something big had already gone down, and the news had missed it as usual, or, more likely, covered it up. Soros and his Arms Fair buddies had had their sex party. The Illuminati had consolidated their secrecy and moved on, and Jack was out there somewhere hard on their heels.

I wondered whether Jack had flipped suddenly, or whether it had been a slow revelation by revelation descent from crazy theorizing into actual craziness. Somewhere along the way Jack had lost it. Either all at once, or gradually, he'd turned from a well-informed pundit who people listened to to a man with the Devil's name in his possession. The world economic system was a death machine, but the death machine all came back to names that Jack knew and nobody else did and the sick fucking evil fucking stuff they're into. It was a form of religious belief, with no possibility of redemption.

I was spending more and more time at Stratford. Staying nights in Stratford was easier than creeping up the stairs to the box bedroom in Islington. I still hadn't spoken to Melissa. I kept putting it off. Every time I decided to set aside a couple of hours to talk to her something came up at Stratford, or else I just had too much on my mind to give Melissa the attention she deserved. I still hadn't read through the petition of divorce properly or filed the receipt of notification but I still had four or five weeks.

I'd brought my books with me. Nights when Natalie wasn't there I escaped from the non-stop party downstairs or Natalie's mother and Nok fighting in the kitchen and shut myself in the bedroom with *The Serpent Power*, *Freedom From The Known* and *The End Of Time*. I left *Bravo Two Zero* in Islington. Andy McNab's

mission behind enemy lines wasn't as crucial as quantum physics
tangled in sexual magic and a new neural setup. In their different
ways, all three books seemed to be based on the traditional idea
of 'maya'—that the world is an illusion. I wondered whether, as a
Buddhist, Natalie believed in 'maya'. Probably not. Her Buddhism
seemed more superstition than metaphysics. She was too alive to
ever countenance 'maya'. At times her 'prince and princess in life
before' drowning in the Phraya River seemed to hark back to a
world even older than Buddhism, to a culture of blood feuds and
vengeance, a primordial world that had less trouble with Hackney
Sauna and 'sex without' for an extra tenner than my bourgeois one
did. In this even more ancient world 'Buddha talked shit.' Natalie
went to the temple. She was into blessing string and joined in the
temple ceremonies but when Buddha said 'bad people dumb' He
talked shit. Krishnamurti preached a new neural setup but he had
his job cut out with hatreds as ancient as that. Hatreds and loves.
The wave function could hover over endless probability without
ever hitting on a configuration as simple and sublime as Natalie's
hatred and love.

I'd seen it the first time I met her, in the blast of the Kilburn fan
heater— that the world is finished before it gets to your eyes, that
this still new-smelling mattress is done-with, long gone, odourless
before it ever reaches my nose, that the central heating is crinking
an eternity ago, in my past and no one else's. By the time I
registered it, even my own body, the thump of blood in my chest,
the hammering in my skull, were so in the past, they felt as
over-and-done-with as the book in my hands. That's the problem
with maya. That's what's wrong with this world-as-illusion stuff.
There's no comfy, flesh-and-blood being plumped down in the
middle of the illusion to observe and enjoy it. There is no being,
certainly no 'I', there's only an illusion looking at illusion, forever
on the cusp, this thread of light, this stinging brightness, the world

turning on a shining hinge, towards something incomprehensible, towards something which can only be feared, and it must be feared because it is the source of evil as well as good. That's what Krishnamurti didn't seem to understand, complacently freeing his mind from the known. *The End Of Time* didn't even address it. The transcendent light sees everything and lights nothing. It brings the past back to life, even this new-smelling mattress, even the central heating's crinking and the book in my hands, it brings the future into the present, except... Natalie was right. 'Buddha talk shit'. So was *The Serpent Power* right. The path it proposed was appalling. The book was a study of something called 'Tantra', the worship of 'She Who Is Outside The Universe, And Goes Upwards'. 'Kundalini' was its name for the unapproachable woman, the one who shone and stung. She is the source. She brings all to life, the past and the future in the now. She makes death and life one thing. She dances with you when you no longer are, on a frozen footpath or a strobe-lit floor. As she approaches you recede, become nothing, the man who should have walked away up the footpath and got on with his life. But you didn't. You walked down the aisle between the bins. You pressed the buzzer by the green star: ORINETAL BABE. Because evil isn't ignorance, evil is more than just dumbness, that's why evil has such tenacity and force. *The Serpent Power* spoke of ignorance not as a lack of understanding but as an intoxication, as *asava*, a Dionysian drunkenness. Ignorance is the inebriation at the heart of desire. Evil intoxicates, and is intoxicating. Since all manifestation is intoxicated desire, understanding is helpless against it. If there really was a 'death machine' running amok in the world, Jack was high on it. If the New World Order was real, then it had got Jack sloppy drunk. Just like I was drunk on Natalie.

I'd assumed that Jack had dropped out of sight, and that maybe— if what he'd told me wasn't simply paranoia— he'd been deported, or else he was sitting with Sylvia in an 'underground' studio somewhere podcasting on the dark web.

I was shocked when, on the third day of the Arms Fair, Jack called me and said he had the money he'd borrowed from me, and wanted to return it.

"Let's meet up, Jim. I've got your two thousand."

He sounded in a hurry.

I hadn't expected to get the money back at all. Jack hadn't given the impression, the last time I'd seen him, that returning my two thousand pounds was top of his list of priorities. Now he spoke like a man with a ticking bomb in his hands, desperate to hand it on to someone else before it exploded. His tone was unsettling, but then Jack had always had a melodramatic side.

"Are you staying in the same place?"

I was in Stratford, just about to drive to over Notting Hill to put in an appearance at work. Jack's hotel in Kings Cross was a bit out of my way.

"Good God, no. Are you out of your mind?" I felt irritated. It was a bit rich being asked if I was out of my mind by a nutjob like Jack. "They busted the hotel weeks ago. I was lucky to get out of there in one piece."

I suddenly felt tired. It was ten in the morning, and I was already exhausted. If I hadn't needed the two thousand pounds so badly I would have told him to keep it.

"Where are you?"

He gave me an address in Wealdstone.

"Wealdstone?"

He was talking about a two hour drive from Stratford, right across northwest London, almost out to Harrow. It wasn't just the length of the drive—two hours there, two hours back— it was hard even picturing Jack way out there in the suburban hinterland.

He gave me an address.

"How long will you be?"

He was hurrying me!

"Can't I pick it up tomorrow?"

"I won't be here tomorrow, Jim."

Jack's games were exhausting. It was like dealing with a willful child, so absorbed in his play world every adult in the vicinity has to participate.

He was giving me the bum's rush *because he imagined our conversation was being tracked!* I could feel it. *M.I.6 were listening!*

"I need to talk to you, Jim."

Christ. He was after something. Jack needed something from me in return for the money.

A month ago, before I met Natalie, I would have let him keep the money. He was an old friend, in trouble. Two thousand pounds was a lot, but I could have afforded it for a mate down on his luck. I didn't want to drag myself all the way out to Wealdstone, but I was running out of money again. The twenty two thousand I'd given Lee to pay off Natalie's contract had eaten into my available cash, and there was another interest payment due on the loan.

I went to tell Jack I was on my way, but he'd already rung off.

Maybe it was only reluctance to waste half my day, but I felt disoriented as I headed out through Golders Green and Hendon, and turned northwest along Kingsbury Road. Suburbia had no end. Northwest London went on and on. There was no such thing as countryside or an ocean out there somewhere beyond, just shopping arcade after shopping arcade, the miles of bungalows and semi-detacheds in between creating an illusion of competition between the Icelands and the Costcos, the IKEAs and the B and Qs. A dingy hotel in Kings Cross was Jack's habitat, not this suburban wasteland. Dubai or Singapore or L.A, anywhere but here. It made me worry about him. These mock Tudor high streets barnacled with brand names from middle-America were the worst place in the world for a paranoiac like Jack. Or perhaps that was just me.

The address Jack had given me— he'd told me not to use my sat nav—was in a long, wide street of nineteen-fifties villas, their front gardens paved over to accommodate numbers of cars that seemed too great for the size of the houses.

The house looked small out front, but when a man opened the glazed front door to a tinkle of wind chimes, I was led through a vista of bare, chic rooms into a marble-floored conservatory out back where the house had been extended into the long back garden. Whoever owned Jack's 'safe house' had money.

Jack looked fatter, physically bigger than when I'd last seen him. He'd shaved and cleaned himself up. He'd developed a pneumatic double chin that had been masked, at our last meeting, by his Steve Bannon stubble. His eyes seemed more pumped up too.

"Hiya, Jim. Glad you could make it." He'd veered from paranoid to businesslike. He introduced me to the man who'd answered the door and a middle-aged Pakistani whose house it was. He informed them: "Jim's the guy leant me the two grand when I had that trouble at Heathrow."

The men thanked me for helping Jack, but made no attempt to give me back my money. I was anxious to get the two thousand and get back to Stratford— work was out of the question now— but instead we sat down round a wicker and glass coffee table and looked out at a hardwood deck bigger than most London gardens.

Jack's situation had become more fraught since I'd last seen him.

"Sorry to drag you out here, Jim, but I'm in danger of my life."

I felt more than exhausted. If I sat here much longer I'd nod off. I just wanted to get my money and go. I tried to keep it light:

"I thought death threats were par for the course for you activists."

Jack was way beyond lightness.

"I'm not talking about the internet, Jim." Irony was wasted on him. "They've put a contract out on me..." Jack had the presence of mind not to mention the Hungarian billionaire by name. "... This thing's big. It could blow the Arms Fair out of the water."

He was serious. Jack's persecutors had gone up a gear from visa hassles at Heathrow to sending armed killers after him. I felt angry. I had enough problems of my own without having to sit and listen to Jack's struggle with the globalist elite all over again. What an egotist the guy was! His take on life was so important people needed to kill him for it. Jack never had mere folks he couldn't get along with. He had to have the New World Order on his case. His solipsism was breathtaking. Jack's enemies weren't mere dodgy businessmen, they were a 'sex ring'. They weren't just sleazy and greedy, they had to hurt women for fun as well, they had to kill women for pleasure. Jack's struggle was so central, the 'sex ring' he'd uncovered at the Arms Fair weren't just a gang of corrupt VIPs, they were criminal 'fiends'. Only the Devil was worthy of Jack's enmity. The guy whose name Jack had, and whom Jack was about to expose— we were talking corporate chiefs, bankers, heads of state—was Satan Incarnate. You need a Satan Incarnate to wrestle with when you're as big a man as Jack.

He couldn't bring the cartel, gang, ring, whatever they were, to book through their business dealings, but he'd found a way to get at them through their sexual proclivities.

"It's sick, Jim. Fucking sick. Fox comes on TV..." Jack's imitation of a ministerial accent sounded more like Mister Punch than Liam Fox. "... 'The Arms Fair provides a platform for international engagement'... blah blah blah... 'UK export license criteria are the most stringent in the world...' blah blah blah... it's a fucking joke."

The export clearance of arms sales overseas— by the FCO and the DIT, whoever they were— was so lax and corrupt, it was impossible, even with the evidence collected by people like Jack, to take the cartels to either the UK courts or the international courts. It was a business run on backhanders and insider trading, lubricated with bribes and murder. The cartel's members came from all over the world. Bringing a legal case against them was out of the question. Getting at them through their personal crimes was the only way to bring the evil doers to book.

"Personal?"

"They're into some sick fucking evil fucking stuff, Jim."

Like all religious nuts, Jack had his mantra.

These guys—they were all men—killed people, in Yemen, in the Philippines, in Afghanistan, for money. Between themselves, in their own circle, they killed for pleasure. The Arms Fair was a get together of the world's sadistic fuckers and this year something big was going down. People who had unbridled power did unbridled things. It was a turn on to hold a woman's life in the palm of your hand. We were talking sex. These guys knew how to party. There's other ways of getting your rocks off besides profiting from the deaths of innocent women and children. They were Satan Incarnate, the Devil himself, and Jack had his name.

"Name?"

"Name, Jim. The big guy himself."

I looked at my watch.

"I'd best be getting back."

"That's what I wanted to talk to you about."

"*Eh?*"

A girl, it looked like the Indian man's daughter, brought me a glass of lime juice with ice cubes in it and some biscuits.

"Look. Jim. We've got hold of this..." Jack held something out to me. "... If you could use it..."

He was insane. I'd worn them before, at engineering conferences and construction industry seminars. The long, blue ribbon to go around your neck. The plastic wallet on the end of the ribbon. The I.D. card with the photo and certification number.

"... Jack, no... this is ridiculous..."

"You can change the photo. It's just a standard passport photo. They don't check it that closely."

I was dealing with children, with little kids playing games.

"I can't front up there myself, of course." Jack leered. "Neither can Siva or Ferdinand. You don't have to do anything..."

"Jack, please."

"... Just check out a face. We've got the stand number..."

He pushed a photograph at me, across the table.

A jowly face. Wavy black hair. A pugnacious nose.

"... We just need to know whether he's here yet or not. If he is he'll be at the stand, we've got all the details... you can't miss him..."

He pushed the photo closer.

So that was him. The Devil. Satan.

It wasn't a prepossessing face. But the jowls were a bit too rosy, the hair a little too pampered, the broken nose a bit too boyish, for it to be the incarnation of Evil.

"If he's arrived, he'll be there tomorrow," said Jack. "Talking to his people."

Jack made talking to people sound like the most heinous crime a human being ever committed.

I looked at the tag.

"How'd you get hold of it?"

There was doubtless strict security at the Arms Fair. The organisers must surely vet visitor applications pretty thoroughly. They didn't want to let any protesters or nutcases in.

Accreditation— the tag said 'security analyst'— would certainly involve background checks.

"Someone I know," said Jack.

"Can't he do it?"

The photo in the I.D. tag, heat sealed into the tag itself, was of an Anglo Saxon face, but it looked nothing like mine.

"He's in America," said Jack. "The Fair gets ten thousand visitors a day, Jim. There's two and a half thousand delegates. You won't have any problems."

Jack was there already, peering through a haze of fiends at a jowly face with a broken nose.

"Just ring me once you've been. He'll either be there or he won't. That's all we need to know."

"Here's your money." The Pakistani man pushed an envelope across the table towards me. "We can give you the same again for helping us."

"No. No." Being financially obligated to them was the last thing I needed.

"He'll either be there or he won't, Jim. It won't take you more than an hour."

I picked up the I.D. tag. Jack gave me a number I could call him on. I stood up.

"I suppose so," I said. "I haven't upgraded my ground to air missile system for a while."

No one laughed.

I'd bin the tag as soon as I got out the door, and forget about the whole thing. This was the last I'd be seeing of Jack O'Grady.

Natalie'd laughed off our string-around-the-neck fuck. She'd laughed it off with a certain grim determination—'only joking, honey', 'just bit fun'— and gone back to spending most of her time with Pra. They'd patched it up. Whatever the rupture had been that put her in such a state the night of the party, they'd sorted things out by pretty much the following morning and she was back to showing her face only at odd moments in Stratford and spending the nights away. Pra had changed his mind a second time. He'd got over his cold feet. They were about to take the big step together. Not even Mrs Leepatawat, with the weight of the East London Thai community behind her, could any longer stand in their way. Natalie certainly looked relieved. She became bright and upbeat, distractedly affectionate towards me in her renewed good fortune on the brief occasions that I saw her. The string had pulled so tight around her throat the marks on her neck had still been visible the following morning, noticeable enough for her mother to see, and glance at me, and comment, Natalie so blithe in whatever excuse she made up I think I may have even learned a new Thai word. 'Mook-daloc!' 'Joke!' But it wasn't a joke. It never had been. It wasn't funny at all. The thing with the string had happened between her and me, and her and me alone. It had nothing to do with Pra or anyone else. Whether it was anger she felt towards me, the rich farang who'd tried to buy her, or she'd been drunk, or Cyril was right and she'd been stoned, her violence had been aimed solely at me, and violence it most certainly was. It had had nothing to do with the 'prince and princess' in old Siam, or the waters of the Phraya River filling our throats. The worst thing of all had been the lack of connection as she climaxed, the disconnected coldness as we fucked. I knew about erotic asphyxiation. Erotic asphyxiation had been in the news a couple of times over the years. David Carradine, the Kung Fu star, found dead in a Bangkok hotel room, trussed up in a wardrobe with a plastic bag over his face. There'd been rumours that Michael Hutchence, the INXS singer, had died from self-strangulation, alone with a heap of porn magazines. But these were just the sleazy kinks of deranged stars. They'd died alone. That was the point. Erotic asphyxiation was a form of masturbation. It

wasn't something you did with another person. Yet Natalie had
tried to do it with me.

Every time I turned up at Stratford there was someone there,
other than Natalie. Her mother and Nok seemed to have had their
fill of London and kept to the house now in a state of suspension,
with the heating turned up.

I went to see them most nights, staying late till I knew my
family in Islington would be in bed. Watching TV with Nok and
eating Natalie's mother's Northern Thai cooking beat sitting alone
in the guest room of my own house. Knocking on the front door
with the TV noise coming through the paneling was better than
creeping up the stairs when my family were still awake.

Nok chattered a little English now, and I added a few words
to her vocabulary— 'giant', 'ghost', 'champion', 'Spiderman'— but
I was glad I couldn't converse with Natalie's mother. I could sense
how upset she was about Natalie spending the nights with Pra.
She'd got over her embarrassment at my having paid to bring Pra
and Natalie together—she'd seen the marks around Natalie's
throat—but the black mark now blighting the family name was far
worse than the mere slur of a daughter's going into prostitution.

Mrs Leepatawat dropped by to scowl and lecture. Her husband
was polite enough, but the old woman assumed an authority that
owning a couple of restaurants hardly seemed to warrant. The Thai
distinction between 'HiSo' and 'Loso' made English snobbery look
egalitarian. Mrs Leepatawat spoke some English but she and I only
made polite conversation. I'd never be forgiven for paying for Pra's
ticket and bringing trouble to Wat Leytonstone. One night she
referred to Cyril as a 'nigger'. I pulled her up on it, but too mildly
to feel that I'd stood up for him properly.

Occasionally, when I turned up, Natalie's mother would be
drinking beer with a guy called Yoot, a tiny, wizened man who
worked as a porter in a block of flats in Queensway. Yoot was a

Christian. He wore a colostomy bag, which he always removed from his trousers and proudly showed me.

Carla and Gigi showed up once or twice during the day, when their escorts were busy at the Arms Fair, but I didn't see anything of Pauline or Amy. Natalie's friends were never there during the evening.

I hadn't seen Cyril for almost a week. Perhaps he was spending some nights with his long suffering wife now that he was forbidden to keep an eye on his girls.

It was time for me to sort things out with Melissa. I still hadn't spoken to her. I hadn't even dealt with the divorce papers, in fact I hadn't even read through them properly, only skimmed. I was scared that if I filled out the response to the divorce petition there and then, at whatever time of day or night it was, in whatever state of mind I was in, I might make some stupid mistake that would turn out to be a major blunder and leave me with nothing. It was better to talk things through with Melissa first.

Now that Natalie was with Pra I'd be crazy not to try and mend fences with my wife. It was over with Natalie, that much was obvious. I'd treated Melissa appallingly, but there was still our family and everything we'd built together over twenty years to weigh against the harm I'd done. Melissa would never respect me again. She might excuse moral collapse brought on by a mid-life crisis, but respect was out the window. She'd forgive me and take me back if I had the courage to speak to her honestly, but even now I wasn't sure if honesty was possible. Admitting that Melissa had been an aberration and that these last six weeks had been a nervous breakdown was even more impossible than wading through all those pages of legalese.

I put the divorce papers aside and went back to *The Serpent Power*. The book fascinated me. I was finishing it for the third time. Arthur Avalon's ponderous Raj prose style no longer put me off. Embodied Consciousness, Energy Centres, Mantras, Cosmic Cycles deserved all the capitals they could get. I felt an obscure gratitude towards the dead hippy girl who'd visited this book upon me.

The Serpent Power seemed to be making the case that consciousness takes primacy over matter. The idea was absurd. It necessitated a belief in magic. It was an arrogant proposition, elitist and hierarchical at heart. Jack would abhor it. I readily understood that materialism is itself a belief system, based on an assumption, but the spray of stars in the skylight and the angle-poise lamp by which I read, even the circle of electric light in which the lines of print filed past, had substance. Consciousness has none. Matter is more real than mind. It was a sort of snobbery to pretend otherwise. Everybody can see a table and smell a pair of dirty socks and hear the wind in the roof, but only the exceptional person, a Buddha or a Zoroaster, or a Soom Bon or a Jack, can magic things back to their conscious source. Even with the odd physicist chipping in and ending time, and the occasional Krishnamurti reengineering his brain, it requires a sort of voodoo to live at the moment where matter emerges from consciousness. And yet that was what *The Serpent Power* seemed to be advocating. That was what She Who Is Outside The Universe And Goes Upwards is.

It all came down to two things: mind control and sex. Both appealed to me. I had so many ghastly thoughts pressing in on all sides, 'emptying the mind' was attractive. Even if 'mastery over one's mental life' means little more than the ability to forget for a few seconds how bad things are, that in itself is precious. The ability to forget is as necessary as breathing. In fact, having a body at all is a form of forgetting. Living in a separate body keeps the unthinkable at a manageable distance, even if it's at the expense of a drastically reduced consciousness and condemns one to the glib assumption that only matter is real and that consciousness is a mere anaemic observer carried along by bodily forces. *The Serpent Power* asserted the opposite: that the body is the mere blurred periphery of an intenser focus.

First, the intenser focus was achieved merely as an idea, thought ascending to intuition ascending to conviction. That's where sex comes in. That's where She Who Is Outside The Universe And Goes Upwards is called Kundalini, the sidelong glance of the unapproachable woman. Only the sexual longing for her has the power to lift the intenser focus past even intuition and conviction into certainty, a certainty that is magical in its power to persuade even stars in a skylight and angle-poise lamps that they are things of the spirit, to convince even the blood thumping way back in the past in my chest that the stinging brightness that's absorbing it is truth.

It's a truth—if it's true— that is doled out in split seconds to chosen people, not through rational argument to everybody. It's a form of elitism, private and idiosyncratic, the very opposite of the globalist type of elitism that Jack railed against. If it's true, one split second of it's enough to fuck you up forever. Once the intenser focussing starts, it's impossible to stop it. I'd lost Natalie. Once Pra left the temple, I'd never see her face or touch her body again, but I didn't care. I saw her face and touched her body in the giddying split seconds when the angle-poise lamp and the stars in the skylight were so far back in the past I could see where they ended, and only the stinging brightness in my spine was real. It didn't matter that the deadness was mine alone, my past and no one else's, because the shining hinge is always turning towards something that's incomprehensible anyway.

All I was going to be left with was the memory of a ghastly fuck, string festooned around my neck and digging into Natalie's throat so tight it left a pale line in her skin, her bottom kicking and jerking on my cock, more a spasm of fear than an orgasm, to which not even my cock could respond, dead and disconnected, sprayed with pipe freeze, let alone my mind, let alone my heart. The irony wasn't lost on me that Natalie's 'just game', 'only bit fun', was a parody of *The Serpent Power*, with its science of breath control and its detailed instructions on how to suspend inhalation and force the syncope that awakens the subtle body. Natalie's flirtation with erotic asphyxiation was a satire on Arthur Avalon's resonant descriptions of the couplings of the Gods. It was almost as if she'd choked herself, and tried to choke me, knowingly—the big Buddha woman riding her corpse mate. The Terrible Goddess Kali straddling the dead Siva. The magic—if that was the proper name for it—demanded that the unapproachable woman mount the disconnected male.

The philosophy behind the magic was nothing if not gender inclusive, at least when it came to polarity. A balance is always struck between male and female, between stillness and movement, between absence and presence, between death and life. The unapproachable woman, she who shines and stings, is drawn into being by the male's non-being. I'd seen it as the string tightened around her throat— the motionless Male with whom the Goddess dances. He wasn't me.

I became so absorbed in contemplation of these matters that I began supplementing my three core texts with other books which I picked up in a bookshop in Camden Town. The bookshop had a big Spirituality section. There seemed to be thousands of books on the subject. I'd never realized what a large area the Occult covered. It wasn't a problem. An inner prompting led me unerringly to the volumes I needed: *The Doctrine Of The Awakening* and *The Yoga Of Power* by an Italian writer called Julius Evola. A nineteen twenties translation of the *Upanishads*. Irwin Schrodinger's nineteen fifties *Tarner Lectures* on the unitary nature of consciousness. A book about *The Corpus Hermeticum* by a medieval alchemist called

Abraham The Jew. *The Art Of Tantra* by Phillip Rawson, filled with stunning photographs of Tibetan mandalas and Rajasthani album paintings of the copulatory positions. *Immortality And Freedom* by Mircea Eliade.

I'd given up going to the office. Things were getting so unpleasant there, with the Rampton Street job and the Arkwright debacle, there was no point in me showing my face.

Work on Rampton Street had stopped altogether. The site had been closed down while Kingsmead Holdings went into liquidation. The liquidators were now trying to recoup their losses by suing us. We'd signed up for impossible deadlines and agreed to swingeing penalty clauses, and now, on top of loss of income, had legal fees to pay.

Bernard and Pippa were trying to thrash out a rescue package, but they were keeping me in the dark about the details. I wanted to be kept in the dark. I could feel my business going belly up, but there was little I could do about it except sign the papers Bernard and Pippa thrust in front of me from time to time.

It was when I was in the office that Natalie's going off with Pra hit me hardest. The yawing dread of being swept under financially was swamped by something far more unbearable. Everything that had ever been important to me, even my family, meant nothing compared to the loss of 'Nok same bird' welling up inside me, or her eye shadow not keeping up with the tapering lift of her eyes, of her body in a pink petticoat and Smurf slippers making a frozen footpath beautiful.

Concentrating on the details of the documents Bernard and Pippa thrust under my nose, or even the divorce papers, which I still hadn't returned, was impossible. I needed all my concentration to focus on the thing that had happened when Pra walked through the Arrivals gate. Those were the details that counted—not money and not even my home were important— the old man with the box of mangoes tied to his suitcase, Nok's reserved, slightly guarded expression, Natalie scolding her for getting chocolate on her dress as the man she loved appeared in a blaze of orange.

I'd thought that the weeks I'd spent with Natalie had been a descent into unspeakable shallowness, but that was completely wrong. It was the office, money, business, even family, that were shallow, life thinned down to a mere surface, and only Natalie's eyes, her stunning face and breathtaking body had depth.

I woke up next morning remembering I'd promised Jack I'd go to the Arms Fair. The I.D tag for the ExCel Centre was still in my pocket. I'd forgotten to bin it.

I'd spent the night at Stratford. The house was empty. Natalie was with Pra. Her mother and Nok had gone shopping with Mrs Leepatawat.

I couldn't face the office. The photo Jack had given me of the fucking sick evil fucking fucker was also in my pocket, along with the tag. I'd promised Jack I'd check the guy out. I decided to do it.

I got dressed, had a shave and drove down to Royal Victoria Dock. It wasn't far from Stratford. I parked in Docklands Road.

I'd been to the ExCel Centre a number of times before, for engineering and construction industry exhibitions, but never on a day as raw as this.

A wind like a bastard rasp filed the shuddering water in the bastardized dock. The yachts had flown south for the winter.

The DSEI flags tugged at their aluminium poles.

Even the exhibition centre's bleak glass entrance managed to look welcoming from out in this freezing morning.

The steps were crowded. A police cordon was keeping a straggle of protesters from harassing the Arms Fair visitors.

As I went in, a masked man carrying a scythe asked me if I enjoyed murdering children.

The photo on my I.D. tag looked nothing like me, but Jack was right. The entrance to the Centre was busy. My I.D. received only a cursory glance.

I grabbed a coffee and croissant from a stall in the foyer and headed into the main hall, Satan's photo in my pocket.

The stand where Jack had told me to look for him was closed.

It wasn't one of the more impressive stands, a featureless cordoned-off space, a row screens, a logo on a placard— something to do with 'intelligent delivery'— and a kitchen table and chairs that looked as if they'd come out of a Swedish design shop, presumably for customers to sit at and discuss intelligent delivery with the sales rep, when he bothered to turn up.

I realized I'd wasted my morning. It occurred to me that Jack hadn't been specific as to *when exactly* we might expect the sick evil fucker to turn up. The Fair opened at ten and closed at eight. The Devil could show his face at any time— now, lunchtime, seven in the evening. He could have popped in and out already. Surely Jack didn't expect me to hang around for ten hours on the off chance of glimpsing the face in the photo in this shuffling crowd. If the photo in my pocket was indeed the death machine's leading light, he presumably wasn't going to man the stand himself all day long, handing out brochures and chatting to time-wasters till I clocked him. I felt irritated. It was typical of Jack. All or nothing. Hypnotize yourself with the big picture, bugger details like time and place. If the picture's global enough, *global elite* enough, the details will look after themselves. The New World Order is so omniscient and so omnipotent even blank screens and unmanned tables and unattended exhibits fit seamlessly into the overall scheme. Jack was a believer in synchronicity. It wouldn't have surprised me if he'd assumed that the moment of my wandering into the Fair and Satan's appearance would be linked by inexorable destiny. Bugger him.

I went for a wander.

The last time I'd been in the ExCel Centre the hall had been filled with bore drilling heads and filtration units, modular cladding systems and surveying drones. The ground-to-air missiles, tanks, jet fighters and advance warning systems that filled the vast space had pretty much the same impact as the construction equipment, except today a draught of despair seemed to be blowing down the aisles between the exhibits, whispering of the uselessness of consciousness in the presence of these slim armatures and aerodynamic fins even more snugly secured from their consummation than the drilling heads from rock and groundwater and the modular cladding systems from vertiginous heights. It was here, exactly here, in the presence of these profiles and casings that consciousness became a mere anaemic observer, carried along. These titanium alloys and polymer resins were the intenser focus that the dealers and the military men and the politicians wandered in the periphery of, along with the murdered and the maimed. I drifted past display tables of handguns that tugged on anti-theft flexi-chains, mannequins modelled fire retardant camouflage outfits on sandbags filled from distant deserts, logistics and communications stands glimmered like command centres under the incoming fluorescence. Perhaps it was just the stuffiness and noise after the cold outside, body heat boiling to the surface from frozen bone, the dire opposite of a footpath in Kilburn afflicting me with the opposite giddiness, no awning to grab hold of, no aisle to walk down between wire bins, no door to take me in, no green star ORIENTAL BABE on the jamb to take me in out of this intenser focus of shapes that mean nothing and have no reality till they take to the air and knock down buildings and tear you limb from limb. I felt bilious. There was nowhere to sit down. Natalie was gone. I'd never see her again. She'd never really existed at all. All she'd done was turn everything to sheer surface, even my boiling chest and the thumping of my heart, to nothing but surface, then vanished into thin air. She'd left me here with non-being and its sleek metallurgy, transcending everything I know to be real. I should have realized. Magic is real, but it comes from outside in, not inside out. Transcendence pushes in from outside, belittling consciousness, crushing reality in the heart, making me nothing. Jack was right. Transcendence is bigger than any system. Evil is stronger than good. Not even the Globalist Elite can hold a candle to transcendent evil. The New World Order is merely evil's concession to illusion. Transcendence can obliterate the ExCel Centre as surely as these aerodynamic fins and titanium alloys will knock down buildings somewhere else. It can crush even five star generals and wheeler dealers under this skeletal roof of ducts and cabling as instantly as women and children under collapsed mud. It's merely evil's concession to delusion that it doesn't do it right now. Evil makes its own allowances for illusions such as the solidity of this rubberized floor or the certainty that the struts and beams above aren't about to fall in. There was nowhere to sit down. There was no awning to hold onto. The claustrophobia grew intolerable. A man in a double breasted blazer sat on tank tracks making a call on his mobile, a Louis Vuitton carpet bag at his feet, taking up the one available seating space. It shouldn't matter that the unapproachable woman was gone— after all, she was only ever unapproachable. It shouldn't matter that the disconnected male had no one to mount him, Siva just a corpse again, no Kali to straddle him. I searched the faces of the men for signs of evil, the mark of Cain on a forehead, Baphomet's horns under a peaked cap, but all the expressions seemed either stolid or innocently bland.

The faces seemed either stolid or bland because none of them were real. Non-entity glazed every eye. Of course the faces lacked being! Even the crushed children and murdered women were no longer real. How could these shuffling perusers pretend to be? It takes more than stars on a jaunty cap or a rosy smile to make dead eyes turn real. It takes more than a double breasted blazer or a phone at the ear to confer reality on a blank expression. Amongst the promenading stares the women's faces were as disoriented as the men's. I wondered if I'd see Pauline on the arm of a chunky Slav, or Gigi relaxing with an African potentate, having a break from Javindra. I laughed out loud. I shook my head. Of course not. Lee's girls weren't allowed in here. Lee's girls were for after hours, the real thing. These women parading in twinsets and pearls and chadors and dhukus were VIPs, the wives of defence ministers and five star generals.

There'd been moments in the last six weeks when I'd felt lost and hopeless, empty and beaten, but this was different, this malice pressing in on me was active, hyperactive. It wasn't just that the heat and the noise were over-and-done-with, that the rubberized floor and skeletal ceiling were way back in the past, that even the Challenger 2 tank painted all over with the Union Jack and BORN IN BRITAIN on the side was already ended, dead before it reached my eyes, this was malice against even anything as simple as heat and noise, a destructiveness turned against even rubberized floors and skeletal ceilings, a hatred aimed at even its own most cherished products, a mocking tank, a snide jet, a sarcastic assault rifle. I was dying. Of course I was dying. Death had been ever-present throughout my body from the day of my conception. The fact that it was my past and mine alone, the private suicide pre-programmed into everything I thought and felt, didn't prevent it from partaking in a destruction that was everywhere and would never end. The shining thread in my spine candesced and blinded me. The stinging was everywhere. The shining hinge stopped turning. Evil is all too comprehensible. Everything to my right— a brochure trampled under a gleaming boot, a tank exploding again and again on a loop on a screen—was heavy and dense. Everything to my left— a

Humvee up off its wheels, a small boy in a tunic holding the hand of a man wearing the same tunic—was light and insubstantial. I felt giddy. I started to lose my balance. I needed to sit down somewhere. I was lost inside the shining thread. I wasn't just giddy. The shining hinge stopped turning and I dropped through blackness. I reached out. There was nothing to hold onto. No awning, not even the incomprehensible. I man stared at me. I was gripping his shoulder. The man glared. He too was filled with malice. My legs gave way.

I came to sitting low to the floor on plywood and carpet. I was sitting on the corner of a stand's raised platform. Hands holding unread brochures, a Dior shoulder-bag on long gold chains, a fist, passed at eye level. The noise and heat were as bad as ever. I wished I was back in the days when I thought the shining thread was just a trapped nerve, the stinging in my spine just something muscular, the presence of evil just a turn. I was even madder than Jack O'Grady. At least Jack had the New World Order to look in the eye. At least Jack had the Globalist Elite to defy. George Soros is just a big pudgy loveable baby compared to the reality of evil. The grim reaper who'd assailed me at the door was right. I enjoyed murdering children. I couldn't get enough of atrocity.

I circulated. I circled back to the stand where Jack's 'sick, evil cunt' was supposed to be, but the stand was still closed. I went for a wander.

In a knot of listeners a face I'd seen on TV, rosy-cheeked, boyish, some politician or other, was entertaining us tour guide style. He was as full of life as a sixth former apple bobbing at a Somerset fete.

A statuesque Asian woman in traditional costume gave me a wonderful smile. Not Natalie.

The carpet bagger again in his double breasted jacket, sitting on his tank track, still on the phone.

I had to get out of here. It was time to leave.

Walls flew away. Children's bodies tumbled in shattered concrete. Women wailed in inconsolable dialects.

The screams and wails gathered in the ceiling.

Like any shopping mall, the visual stimulus at floor level was deemed significant enough to warrant a cut-price ceiling complete with casually exposed cabling and banks of conduits. Billions of pounds worth of hardware was showcased on the shiny floors, while above our heads the building's innards were on display. I could only stare, not hear or feel. Hearing and feeling were forbidden by these inexplicable machines staring back at me.

I made my way back to Jack's stand. It was open. The screens had been switched on. The display cabinet was lit. The sales rep hovered.

Two men sat at the kitchen table. I recognized both of them. The flushed jowls, wavy hair and broken nose weren't exactly the same as the face in the photo in my pocket, but Jack's 'sick, evil cunt' was easily recognisable. The other man's affected scruffiness, his boyish face and hint of early double chin were even more recognisable. Jack's incarnation of evil was talking to Adrian Whitely.

The sun had come out, but as I left the exhibition centre the day felt rawer than ever.

Down by the water bronze dockers froze in a headache-y dazzle.

Beyond a chaos of access roads and municipal landscaping the curved, curtain-window façade of a hotel moaned like a musical instrument.

I rang Natalie. Her phone was still switched off. I needed to speak to her badly.

I thought of going to the temple, but she and Pra wouldn't be at Wat Buddharama now. They were holed up in a hotel somewhere, or else staying with sympathisers in the Thai community.

I tried Cyril. Talking to Cyril might help.

His phone rang for a long time but Cyril didn't answer.

I thought about ringing Jack and telling him that I'd seen the man in his photo, but decided to do it later when I'd had time to think about the fact that it was Adrian Whitely that Jack's 'sick, evil cunt' had been talking to.

As I unlocked my car, my phone rang. Thank God. Cyril had rung back. Maybe even Natalie.

"Jim?" It was Melissa. It was the first I'd spoken to her in nearly a week. She sounded hysterical. "It's the police. The police are here. They want to speak to you. They say it's urgent."

I was handed over to a man with an anxiously bland voice like one of the Channel Four newsreaders, I couldn't think which one.

He asked me if I knew Jack O'Grady. I said yes, and he told me to go to Paddington Green police station at once. It wasn't a request, it was an instruction. I asked him why but he wouldn't say.

I disconnected before he could hand me back to Melissa.

A second later my phone rang again.

"... Jim...?" It was Natalie. "... Can take Mum Nok airport...?"

"Eh?"

"Morning two morrow. You can?"

It took me a moment to realize what she was talking about.

Her mother and Nok were flying back to Thailand in the morning. It didn't make any sense. They'd been here for a little over a week. We'd arranged for them to stay three months.

"Look. Natalie..."

"I speak you later."

She disconnected. I called her back but her phone was switched off.

I started the car.

Paddington Green Police Station was where they held terrorist suspects. Fucking Jack O'Grady was in trouble again. God knows why he'd given them the house number instead of my mobile. M.I.6 or some frigging thing. He probably wanted the two grand back.

I had a million more important things to do than sorting out Jack's latest fuckup. I resented having to drive all the way over to Paddington, but I'd promised the police so I'd better go. I seemed to have spent most of the last week in the car.

So.

They'd finally caught up with Jack.

His story about being hassled at Heathrow over the Arms Fair hadn't all been fantasy.

Jack was a British citizen. They couldn't be deporting him.

It must be money again. Jack needed a bond to get bailed out till his court appearance. I prayed it wasn't too much. He'd certainly abscond.

Jack was dead. The police wanted me to identify his body. Jack's phone had disappeared but they'd got my address from a scrap of paper they'd found in his pocket. Jack had always cared too much about the big picture, and overlooked the details.

Two policemen took me to a morgue facility in the basement of St Mary's Hospital. The one in plain clothes gave the impression that he was pretty senior.

He asked me why my address had been on Jack's body. I told him that I'd loaned Jack two thousand pounds.

Had Jack payed me back? No, not yet.

He asked me if I knew why Jack had returned to England at this particular time, and whether I knew what Jack's activities had been since his return. Had Jack spoken about the Arms Fair to me?

I answered no to both questions.

The detective asked me if I'd seen Jack since the day I'd leant him the money.

I hoped like hell that Jack's sat nav fears had been paranoia, and didn't mention my visit to Wealdstone.

The bullet had entered Jack's face just under his left eye. Someone had closed his right eye, but the impact had left a mess of tissue where his left eyeball should have been. He looked like a man squinting into a telescope.

By the time I'd been questioned by a number of different officers and filled in some forms, it was almost five.

I felt bad not speaking to Melissa after I'd finished talking to the police on my phone. I'd put off speaking to her for far too long. It was time to go home and have it out.

When I got back to Islington Melissa was sitting in the kitchen, alone, not doing anything, not cooking or washing up, just sitting at the table.

I realised how much we'd been avoiding each other these last weeks, she avoiding me as much as I'd avoided her, even though we were, at least some of the time, living in the same house.

Talking at the kitchen table felt strange and awkward.

Pra. The Arms Fair. Adrian Whitely. Jack. Jack's 'sick, evil fucker'. My mind was all over the place, it was everywhere but here.

Melissa looked terrible. There was a nervous tremor around her eyes that made her look old. She'd got thinner.

"Gordon says you haven't returned the papers yet."

It hit me that I'd walked into Paddington Green Police Station with Jack's photo of some renegade arms dealer in my pocket. I'd binned the I.D tag but forgotten the photo. If the police had searched me, God knows what sort of trouble I might have been in.

"You haven't even signed the acceptance of service."

It was me, not the face in the photo, who was the 'sick, evil cunt', doing this to someone I loved.

"... Yeah, well... I thought we should talk about it first... before I sent the papers back... there's plenty of time..."

I'd forgotten the exact length of time I had to return the papers, but it certainly hadn't expired yet.

"*Plenty of time*? Jim, this is killing me."

Tears sprang up from the tremor around her eyes.

"... No. Of course. I meant... time... time to talk..."

Each time I'd put off looking at the divorce filings I'd told myself that I needed to talk to Melissa first, but now that we were talking , I didn't know where to begin. Natalie's staying with Pra had hurt me worse than I thought. I'd imagined that now that Natalie was living with Pra getting it together again with Melissa would be easier, or at least more urgent. But the opposite was true. I was missing Natalie so badly I felt a numb inability to love my wife.

"Talk about what, Jim? You're spending more and more time in Stratford."

Up in the guest bedroom, putting off dealing with the divorce papers, there'd seemed as if there were a million things we could talk about, not so much excuses for my behaviour, or even remorse, as a reaffirmation of all the good things that Melissa and I had had together before, an assertion that this thing hadn't happened because there'd ever been anything wrong with our relationship.

"Perhaps you should move out, Jim. Go and live with her if that's what you want. Carrying on like this is unbearable."

"No. I don't want that. Not yet."

I knew that I ought to tell her that Natalie had another man and that living with Natalie was no longer a possibility, but my pride wouldn't let me.

"I'm not giving up my home, Jim."

I was appalled.

"No one said you should."

"I know that's why you you're staying here, upstairs."

"Eh?"

"You've brought this on yourself, Jim. I'm not having you sell this house over my head!"

I felt my jaw drop.

"I never even considered that."

Her voice shook.

"And don't think I'm going to buy you out either."

"I never said you should."

I hadn't really thought about what would happen with the house. Melissa and I had joint savings, but most of our equity was in the house.

"That's why you're staying here. Isn't it? So you can hang onto your half of the house."

"... Look.... Melissa... let's talk about this some other time..."

"It's Ralph and Meredith's house too! They still live here!"

"Later. When we're not so upset."

"*We*?! *We're* upset? Good God, Jim. You've got some fucking nerve."

I stood up.

"... No... I meant..." I didn't know what I meant. "... Jack... Jack's dead... That's why the police came.... Jack's been shot..."

Her fist thumped the table.

"Damn Jack! I don't care about Jack. Why do you always bring Jack up?"

I headed for the stairs.

"Later. Let's talk about it later."

Natalie hadn't said what time in the morning her mother and Nok were flying.

I set out for Stratford early. I got to the house just after seven.

I felt a prickle of apprehension. Natalie would be there to see her Mum and daughter off. There was the drive out to Heathrow.

I'd hardly spoken to her since the night with the string. My eagerness to see her face again struggled with an anxiety that there'd be an announcement about her and Pra.

The house was in pandemonium. The East London Thai community had turned up to see the travelers off.

Yoot and his wife were there.

Mrs Leepatawat sat on the sofa barking out instructions. There were people I'd been introduced to at the party but forgotten their names.

Nok was thumbing her keypad, playing Angry Birds on the TV.

The amount of suitcases and carrier bags and Disney rucksacks scattered round the living room, I was looking at a hefty excess luggage charge.

Natalie was in the kitchen with half a dozen other women. They were sitting cross-legged on the floor cutting up meat and pounding chili in mortars!

The kitchen table, crowded with bowls and sachets of blood and bags of curry, had been pushed back against the wall so the cooks didn't bang their heads. The chairs were stacked out in the yard. Natalie had said morning, but Nok and grandma clearly weren't leaving till after lunch.

Natalie smiled up at me.

"Making North food, honey!"

Her eyes shone. It was hard to believe they were the same crazed eyes that had stared and goggled as the string tightened round her throat. I'd forgotten how broad and sensual her lips were. The dimples, swift as surgical incisions, were happy.

"Must eating be fore."

'Must eating be fore' seemed to be a Thai tradition.

Gigi was helping with the cooking, dismembering a complicated looking vegetable, a bit like coriander but with yellow flowers. Her curvy body seemed at home in an apron, more relaxed than usual, or maybe it was just not having Javindra on her case.

Pauline and Carla were frying fish, both of them poking at the sizzling wok. Nok and her grandma's departure must be a major event, if the girls had got time off from their Arms Fair dates.

"Plane go four clock, honey."

That was good. Four in the afternoon. We wouldn't need to leave for Heathrow till noon, or one at the latest.

I wandered upstairs to our bedroom.

Three teenage girls sat on the bed, comparing posts on their phones. Even the bleak bedroom felt good this morning, the magnolia woodchip more lived in, our dismal fuck and Natalie's erotic asphyxiation kick forgiven.

"... Okay...!" I raised my hands surrender style and backed out the door. "... Sabai! Sabai!"

I retreated down the stairs. I looked at my watch.

Sitting in the living for four hours listening to Angry Birds and Mrs Leepatawat didn't appeal. The pandemonium was convivial but my dozen or so Thai words would never stay the distance.

I decided to go out and grab a coffee.

I went down to Stratford mall and wandered around the shops for a while then found a Starbucks to sit in.

When I got back, Cyril was spread out on the sofa. I was pleased to see him. It was a pleasure to endure his bone crushing handshake.

"Where is everybody?"

Nok was still playing Angry Birds, Natalie, her mother and a few of the cooks were still working in the kitchen, but the crowd in the living room, including Mrs Leepatawat, had vanished.

"They're takin' the bus to the temple," said Cyril. "The old duck's gone in her car."

"Eh?"

"Yeah, man. We're all off to the temple."

"The temple? To say goodbye to Pra?"

"No. For good luck. So their plane don't fall outta the sky or nothin'. That's what they've cooked all that food for. For the monks." Cyril looked at his watch. "We better get a move on. Monks have to finish eatin' before twelve thirty."

I began to worry. It was nearly twelve already. They were going to miss their plane. The food they were cooking—there was a hell of a lot of it— all had to be taken to the temple, for the monks' lunch! Temple regulations said the monks had to finish eating before twelve thirty on the dot, but after lunch there was going to be some sort of ceremony to wish Natalie's mother and Nok bon voyage. No one seemed to be in any sort of hurry. I'd expected to be setting off for Heathrow by one at the latest. We were cutting it a bit fine. The only chance I'd have to speak to Natalie would be racing flat out to the airport, stressed that they'd missed the check in.

"Hey! Babe!" Cyril called through to the kitchen. "Reo! Reo!"

Natalie called back something in Thai.

"Cooking laarp, bro. Beatin' six bells out of a piece of liver. Cannot be hurried."

Laarp was a favourite dish of Natalie's. Diced raw liver with enough chili to take the paint off the gate. I couldn't stomach it myself.

Natalie certainly wasn't being hurried. She sat on the kitchen floor with a chopping board between her legs and a knife so big and heavy it was pretty much a machete, pounding the liver into an all but translucent paste.

It was five past twelve! The monks had to finish eating and begin their fast by half past!

"Thais, bro. They aint got no sense of time," said Cyril. "Even the language. There's no tenses or nothin'. You just gotta sorta guess what time you're at."

Cyril's knowledge of Thai impressed me. He'd only worked for Lee for a couple of years but he'd picked up enough of the language to joke with his girls and understand what they were saying when the chatter got serious.

Natalie finally scraped the liver paste into a bowl, added mashed chili and lemon, and tipped in a litre sachet of blood. Where she'd got the blood from, God only knows. I'd never seen it in Tesco.

She mixed the contents of the bowl together for a few minutes then spooned the laarp into a plastic bag and sealed it with an elastic band.

We were ready to go. With all the luggage, Nok, Mum, the food and the cooks, we needed both Cyril's car and mine.

We got to the temple fifteen minutes before the deadline.

The two-up, two-down house in a back street of Leytonstone didn't look at all like a religious establishment.

From outside, Wat Buddharama seemed too small to accommodate either the seven monks who lived there, or the hundred or so worshippers who'd shown up for Nok and Natalie's mother's send off, but there was a large annexe at the back where the kitchen had been extended, none too professionally, out into the garden.

I was desperate to speak to Natalie. With Nok and her mother in the back seat, and Natalie fretting about her laarp, I hadn't had a chance to talk to her on the way.

We crowded into the annexe. The kitchen area was packed with women jostling each other to get at the oven and microwave.

Smokers huddled in the yard. Children were running around outside. Nok rushed off to join them.

I noticed a few farangs, besides me and Cyril, short-arsed working class guys pleased as Punch with their oriental princess wives.

There were so many people I wondered if perhaps today's ceremony was going to be for more than just Natalie's mum and Nok's departure.

Through some double doors a life-size statue of the Buddha stood in front of the mantelpiece in what had once been the front parlour.

The hubbub in the annexe was deafening.

"Feedin' the monks, bro," said Cyril. "It's a blood sport."

The table where the monks sat eating their lunch groaned with bowls and tureens and bottles and plates. There wasn't room for all the food that had been brought for the holy men's repast. The seven of them, in their orange robes, sat eating fixedly. Cyril was right. The women, reheating their gang pet in the microwave, barging for a ring on the cooker to fry their fish, seemed to be competing to win the monks' approval. Bowls were replaced before the holy men had a chance to dip in. They were urged to try this and try that with cackles of barracking merriment. The monks hardly talked as they munched and sipped. They didn't have much chance. It was twenty five past twelve. In their orange kit they looked like professional eaters giving an exhibition.

The food smelled out of this world. I suddenly felt ravenous. A couple of cups of coffee was all I'd had all day.

"Fit dude." Cyril nodded at Pra. "Word is he's a big monk back in Thailand."

I still hadn't worked out what it meant when Thais called someone 'big'. Applied to ordinary people 'big' meant 'rich', but applied to monks it seemed to take on much broader connotations.

"Which one's the head monk?"

"Dunno," said Cyril. "The little old guy's the abbot."

He nodded at the elderly monk sitting at one end of the table. The abbot's wizened face and hunched shoulders were in strong contrast to Pra's sleek, powerful physique.

"I thought they were particular about who sits where."

Pra was at the other end of the table from the abbot.

"Yeah. They are. The abbot's the abbot, but Pra's, like, further up the spiritual pecking order or something."

Pra looked completely at home. Even with his leaving the sangha to marry Natalie and all the ructions that that had caused, his demeanour was as unruffled as the day he stepped off the plane. He didn't pay any particular attention to Natalie as she jockeyed with the women in the kitchen, but the connection between them was palpable. It was there, out in the open, there to be seen by every person in the room— seen but not questioned. Whether it was his personal charisma or being further up the spiritual pecking order, Pra's aplomb was perfect, even in the midst of the waves he and Natalie were making.

He was certainly the focus of the women's attention. They thrust their food at him with everything from motherly solicitude to blatant seduction. Pra seemed equally unmoved by either.

Mrs Leepatawat fussed proprietorially around him, spooning steamed fish prepared by a chef in one of her restaurants onto his plate.

"Arroy!"

The woman who ran the Thai grocery shop in Earls Court tipped glazed chicken feet on top of his curry.

"Arroy maak!"

A working girl in a cowboy hat was cheating with a mandarin duck takeaway from London's premiere Chinese restaurant.

"Arroy thii soot!"

Natalie's mum was fretting. Her North Thai delicacy was superior to anything these London Thais could throw together, and the monks weren't going to get a chance to try it.

"Look's like the English cold's got to him," said Cyril.

"Eh?"

Cyril nodded at Pra.

"The English winter. He's got the flu."

Pra's nose was red. He certainly had the sniffles. He kept producing a handkerchief from a pocket of his robe and blowing his nose.

"Maybe it's all the stress he's under."

"Stress?"

"Leaving the sangha. Everybody angry."

"Leaving the sangha?" Cyril rocked backwards, eyebrows raised. "Pra's not leaving the sangha."

"To live with Natalie."

For a second I thought his look of puzzlement was put on. He must surely know. But it wasn't. Cyril was genuinely incredulous.

"What are you on about, man?"

"He's Nok's father."

Cyril frowned.

"So?"

At least Cyril knew that much. I explained about Natalie spending the night with him.

"Jim. You're out of your mind." Cyril chuckled. "That girl's driven you crazy."

I explained about how manic Natalie had been since Pra arrived, one moment euphoric, the next, on edge. Everybody coming down hard on her for making Pra leave the temple.

"What are you on about, Jim? Pra's not leaving the temple." Cyril thought he was the only one who knew what was going on.

He didn't like it when one of his girls kept him in the dark. "I toldya. She's seein' Adrian Whiteley. She promised Lee."

Cyril was miffed. A couple of people glanced in our direction.

"No. You don't understand. When I met them at the airport..."

I explained about how pleased Pra had been to see Natalie again, and how delighted the three of them, Pra, Nok and Natalie, had been to be together again.

"Pleased? Of course he was pleased, man. That doesn't mean him and Natalie want to hook up again."

Cyril was a nice guy. He spoke Thai. He understood Thai customs better than I did, but when it came to *his* girls he was as off the radar as Soom Bon. Cyril was as much a fantasist as Natalie. Cyril knew that 'sister', in Thai, could mean almost any woman, yet he took Soom Bon's story about the arms trader killing Natalie's 'sister' seriously.

He was so gullible I almost told him about the night with the string.

"You saw the state she was in that night she came home during the party."

I could feel Cyril starting to get angry with me.

"I told you, man. She's on the sniff. All the girls are. These Arms Fair dudes are into their coke. Particularly when they're with a pretty lady."

I liked Cyril a lot, but he was so caught up in his gangland trip, he was so high on being bodyguard to a dozen hot girls, he couldn't see what was staring him in the face.

I looked up.

Natalie was standing at Pra's elbow. She'd pushed her way through the throng of women and was spooning her laarp onto Pra's plate, every inch his wife-to-be.

"*Laarp*, bro!" End of conversation as far as Pra and Natalie were concerned. "Don't go there! It's only for the initiated!"

The change of subject was abrupt enough to see that Cyril's
nose was out of joint. Talking about Pra and Natalie upset him.
He didn't want to see the naked affection with which she served
the monk. Cyril was totally blind to the pleasure on Pra's face, his
delighted 'arroy!'

I shrugged.

"She certainly whanged a load of chili into it."

"Give you worms if you haven't got the stomach for it. It's a
Northern Thai speciality. Chiang Rai. Up where Pra and Natalie
come from."

Pra tucked into Natalie's laarp. The love between them was
palpable.

The Red Bull tattoo flexed on his shoulder as he spooned
Natalie's food into his mouth.

"What's that tattoo?"

The bull's head, with its elongated horns, glistened on Pra's
bicep.

"A Carabou," said Cyril.

"It looks a bit like the Red Bull logo."

Though crudely inked and fading, the tattoo was very much
like what you saw on a can of the energy drink.

"It is," said Cyril. "Same thing. 'Carabou' means Red Bull in
Thai. Not the energy drink, but. Carabou's Bangkok's biggest rock
band. Thailand's answer to the Rolling Stones. 'Cept instead of a
tongue hanging out, they've got a Red Bull."

Pra was cleaning out his bowl with a ball of sticky rice.

"Like a priest," I said. "Having a Nirvana tattoo."

"Yeah. Well," Cyril's eyes sparkled, "word is, Pra was a bit of a
wild man when he was young."

Pra polished off the last of Natalie's laarp. He hadn't offered any
to his companions.

"Before he was a monk?"

"Yeah. Hung out in the fast lane. Pra was into drugs big time. They reckon Pra was the major dealer round the Bangkok music scene. Before he found the Path."

I almost laughed out loud. Cyril had just proved my point. He'd confirmed everything I was telling him, without putting two and two together. Now that he was leaving the sangha Pra was celebrating the same way he used to celebrate before he found the Path. That was why Natalie came home stoned the night of the party, from wherever she'd been partying with Pra. It was probably when Pra was in the fast lane in Bangkok that she and Pra had met.

The monks finished their lunch and everybody trooped into the shrine room.

Although the front room had been converted into a shrine, it still felt like a parlour, even stripped of its furniture so worshippers could sit on the floor. The gilded Buddha sat in meditation with his back against the fireplace, the grate filled with freshly cut flowers. It was a big statue for such a small room. The Awakened One's topknot poked up past the mantelpiece, on which a large portrait of the Thai king in a heavy gilt frame leant perilously against the floral wallpaper. The room's original acanthus leaf cornice had been painted gold.

A row of thin red cushions with red vinyl backrests edged with gold filigree, like fold-up thrones without legs, had been set up on the carpet for the monks to sit cross-legged on, four on one side of the Buddha and three on the other. Pra took the central throne.

Even squeezed in cross-legged on the Axminster carpet there wasn't enough room for everyone. A lot of the worshippers watched through the double doors from the kitchen.

I went to sit down the front with Natalie and her mother and Nok, but Cyril grabbed me. He'd nabbed a place for us at the back.

"Gonna take a while, bro. It's murder on your knees."

Even after a couple of minutes sitting cross legged I was glad to
be able to lean against the wall at the back. There were dents in the
carpet where a piano had once stood.

The room was packed. Down at the front, Natalie was almost
knee to knee with Pra.

She swung round and beamed at me above the sea of heads. The
trippy smile was gone. She looked happy.

A smell of ginger grass and washing up liquid wafted in from
the kitchen and mingled with the sickly sweet scent of the joss
sticks burning on the mantelpiece.

Through the net curtains the red silhouette of a double decker
bus changed gears beyond the bay window.

The monks got themselves comfortable. They each had a prayer
fan, like an embroidered canoe paddle, which they held upright in
front of their faces by its bamboo handle.

I glanced at my watch. It was five past one. The monks had
stopped eating at half past twelve, but had sat on, digesting their
lunch and chatting for another twenty minutes.

Pra began to chant.

"... Buddham saranam gocchami..."

The other monks answered him. Their voices, some high, some
low, reverberated in a single drone.

"... Sangham saranam gocchami..."

Maybe it was the repetitiveness of the responses or simply the
fact that I didn't understand what the monks were chanting, but
I felt a pleasant lulling sensation, the lift and calm of anxieties
suspended, almost like the cessation of pressing worries on a long
haul 737, strapped into a seat, engulfed in the drone of the engines,
absolved of any need to act for ten or twelve hours. I could almost
have been on the plane with Nok and her grandma, the monk's
voices the din of the CFM engines. It went on and on. They were
going to miss their flight.

"... Buddham saranam gocchami..."

I was grateful to Cyril for sitting us at the back of the room. Even leaning against the wall it was hard to get comfortable.

"... Sangham saranam gocchami..."

Without hint of a coda or a final flourish the chanting stopped dead.

The religious ceremony abruptly turned into a social occasion.

The monks laid their prayer paddles aside and chatted with the worshippers crowded onto the carpet. They joked and gesticulated and laughed out loud like folks who'd just run into each other at the market or met up in the pub.

The monks distributed gifts to the children, pencils and sweets they produced from their shoulder bags. It was like a family get-together, holy men and worshippers catching up on each other's news.

Stray English words...'Lotto'... 'Manchester United'... 'visa'... bobbed in the hubbub of Thai.

Pra was the only one who didn't join in. He leaned forward, toward Natalie. He was speaking urgently to her.

Natalie shook her head.

Cyril nudged me.

"I'd watch out for him if I was you, bro. Pra's putting the word on your old lady."

Cyril didn't have a clue.

The monk whispered in Natalie's ear. Sternly. Urgently. Deadly serious, laying down the law. I envied him his authority with her.

Natalie shook her head again, more adamantly this tie. Even in the hubbub of conversation, people started noticing their conversation. Even Cyril noticed.

Nok! Of course! How foolish I was not to have realized!

They were arguing about their daughter. I'd been surprised when I heard that Nok was going back to Thailand with her

grandmother instead of remaining in London with Natalie and
Pra. There'd be visa issues to sort out for Nok of course, especially
as Natalie was here illegally, but they'd be easier to sort out if the
three of them stayed together here in England. Pra shook his head.
He was angry. Natalie's replies were growing definat, his status as
a monk swept aside. They were having more than just a minor
disagreement. One of them— it was impossible to tell who—
wanted Nok to stay in London, the other was insisting she go back
to Thailand.

Pra gesticulated. Natalie shook her head. Natalie's
stubbornness was more than a match for the monk's authority.

The Leepatawats looked nervous. Mrs Leepatawat was
frowning. Mister Leepatawat fiddled with a ball of blessing string
he had in his lap.

Yoot stared out the window. His wife whispered to a
neighbour.

Pra hissed an ultimatum. Natalie shook her head.

Mrs Leepatawat sat bristling.

Mister Leepatawat offered the ball of string to Pra, but Pra
ignored him.

Natalie's mother looked at her watch:

"... Bai mohng sip haa natee... Heath Low glai mai?"

Pra slumped backwards into his throne. Natalie sat up straight.
Pra grabbed the ball of string out of Mister Leepatawat's hands and
almost shouted:

"Maa nii! Maa nii!"

He unwound a length of string, about a metre or so, and
handed the ball back to Mister Leepatawat. It was a large ball.
People were jostling on their knees towards the row of monks. I felt
an acute anxiety about time. They were going to miss their plane.
The whole room was milling too have their wrists tied with string.

I felt an almost insane relief when the other six monks produced their own balls of strings and those waiting to be blessed divided into chaotic queues.

"We're never going to make it."

"Can't skip the string tying, bro."

"It'll take hours."

Some of the monks had devotees assist them, like Mister Leepatawat was assisting Pra, unwinding strings from the balls.

Pra nodded at Nok.

"Luuk sao!"

Daughter.

Nobody seemed shocked. I realized that 'daughter' must be the same as 'sister'. It can apply to any female child, not just one's own blood. Most of the people seemed to know that Nok was Pra's daughter anyway.

Nok knee-walked across the carpet to him, bobbed him a wai, and held out her hand.

She gazed up at her father with wide, round eyes. She knew now that Pra was her Dad. Natalie had told her.

The monk gazed down at her with transparent delight.

He blew on her wrist, passed the string three times up and down the delicate veins above her palm, then wound the string round twice and tied a knot.

He severed the string with his thumbnail.

Nok held out her other hand. When he'd tied the string round her other wrist, Pra placed his hand on Nok's head, closed his eyes and murmured something. It sounded more like a fatherly admonition than a religious formula.

Nok knee-walked back to her place. Pra nodded at Natalie's mother.

"Mair!"

Mother.

'Mother' was the same as 'sister' and 'daughter', just a term of affection.

Natalie's mum knelt before him and held out her wrist.

Instead of tying the string himself, as he's done for Nok, Pra unwound another metre or so from the ball ball and gave the end of the string to Mister Leepatawat.

"Monks aint allowed to touch women," whispered Cyril.

I couldn't help smiling. Since he'd arrived in England, Pra had spent almost every night with Natalie.

"He touched Nok," I said. "He patted Nok's head."

"That's cause she's a child. Pre puberty. Monks aint allowed to touch a woman post puberty."

"Right."

Mister Leepatawat tied the string as efficiently as any of the monks. He severed it with some scissors and Natalie's mother crawled back to her place.

"Thii rak!"

A murmur ran round the room.

Natalie shook her head.

"THII RAK!"

Darling. Sweetheart. Beloved.

Natalie turned her back on him.

Pra grabbed a handful of her hair.

The murmur turned to a hubbub.

The monk jerked her head towards him, hard.

"Hey!"

I was on my feet.

The string got tangled under her knees. The ball rolled onto the floor. Pra pinned her arm to her side with his elbow. Natalie struggled but he wouldn't let go of her. He was winding the string round her wrist, except she thrashed so much some tugged up near her elbow. It dug into her skin.

Mrs Leepatawat was shouting at Natalie. The room was in pandemonium.

Pra jumped to his feet. His voice boomed out. He bellowed at Natalie.

"THII RAK!"

Natalie was crying.

A shocked silence gripped the room.

Pra was taking his robe off! He dragged the saffron cloth from his shoulder. The Carabou tattoo flexed on brown muscle. He fought the robe down around his waist like a contortionist struggling in orange chains.

His back and chest were covered in scratches. Five-finger tracks of red welt, where her nails had raked him, criss-crossed his pecs. There were bite marks on his shoulders and chest, where she'd kissed him.

He spat on the carpet and walked out.

Natalie hurried after him, wailing and pleading.

In the stunned silence, everyone heard their footsteps mount to the room upstairs.

"Fuck me," whispered Cyril. "They conned the lot of us."

"Sennambin...?"

Natalie's mother was saying something to me. We were out in the yard standing in a knot of people shouting and talking all at once.

"Sennambin...?"

Cyril was in the kitchen yelling at one of the monks. Cyril looked as if he was going to hit someone. He took a step towards the stairs. The abbot blocked his way, shaking his head.

Nok clung to her grandmother's dress.

"Sennambin...?" Natalie's mother pointed at her watch. "... Sawng mong... Heath Low...?"

It was nearly two o'clock. She and Nok needed to get to Heathrow. Their flight was at four.

Natalie didn't come down to see them off.

We stood in the queue at the check-in counter. We were desperately late.

Nok had had a tantrum in the car. Natalie's mother looked distraught. I waited in line with them. I'd only known Natalie seven weeks. I hadn't picked up enough Thai to make light conversation.

Their passports were checked, they received their boarding cards and we dashed to the Departures gate.

"Swaddee ka, Loong Jim."

"Swaddee ka, Daddee."

I wai-d. I wasn't sure whether a wai was appropriate or not.

"Sawaddee khrap."

I didn't know the words for 'have a nice flight'.

By the time I left the terminal it was dark.

When I got back to Stratford, the house was empty. Natalie wasn't there. Of course she wasn't. She was with Pra. It was over.

I had no idea what the trouble had been between them. It was obviously something serious, more serious even than Nok going back to Thailand. God only knew what went on between them. The way Pra's chest was lacerated, the welts from her nails down his back, it was something pretty crazy. It was none of my business.

The living room was neat and tidy, the mats rolled up and stacked in the corner.

Someone had done the washing up before we left for the temple. The pots and pans for cooking the monks' lunch were stacked in the drying rack.

Everything was spick and span, but they'd forgotten to switch the heating off. The house was sweltering.

I watched TV for a while then went up to our bedroom. The girls who'd been sharing posts on their phones had straightened the duvet before they left. I didn't feel like sleeping.

I decided to go home to Islington and try to patch things up with my family. I'd been right putting off dealing with the divorce papers. I'd known that this was going to happen, and some right instinct had kept me from responding to Melissa's angry declarations with an irrevocable reply.

I switched the heating off. Checked to make sure the back door was locked. Went up to the bedroom and packed my bag. Natalie's clothes were still hanging in the wardrobe.

Even with the radiators ticking down, the room was unbearably hot.

I was on fire. I felt feverish. There was a ticking in my head like a thermostat stuck on high. The thread of light in my spine roared and prickled. Everything stung. The room envenomed the lie called consciousness. The unapproachable woman was everywhere, now that Natalie had gone. She didn't need me to make her presence known. I was burning up, but my skin wouldn't sweat. My clothes itched like sandpaper.

I double-locked the front door. I'd need to keep hold of the keys to return to the agent when I cancelled the contract. Natalie had the second set.

I posted my set through the letter box. Natalie could deal with it. If she wanted to carry on living here, Pra could sort out the arrangements. I couldn't go home to Melissa and keep on paying the rent on this house. Even leaving my name on the contract was impossible. I'd have to ring Natalie at some stage and tell her how to transfer the rent to Pra's name. Not now. In a day or two. She was busy. She was with him. The need to know *where* was so urgent I almost howled out loud.

I needed to calm down. I started the car. I'd ring her in a day or two and wish them luck. Tell her I still loved her.

I couldn't face my normal route back to Islington. My pilgrim's way? The pilgrim's path? I felt ill. Lea Bridge Road was out of the question. Stoke Newington was unthinkable.

The Saturday night traffic was heavy heading north on Romford Road. This wasn't the way to Islington. I turned left at Forest Gate.

The clock at Forest Gate station said eleven thirty. I hadn't realized how late it had got.

I checked the climate control.

OFF.

I was burning up. My body was on fire.

I knew I was returning to a shambles. Things would never be the same. I was going back to the empty shell of what I'd once had, but it was better than nothing. Melissa's generous mind wanted to forgive me, even if her heart couldn't. I'd have to accept her forgiveness on whatever terms it was given. If she needed to believe I was sick, I'd be sick. If she wanted the last seven weeks to have been a nervous breakdown, I'd admit that I'd had a nervous breakdown. Maybe I'd have some therapy. Admitting I was ill would be better than this scalding sensation in my chest.

A stream of festive headlights cut across Wanstead Flats, Saturday night reds and whites jockeying in the blackness.

The turnoff for Leytonstone took me past the temple.

The lights were off upstairs and down. He'd gone away with her somewhere. They'd left together. They were in a hotel somewhere now. The need to know *where* grew so acute, everything went black. Their love was miles beyond me already, I just needed to know *where*.

I had no idea whether my family would be awake or not. Melissa liked to go to bed early. Ten or ten thirty on a weeknight, but she sometimes stayed up later on Saturdays. Ralph was a night bird. He'd certainly be up, watching a movie or listening to music. My son's anger frightened me. I hoped his girlfriend would be there to calm him down. I didn't know what I'd say to Meredith.

Stoke Newington turned into Islington. I felt sick to my stomach. The heat scorched worst of all in my stomach. Before there could be any talk of forgiveness, or a chance of me hiding away in therapy, I'd have to discuss money with Melissa. I'd need to reassure her about the house. I'd have to ask her to lift the block on my withdrawals from our joint account. The money Jack had repaid me was starting to run out.

It was after midnight when I turned onto our street. There was a parking space directly in front of the house.

All the lights were off.

They were asleep. Even Ralph's bedroom window was in darkness.

The living room curtains were drawn back. I could see through the windows that the lamps and the TV weren't on.

The kitchen shutters on the ground floor were closed, as they were every night. No crack of light came from inside.

I opened the gate. The front steps shone in the moonlight. The Portland stone looked as if it had been scrubbed with milk. The front door was a black mirror, immaculately glossed.

My key wouldn't go in the lock.

I tried again. My key no longer fitted.

The lock had been changed.

As I turned to go, my foot hit something, under the parapet, next to the milk bottles.

It was a pile of books.

I drove back to Stratford. It was only as I parked the car that I remembered that I no longer had the keys. I'd shoved them through the letterbox when I left. I couldn't get in.

A light shone in the living room window.

I knocked.

Natalie's face was a flux of clotted white. Whorls—arches and loops—of pallor pitted her forehead and cheekbones. She stood shivering in her dressing gown on the doorstep.

There was a sour, yeasty smell.

The upward tilt of her eyes looked steeper where the ghostly curds ran up under her lashes. Yoghurt. She'd painted her face with yoghurt.

She drew the dressing gown tight around her throat.

"Fleezing."

I was so hot, I felt as if my skin was melting the frost on the brickwork through my clothes.

Her hold-all sat on the sofa, zipped-up, ready to go. She'd come back to get a few things to take back to wherever she and Pra were staying. After the scene in the shrine room there was no way they could stay at the temple. Pra had disrobed already.

My keys lay on the carpet beneath the door.

I couldn't stop staring at the yoghurt.

"Must give skin beautiful."

The scene in the shrine room had freaked her out worse than I'd thought.

She moved her hold-all so I could sit down. Her dressing gown fell open.

She must have used five or six cartons. Her stomach was smeared with the stuff. Her nipples stood up as if they'd been artex-d. Her bush was a wire brush loaded with emulsion. She wanted to erase her skin, not beautify it. The scene with Pra had driven her out of her mind.

She shivered. Her eyes told me not to speak about him. There were things we needed to sort out, rent, the keys, the agents, but I musn't talk about them now.

She shuddered.

"Cold, honey."

Goose pimples showed through the yoghurt on her breasts.

My skin felt as if it had been glazed in an oven. It would have felt better if I could have sweated, but the heat was baking the perspiration out of me.

She went into the bathroom. I heard the shower come on.

I went upstairs, took off my clothes, and dropped onto the bed. I was desperate to know *where*. I wanted to ask her where she was going, with her hold-all and her skin made beautiful, but it was none of my business. It was good to be alone together one last time, but *where she was off to* wouldn't let me be with her.

A radiator throbbed, inches from the back of my skull. She'd switched the heating back on.

I was too tired to reach around and turn it off.

The heat tugged at the back of my head like a suction cap.

I pulled my singlet and underpants off. Kicked the duvet away. The sheet prickled like an unshaven cheek.

Natalie walked in with a towel wrapped around her. Her teeth were chattering. The yoghurt was gone.

It had done the trick. It had lifted more than grease and dead skin from her face. Her cheekbones were stripped to a freezing nudity. She'd peeled her eyes back to the shuddering quick.

She dropped the towel on the floor and climbed onto the bed beside me, and pulled the duvet over us. Her feet were like blocks of ice.

The light was still on. I felt a moment's exasperation that she'd forgotten to switch it off. I shut my eyes tight. The glare from the unshielded bulb still pushed between my eyelids.

I was desperate to get to sleep.

I rolled onto my side, but the glare from the bulb slanted down into my brain. Natalie laid her body against mine, face to face, belly to belly, knee to knee. We held on to each other.

Luxurious coolness poured from her skin. The heat that burned me grew blissful as it covered her. Neither of us moved.

Her breasts inched their way up my chest on a ladder of slow breaths.

We reached the bottom, where consciousness ends; the floor, where dreams dissolve into blackness.

The right side of my body dragged me deeper; it pulled me down through the floor to where weight comes from and density begins. I sank down and down. The left side of my body was a husk of light dissolving in a glare from somewhere far above me.

I felt a woman holding me.

It wasn't Natalie. The woman was younger than Natalie, slighter. Her breasts weren't fully formed. A nipple, nestling against my chest, puckered like a milk blister on a baby's lip.

She threw her leg over mine. The leg was a teenager's, lighter than Natalie's. The down on its shin grazed my calf like blown dandelion.

The girl who wasn't Natalie rubbed her belly against me. She lifted herself and pressed her abdomen into mine. I felt an untouched smoothness. There was no caesarean scar.

Hair swarmed over my face. Some strands found their way into my nose.

She was the only woman I'd ever wanted. It didn't matter that she wasn't Natalie. It was a small price to pay that I was another man. It wasn't important that the only way I could hold her was to be another man— Pra, Adrian, the man in Jack's photo, it didn't matter who— holding her, in another body, at another time, somewhere else.

Her breath grazed my lips. I knew we mustn't kiss. She knew it, too. It was essential that our mouths shouldn't touch. If we kissed, she'd change back into Natalie. I'd change back into me. Our eyes would open. The glare from the ceiling would blind us.

The glare was too strong. It wasn't a naked bulb behind a crooked shade at all. *Its light was purple, not white.* It beat down from an immense height. From fifteen, twenty, twenty-five storeys high. From a purple pulsation on a high balcony.

Our breaths mingled, but we didn't kiss. Stillness took hold of us, an utter stillness we knew we mustn't lose. The room—it was a suite in a luxury hotel, not this bedroom in Stratford— spun from my body in a wash of purple light. An instant in time—not this one, here, lying under a light bulb—spiralled out of me. The taste of champagne, the smell of semen—not a chaste, desperate cuddle with a woman I'd already lost—came from inside me, from inside her. We were high above the city, holding each other on a balcony. London spun from our bodies far below, twenty-five storeys down, a wash of purple light on a river, each lit wavelet and oily reflection pulsing from our skin.

Then darkness.

When I came to, Natalie was curled up in my arms, warm as toast, still face to face—her pelvis arched away from me, one knee hooked over my knees, her toes grazing my shins.

She muttered and, with the painstaking slowness of a determined sleeper, rolled over.

By the time she'd got herself comfortable, the crook of her knees around my kneecaps, her backside squashed against my flaccid penis, we'd made love more thoroughly than any two people can.

CHAPTER SEVEN

A winter's sun was shining out of a Homebase lampshade.

I opened my eyes.

Daylight slanted through the window. She'd switched the light off when she left.

Late afternoon sunlight glared through the crack where the blind was off its runner. I'd slept for nearly fifteen hours.

I hurried downstairs.

Her hold-all was gone.

She wasn't in the bathroom. The kitchen was empty.

I looked at the clock. It was quarter to five. It was starting to get dark outside.

I felt a crazed desperation to know where she was. It was insane. She was with Pra. That was all that mattered. *Where* wasn't important.

I missed her so badly, going back to Islington was no longer an option. I couldn't speak to Melissa feeling like this. There was no way I could discuss the house and money and the future, longing for Natalie so much.

It was as if a sort of magic had happened during the night. Not Soom Bon magic. Not even Big Buddha Woman magic. She'd felt too childlike and cold in my arms to be an angel girl. But something had happened never-the-less. Remembering what it was that had happened was as impossible as getting her back. There'd been no desire. My body pouring its heat into her body, her body pouring its coldness into mine, without desire. Lying skin to skin, arousal out of the question. Her arousal was for Pra. Her desire was for her daughter's father. I felt raw and lonely. Stillness had taken hold of us during the night, but now it was gone. Something magical had occurred, and it meant nothing.

I switched the TV on.

I watched the end of a film and the football results.

The News at Six.

The Arms Fair was over. The Defence And Security Equipment International Trades Fair had closed today. There was a live report from the ExCel Centre. The Fair had been a success, a boost for Britain's aerospace industry, a shot in the arm for international engagement. A final-day protest rally had been broken up by police. It was Sunday. The Fair had closed at five p.m.

So much for Jack's 'sex ring' and 'girls ending up dead' and Cyril's worries about Adrian Whitely setting Natalie up for 'somethin' heavy' at the Arms Fair. The 'sick, evil cunts' were on their way home. Satan was flying out. The guy in Jack's photo was probably on a plane at this very moment going back to wherever it was he came from with his 'intelligent delivery' contract in his pocket. It was sad Jack had had to die for nothing.

I wandered around my new home.

It was me who'd ended up here after all.

The living room was as bare as the day Natalie moved in. There were no homely touches, no flowers or knickknacks, no calendars or pictures on the walls, not even the Thai King.

A Glade dispenser in the kitchen squirted 'Zesty Jasmine' every time you walked past it, the one feminine touch. Natalie was certainly no nest builder. Pra would have to do the home improvements wherever it was they ended up living.

I found Mister Leepatawat's bottle of Johnny Walker stowed in a cupboard in the kitchen. I poured a glassful and toasted the leader of East London's Thai community.

"Bottoms up, Mr. L. There's no standing in the way of love."

I went back upstairs to the bedroom. I took the glass and bottle with me.

I opened the wardrobe and went through her things.

Her three or four best dresses were missing, the high-class ones she loved, not the sexy things she wore at the sauna. The elegant black chiffon she'd worn to White's with Adrian. The hand-woven skirt with the embroidered tunic. Her best black slacks. The silk top with the oyster grey pleats and the glittery shoulder strap.

The hot pants and see-thru tops, the halters, and crotch-length mini-skirts were still hanging on the rail. Pra wasn't a plastic bra and G-string man.

I rummaged round the bottom of the wardrobe. She'd packed three pairs of shoes— her trainers, her glass high heels, and the Jimmy Choo stilettoes I'd bought her.

I opened her underwear drawer. It was nearly empty.

There were a couple of bras and a few pairs of knickers in the wash basket. Not many. She'd taken at least five changes.

So much for the sex party.

I opened the drawer. Her jewellery was gone, the gold bracelets and her necklace with the King Number Five pendant, some rings and earrings.

I checked in both bedside cupboards, pulled open the drawers, and double-checked the wardrobe. The wallet of photos of Nok was gone too. That clinched it. Pra was Nok's father. He'd make a good one. They'd have more children. Raise a family. Be happy.

I looked at the unkempt bed.

Snapshots I didn't know I'd taken floated up: Pauline's navel, Carla's split, the curve of Gigi's arse. I had a couple of hundred quid in my wallet. Anything was better than being alone.

I sat on the bed and finished off Mister Leepatawat's Johnny Walker.

Lying in each others arms last night something magical had occurred, but it meant nothing. A wonderful stillness had taken hold of us. Or had I just dreamed it? It was certainly gone now. My willpower was too weak, my mind too numb, for magic. Something weird had happened, but remembering what it was that had happened was as impossible as getting her back. All I was left with was this frantic need to know *where she was*, not even with whom, or doing what, just where, as if a place alone can stay real as events and people vanish into a blur of deadness.

I'd always felt places more vividly than people, especially the further back into the past I went. When it comes to the past, people are just the unseen presence of places. Human presence is real enough, but it needs a place, or at least the memory of a place, to cling onto if it's to be really felt again. Natalie was gone. She was so deeply gone she no longer existed, and yet the bedroom in Kilburn was still here, with its pink lampshade and the fan heater blasting. Natalie had ceased to be real, yet the Holiday Inn bedroom carried on. The room in the Holiday Inn *was still here*, its Spartan furniture and its window that only opened as wide as the building regulations allowed. Places. There were so many of them. The restaurant in Hornchurch. ATIK in Romford. A cubicle in Hackney Sauna. Islington. There were enough places, back there in the past, to keep me going for the rest of my life. I could still cling onto them *because they were past*. It was what I'd seen in the bedroom in Kilburn, that first time I'd been with Natalie. By the time it reaches your eyes, let alone your ears or nose or touch, or even your mind, a room is dead. It's already over and done with. It's merely its own past. Only the fact that the place has ended reaches the present, whereas a person is something more. *The Serpent Power* spoke of *akasha*, space transcending time, but that way madness lay.

All that mattered was to know where she was. I had an infinity of places to hold onto, out there and in my memory, but that the only two that counted— this bedroom in Stratford and *where she was*— were unknowable.

Bang. Bang. Bang.

Downstairs someone hammered at the front door.

It took me a few seconds to gather my wits and get down the stairs to the living room.

Bang. Bang. Bang.

Whoever it was, they were insistent. The flimsy paneling shook. The fanlight rattled in its beading.

I got to the door and opened it.

It was a Cyril.

A blaze of orange stood at his side.

Pra.

The man I'd seen this morning at the temple wrestling with Natalie, fighting his way out of his robes, stood next to Cyril, calm and imposing, swathed in saffron.

Cyril barged past me.

"Where's Natalie?"

Pra smiled benignly.

He'd called her 'THII RAK!' He'd yanked her hair. He'd grabbed hold of her and tried to tie string around her wrist. I'd seen the scratches on his chest and back, where her nails had raked him.

He stepped into the living room, unnaturally serene.

"She's not here," I said.

Cyril strode into the kitchen. He didn't believe me. I'd hidden Natalie in the kitchen. He strode back out.

"Where's this party, man?"

"Party?"

"*PARTY!* Did she tell you where it was?"

"No. I thought she was..."

I looked at Pra.

Cyril groaned.

"So did I."

He stalked to the foot of the stairs and grabbed the newel post as if he wanted to rip it out of its fixings.

"Fucking Javindra, man. Gigi told him there was a party tonight, and he never even said nothin'." Cyril's face was ashen. "I'll kill Lee, man. Anything happens to those girls I'll fucking kill him."

"Which girls?"

"Gigi, Pauline, Carla n Amy. N Natalie too now. I thought somethin' heavy was goin' down, but I never knew it was the guy killed Natalie's sister."

"*Eh?*"

Pra looked at me.

"Poo chai kha naawng-sao Nam Huan."

"Killed Natalie's sister?"

"The five of them coked up all week. I didn't think nothin' about it." Cyril grabbed the back of the sofa. He rammed the sofa against the door. "Bit of sniff. I know how these cunts party." I was drunk. I wasn't hearing right. "Then Javindra mentions, casual as fuck, like it's a fucking everyday occurrence, that Gigi's been coming back with these marks on her throat, string marks or some fucking thing round her throat. They're doing that sex game, you choke yourself."

Pra stared round at the room. He'd never seen an IKEA sofa or a HomeBase Monet before.

"I thought Natalie was with..."

I nodded at the monk.

"Yeah. I'm an idiot." Cyril's eyes bulged. "That thing at the temple yesterday. So did I."

"Nam Huan mii luuk-sao," said Pra. "Kah khon mai dai!"

Cyril glared at me.

"You sure she never said nothin' to you about no party?"

"No..." I felt bilious. "... I've hardly seen her these last few days. She packed a bag. She took a load of stuff with her. Her gold. Her photos. Changes of clothes."

"So'd Gigi." Cyril groaned. "So'd Pauline 'n Carla. Jesus Christ! They're ready to go to ground if somethin' goes wrong." Cyril looked at Pra. "Nam Huan mai phuut yuu thii-nai?"

Pra shook his head.

Cyril's fist clenched and unclenched. The big gold C on his signet ring jerked on his knuckle.

"I go to the temple just now, thinkin' Natalie's with Pra, I could speak to Natalie, Natalie must know where the other girls are, n Natalie aint there, she's with the others, n Pra says the guy she's seein's the one who killed her sister... her real blood sister..." I stared out the window. I had his photo in my pocket. "... Pra says Natalie's gonna kill the guy, pay him back for killing her sister, cause she's a big Buddha woman n all that shit..."

People wrapped up against the cold hurried by in the blackness. I stared at Cyril.

"She wouldn't tell me about her sister. She refused to even speak about her."

"Pra says it was her real sister, her blood sister. They found her dead in Dubai. In a hotel room with string around her throat. Big load of fucking blessing string."

"Natalie's with him?"

Cyril covered his eyes with his hand.

"Coupla hundred grand they've given Lee. That cunt's disappeared too. I catch up with 'im, Lee's fuckin' dead, man." He glared at the wall as if he wanted to put his head through it. *"Where are they?!"*

"There's that hotel at the ExCel Centre," I said. "We could try there."

Cyril glared at me. It was hopeless.

"Yeah. Come on."

By the time I slammed the front door, half in, half out of my coat, Cyril was in his Audi, gunning the engine so hard it screamed.

Pra's robe glowed in the front passenger seat, like a live ember in the orange fire of the streetlamp.

The Audi swerved out into the road!

Cyril wasn't waiting for me! He couldn't hold on for half a second to head off on a search that was totally pointless.

The Audi screeched round the corner and was gone.

I got into my car.

I was drunk but sobering up fast.

The clearer my head got, the sicker I felt. I should have spoken to her, confronted her, reasoned with her, not wallowed in some dream stillness from which she could slip so easily, her face painted with yoghurt, her teeth chattering.

I turned right into West Ham Lane. It was the way to the ExCel Centre, if that was where Cyril was going.

I caught a glimpse of the Audi jumping the lights south onto Stratford High Street.

I followed him over.

Cyril was stuck in a snarl up at the turn-off to the station, by the roundabout with the modern sculpture in the middle.

I joined the turn off tailback ten cars behind him. Even ten cars back I could hear Cyril revving his engine. We weren't going to find them, but the need to just drive, just gun the engine, blast the horn, 'Outta my way!', was better than mooning around an empty house dreaming about some magical *where*.

I was a fool, right the way down deep, where folly turns into evil, becomes a willful violence against reality. There'd been no reason for me to be jealous of Pra. Pra and Natalie hadn't given me the slightest reason— not even the ruckus at the temple yesterday— for making all the assumptions that I'd made. The fantasy about Pra leaving the temple and Natalie marrying him had turned up in my head out of nowhere. The world itself turns up in your head out of nowhere, but that was no excuse.

I held her in my arms, the stinging heat pouring out of me into her, the frozenness pouring out of her into me, and reached the bottom, where consciousness ends, the floor, where dreams dissolve into blackness, where *where* is a wash of light beating down from an immense height and rippling on river wavelets, but the stillness that took hold of us when we didn't kiss was even more pointless than Cyril's revving his engine and blowing his horn and our dashing all over East London like a pair of headless chickens.

The roundabout was paved with pyramid-shaped blocks, to stop people walking there and touching the sculpture presumably, a ten foot high clutch of bent girders.

The queue inched forwards. Cyril wouldn't stop blowing his horn. I could feel the steam coming out of his ears. It was pointless. Totally and utterly hopeless.

Another halt.

Cyril reversed, clipped the car behind him and mounted the roundabout. He bumped past the snarl-up, bounced back down onto the road and accelerated away down the southbound carriageway.

I went after him, my wheels jiggling on the pyramid points as if I was barefoot on broken glass.

The ExCel Centre was surrounded by a maze of service roads, one-way systems and signs pointing to car parks.

When we finally got to the entrance, the glass pyramid was in darkness.

Workmen in a cherry picker were dismantling the Arms Fair sign, struggling in the wind with the sheets of vivid canvas.

Flyers and placards littered the empty forecourt and scuttled off down the steps towards the water.

The curved, curtain-window façade of the hotel was at the back, on the far side of the complex. It was impossible to reach it without getting back onto the main road.

The hotel lobby was as devoid of life as the exhibition centre.

"I'm lookin' for five Thai girls," said Cyril.

The woman at reception stared from Pra's robes to Cyril's corn rows.

"Thai girls?"

"With some guys!"

The woman looked nervous. Cyril was ready to head for the lift and bang on four hundred doors.

I still had the photo Jack had given me in my pocket. I showed it to her.

"No. I..."

She looked even more nervous.

"FIVE THAI GIRLS!"

"Cyril. Cyril."

"Women?"

"Yes. FIVE THAI WOMEN. With some wankers from the Arms Fair. PARTYING!"

The receptionist glanced across at a bellboy stacking some suitcases that had fallen off a trolley. The foyer was empty.

"... Erm..." She put on a thoughtful look. "... Well... I know there's a big party being held down near London Bridge..." She was making it up. She was scared and she just wanted to get rid of us. "... I heard there was... a big party... some of the delegates... on a boat... on the river... down near London Bridge, I think..."

It was hopeless. We were on a wild goose chase.

"Yeah. I know the one," said Cyril. "Thanks."

It wasn't a boat, it was a warship, a World War Two cruiser moored by the embankment.

It made sense to Cyril— Arms Trade pleasure seekers choosing a battlecruiser to have their fun on— it made no sense at all to me.

The woman at the hotel had been right about the party, but. The decks were lit up. Guests in evening dress were arriving. A

Sinatra classic segued across the water. The ship had been hired out
for an event.

A red-carpet gangplank with a chrome rail led up from the
embankment to the lower deck of the cruiser. At the top of the
gangplank a tasselled rope hung between two poles.

There was a bouncer.

"I'm lookin' for some Thai girls, bro. Five Thai girls. With a
party from the Arms Fair."

"Sorry, bro. Private event."

"FIVE THAI GIRLS, BRO! With some dudes from the Arms
Fair."

The bouncer planted himself behind the dip in the rope.

"Would you ask the Dalai Lama to step aside, bro? He's
blockin' the gangplank."

A woman in a blue cocktail dress tried to squeeze past Pra's
bulky form.

"Can I help you, sir?"

The manager was as small as the bouncer was big.

"I'm lookin' for five Thai girls," Cyril repeated through his
teeth.

"I'm afraid it's invitation only, sir" said the manager, smiling the
woman in the blue cocktail dress through.

The slope of the gangplank gave the doorman an inch or two
over Cyril.

"What's your problem, bro?"

"I just toldya, nigga..."

Pra's voice rang out:

"Sabai, sabai."

Pra inserted himself between Cyril and the bouncer. He was as
big as either of the two men.

"Phom yaak bpai haa..." The monk spoke slowly and
persuasively to the manager, unperturbed by the fact that the small

South Londoner couldn't understand a word he was saying. "...
Hahn poo ying mii and-ta-rai..."

A queue of guests built up behind us.

"Aint fancy dress event, bro," said the bouncer.

"Look, man. I've worked the door."

"... Haa hah poo ying Thai nai and-ta-rai maak..."

Pra nodded down at his feet. He nodded at the ship.

He wai-d the manager!

"... Well... only if I... two minutes..."

The manager unclipped the rope and ushered Pra aboard.

Cyril and I waited on the embankment, Cyril pacing up and
down in the lamplight, shaking his head.

"I'll never forgive myself, man. I'll never fucking forgive
myself."

Twenty minutes later Pra came down the gangplank.

"Mai mii."

Cyril muttered something about the 'West End' and jumped in
his car and sped off.

Pra was left standing on the footpath. He had to go with me in
my car.

It was crazy. We had no hope of finding them.

We tobogganed down a tunnel-like freeway beside the river.

The blur in which I was being swept along came into focus:
this morning she'd left without waking me; we'd hardly spoken
the whole time Pra had been in London; even last night, lying in
each other's arms, heat pouring into cold, cold pouring into heat, at
the bottom, where the world ends, we'd been separate; even *there*
she'd been as impermeable as the concrete ceiling of *this* overpass,
she'd been as headed in her own direction as *these* streaks of white
flashing under my wheels, she'd been as trapped in herself as these
stacked cubes of fluorescent light. I'd never see her again.

I glanced across from the go-karting zip of taillights.

Pra sat calm and silent, his profile grave and absorbed, taking in Tower Bridge as if it were a postcard of the moon.

I pumped my horn.

Cyril was getting further and further ahead. I couldn't keep up with him.

We careened down an incline towards some traffic lights.

The lights turned orange.

Cyril picked up speed. His determination to beat the opposing stream of traffic across the intersection was as crazy as the furry dice bouncing in his back window.

The lights turned red.

A bus jumping the green light pulled out in front of him. Horn blaring, Cyril skidded to a halt inches from ramming into it. The traffic piled up behind him. I was six cars back.

I had a sickening hallucination.

We'd found her. She was here, now, somewhere nearby, but it was too late.

I stared out at the street: office buildings; the entrance to a railway station; a section of river cut off by the mezzanine floors of tower blocks. Concrete. Glass. Asphalt.

It was impossible.

This stillness was impossible, shining, stinging, taking hold.

She was here, now, pressed against me, holding me, warm, her hair swarming over my face, some strands finding their way into my nose, muttering something as she rolled over with the painstaking slowness of a determined sleeper.

The street was a void. Its asphalt was glassy. The concrete rang. The road was a transparent ringing.

Purple light rippled on a cut-off section of river. A wash of purple light rocked on lit wavelets and oily reflections.

I looked up.

The glare came from high above, fifteen, twenty, twenty-five storeys up, from a neon sign, the name of a hotel in purple, on a concrete curtain wall below a balcony, the building's penthouse suite.

I jumped out of the car. The lights were turning green. I dashed towards Cyril's car.

He was pulling away. I banged on the window. I thumped so hard I thought I'd smash the glass. He braked. His door flew open. Cyril jumped out. Angry. Ready for a fight.

"What the fuck, man?!"

Traffic surged past us. The cars behind were pulling out around us, their horns blaring.

"She's here! They're here!"

"What?!" He was going to hit me.

I looked around. Speeding cars. The traffic lights green. Offices. The hotel entrance was on the other side of the road, across six lanes of traffic.

I pointed up at the railing of the penthouse balcony.

"Up there!"

The commissionaire wore a top hat and a greatcoat. I nodded to him as we strode in.

"We're wastin' precious time, man." Cyril's voice echoed off cut glass and polished stone. "They're in the West End. Not a shit hole like this."

An expanse of marble and chandeliers. A grand piano. Some rockery. A display of ferns. The tinkle of a fountain. But Cyril was right. The place felt cheap and nasty. The hotel was a transit dormitory with five-star pretensions.

Three clerks sat at the reception desk. They didn't greet us as we passed. The lobby was empty. We seemed to be the only guests.

"This is crazy, man. They're not here."

There were two lifts. I banged both buttons.

One of the receptionists picked up a phone.

The lift had a mirror. Rising floor by floor, I studied my face. Cyril was right. I looked crazy. With his ashen jaw and Old Testament eyes, so did Cyril.

Pra hadn't wanted to come. We'd left him in the car. I didn't judge him. He'd taken a vow of nonviolence.

We reached the penthouse floor and a bell pinged.

We stepped out into a smell of stale champagne. Half a dozen uncorked magnums stood on a trolley outside the only door on the landing.

Music thudded from inside. An engineered beat with playgroup vocals. Disco funk for non-dancers.

I tried the handle. The door was locked.

Cyril banged with his fist.

The door opened.

The guy was bigger than Cyril.

He looked at me.

"Are you Adrian?" He was stoned. He was out of his tree. His eyes had trouble dealing with the picture of us walking past him. "Lee said to wait for Adrian." Gigi lay on the carpet outside the bathroom. "Lee says, Adrian'll sort it out. No one's to leave."

A guy walked out of a bedroom with his dick in his hand. He thumbed the foreskin like a rosary medal. Carla sat on the bed in the room behind him, spitting into a tissue.

"Where's Natalie?"

The guy grinned and kept thumbing.

Pauline and a fat blonde girl were dancing naked in front of a home movie plasma screen showing hairy buttocks and an anus pumping in and out, watched by a guy swaying in time to the disco music. Pauline and the blonde twined in each others arms, kissing as they danced. They didn't even see us. The guy swayed sideways, weaving his head. The girls were blocking the screen.

The security guy looked from me to Cyril and back again.

"Are you Adrian? Lee said Adrian'll bring some people'll sort it out."

"Where's Natalie, man?"

"Natalie?"

The bathroom floor was flooded. The bath was stacked with bubbles. Someone had left the tap on. A skin of water ran down the bath board. Red scum capped the heap of foam.

The second bedroom was empty. The contents of Natalie's handbag were spilled out over the floor.

In the third bedroom, a man lay on his back on the bed. His thighs and belly were matted with thick, black hair. It was the guy in Jack's photo.

His goggling eyeballs and florid jowls had been pumped larger than life. A complicated cat's cradle of white string around his genitals fastened the triple strands round his throat. He wasn't breathing. His eyes saw nothing.

The security man followed us into the bedroom.

"Are you...?"

Cyril had been waiting to hit someone all night.

There was a crunch of knuckle on bone, a squelch as his signet ring buried itself in facial tissue and broke the man's jaw.

The guy didn't fall over. He hardly staggered. He wasn't stoned anymore. He pulled out a knife and sank it into Cyril's stomach.

The man who'd come out of the bedroom was putting his trousers on. The guy who'd been watching TV was hurrying into his jacket, banging his pocket for wallet and keys. The security man had disappeared. Pauline and the fat girl were still dancing.

Carla came out of the first bedroom hugging her shoulders, covering her breasts with her elbows. The hair between her legs was wispy, like a new beard.

"Where's Natalie?"

Natalie was out on the balcony. She was slumped against the railing with her back to me. There was a festoon of string around her neck. For a second I thought she was going to jump.

The balcony door was locked. I couldn't get out to her.

Her frock's plunging neckline plunged from her shoulder blades. It was on back to front. She held a bottle of champagne by the neck, behind her leg, like a baton in a relay race.

I found the lock on the door and got it open. Out on the balcony a freezing wind blew.

Her face was cold and pale. I couldn't tell if she was breathing or not.

A tangle of loose ends hung from the knot around her throat. She must have severed the string that tied her to the dead man with her fingernails like I'd seen Pra do in the temple.

The string around her throat had been drawn so tight I was scared I'd choke her if I tried to get my fingers under it. I plucked at the knot. She made a dreadful gurgling sound. Spittle and lipstick bubbled from the corner of her mouth.

The bottle slipped from her fingers and smashed on the tiles. Champagne swilled round her feet.

I picked up a sliver of glass and cut the string. Blood blossomed on her throat but I got the knot free.

She fell against the railing. Her shoulders quivered. Something was stopping her from breathing. Her shoulders kicked. There was a place, between the red line left by the ligature and her collarbone, where the air wouldn't go down. I could see it as she struggled.

She slumped against me. The shuddering reached down past her shoulder blades, down past her collarbone, down past her heart. I held her against me as the oxygen fought its way down towards the terror that paralysed her lungs.

"Natalie..."

I wet her hair with kisses.

Twenty five floors below headlights streamed down a hill towards a set of traffic lights. In a gap between tower blocks purple light rocked on oily water.

A car swept up the ramp to the hotel entrance. Some men jumped out.

I carried her inside.

Cyril was sitting on the sofa with a lapful of blood.

"Okay, man. I'm okay," he said. "It's nothin.'"

Pauline and Carla were getting dressed. The blonde girl was walking around with a shoe in her hand, clomping on one heel. Her Slavic eyes were stare-y.

"There's some men coming up!"

Blood glistened in the flies of Cyril's trousers. He dragged Gigi to her feet. She smiled at him. She'd been punched, but she wasn't unconscious. She must have pretended to be drunk when things kicked off.

Amy was in the toilet, trembling too much to speak.

Natalie had lost consciousness again. She grew heavy in my arms. She could have been dead if it weren't for the way she was shivering.

I grabbed a man's jacket from the back of a chair and covered her with it and carried her out through the door.

We headed for the lifts.

By the time we were all out on the landing, one of the lifts was on its way up.

I banged the button of the other lift, praying to God it wasn't somewhere down on the ground floor.

The door trundled open. We crowded in. I pressed DOWN.

The foyer was empty. So was the reception desk. The commissionaire had made himself scarce.

There was a stampede of high heels on marble. Pauline and Carla had their coats over their faces, their dread of deportation was stronger than their fear of death. The blonde girl clomped along in one shoe, a silver lamé stiletto in front of her face.

Cyril had his coat over Gigi's head, holding her upright as he stooped out through the automatic doors. Drops of blood pursued him across the marble.

Natalie was slumped in my arms, her head dangling back from under the coat, her face uncovered. I glanced up at the ceiling, looking for cameras.

A black Mercedes was parked on the ramp outside the hotel.

We hurried down the slope to the footpath. Heavy traffic blocked our way across the road to the cars.

I looked up at the penthouse suite twenty-five floors above us. Tiny figures stood at the balcony railing looking down through the glare of a streetlamp.

We ran through blaring headlights.

Pra was asleep. He was curled up in my front passenger seat, his feet tucked under him and his head squashed against the window. A circle of shaved scalp stuck to the glass like a sun-browned decal.

I opened the back door and lay Natalie down on the backseat. She was still unconscious.

Pra sat up. He was wide awake in an instant. He swung around and stared at Natalie.

I slammed the door shut, ran round to the driver's side, jumped in, and started the engine. As I pulled away, the passenger door swung open towards the footpath. Pra was half in and half out of the car.

He glanced at me and then at Natalie unconscious in the backseat.

"Mai dai! Mai dai!" He was in enough trouble with the sangha already. "Phom bhai rot Cyril."

He hurried back to the next car. Natalie and I were alone.

As I pulled out into the traffic, the fear that had got me into the lift and out of the hotel hit me as if I'd touched a live cable. The terror that had managed to carry Natalie dead weight across the foyer and over six lanes of traffic locked me in its current.

Cyril's gasp as the blade went into his stomach, the retching gurgle in Natalie's throat when I tried to undo the string, the thick black hair on the dead man's belly, a red light ticking off the floors as the other lift came up—rushed up, as close behind me as the headlights in my rear-view mirror.

I had to find a hospital.

I sped north. I was in the maze of roads somewhere around Liverpool Street Station.

The Royal Free was the only hospital I could think of. It was miles to the north, in Hampstead. I held a picture of its floodlit entrance to Accident and Emergency in my head as I sped up Gray's Inn Road.

She'd killed a man; if I took her to hospital, we'd be arrested; if I didn't take her, she might die.

"He don die I... I big Buddha woman..."

The rasping whisper in the backseat was like a voice in a dream.

"...I vics woman...do magic big more than he..."

The ligature had damaged her throat.

"He don kill I... cannot... I big Buddha woman... fuck he dead..."

Convulsive shudders ran up and down her body, like a snake shedding its skin.

"... I number one vics woman..."

The hospital entrance was brightly lit. A concrete ramp swept up to the doors of Accident and Emergency.

"WHA?!"

She clambered between the seats like an out-of-control child. She dragged at my hands on the steering wheel.

"No! No! No do, honey! Cannot!"

"You're hurt. We've got to."

"They send I back!"

She needed medical attention. She could die. It was more important than getting deported.

"I kill he! They put I prison!"

I didn't know what to do.

"I okay! Don't must go!"

I pulled away and headed for Stratford.

She sat in the front passenger seat, her cheek against the glass, staring out at the empty streets. She kept on muttering.

"He think he big devil."

Her voice croaked painfully.

"More big than I big Buddha woman."

She wouldn't stop.

"He do string strong. I do string strong more than he."

She was driving me crazy.

"Natalie..."

There were things she needed to be told. Far more important things than 'he think he big devil' and 'I big Buddha woman'. She needed to shut up and listen. There were things she needed to urgently understand.

"I knew where you were!"

"... I do string good..."

"I saw the light on the water! The purple light from the hotel. I knew where you were!"

"... I cannot breathing...I don care... I angel girl...!"

"If I hadn't found you when I did...!"

In each other's arms, asleep but awake, making love without making love, we'd gone outside space and time, we'd spun a moment that had yet to be, and a place that had yet to be, out of our bodies—and it had brought me to her on the hotel balcony. She wasn't interested.

It was only as I parked outside the Stratford house that I realised it mightn't be safe to go inside. Whoever these people were, they'd found Jack and killed him easily enough. Lee knew about the Stratford house. He'd been here. But Cyril said that Lee had vanished. Adrian Whitely couldn't have the address.

The bay window was in darkness.

The knife going into Cyril's belly, Natalie's choking gurgle, the thatch on the dead man's stomach, stepped up behind me as I put my key in the lock.

I'd seen at least two of the faces of the men at the party before, on TV or in the newspapers somewhere. Jack had said there were big businessmen, with powerful connections, and politicians too in the cartel or gang or sex ring or whatever it was. Perhaps I should go straight to the police. The party alone was enough to put them in gaol even if their arms deals weren't, except... Natalie had killed a man.

The front window was in darkness.

I felt sure I'd left the lights on, when I dashed out after Pra and Cyril.

They were already her. They'd got here before us.

I pushed the door open and felt for the light switch.

The living room was empty. The empty whiskey bottle stood on the coffee table exactly where I'd left it.

Natalie headed for the stairs.

"... I do string good... I fuck he dead..."

I didn't want to think about it.

I followed her up the stairs.

"I knew where you were!"

The bedroom light was on.

Her fingers groped up and down her back, searching her frock's neckline for a zipper. She didn't realise she had it on back to front.

She gave up and dragged the dress off over her head. She was wearing nothing underneath.

"Natalie, I went outside space..." I stepped out of my trousers. "... And time."

She plugged my mouth with her tongue. She didn't want to know. The big Buddha woman was as scared as I was.

She dropped backwards onto the bed. I lay on top of her.

Her pussy was so wet and wide open she could have given birth. My cock was flaccid. It felt as flaccid a used condom.

"We did something magical!"

Downstairs, I heard a click as the lock on the front door was slipped.

She groaned.

"He wan scary I. *I no scary*!"

Her fingers tugged at the tip of my cock. She pinched and kneaded my glans. The tip of my cock felt like a teatful of someone else's semen.

Downstairs, footsteps crossed the living room.

"The hotel. The balcony. They came out of my body... and your body..."

We were trapped in the bedroom.

She rolled over and climbed on top of me.

"He fuck I big..."

She stuffed my cock into her pussy. It barely stayed inside her.

"He do string big..."

Footsteps were coming up the stairs.

"I was someone else! You were..."

I tongued the red mark around her throat. The cord had burned the skin. Her Adam's apple reared and bucked.

"... He think I cannot make he cum..."

She rolled my cock around inside her pussy clenching and letting go. It didn't fall out.

"...I big Buddha woman..."

"I was him! Up there! With you!"

"He think I die... *I don die...!*"

Her pussy was slippery as a potter's hands working a lump of clay, insisting it stand up.

"... I look he eye..."

"I thought I was Pra. But I wasn't. I was him. The guy in Jack's photo."

A floorboard creaked softly beneath carpet. They were outside the bedroom door. It sounded as if there were at least three or four of them.

"...He cum so big, he dead before he stop..."

Her fingers went round my throat. Her thumbs jammed my windpipe.

"... Hold I, Jim..."

The unapproachable woman reared upwards, poured burning and candescent, up past where her fingers gouged, beyond where my tongue traced the line in her throat, behind my eyes, up past my brain, which needed air, but the woman who shone and stung didn't. She continued out, through the roof of my skull and the crown of her head, past the unshielded bulb and woodchip ceiling. Natalie was right—a Buddha woman looked back from her face, shone full-featured from every pore of her skin, as many-eyed as there were pinpoint jewels in her face, a tegument made of seeing, up which I travelled, diamond by diamond, towards her eyes.

CHAPTER EIGHT

My phone rang.

The bedroom was in darkness.

The ringing came from somewhere down on the floor.

I rolled out of bed and stood on it, the vibration massaging my foot through my trousers' pocket.

"Jim!"

It was Cyril.

"Cyril! Are you okay?"

"Yeah, I'm fine." I heard him wince. "Know this doctor. Look, Jim..."

"Where's Gigi?"

"With me. Everyone's okay. We're safe. Somewhere. The Albanian bird's headed off, Jim, where are you?"

"At Stratford."

"Natalie?"

"She's okay, too. She's here."

"You gotta get out of there pronto, man."

"Yeah. I suppose."

"NOW, Jim! I'd let you come here, but it's too late." There was a sharp intake of breath. "Get outta there, Jim. They'll trace you in no time. They know Natalie was the dead guy's girl."

"Cyril. She didn't kill him. It was some sort of sex act. He initiated it."

"Tell that to his mates, bro."

"Maybe I should go to the police."

"FUCK MAN! Don't even think about it."

"If the police know Adrian Whitely's involved..."

"Jesus, Jim! No! They know already. Get outta there, man. Adrian Whitely's connected. So's the guy Natalie killed. They'll put her in prison n throw away the key. If she's lucky!"

345

"I told you. She didn't. It was him. Some sex thing."

Cyril groaned.

"The *cops* are lookin' for Natalie, Jim. Already. The cops're in Adrian's pocket. These dudes control everything, man. She'll never even see prison."

"I still think..."

"For fuck's sake, Jim, NO! Get outta there. NOW! Switch on the TV. Have a look at the news, if you don't believe me..." It took ages for him to catch his breath. He was hurt worse than he was letting on. "... Those guys we saw, comin' up in the lift. They came to get the body. With Adrian Whitely. To get the body n kill Natalie n the other girls too n get the body outta the country on the quiet. But for some reason... I don't know what... they didn't...oh fuck..." There was a long pause. "... For some reason they left the body n contacted the police instead. The police are workin' for them.. The cops are lookin' for you n Natalie already. Me n the girls too. They got us on CCTV..."

"But..."

I waited for him to continue. I could hear that it was hurting him to speak.

Even if Natalie got into trouble, it was better than these guys catching up with us. I had to go to the police. They'd deport her, but surely they couldn't put her in gaol. The guy had killed himself. Natalie hadn't done it, even though she kept going on about 'I fuck he dead'.

"GET OUT OF THAT HOUSE, JIM! NOW! For Jesus's sake. DON'T GO TO THE COPS! I don't trust 'em. I dunno why Adrian Whitely went to the police. There must be people higher up he's got somethin' on. Fuck knows who else was at that party with the dead guy."

"Where will we go?"

"I dunno. Not here. N listen. Throw your phone away. Get rid of it. N Natalie's phone too. They'll track you."

He'd taken a risk ringing me. If Cyril hadn't come knocking yesterday, Natalie would be dead.

"Look. Cyril. Thanks. If you hadn't..."

"Fuck off, Jim. There aint time..."

"Okay. I'll speak to you soon..."

"No you won't. Get rid of your phone Jim. Natalie's too."

The thought of losing contact with him scared me.

"Okay, Cyril. I'll..."

He'd already rung off.

I threw some clothes into a hold-all. Natalie found an old pair of jeans and some T-shirts among the thongs and see-thru tops in the wardrobe.

I switched on the TV while we were getting ready to leave, and looked for a news channel. There was a report on the worsening situation in Venezuela.

Natalie wasn't keen on handing over her phone, but she realized it was urgent and gave it to me.

I took the phones into the back yard and smashed them with a brick. There was a container of mouldy weed killer and I immersed the remains in that.

When I got back Natalie was in the kitchen packing herbs and spices into a cardboard box.

The newsreader's voice came from the living room:

'...Where a senior delegate was found murdered last night...'

We forgot about packing.

'... Police are hunting for several people seen leaving the hotel...'

My glance up at the balcony had been disastrous. A camera on the streetlamp stanchion had caught me looking straight up into it, with Natalie in my arms, the jacket covering her shoulders but not her head. Both our faces were clearly visible.

'... The killers were amongst a group attending the party where the businessman died...'

The top of Cyril's head. His dreads bobbing. His coat held like a toreador's cloak over Gigi's face as she ran crouched beside him. Carla, Pauline and Amy with their faces covered. The crown of a blonde head, a high-heeled shoe pressed to its eyes, hobbling across the footpath.

'... A reward is being offered for information leading to the arrest of suspected...'

Suspected? They already knew who we were.

Cyril was right. Adrian Whitely had contacted the police. Keeping details of the party out of the news must surely have been a top priority, yet Adrian had gone to the authorities. For some reason catching us was more urgent than questions being asked about what had gone on at the party or who else was there. It was inexplicable. Unless something had happened while we were in the penthouse suite, something we'd seen or done that they needed to keep from being known.

Natalie stood in the doorway. Her eyes were grave.

"I making bad luck."

"No."

"Life be fore. You I drown two gether. Now this life."

"Don't say that."

I didn't want to listen to all that stuff now. There was no time.

"I kill man."

"He was bad."

She shrugged.

"Bad luck same same."

"He killed himself. It wasn't you."

"Was I. I kill he in I heart. I wan do."

She put down the carrier bags she'd packed. She was taking rice, chili, ginger grass. DVDs of Thai soap operas. The rice steamer. She seemed disoriented. She was still in shock.

"Your fault, too."

"Yes."

"You don stop I go party."

"I know."

"You think I stay with Pra. You crazy, same me."

I switched the TV off.

"We've got to get out of here."

She shuddered. "Yes. Must going. Quick lee."

Outside, wintry morning light was seeping into the darkened street. Wisps of white breath clung to our mouths in the silence.

Natalie ferried the rice cooker and her carrier bags and boxes to the car and assembled them on the footpath. I couldn't bring myself to tell her that we weren't going to need any of it. She'd brought hardly any clothes.

I opened the boot.

My books lay scattered around in the bottom where I'd thrown them the night I went back to Islington. *Freedom From The Known*, *The End Of Time*, *The Serpent Power*. Alchemy. Tao. The Tantras. Buddha. Melissa had dumped my whole library on the doorstep.

I didn't protest about the vacuum cleaner when Natalie slung it in on top of the *Corpus Hermeticum*.

I drove south. I headed for the Blackwall Tunnel.

It was still too early for the rush-hour traffic to have begun. We were one of the few cars on the road, out with delivery trucks and the first buses.

Careening under the river, the tunnel was as empty as a bobsleigh run.

Even if my BMW hadn't been caught on CCTV outside the hotel, the police would have traced it by now. My vehicle make and registration number would be on their computers already. On the deserted roads, we were an open target.

Natalie surveyed the streets of Greenwich as blankly as the tiles of the Blackwall Tunnel.

"I make you bad luck."

"No you don't."

"I do bad for you."

"Stop it."

I had no idea what had happened in the hotel, between her and the guy in Jack's photograph. I'd heard about erotic asphyxiation, suffocation at the moment of orgasm to obtain some sort of high, but he'd participated in it as much as her. It wasn't her fault that it had gone wrong. Even if Soom Bon's story about her sister was true, and she'd deliberately sought the guy out, it still didn't make it murder.

"Better you don be with I."

"Don't say that."

"More safe you I don be two gether."

Up ahead, the wail of a siren sped towards us.

The police car was a quarter of a mile ahead of us, travelling fast.

We were on a dual carriageway, with a central reservation, on the other side of the reservation from the police car's blue lights as it flashed past.

I swung left onto a side street.

Five hundred metres behind back, at the traffic lights, the police car was doing a U-turn through the red.

I drove down back streets and across junctions. I tried to stop speeding. Speeding attracted attention in these narrow suburb thoroughfares. There was no sign of the police car behind us, but I could still hear sirens.

I had no idea where I was heading or what I was going to do. The longer we stayed in the car, the sooner we'd be caught. I couldn't phone Cyril.

The streets began to fill with rush-hour traffic. Crowds of people hurried along the footpaths to bus stops and the underground.

I wondered if we wouldn't be better off dumping the car. We could mingle with the throng of commuters, and maybe head back into central London. There was CCTV everywhere, but it was preferable to staying in the car. I avoided anything that looked like a main road, and kept my eye open for an Underground sign.

We got caught behind a bus picking up passengers at a bus stop. Several of the people glanced at us. It took ages for the bus to move. I stared straight ahead into a blaze of sunlight.

It was half past eight. We were still behind the bus, inching along in a queue of vehicles dropping children off outside a school.

South London meant that we weren't all that far from the sea. We could head for Brighton or Eastbourne. Maybe a seaside hotel or a holiday B and B on a cliff. Bad idea. They watch the news at the seaside too.

The lollipop lady frowned—a middle-aged man and a young Asian woman in a fancy car—as we crept past.

We were in a one-way system north of Croydon.

"Hungry."

I couldn't believe my ears.

"Later."

"Must eating." There was enough chili and ginger grass in the boot to prepare a banquet, but there was nowhere to plug in the rice steamer. "That one. Okay?"

She pointed at a workman's café. The café was packed with builders and truck drivers digesting our faces on the front page of their *Suns*. Through the window I could even see a TV set glimmering on a shelf behind the counter.

"Natalie, we can't just walk in there."

I was ravenous myself. I hadn't eaten for over twenty-four hours. The only thing my stomach had seen since yesterday morning was a bottle of whisky.

"I hungry." She'd probably eaten at the party. "Must eating breakfast."

She spotted another greasy spoon behind Selhurst station. This early, workmen's cafes were the only places open. Here too, a TV set glimmered on a shelf above the counter.

"Natalie." I tried to be patient, "you saw the CCTV pictures. On TV. If we go in there, someone will see us." I resented being made to sound like a schoolteacher. "They'll call the police. The police'll be here so quick you won't even get your breakfast."

"Don eating breakfast. Get sick."

I felt like tearing my hair out.

We passed a supermarket. I dived into a parking space.

"I'll get something in there. Bread or cheese or something. This is crazy."

"Must eating hot, honey. Don eating hot breakfast. Stomach get sick."

I panicked. I was as disoriented as she was. Driving around South London made as little sense as walking into a cafe and getting arrested on the spot. It was wrong getting angry with her for being hungry. I was staring ravenously at the suburban streets myself, as if a roundabout or an arcade of shops might suddenly fold back, like a page in a street directory, and let me in somewhere safe and warm and comforting as a hot breakfast.

I wasn't just disoriented. The purple light on the river last night had done something to my sense of space. That was why this felt so lost and aimless and lonely, driving around South London without any real direction I was going in, last night's hallucination getting mixed up with ideas from the books in the boot: There's no such thing as time; there's only space. Time is a hallucination created by the complexity of space; not three-dimensional space—these rows of snug houses, these purposeful fences, these sedate billboards, these self-assured parks—but a multidimensional space so folded in on itself that it seems to move, even though it's static. I seem to be driving past a stranded cinema, but the cinema's a fairground I'm running towards, aged eight, and the fairground's a police cell I'm sitting in, in the near future; and the only thing this infinity of cinemas that I'm driving past has in common is that, in spite of the rush-hour traffic and the throngs of commuters, there's no one there, not even Natalie, just me.

"Thai, honey! Thai!" She was jumping around in her seat like a child at Christmas. "Is open!" We were in a hilly area somewhere outside Croydon. Steep inclines offered up glimpses of a radio tower. Gridlocked traffic blocked the main road. "Thai, Jim! Thai!" I'd turned down a side street towards a railway cutting. The light stanchions and grandstands of a football stadium appeared on the hill to our left. Crystal Palace Football Ground. There'd be a station at Norwood Junction. I could dump the car there and we could head back into central London by train. "Thai restaurant!" It was a tiny place, jammed between a betting shop and an upholsterer's workshop. There was a picture of a royal elephant in the window, and a sign: CRYSTAL PALACE ROYAL RESTAURANT. THAI CUSINE. ENGLISH BREAKFAST. "Can get takeaway."

It was lucky I'd slowed down. She was already climbing out of the car.

I grabbed her arm.

"I'll go." There was slightly less chance of me being recognised than her. "Wait here."

She laughed.

"You don speaking Thai!" She was out on the footpath. "You don know how order!"

The restaurant's being Thai exempted it from the real world.

Inside, CRYSTAL PALACE ROYAL RESTAURANT was poky— two rows of four-seater tables, with a central aisle so narrow I had to walk behind Natalie to get to the counter at the back.

Posters of Thai tourist attractions decorated the walls: Phuket. The White Temple. Ko Samui.

Four Crystal Palace football scarves, pinned to the wall at right angles, framed a poster of the nineteen ninety Cup Final team.

There were half a dozen customers eating breakfast.

This place had a TV set too, perched on a shelf under the ceiling, the screen speckled with cooking oil.

The sound was turned down, but the omnipresent news program was showing. A newscaster mouthed silently through spots of oil, above a ribbon of rolling headlines.

"We order..." I whispered. "... And get out quick!"

We waited at the counter. Ten seconds. Twenty seconds. Forty. A minute. A minute and a half. Two minutes. We were still waiting.

There seemed to be no one serving. Behind a bead curtain, the kitchen stood silent.

Natale pointed at one of the posters.

"Wat Suthep!" BEAUTIFUL CHIANG MAI. A golden jedi. Multi coloured dragons. A row of temple gongs. "Wat Suthep be north. I go there I little girl!"

It looked beautiful.

I glanced round at the other customers.

There were four builders reading newspapers at a table covered with finished breakfasts, the ketchup cold, the baked bean sauce congealing, their empty plates uncollected.

A young woman in a blue skirt and an Argos blouse picked at the last tomato ring of her salad and stared up at the TV.

An old man was stretching out a mug of tea.

None of them volunteered any information about the lack of service.

"Let's go."

Up on the screen, a crowd of demonstrators jostled with police. Venezuela again.

ARMS DELEGATE MURDERED AT HOTEL SEX PARTY scrolled across the bottom of the picture.

"Natalie!"

"Hungry, honey."

I stepped around behind the counter and pushed my head through the bead curtain.

Blackened saucepans. Woks. A tray of eggs. A jar of chicken feet. The kitchen was empty.

"That's it. Come on."

A man lay asleep under the counter wrapped in a duvet.

His eyes shot open.

"Sawaddee krap! Good morning, sir! SawaddEE? How I help you? What you want?"

He jumped up, bouncing on his toes, shaking the sleep out of his head, like a boxer warming up before a fight.

"Sorry. Very tired. Sleep bad bad last night. You want eat some breakfast?"

He saw Natalie and beamed:

"SawaddEEEEE!"

"Sawaddee ka!" said Natalie. For an instant, I thought they knew each other. The man was short and tubby. He had a diamond stud in his ear and a bald, shiny head. "Mii ahaan chao baang rai?" Natalie was ordering our breakfast. "Honey. This Sam. Sam come from North same I." Sam shook my hand. "Sam. This Jim."

"Swaddee krap, Loong Jim! Good see you!"

I glanced up at the TV. A weather chart of England, Scotland, Wales and Northern Ireland. MUELLER REPORT MAKES INDICTMENTS scrolling underneath.

"I'm sorry," I said. "But we're in a hurry."

"No problem!" Sam beamed. "I cooking everything!"

He pointed at a menu board on the wall behind the counter. The board was enormous. It took up half the wall.

The menu hypnotized Natalie. She stared wide-eyed, a tourist at a banquet.

Sam had a gravelly racetrack barker's voice, reading off from the menu in Thai. Natalie kept interrupting him with questions.

"What you fancy, Jim? English breakfast? Or Thai?"

I felt giddy.

The menu had six columns, each column cross-referenced between lines of dotted red paint, to the other five.

FULL ENGLISH BREAKFAST was served between six thirty a.m. and one p.m.

Between eleven a.m. and one p.m., FULL ENGLISH BREAKFAST shared a slot with FULL ENGLISH LUNCH.

FULL ENGLISH LUNCH lasted till four thirty p.m.

From noon to six p.m., FULL ENGLISH LUNCH was joined by SPECIAL THAI LUNCH.

From six p.m. till midnight, SPECIAL THAI LUNCH blossomed into FULL THAI DINNER.

Customers who wanted a FULL THAI BREAKFAST or a FULL ENGLISH DINNER were enjoined to speak to the manager.

The old man with the mug of tea returned a *Daily Mail* to Sam's heap of newspapers:

ARMS FIXER DIES IN HOTEL ORGY

"Natalie!" Natalie didn't hear. She was still ordering. "We've got to go! Please!"

Sam raised one finger.

"Two minutes!"

He bounced off into the kitchen.

We sat down at a table. I looked up at the TV screen.

The newsreader was staring down at his desk. His mouth had stopped moving. He shuffled a sheet of paper, and came up reading.

The instant our faces appeared on the screen, one of the builders glanced up from his *Sun*.

"Natalie! Please!'"

"Is okay, honey. Sam good man."

"That guy's seen us," I nodded. "The one in the blue jacket."

Her head dangling back from under the coat as I carried her, her face upside down but clearly visible, my face, larger, above hers, craning around and upwards, straight into the camera.

Cyril and Gigi. The blonde girl hobbling. It lasted ten or fifteen seconds. Shots of the hotel facade. Footage of the Arms Fair. A senior policeman making a statement.

It took forever to roll on to the next item.

Our food still hadn't arrived.

"Natalie. Please."

"Must eating, honey."

The builder in the blue jacket was looking at us.

Sam came out of the kitchen.

"I said takeaway!" He carried two plates in one hand, three in the other, with more dishes balanced on his forearms. "NATALIE!"

Sam plonked the plates on the table and Natalie tucked in. She'd ordered dried fish, glazed pork, chicken feet, chili salad, and rice soup, with a dessert of fried bananas in coconut milk for herself, and a sausage, egg, bacon, beans, and tomatoes gut-buster for me.

"Must eating. Make strong."

The builder in the blue jacket was leaning across his empty plate, whispering to his mates. The two that had their backs to us turned and looked.

Sam sat down at our table and chatted with Natalie while we ate. He was pleased to have someone to speak Thai with.

"Gin khao, honey!"

My sausages were delicious, except they were dropping through a hole in the bottom of my stomach.

"Natalie! Hurry! *Please!*"

"Is okay, honey. Sam good man." Sam was Thai. It made him magical. She tried a chicken foot. "Alloy maak maak, Pii Sam."

Sam beamed.

"Pet arroy!"

She was incapable of hurrying her food.

Sam asked her:

"Sammee mai?"

Your husband?

"Chai."

Something melted inside me.

"Poo chai geng dii!"

Sam thought I was a nice man.

She gazed at me.

"Chai. Dii maak jang looei."

The builder in the blue jacket had his phone in his hand.

I stood up.

"Thanks, Sam. How much do I owe you?"

Sam took an eternity totting up the bill. The amount was ridiculously small. I gave him a twenty pound note and told him to keep the change. He refused and scuttled off to the till. I'd insulted him.

"Yeah. Hello. Is that? Just a sec..."

The guy hurried out to finish his call on the footpath.

Sam was still arguing about the tip as we left.

The builder was five metres away, on the footpath, by the furniture workshop window. When he saw us, he stopped talking.

He was scared. The police were telling him not to confront us. We'd just killed a man.

I started the car. For a moment, I thought there was something wrong with the engine. A battering noise shook the roof. The sound pressed down on me, drumming through the top of my skull. It came from above us.

The helicopter was half a mile away to our left. I couldn't tell whether it was circling towards us, or heading south along the route we'd originally taken.

The builder's sighting had narrowed down the search area.

The roads were still busy. I took the shortcut towards Shooters Hill.

I had to dump the car. I should have ditched it hours ago. It was getting late. By now everybody on the bus or the train would have seen our faces in their newspapers or on TV.

We were on a stretch of a road where the sort of hotels used by sales reps and travellers for small companies alternated with Social Security bed and breakfast hostels. Even these were impossible. Even if the receptionist didn't recognize us, they'd ask for our IDs.

I was running out of money. I barely had enough cash on me for a couple of days stay in a hostel, even if that were feasible.

There was a little left in my bank account, but using an ATM would be suicide.

East of Shooters Hill, we turned onto a long, non-residential stretch of road. Industrial estates. Garden centres. Car showrooms.

The helicopter was miles to the south, soundless and tiny, like a hawk hovering in the sunshine.

Some of the car dealerships sold second-hand cars.

I turned back at the next roundabout and cruised past the used car lots.

"What you do?"

I didn't answer. My heart was thumping. I had less than two hundred pounds in my wallet. My BMW was worth forty-five grand.

I doubled back again.

"Cannot, honey. Danger."

The first of the car lots was classy. There were Jaguar and Mercedes flags. A copperplate "...Quality..." on the sign. A silver-haired man in white running shoes was sweeping the footpath.

I drove past.

The next yard had enough bunting to celebrate a royal wedding. Rows of bonnets shone in the sun. AMAZING DISCOUNTS! blazed in the windshields.

I kept going.

The third lot looked more like a breaker's yard than somewhere you could sell a BMW. The forecourt was caked with grease. The shells of stripped down cars stood on breeze blocks.

The office was a caravan. A sign read: TOILETS FOR CUSTOMER USE ONLY.

I pulled in.

"Cannot, Jim! No!"

I saw the panic in her eyes. I was as irrational about my BMW as she was about her Thai breakfast.

"You stay here."

I walked over to the caravan. I could hear the sound of a television through the door. I knocked.

"Door's open."

The accent was cockney. It sounded wrong south of the river.

A short, dumpy man sat in a swivel chair, his boots up on the littered desk. His shoulder-length hair was as greasy as his yard.

He was watching me look up at him, Natalie in my arms, on a fourteen-inch TV balanced on a pile of maintenance manuals.

He glanced from my face to the screen then back again.

'Police are hunting for a man and woman seen leaving the hotel where a delegate to the London Arms Fair was found murdered last night...'

He double-checked. There was no mistaking. He swung his feet off the desk.

'... The killers, believed to be a prostitute and her pimp, were in a group attending the party where the businessman died...'

I turned to go.

His beady eyes were flu-glazed.

"Yep?"

He wore a gold earring. He looked like a heavy-metal roadie gone to fat. Tattoos climbed from the collar of his jacket and all the way up his neck.

I hesitated.

One of the tattoos was a red and black three-pronged circle.

"I want to sell my car."

He held my eye.

"Oh yeah?" He knew why I was here. "What make?"

A kerosene heater smoked in the draught from the door.

"BMW. 4 Class. Sports Coupe."

The ring in his eyebrow lifted.

"Mm..." He grinned. "... Better have a look at it..."

We went out. He ran his eye over my BMW. I'd left the engine running. The gates were twenty metres away. I might be able to get to the car and reverse out before he got them shut. "...Very nice..."

The newsreader droned on inside the caravan.

'... A reward is being offered for information leading to the arrest of...'

The chain-link gates looked flimsy. I could ram the car through them. I decided to make a dash for it.

Natalie got out.

A sparkle surfaced through the flu-y haze.

"She come with the motor?"

"No."

"Look, mate." He nodded at his yard. He sold the sort of cars poor people buy to get them around for a few months before the road tax expires. "You don't wanna sell that motor to me."

"That's right. I'm here to use the toilets."

He smiled.

"Thing is...?"

"Jim."

There was no point in lying about my name.

"Frank."

Frank glanced at a shed at the top of the yard. He was waiting for the person who was inside to come down and help him grab me.

"Thing is, Jim. You could get twenty-five grand for that motor. This morning. BMW, Kensington. As we speak."

"It's a long drive."

"Honey! Must going!"

Natalie opened the passenger door. She jumped back in. She waved at me to hurry. Her hysteria was patently obvious.

Frank nodded toward the highway, in the direction from which we'd come.

"Grandad up the road'd give you ten."

"I don't like his running shoes."

Frank resembled Meat Loaf when he smiled.

"Five, tops, Jim. I'll have trouble raising that." He was toying with me. The reward for our arrest was going to be much more than what he could make on a BMW the police were already looking for. "I don't wanna rob ya, Jim."

"Five's fine."

"Better take it up the workshop then."

He nodded at the shed, beyond the heap of gear boxes and the pungent toilets.

I got in and drove the car up.

The shed doors were skewiff. Frank grappled with the padlock.

"Don't get your shoes dirty, love."

Inside the workshop, under a fluorescent tube, away from the busy road outside, Frank took a longer, closer look at the car.

A respray. New plates. A forged logbook. A trip to the continent. It was a huge risk, compared to a legally-earned reward.

"Take me an hour or two to get the cash for you, Jim."

Frank locked the workshop and took us back to the caravan. He brought a plastic chair in from the yard. He brushed ice and dead leaves off the seat.

"You n yer missus make yourselves comfy." The air swam in kerosene fumes. I felt exhausted. "I'll have to lock the place up. Ya don't mind do ya?" He nodded at the front gates. "Kids around here are murder, man. Trash me fucking toilets."

As soon as Frank was gone, I switched the TV off.

"We crazy," said Natalie, settling down in Frank's swivel chair. "He bring police."

The plastic chair was freezing. I leaned my head against the wall.

Thoughts of climbing Frank's fence and looking for a bus stop floated away on the kerosene fumes.

It was too cold to move. If we were going to get busted, here was as good a place as any.

Through a nodding doze I heard the sound of the caravan door opening.

It was Frank. He had five thousand pounds in used fifties.

We needed transportation.

Frank sold me a Micra for eight hundred quid.

"Bit of rust, Jim. But she's a runner."

We loaded our stuff from the BMW into the Micra. I double-checked the glove box and under the BMW's front seats. I didn't want to leave anything that might get Frank into trouble.

The jacket from the hotel—the one I'd covered Natalie with last night—lay on the floor in the back. It had slipped off her shoulders when she clambered between the seats.

I stuffed it in the boot of the Micra with the rest of our stuff.

Ice floated on the oil in the puddles in Frank's forecourt. The cobbles were slippery with frost. The Micra started first go.

I headed East. East felt better than North, South, or West. The Star in the East. The Orient. Where Natalie came from, eight thousand miles East of the Thames Barrier.

She laughed as we passed an underground station.

"I do magic. See Sam. You do magic. See Frank."

"That's not magic. It's luck."

"Same thing."

Driving around southeast London with nowhere to go didn't feel much like luck either, let alone magic.

The real magic had been last night, in the bedroom in Stratford. It had been wild and scary: *the unapproachable woman looking back from her face, shining full-featured from every pore of her skin, as many-eyed as there were pinpoint jewels in her face, a tegument made of seeing, up which I travelled, diamond by diamond, towards her eyes.*

"You vics man." She didn't mean it. She was hysterical. She was still in shock. "I big Buddha woman."

"I'd rather just be myself."

Her eyes went bleak.

"Same I."

The Crystal Palace Royal Restaurant and Frank's Used Cars were just pinpoints on a timeless map. Sam and Frank were where space folded back on itself and hid us. But you have to pay a price for luck or magic. The price had something to do with her rice steamer and carrier bags of food, and my books, in the boot. 'I'd rather just be myself' and 'same I' were becoming more and more impossible.

It was after eleven.

"We've got to find somewhere to stay. I'm bushed."

"Chai."

I explained the hopelessness of finding anywhere. I had money now, but there was nowhere we could go. We'd be recognized in B and Bs and hotels. Renting a room or a flat was impossible. The landlord would demand IDs, bank checks, references. I couldn't turn to any of my friends for help, their addresses would all be on the police computers by now.

"Sam give I this..."

She sounded uncertain.

She took a slip of paper out of her pocket. It was the chit from Sam's restaurant. The bill for our breakfast. There was a telephone number on the back.

She handed it to me with a questioning look. She hadn't wanted to use it.

I bought new phones and sim cards in an Internet cafe.

"Sam good man."

"Yes."

I wasn't so sure.

"Sam say woman okay. She help you I."

I looked at her.

"Why? Why would she help us?"

Natalie shrugged.

"Don know."

I stared out at an arcade of shops, terrace houses petering out into an industrial estate. The city was endless.

"Alright. Give her a ring."

We pulled over and Natalie rang the number. It was a mobile number. Natalie talked for several minutes in Thai, looking at me and nodding.

She thrust the phone at me.

"She want speak you."

The woman had an accent that sounded Asian, but not Thai. She was a Mrs. Fairhazel. She spoke with the clucking breathiness of someone who's always busy. Her English was good.

She had a place we could stay. She gave me the address. I wrote it down on Sam's chit. It was back the way we'd come, past Bexleyheath.

"Two three seven Clay Pit Road." She was wheezing. She sounded stressed out. There were some arrangements she had to make before she could meet us there. "Two-thirty?"

It was only half past eleven.

We entered an area of stunning suburban-ness.

Street after street of small, identical bungalows; each on a small, identical, quarter acre block, each block just wide enough for a house and a driveway down one side of the house to the garage in the back garden. Tudor lead lights in one bay window, a lava lamp in the next, a Greenpeace decal in the next, couldn't mask the appalling sameness. We drove around crescents and along avenues without once seeing a corner shop or liquor store. There were no pedestrians, and almost no trees— these lightweight houses couldn't take root heave. It went on and on. It was as if an expanse of seaside chalets had been lifted from its cliff and plonked down in an urban vacuum. It was the sort of neighbourhood where not an uncollected milk bottle or unclipped privet leaf goes unnoticed.

"Is very quiet."

"We could try somewhere closer to the centre."

We'd spent three hours parked in some woods, telling each other stories about our radically different childhoods, pretending to kiss when dog walkers came too close. The three hours had flashed by, but it was still plenty of time for Mrs Fairhazel to have called the police, for the police to have contacted Adrian Whitely's people, and for Adrian Whitely's people to be waiting for us at two three seven Clay Pit Road.

The house had pink curtains. A JESUS DIED FOR OUR SINS poster hung in the bay window.

"I think we'll try Finsbury Park."

I started to pull away.

A door at the side of the house opened. A tubby woman in shiny, multi-coloured slacks came running down the drive, waving a piece of paper.

"Hello! Hello there!"

She'd seen our car; she'd quite possibly taken the license number from inside the house; she knew from Sam who we were.

I stopped the car, and let down the window. The woman leaned in. She had bronze, Malaccan features.

"How are you? So nice to meet you! You can park in here. In the drive." She trotted along beside me as I parked. "Careful of the asters!" There were orchids on her slacks. "I'm Mrs Fairhazel. Your letting agent."

My heart sank. I'd got the impression that Mrs. Fairhazel was a friend of Sam's, not an estate agent.

"Christian Home Finders!" She was panting from her sprint. "Dear me!"

She jammed her hand between her legs and bent double. For a second it looked as if she was struggling not to wet herself.

"My card!"

She handed me a business card. The card featured a silhouette of a church. CHRISTIAN HOME FINDERS' head office was THE VICARAGE, ST. DUNSTAN-ON-THE-HILL.

I gazed away down Clay Pit Road. It was very long. I couldn't see any hills.

Mrs Fairhazel beamed. She had a face like lovingly polished brass and a smile like a vase spilling lilies.

"My husband's the vicar. You're most welcome to join us. Morning Fellowship. Eleven o'clock. Every alternate Sunday."

I felt exhausted. Natalie's face was ashen.

"Actually, Mrs Fairhazel. We're not Christians."

Mrs Fairhazel's smile grew evangelical.

"Oh well. Never mind."

"We're... Buddhists..."

"Yes. Sam said. Not to worry. It's never too late to let Jesus into your heart!" The JESUS DIED FOR OUR SINS poster was black and white. The Cross. The Nailed Feet. The Crown of Thorns. Zig zag lettering like you'd see on a flyer for a Goth Rock venue. "Here's your tenancy agreement!"

I felt like crying. This wasn't refuge. We were getting tangled up and weighed down.

She handed me a pen.

The document was crumpled from her dash down the drive. Mrs. Fairhazel smoothed it flat on the Micra's bonnet.

The tenancy agreement lasted for one year.

I wondered if I should mention my inability to supply references.

"I know you'll be happy! The Handleys are such lovely people!" Mrs. Fairhazel waved at the pink curtains. For a moment, I thought the Handleys were inside, still packing. "I'm sure you'll look after the place!"

There was a degree of threat in her certainty.

"Yes. Yes, of course."

"The Handleys are off to toil in the field! They've taken the children, too! Isn't that wonderful? Africa!" Mrs. Fairhazel beamed down Clay Pit Road. It seemed even longer than before. "What an opportunity for Lisa and little Freddy!"

Mrs. Fairhazel nodded at the pen into my hand. She only wanted a month's rent as deposit and a month's rent in advance. She wasn't demanding references or bank checks. Sam had vouched for us. She must have seen our faces on the news and known what we'd done, but for some reason—Sam must have passed on something Natalie confided in him— we were a Holy Family on the run from Pharaoh.

I signed on the dotted line. The ballpoint ground against the paintwork. I handed over the cash for the deposit and two months rent in advance.

Mrs. Fairhazel took Natalie by the arm.

"You'll love the kitchen when you see it, Mrs...?"

Natalie looked dazed.

"Blight."

The house belonged to a window cleaner and his family. It was a small two-bedroom bungalow. It felt even tinier inside than it had looked from the road.

Mrs. Fairfield showed us around.

The kitchen was spotless. The sink gleamed. The work surfaces shone. The linoleum was white with grey flecks.

A letter, written in a child's hand, in every shade of coloured pencil imaginable, was attached to the fridge with a smiley magnet: WELCOME TO OUR HOME.

The capital letters were charmingly uneven. The writing was a young child's, but the words weren't. I could almost see the Handleys sitting at the kitchen table with Lisa or little Freddy and a box of crayons, dictating:

PLEASE. KITCHEN DOOR CLOSED AT ALL TIMES WHEN COOKING. SMELLS GREAT IN THE OVEN. NOT SO GREAT IN OUR CURTAINS.

Natalie's chili and ginger grass could make it through most kitchen doors I'd ever seen.

PLEASE. NO FOOD IN THE LIVING ROOM. STAINS LOVE CUSHIONS. CUSHIONS DON'T LOVE STAINS.

Natalie would have to spread her mats out on the linoleum.

ABSOLUTELY NO SMOKING. OUR HOME IS NOT A PASSIVE SMOKER. THE GARDEN IF YOU MUST.

I leaned over the sink and peered out through flounced gingham.

A wheelie barbecue hunkered under its hood. Hibiscus and choisya cowering against a fence. A tarpaulin-shrouded trampoline on a frost-stiffened lawn.

Natalie smoked thirty cigarettes a day. At five minutes a cigarette, that was two-and-a-half hours she was going to have to spend out there daily.

The DOs were less specific than the DON'Ts.

HAVE A GREAT STAY.

PLEASE RESPECT OUR NEIGHBOURS. THEY ARE: JEAN AND PHIL (NUMBER 235, LEFT SIDE FACING HOUSE) AND CRAIG, MERYL, SANDY, AND SIDNEY—THE HIGSONS— (NUMBER 239, RIGHT SIDE FACING HOUSE.)

DO USE THE TRAMPOLINE. (CHILDREN ONLY.)

WATCH OUT. THERE'S A THIEF ABOUT.

Mrs. Fairhazel showed us the bedrooms.

The first was a tiny box bedroom with double bunks, toys neatly stowed in plastic boxes, and finger paintings on the walls.

"The children's bedroom!"

Toilet roll sculptures on a kindergarten table. Disney posters: Beauty and the Beast. The Lion King. A reproduction I hadn't seen since I was a child: Jesus with a lantern in his hand, standing outside a gothic door in the middle of the night. Inside, little children visible through a lit window: 'Behold I Stand At The Door And Knock!'

I already felt claustrophobic. Part of me wanted to ask for my money back and get in the car and go. If the Handleys were toiling in the field in Africa, perhaps Natalie and I were the object of Christian charity and maybe even Christian opposition to the arms trade, but I still felt uneasy.

"The master bedroom!"

The master bedroom was bigger.

The floor was carpeted in white synthetic fur. The tubular steel bedhead had enamel finials, like bathroom fittings. The bed itself was encased in a quilted bedspread, with gussets for the pillows, and corded piping round the edge, where the floor-length quilting hung down neatly to the carpet. It was not a bedspread that was meant for sleeping under. It would require careful folding every night.

Mrs. Fairhazel pulled up the venetian blind, and there was Clay Pit Road.

"I'm sure you'll be comfortable."

"I'm sure we will."

I gave the bed a propitiatory bounce. The mattress had an evangelical springiness.

"And don't forget! Alternate Sundays at eleven!"

The minute she left, Natalie and I hurried back to the bedroom. We took our shoes off and crawled under the bedspread without undressing, and fell asleep in an instant.

When I woke, it was dark. Something flat and heavy lay on top of me. I couldn't kick it off. I was pinned under a sheet of lead.

Natalie was sound asleep.

The lead was quilted. It overflowed the edge of the bed and bound me down with its weight.

I thrashed my way out from underneath. Natalie didn't stir.

My feet sank into fur.

An electric clock read 21.43.

The Ten O'Clock News!

I hurried downstairs to the living room. There was no downstairs. I was in a bungalow.

I bumped along a narrow corridor towards a stream of light. The light came from a streetlamp somewhere outside the house. We'd forgotten to draw the curtains when Mrs Fairhazel left.

Each of the windows, across the road, was tinged an identical blue. I fumbled in the dark for the curtain strings.

The streetlamp shone like an x-ray through the crucifixion poster. The poster was even more hideous close-up, and back to front, than it had looked from out in the street.

The nailed feet took up the whole bottom half of the picture. A dizzying perspective swept upwards, past stretched-out arms, reduced at mid-height, to a tiny grimace under a pinhead crown of thorns. He looked like an aeroplane screwed to a runway.

SNIS RUO ROF DEID SUSEJ.

I picked at the sticky tape that fixed Him to the glass. It was ghastly. I had to get the thing down.

"No, honey! No! Can not!"

Natalie's hair was mussed. Her eyes were wild.

"Not you I house."

A carriage clock ticked on the mantelpiece. A shepherd girl glazed with streetlight watched from a china cabinet.

Natalie pointed at the windows opposite.

"Them see. Know you I here."

She was right.

I smoothed the poster flat against the glass and refastened the tape and drew the curtains. The room plunged into darkness.

"It's ten. The News!"

There was something wrong with the curtains. Natalie was drawing them apart and sweeping them together again, over and over, chopping at the satin folds to make them hang straight.

"Must do properly. Can not do no tidy."

She thrashed at the swags of satin. They were getting out of control.

The TV wouldn't work. I wondered if I'd broken it trying to turn it on.

The set had been switched off at the wall and the cord unplugged. I groped for the socket, plugged it in, switched on the power, and felt around the bottom of the set till I found the ON/OFF button.

A swarm of butterflies appeared on the screen. A cloud of Red Admirals was being blown sideways across the plains of Montana by a strong wind on the Discovery Channel. The butterflies were migrating to the warmer south, three thousand kilometres away.

They'd reached Arizona before I found the remote control.

The carriage clock chimed ten.

We sat on the sofa. The upholstery was shiny in some places and not shiny in other places, a mixture of silk-like smoothness and woven coarseness. The seat had a high camber. The backrest was too low. It was more like a shelf for the row of paisley cushions balanced perilously behind our heads than something to lean against.

The News At Ten fanfare zapped the murmuring butterfly commentary. The newsreader's voice homed in on the darkened room.

Venezuela. Mueller. A riot in Pakistan.

We sat very still and waited.

'... A woman linked to the Arms Fair hotel killing has been found dead in Stepney...'

Gigi. Pauline. Carla. Amy. Cyril hadn't been able to protect them after all. His safe house hadn't been safe at all.

'... The body of a woman, believed to be that of a prostitute seen leaving the Royal River Hotel in East London, was found this morning in a garage in Stepney...'

In an alleyway, a crowd of people milling behind police tape. A garage door hanging off its hinges. Something being carried out.

"No, honey! No! Can not!"

Natalie was tugging at my legs.

"No you I house! Don do!"

My feet were up on the coffee table! I'm not usually a slovenly person. My feet were sitting on the polished rosewood, rucking up the doily! I swung my heels off and she straightened the rucked-up lace with swipes like rabbit chops.

'... The woman, thought to be Albanian...'

A rerun of the CCTV images, a red, identifying ring around the blonde girl hobbling on one high heel as we fled down the footpath, stopping at the kerb to put on her second shoe.

'... Police believe the five women and their male accomplices may have stolen documents relating to high profile arms deals made at...'

Cyril, his face covered, just his dreads bobbing, shepherding Pauline, Carla, Amy and Gigi across the footpath, their heads buried in their jackets.

Natalie and I staring up at the camera; Natalie's eyes closed, mine open wide.

'... One of the men has been identified as James Leslie Bright...'

Melissa and the children would have received a visit by now.

"Can not stay, honey. No you I house, honey. Make no tidy."

Her shoulders were trembling. The Handleys had left the doily neatly draped over the coffee table, on the diagonal, with two corners hanging equidistant over the rosewood rim.

She pushed the square of lace backwards and forwards, left and right. She couldn't get the overhangs equal.

The house was freaking me out, too.

"We've got nowhere else to go."

"Must go. No you I house. Can not look after properly."

I took the doily away from her. I threw it on the floor. She was doing my head in.

I held her against me.

"It's okay. Gigi and Carla and Pauline and Amy. They're alright."

She was shaking. Her shoulders quaked. She was rubbing the seat of the sofa with the flat of her palm, trying to brush the coarse weave pattern smooth. She didn't understand that that was how the sofa was meant to look.

"She name Darya. She good girl."

"She should have stayed with Cyril."

"Give I sandwich." She gazed bleak-eyed round the dollhouse room. "They have caviar. They have oyster. Have staff give high class. Darya not eating. Bring sandwich."

She swatted at my shirt. My shirt was a crooked doily. My shirt pocket was a curtain that wouldn't hang straight. Her palm was clammy, brushing at my chest. It was a sofa we were getting grubby.

"Sandwich?"

"Albania girl like fish paste. No like caviar."

I crushed her in my arms. I couldn't stop her shaking. She was trembling so badly her breath came out in heaving gulps. The mark the string had left round her throat was still white and deep.

"It's okay. It's okay."

She didn't know me. I was a stranger, a jowly face, wavy black hair, a boyishly broken nose, a paunch thatched with thick black hair, crushing the life out of her.

"Can not stay, honey."

I didn't know her. She was a stranger, in a pink petticoat, swilling Listerine on a freezing footpath. I crushed her against me.

"It's alright."

"Must go. Can not live. Make dirty."

She swatted at my shirt. She hated me.

Maybe she was right. Perhaps we should leave. Right now. I didn't trust Mrs Fairhazel. I didn't want the Handley's charity. Their house was getting on top of me already.

"I love you, Jim."

"I love you too."

Her fingers slid under my belt.

"Wan do sex?"

"Okay."

I pushed my hand down the front of her jeans.

She unbuckled my belt.

The elastic of her panties was tight. I couldn't work my fingers under the waistband.

She rooted around for the slit of my Y-fronts.

Her labia were sopping. I got three fingers inside her. I was holding onto a slippery window ledge, about to drop.

I pushed her onto her back.

She stared up at me.

SPUNK LOVES OUR CUSHIONS. OUR CUSHIONS DON'T LOVE SPUNK.

She started to cry.

SMELLS GREAT IN THE SAUNA. NOT SO GREAT IN OUR CURTAINS.

We stumbled into the kitchen. My trousers were around my ankles.

The kitchen linoleum shone white in the moonlight, with a pattern of grey flecks like the shadows of blown sleet.

I put my hand inside her T-shirt. She was wearing a stiff, boxy bra, clipped at the front. I needed both hands to unfasten the clips.

She sat down on the kitchen table. I pulled my underpants off. The table squeaked. PLEASE. The Formica groaned. KITCHEN DOOR CLOSED AT ALL TIMES WHEN FUCKING.

The bathroom was too small. The bath glared coldly at us. There wasn't enough room on the floor under the basin. A half-empty bottle of lavender water stood on the window ledge. DO HELP YOURSELF.

We'd forgotten to turn the boiler on. The bedroom was freezing.

We pulled our clothes off and removed our socks.

We looked at the bedspread.

There wasn't a wrinkle or bump. Natalie had straightened it when she got out of the bed. She'd straightened the bedspread as smooth and perfect as the Handleys had left it. Even smoother. Even more perfect. We couldn't fuck underneath that, let alone on top of it.

"Ai-eeegh."

We pulled the bedspread off the bed and began folding it. We turned the pleats up into the middle. The pillow gussets wouldn't lie evenly. I rabbit-chopped them flat. We picked up the bedspread by its four corners, two corners each. It sagged in the centre. We folded once, twice, and marched towards each other with the bedspread at arm's length. I braced my buttocks backwards so my erection wouldn't touch the plumped nylon.

"Do again!" Natalie was in tears. "No do properly."

We had armfuls of pleats and quilting, a leaden tent dismantled in a gale. I stuffed it in the wardrobe.

We slid under the blankets. They were tucked so tight it was a struggle to get on top of her. We began to fuck.

"Can not, honey. No. No good." Her body was rigid. "Feel bad."

"Jesus!"

"Feel very bad."

My cock was wet and slippery. She held the sheet away so it wouldn't get stained as I pulled out.

"Outside."

"It's freezing."

"In car. Car better. Can put heating."

We stumbled down the hallway. My feet were blocks of ice. My cock ached in the cold. Her juice had turned freezing cold on my erection. In the moonlight from the kitchen window, her legs were the colour of hammered pewter.

The door of the children's bedroom stood open. The moonlight shone in.

"NO, HONEY! NO!"

The children slept in double bunks.

There was a Thomas The Tank Engine duvet on the top bunk, and a My Little Pony duvet on the bottom bunk.

A Brio train set had been packed away in a plastic crate.

A buxom doll ruled the bottom bunk, her long white skirts spread out on the pillow.

A box of coloured blocks and a Rice-Crispies-packet-and-toilet-roll-sculpture stood on a low kindergarten work table next to a Winnie The Pooh lamp.

The Handleys were good parents. They were starting Lisa and Freddy early with their writing and art.

Finger paintings and spidery crayon drawings shared the wall with the Disney posters and 'Behold I Stand At The Door And Knock.' A stick insect 'Daddy' and a fireball 'Mummy' had been framed.

The bottom bunk was too small for the two of us. The doll was daunting.

I pulled the duvet out from under her, and spread it on the floor.

Natalie stared down at the My Little Pony cover with blank, animal misery.

"Can not." I grabbed one of the kindergarten chairs and set it in the middle of the duvet. "No. Don want."

She stooped and switched on the lamp on the kindergarten table. It was shaped like a spreading oak tree. It shed green and brown mottled light on plastic animals sitting around the trunk eating honey. A droopy donkey. A bouncy tiger. A dopey bear.

"Fleezing." Her eyes were empty. No Buddha woman looked back from her face. The tegument made of seeing had turned to cold skin. Her pupils were black holes reflecting the brown and green of the lamp. "Wan I do oral?"

"No." I laughed out loud. I sounded crazy. "I just want to talk."

She frowned. She didn't get it.

I took her in my arms and stumbled. I fell backwards against the wall.

The ridges and hollows of finger paintings scratched my arse. BEHOLD I STAND AT THE DOOR AND KNOCK rustled beneath my occiput.

A smooth, bony mound ground against my erection. She'd shaved before she left for the party.

She grinned at me.

"Don do anal."

She got it after all. Our bodies were back in the past. They'd already ended.

She stood tiptoe on my foot. The ball of her right foot sank into the instep of my left foot.

"Ow!"

Her leg shot up around my hip.

I grabbed her bottom with both hands. She wanted me to lift her onto my cock, porno stud style. She wanted me to lift her off her feet and impale her rodeo manner. I cupped her bottom with both hands.

"No!"

For a second I thought she was dancing. Maybe this was some Thai style temple dancing thing. Her arms around my neck, lifting herself, gracefully, hieratically, her knee climbing my side like smooth-skinned forked lightning, her foot snaking into the small of my back with a sound of tearing paper as I entered her.

I couldn't move. She was too heavy. She dragged at my neck to pull herself up, but she was too heavy. Only her cunt kept climbing, swarming up my cock like a child shinning up a tree.

I tried to kiss her. She didn't want to kiss.

Her face was turned adamantly side-on, away from me, staring over her shoulder, craning further and further away from me.

Something was pursuing her. She slit her eyes at it, driving it back, away from her, her gaze a threat.

On the far wall BEAUTY AND THE BEAST came after her. A prince and princess— it was following the Beast's transformation— beside a fairy tale lake, rapturously enfolded in each other's arms.

The unapproachable woman roared in the back of my head. A vacuum lifted my scalp away from my skull, draining the light from the backs of my eyes, sucking the consciousness out of my brain. The stinging brightness held my neck in a radiant splint.

She pinned me to the wall. She shoved and slithered. Cold muscle slid from her cheekbone. The bones of her face shucked off their skin. She climbed me and collapsed, her frozen slip and slither white-hot in her cunt. We'd go on like this, fucking and fleeing, when we were two skeletons locked at the pelvis.

The night before the party, holding an unapproachable woman in my arms, who was and wasn't Natalie, I'd been another man. I'd ceased to be and come back into existence as someone other than myself. Her unapproachable body and someone other than me had gone together, deep into the darkness below dream, and seen a wash of purple light on a river, each lit wavelet and oily reflection pulsing from the touch of our skin. It had saved our lives, but we hadn't gone deep enough.

We saw it at the same instant—that we hadn't gone deep enough. BEAUTY AND THE BEAST let go of her. The prince and princess stopped chasing her. The fear of dissolution loosened its hold on me.

Our eyes met. She smiled, a crooked, girlish grin, a sublime smirk. A broad delight buckled her lips, laughter wincing at the corners. It was every smile she'd ever smiled. I was everyone and everything she'd ever smiled at. It was an unscarred smile, and a raw welt of a smile. It was a nubile smile and an old woman's. It was a shy grin at the fact that she was a Big Buddha Woman. It was the pleased smile of an angel girl. It was a smile that knew we'd thought the same thing. It was a smile that knew we were about to cease, together.

The unapproachable woman roared in the back of my head. I felt myself being drawn backwards, as if the clotted paper and crests and hollows of crumpled finger painting against my bum were a cloth through which I was being strained, backwards out of myself. The void into which I was being drawn was unbearable, but every time I became afraid of it, Natalie exploded in my mind. The smell of her hair erupted and vanished. The taste of her lips was an explosion, in another place, at another time, at the far end of the universe. It erupted and vanished. The depths of her eyes erupted and vanished. Her skin was an explosion, everywhere, at all times. It erupted and vanished. Her shapely weight on my cock, the ball of her foot on my instep was an explosion, a million miles away. It erupted and vanished. Her smile erupted and vanished, leaving me with just her.

Each eruption vanished into a pinpoint of light that turned up again a million miles away, on the other side of the universe, in another place and time, erupting and vanishing into a pinpoint of light that turned up again, in another dimension of space, somewhere where there was no time, erupting and vanishing and turning up again and again, the cat's-cradling points of an invisible dance, a hidden dancer steeple jacking from instant to instant, a new body pirouetting from two dead weights coupling against a wall, cart-wheeling from simultaneity to simultaneity. Not stopping. Dancing on and on. A stepping into the void, with nothing to prevent it. The void itself dancing. No spasm locking it to the shock of being.

CHAPTER NINE

We lived quietly. I risked a trip to the supermarket and brought back enough food to last us a month. We didn't go out for walks or use the garden. It was too cold to go outside anyway. The trampoline stayed wrapped in its frosted tarpaulin. We were happy.

Winter brought a late cold snap. Raw wind tossed handfuls of sleet at the house, like polystyrene pellets whispering against the windows.

When I wheeled the bin out—BINS NOT LEFT ON KERB (THURSDAY A.M.) WILL NOT BE COLLECTED—my feet skidded on black ice, and over I went. Peeking through the curtains, Natalie laughed like a child.

We were the only residents of Clay Pit Road who were not working.

For two hours every morning, a stream of headlights drove off into the dark. For two hours every night, the stream of headlights came home.

At seven fifteen each weeknight, Phil's headlights, Jean sitting beside him silhouetted in the dazzle, swept through our curtains and into their drive.

The worst hour of the day, four in the afternoon, as the approaching darkness drove a wedge of glare between the clouds and the rooftops, Meryl Higson brought her kids home from school in a blue Fiesta. Natalie and I watched through a crack in the venetians, a pair of seraphs gazing from a weightless world, as Meryl lugged the baby seat, the baby asleep in it, the shopping, and Sidney into her house.

Natalie stayed inside the whole time. Our kitchen door was at the side of the house, facing Phil and Jean's kitchen window. Slipping out for a cigarette was impossible. I suggested she use the bathroom—the bathroom had an extractor fan— but she was too fond of OUR HOME to make it A PASSIVE SMOKER. She stopped smoking instead.

She cooked and cleaned. She'd never had a home to look after before. There was a washing machine in the kitchen. She used it every day, hanging the wet clothes, sheets, table cloths, and cushion cases on a line in the bathroom. She ironed in the living room, watching the Discovery Channel and reruns of Columbo.

The house was spotless. The Handleys could have walked in at any hour of the night or day, and, except for the paintings missing in the children's bedroom, not been disappointed.

We didn't use their wardrobes. We kept our clothes, freshly washed, ironed and packed, by the front door in our suitcases, the jacket I'd picked up in the hotel draped over the top.

Alcohol wasn't mentioned in WELCOME TO OUR HOME—booze probably came under UNWRITEABLE— but we both stopped drinking. We were too keyed-up to drink. Alcohol would only have dulled the excited closeness that we felt.

The same went for sex. We'd woken up on the floor of the children's bedroom wrapped in a My Little Pony duvet, knowing that there could be no repeat of what had just happened against the wall, where the torn paintings hung forgivingly. Later. The future. One day when we'd made it out of here and were living our own lives, in a place of our own.

We'd been in the bungalow ten days without a knock at the door.

The SEX PARTY KILLING was still in the news, but the CCTV footage of Natalie and me was being shown less and less frequently.

The questioning of the dead girl's boyfriend, and her contacts with an Albanian gang, had resulted in some deportations, but failed to produce any fresh evidence in tracing 'James Leslie Bright and his Thai girlfriend.' It was hard to imagine what was going on in Islington, or how my family felt every time 'James Leslie Bright and his Thai girlfriend' were mentioned.

Natalie and I began to think ahead. We couldn't stay in Clay Pit Road forever. Even at Mrs. Fairhazel's reasonable rent, we were going to run out of money in three or four months' time. The neighbours' inquisitiveness as to who the Handleys' tenants might be, and why they never showed their faces, came through the walls tangibly, getting stronger by the day.

One Saturday afternoon, I heard Phil's leaf blower out in our drive, rounding up some debris that had blown in from the street, which I should have dealt with.

The following day, our doorbell rang. We crouched behind the living room curtains like children playing hide-n-seek.

The ringing went on and on. Whoever it was started thumping on the door.

Several minutes passed. The thumping stopped. Through a crack in the curtains, we saw little Sidney Higson marching home, bottom stuck out like a bailiff.

That evening, Natalie noticed a soccer ball on our back lawn whitening in the indignant frost. I darted out and threw it back over the fence.

We'd be safer out of the country, but my passport was in Islington, and Natalie didn't have a passport.

There were periods of claustrophobia when we set aside the practicalities of getting out of Clay Pit Road, and simply dreamed. Laos. Cambodia. Burma. Somewhere near the border with Northern Thailand. Natalie would never be able to go back to her village, but at least she'd be closer to her family. We held rambling conversations about a village somewhere in the mountains, a temple bell in the mist, Natalie singing by the fire, me chopping wood and carrying water, our unapproachable body dancing in the dew as the mist cleared.

I yearned to ring Cyril, find out if he was alright. That wince on the phone the last time I spoke to him, Cyril had been wounded worse than he'd let on. I longed for the reassurance of his unruffled voice, to plug in to some of that underworld knowhow. I reran his parting words to me over and over in my head: '...Those guys we saw, comin' up in the lift. They came to get the body. With Adrian Whitely. To get the body n kill Natalie n the other girls too n get the body outta the country on the quiet. But for some reason, I don't know what, they didn't... for some reason they left the body n contacted the police instead...' I'd missed something. I'd overlooked something important that Cyril had been trying to tell me. '...I dunno why Adrian Whitely went to the police. There must be people higher up he's got somethin' on. Fuck knows who else was at that party with the dead guy...' I was desperate to speak to him. There were times when, if I'd had his number, I might even have risked calling him.

I'd never in my life had so much free time. Even what I could remember of my childhood had been regimented in comparison. I used the time to study.

I got my books out of the car and lined them up in the kitchen, on the work surface between the microwave and the fridge.

I read at the kitchen table, while Natalie peeled garlic and pounded chili at the sink, the living room door closed, a draught stopper fighting the garlic, the curtains flapping in the open window, both of us too absorbed to feel the cold.

If Natalie was in the living room ironing, I'd sit on the sofa and read. My concentration had never been so sharp. I could get to the bottom of the Tao Te Ching and at the same time follow Columbo as he tangled the murderer in their own web of deceit.

I took copious notes, cross-referencing the Taoist, Tantric, Buddhist, and Alchemical texts. It was soon clear that they were all talking about the same thing. I composed the odd Tantra of my own. I had two degrees, but I'd never enjoyed university like this.

Natalie couldn't read, in Thai or English, but when she saw me absorbed in my books, she became curious about them. She picked them up, frowned at the covers, peppered me with questions. She asked me to explain what the books said. I got a real kick out of discussing metaphysics with a thirty-word vocabulary.

I explained the Buddhist doctrine of impermanence.

She shrugged.

"I know already."

She smiled as I raved on about the awakening of Unconditioned Consciousness.

"I do long time be fore."

She always knew more than I did.

We'd been granted an instant's precognition: *twenty-five storeys down, a wash of purple light on a river, each lit wavelet and oily reflection pulsing from our joined bodies.* The precognition had something to do with sex. It had happened during an out-of-body act of love—'out-of-body' was the wrong phrase—during *an intensification of consciousness* in which the body became husk-like, forgettable, the fact that it was over and done with superseded.

If Cyril hadn't come hammering at the door, the moment would have remained meaningless, a hallucination. If Cyril's concern for Natalie and the Thai girls hadn't dragged me through East London, along the embankment motorway, *the place, the moment, where she was* would have been just a sex dream. That particular intersection of space and time would have stayed unembodied. The fact that we'd found Natalie, the fact that the wash of purple that rocked on the water came down from the hotel balcony, where Natalie was, could only be explained if it were part of a larger, instantaneous pattern; a pattern that included Cyril and Pra, the bouncer on the boat; the security man stabbing Cyril;

Carla spitting into a tissue; Natalie out on the balcony; the river, the traffic, the whole of East London, and beyond, the ocean, the night, the stars, everything. It was crazy, yet it had happened.

It was insane, and yet there was an intelligence, even if only an impersonal intelligence, at the heart of the pattern. Intelligence has more energy than matter. Psyche is more real than soma. Consciousness is the source of the body. It's not the other way round, like people think. In fact, matter *is* intelligence. I pored over Hindu texts that spoke of a 'subtle body' that connects absolute spirit with absolute matter, a body made neither of vibrating electrons nor thought. *The Corpus Hermeticum* called it 'mercury'. Chuang Tzu said it was 'the circulation of the light'. It was the Linga Sarira, or unapproachable body, of Tantra. It was spoken of through metaphors of flow and current and descent, because it is the 'body' through which transcendence 'falls' and through which the Unmanifest is made manifest. It's the thread of light in the spine. It's the shining hinge in the backbone on which the world is constantly turning towards the incomprehensible.

By chance, or luck— and luck can be either good or ill—or an act of will, or a moment's love, the hinge stays still as the door slams and I'm shut out of transcendence by a door with a green star, ORIENTAL BABE on it, slamming, and suddenly the unapproachable woman is everything and everywhere, She Who Is Outside The Universe And Goes Upwards stands on a frozen footpath in my body.

The trouble is that, once the door has slammed, and infinite probability has collapsed into being, transcendence becomes the source of pain as well as of joy, as equally the source of evil as of good, and you've given up all your codes of conduct and personal principles to arrive at this terrible place. There's no way back. The collapse of spirit into unspeakable shallowness and the collapse of consciousness into the body's loneliness, that shuts out compassion, can only be taken back to its source in transcendence, knowing nothing and expecting even less. There's a necessary nihilism at the heart of a world that is only material, and once I'm in its grip there's no way back into simple goodness. Even simple goodness is downwards. Upwards, She Who Is Outside The Universe And Goes Upwards, is all that's left.

The *End Of Time* guy was right. Time feels all-powerful, but space is more powerful still. That was why I'd always remembered places more vividly than people. That was why, when it came to the past, people were the unseen presences of places. A bedroom in Kilburn. Islington. A cubicle in Hackney Sauna. The Handley's bungalow. Human presence is more real than place, but it needs a place, or at the very least the memory of a place, to cling onto if it is to be felt. *Where* is the ultimate emptiness at the heart of *who*. Space at the quantum level of multiple dimensions that Julian Barbour speaks about is something other than, and stronger than, the three-dimensional thing out there of which my body occupies a tiny volume. 'Space' is best understood in the Tantric sense, as an intensity, an essence, an infinity of possibilities focussing on fixed points. The universe is the wave function—all imaginable universes at all imaginable moments—hovering above a quintessential landscape. All of the past, all of the future, and all of the present are here, as configurations of space, in a *now*, which isn't a time at all.

Everything comes into its being, into the fact that it's over and done with, already ended, in the polarity of male and female. Sex is the only way Upwards. My tailbone yearning for her tailbone, two points of light fusing into the one brightness, rising like the candescence up a hurricane lamp, towards the source of all joy, and of all pain too, is all there is. Sex candescing into love. Lying in each others' arms, stinging heat pouring out of me into her, her frozenness pouring into me, at the very bottom, where even consciousness ends, the floor where dreams dissolve into blackness and all that is left is *where she is*.

Magic is real. We'd been granted an instant's precognition, and something deeper, even more precious than precognition.

'When the brain discovers something new, a new function is born, a new organism comes into being. We must challenge the brain itself, to find out whether it has the capacity, the energy, the drive, the intention, to break down this continuity of the past, so that, in the act of ending, the brain cells themselves undergo a change, a transformation.'

The challenge was correct, the only one worth making—but who or what does the challenging? *It can only be done*—who or what does it, can't be known. Who or what does the challenging, is already over, already dead. No matter how swift and seemingly instantaneous the signals are, that carry everything to the brain, everything is finished, it's dead by the time it gets there. This is the real terror of time, and not just regret for the past or fear of the future. I live in a dream state, in an illusory world—not because the world, the state I am in, doesn't exist—but because I can't see that everything, even the brain itself, is constantly, instantaneously finishing; and, that what, constantly, instantaneously resumes is new, something else, another reality. This is why the who or the what, or even the where, is a new body, dancing. It's a pinpoint vanishing and an unforeseeable turning up, consciousness jumping from place to place in two bodies as they make love, intelligence dancing in darkness, encompassing strangers, distances, fearful weights and forces, in its swaying hips, stamping feet, and in the ecstatic dip of its head.

Natalie was vacuuming in the hallway. She was singing to the tug and knock of the nozzle against the skirting board.

I sat in the kitchen, with a book open on the table, and listened.

She was singing a country-style ballad, a song of farewell. I'd seen the song's video on one of her Thai DVDs: a sultry chanteuse, a beautiful young girl on a starvation farm forced to leave her village for the big city, the tyres of the bus throwing up a plume of golden dust across the paddy fields as it carries her away. It was a sad song, but Natalie sang it happily.

The TV was on in the living room. It was four o'clock in the afternoon. Teletubbies was on. I remembered sitting with Sandra, watching the children's programme, while Natalie saw her last customer. I felt a rush of simple, unmitigated joy.

The book I was reading—Chiang Tzu's song of the hollow reed— wove in and out of the roar and knock of the Hoover and the Teletubbies' theme tune and Natalie's singing.

The vacuum cleaner stopped. Natalie came into the kitchen and searched for something under the sink.

In the living room, Teletubbies broke off. A news flash slice of fanfare interrupted the sudden silence.

'...A second body has been found in the hunt for the hotel killers...'

I got to the living room before Natalie did.

'...The body of a man, believed to be involved in the murder of the Arms Fair delegate, has been found in woods near Harold Hill...'

"Uh?"

Police vehicles. Officers in flak jackets milling in a clearing amongst trees. Men in white overalls ducking under police tape. A body bag.

'... Cyril Wainwright, sought by police in connection with the death of an arms' trader at the Royal River Hotel...'

I couldn't hear the TV.

Natalie was screaming. The screaming went on and on, a keening, wailing cry like I'd never heard in my life.

She had her hands over her ears. Her eyes were shut tight.

"Ai-eeeeeeeeeeeeeeeeee!" Leon helping a tall black woman into a car, jostled by cameramen, outside Shenfield police station. "Ai-eeeeeeeeeeeeeeeeee...!"

Natalie clutched her stomach and shrieked. The sound was high-pitched and relentless.

I put my arm around her shoulder. She threw it off. She rocked from side to side.

The newscaster's mouth moved soundlessly, drowned out by her keening.

There was a rerun of the CCTV footage from the hotel. Cyril's beads and corn rows ringed, as he shepherded Gigi across the footpath.

Another slice of fanfare. A toothy teenager was introducing the next program.

Natalie's screaming became punctuated by breathless, gabbling sobs. I was grateful for every one of them. She was saving me from having to face what had just happened.

"Is I do!"

"No. No it's not."

She yelled:

"IS I DO!" Snot and tears streamed down her face. "Cyril love I..."

"Yes."

"Cyril love I number one he girls..."

"Yes."

"... I KILL HE...!"

"No, you didn't."

"I go party."

Her whole body shivered, as if she were standing up to her neck in frozen water.

"Stop it. Lee made you go."

"No Lee! I! I wan kill man. Now Cyril die! IS I DO!"

"Don't be ridiculous. It's not your fault!"

"Police gon find us. Men come kill us. GOOD! I WAN! Is I do every thing!"

"Natalie," I said. I made her look at me, "it isn't just your fault. It's mine, too."

If I hadn't let my jealousy over Pra blind me, Cyril would still be here.

"I DON WAN LIVING! I wan die!"

She meant it.

One programme followed another. 4 O'Clock Club. Blue Peter. ChuckleVision. I switched off before the Six O'Clock News.

We went to bed. We didn't fold the bedspread. We crawled under it in our clothes. When I put my arm around her, she rolled away.

She was right. It was her fault that Cyril was dead. If she hadn't got involved with Adrian Whitely, Cyril would still be alive. If she hadn't exacted her bizarre vengeance for her sister's death, Cyril wouldn't have needed to protect *his* girls. Natalie was responsible for his death, but it was my fault as much as hers. If I'd seen the risk she was taking, instead of letting my jealousy about her and Pra blind me, Leon would still have a father, the tall black woman being helped into the police car would still have a husband. They'd lost everything. Natalie and I still had one another, even lying back to back in sleepless silence.

I listened to the wind keening around the corner of the house.

Cyril's underworld knowhow hadn't saved him. His safe house hadn't been safe enough.

I regretted never speaking to him since the morning he warned us to get out of the Stratford house. He'd scared me the first time I saw him, in Kilburn, he'd punched me, outside Adrian's Holland Park mansion, he worked for Lee, and yet now that he was dead

I yearned to talk to him again, about Leon's maths, the 'door', Thai birds on the sniff, anything. Natalie's childlike trust in Cyril's 'security' had got into me. Cyril could still save us, if he were still alive. If I'd been able to talk to him, he might have explained why the hunt for us involved both the police and Adrian Whitely, and not just the dead man's people. '... Those guys we saw comin' up in the lift. They came to get the body. With Adrian Whitely. To get the body n kill Natalie n the other girls too n get the body outta the country on the quiet... but for some reason, I dunno why, they left the body n contacted the police instead...' If I could speak to him, Cyril might have had time to figure out why Adrian Whitely had gone to the police instead of removing the body himself and hunting for us with his own people. Something—not just Natalie's escape—something tangible, that was even more important to Adrian Whitely than vengeance, had forced a change of plans. Cyril, with all his inside knowledge, might have worked out what it was. Now Cyril's knowhow, and the big, generous 'security' he offered, were gone.

Natalie's breathing grew lighter and gentler. She inched backwards in her sleep till our bodies touched.

I thought about dying.

Our only hope of staying alive was to separate. We were safer apart. Natalie would be less recognizable if she were on her own. On her own, she'd be just an Asian face, lost in the crowd. I would stand out less obviously as the man in the CCTV pictures if I didn't have Natalie with me. If Cyril's safe house couldn't protect him, Natalie and I stood no chance here. Sooner or later, Phil and Jean would catch us together. The Higsons were already wondering what was going on behind our drawn curtains. Neighbourhood Watch would figure out who we were.

I thought about dying. When it came, I wanted to be with Natalie. Separating was out of the question.

When I woke, it was still dark.

Natalie wasn't in the bed next to me.

I hurried into the kitchen.

There was a sheet of paper on the work surface, weighted down by a Thai-English dictionary.

'... Jin...' She'd only just started to learn to write English letters. '... love... *******'

She'd signed in Thai writing. I couldn't tell whether the courtly script said 'Natalie' or 'Nam Huan'.

I checked the suitcases by the front door.

She'd taken a small hold-all.

She didn't drive. She would have had to walk the mile and a half to the bus stop.

I had three thousand pounds in my wallet. It was still there. If she'd taken any money, it was only a twenty, or a fifty at the most.

I got ready to go. I had to find her before she did something stupid.

'I DON WAN LIVING! I wan die!' 'IS I DO!'

I could see her at the bus stop, trying to give the driver a fifty pound note, and not being let on.

'We drown our self.' Her eyes filling with tears. 'We drown our self two gether. Make this life bad for you I.' She was quite capable of killing herself over some junkie waiter's 'vics' fantasy.

She'd taken hardly any money. She intended staying in London, if she had any intentions at all.

She didn't have a passport. Surely she wouldn't attempt to leave the country.

I went through the suitcases, grabbing a few things.

I slung the jacket aside that I'd picked up in the hotel.

I stopped, and picked it up again.

It was a suit coat, stylishly cut, an expensive piece of tailoring. There was a maker's tag in the collar, a tailor in Dubai. The jacket was an Extra Large size, cut for a big man, with plenty of room at the front.

There was a passport in the inside breast pocket, a gilt and blue UAE passport with an eagle insignia, and a British Airways ticket poking out from inside it. Heathrow-Dubai. Monday the eighth of February. The day after the party.

Jowly face. Wavy black hair. A boyishly pugnacious nose. The photo on the passport was the dead man's.

His wallet was in the other inside breast pocket.

Credit cards. Cash. A memory stick tucked into an inner compartment.

I removed the money from the wallet. I didn't count it, but I knew it was quite a lot. I stuck it in with my own cash. I'd signed a year's tenancy agreement with Mrs Fairhazel, but I needed money more than Christian HomeFinders did. I left Mrs Fairhazel a note apologizing for our sudden departure and hoping my deposit would cover any inconvenience.

I put the wallet, the passport, the cash and the memory stick in my overcoat pocket.

I locked up the house, posted the keys through the letterbox, and hurried out to the garage, threw my things and the dead man's coat into the back seat of the car.

The Micra took forever to start.

I drove up and down Clay Pit Road. I passed St Dunstan-in-the Hill. The bungalows went on and on. I found the bus stop. There was no sign of Natalie. The driver must have let her on with her fifty pound note.

The suburban hinterland wasn't all bungalows. I passed the woods where we'd parked up, waiting to meet Mrs Fairhazel. Early morning dog walkers were walking their dogs around a lake. If she'd drowned herself there was no sign of it.

I took the memory stick out of my pocket. It was a 32 G
SanDisk, small enough to fit in the inner compartment of a wallet.

My laptop was in Islington.

I drove through a couple of suburban shopping centres. The
morning rush hour was picking up, but the internet cafes were still
closed. It was after ten, when I found one open in Bexleyheath.

The proprietor was Afghani. A photograph of the mosque in
Kabul hung on the wall amongst the phone card ads.

I paid my pound.

"Number one, boss."

There was a long row of computers, each with a battered chair
in front of it. Number one was by the window.

"Can I have the one at the end?"

The last computer in the row was at the back of the shop, next
to a door with STAFF ONLY on it.

"Number twenty four, boss."

He studied my face.

There was only one other customer this early, a dark-skinned
man on number nineteen, talking on Skype with a woman wearing
a veil.

I squeezed past him to number twenty-four.

My chair's backrest faced the ceiling. The legs shot around on
castors.

I opened my computer and plugged in the memory stick. The
proprietor was looking at me from behind the counter.

A sign above the row of computers said: NO PORN.
CUSTOMERS VISITING PORN WILL BE ASKED TO
LEAVE. NO REFUND.

The memory stick was locked.

The dark-skinned customer nodded his headphones, grunting
brusque replies.

I took out the dead man's wallet and emptied it on my desk.

Credit cards. Business cards. ATM receipts. A note in a script I couldn't read. A payment chit for a restaurant in Singapore. The receipt from a deposit slip for a bank I'd never heard of.

The contents of the wallet filled the desk.

The proprietor watched me as I sifted through the scraps of paper.

On the back of the bank receipt, some figures had been written in ballpoint pen. They appeared to be exchange rate calculations. Amongst the numbers there was a single letter: Q.

I typed in Q with different combinations of the surrounding numbers.

"Can I have another hour, please?"

"Okay, boss."

Forty minutes later, the memory stick opened.

It was a video, logged under its opening frame. A man standing over a woman. I clicked play. The video began to run.

I saw why Adrian's people would stop at nothing to get it back.

The proprietor strolled down the row of chairs. Picked up a Coke can. Glanced at the skyper's screen.

I clicked back to desktop.

The proprietor opened the STAFF ONLY door at my elbow, left it standing open, and went into a jumbled storeroom. He stepped over cardboard cartons and dusty monitors, and went out another door at the back.

I reopened the video.

It had been made to blackmail the men performing the sex acts it featured. Jack had been right when he spoke about sick, evil cunts.

A face I'd seen on TV, on Question Time, raping a young girl. She pleaded with him in a language I didn't know. I took my earphones off.

The girl stared straight at me. She couldn't see the camera. She didn't realize she was being filmed.

The proprietor's footsteps came back through the storeroom. I clicked back to desktop. The door shut. He glanced at my screen as he strolled back to his counter.

Black Ops. Judge Dread. Super Mario.

To go back to the video would be evil. I'd seen enough already.

Most of the sex acts began consensually but became abusive as the men lost control. A familiar diplomat, playacting with a whip, picked up a length of reinforcing rod and blood speckled the lens.

The women's faces swung from tough complicity to blind panic.

The videos appeared to have been shot in different locations around the world. In most of the clips the participants seemed unaware that they were being filmed—the women too terrified, the men too aroused to notice the camera— though in one or two of the segments the men participated in the filming too, their sadism not exciting enough, unless it was being recorded.

I'd seen enough. It was horrific. Simply looking at it was wrong. There was no reason for me to watch it to the end. I needed to tidy up the paper and credit cards that littered the desk and get out of here before the proprietor confronted me.

The clip featuring Adrian Whitely had been filmed in a hot country. In the background, a tamarind tree shimmered in an open window. I put my earphones on. Above murmured grunts and slapping sounds, birdsong of a brilliance you don't hear in England, jarred and shrilled. The multi-coloured wings of parrots flapped in the tamarind tree.

The camera slowly panned down from the tamarind tree in the window to Adrian and a woman on a bed. Adrian was having trouble getting it up. His clip took longer than the others. The woman sucked and gobbled. She was frantic. She was frightened.

She was making him angry. He slapped her face a couple of times with a bored liege majesté. He was still half flaccid when he entered her and picked up a small brown bottle, like a whisky short bottle. He unscrewed the lid, placed the mouth of the bottle to his nostril, and snorted it. A short time later there was what looked like a climax, the woman noisy, Adrian silent, recoiling with a grimace of distaste, glancing round at the tamarind shimmer and the squawks of the parrots, as if he'd sensed someone was watching.

As his body twitched, the woman's mesmerized stare relaxed into a dislocated smirk, of relief or pleasure it was impossible to say.

I decided to go and see Adrian Whitely. There was no way he'd want the contents of the memory stick made public, either the video of himself, or the clips of his colleagues. Cyril had said that Adrian had contacts with the police, and that it was Adrian who'd brought his people back to the hotel to kill Natalie and dispose of the dead man's body. *He'd come back to the hotel to get the memory stick.* It was clear why he wanted to get hold of it so badly. If I took it to the newspapers he and his sadist buddies, his ministerial contacts and arms trade fixers, would go down with him. It was no wonder Jack had been pumped up and paranoid. Jack had been right all along.

Seeing Adrian Whitely was even more urgent than looking for Natalie. Natalie was somewhere in London, maybe walking around steeling herself to 'I wan die', sitting on a station somewhere considering how to 'I NO WAN LIVING', unless she'd gone to the Leytonstone temple, or her mother's friend Yoot, or perhaps even Mrs Leepatawat. She might already have been picked up. She could be in a police station somewhere right now. It was imperative I get to Adrian. It was Adrian who was the real danger. Only Adrian could stop something dreadful happening. I could offer him the memory stick in return for Natalie's safety, and my own safety too. I needed to be careful how I did it, but there had to be some way I could let him know I had the video and use it to guarantee Natalie's safety, if Adrian did indeed have the power to call the sick, evil fuckers off.

I walked up to the counter and bought a memory stick. The proprietor looked at me. He knew I was copying porn. I made the copy as quickly as I could and left.

I had to find someone I could leave the copy of the video with, while I went to see Adrian. Adrian Whitely might have me killed if I couldn't convince him that there was someone holding a copy for me.

It was a lot to ask of anyone. Whoever looked after the copy would have to know what its contents were. Their life would be in danger. They'd be taking an enormous risk for my sake.

There wasn't a single person I could ask.

Before I met Natalie, I'd had lots of friends. Mates from university I'd known for decades, buddies I'd met through work, friends with kids I'd made while bringing up a family. They hadn't all turned their backs on me. A few had stayed in touch, but I couldn't repay their loyalty by dumping this burden on them now.

I could lie. I could tell Adrian I'd left the copy with someone and hope he believed me. If he didn't believe me, he'd simply take the memory stick and have me killed. Adrian would find Natalie, if she hadn't been picked up already, and Natalie would be killed too. I could risk it, but I felt too frightened to make the attempt. If I faltered in the lie, Adrian would know. He'd raise my bluff. If I lost my nerve, Natalie and I would both end up dead.

I drove around for several hours, uncertain what to do.

Ralph! Ralph was angry with me. He'd never forgive me for abandoning his mother. But he was still my son. Ralph was intelligent and brave. He'd look after the copy for me. I'd have to tell him what was in it, but he wouldn't refuse, he'd keep it for me, and if I never came back Ralph knew enough about the way things worked to pass the copy on to someone in the media. The media would take it. There was a journalist lived down the road from us in Islington, Chris Woodrow, whom Ralph could give it to.

I decided to take the memory stick directly to Chris myself. It was better than getting my son into trouble, especially with things being so difficult between us. I felt nervous about facing Ralph at all, let alone asking such a favour of him. Especially at university, in the middle of the day, during his lectures. Except... if I left the copy with Chris, Chris would have to know what was in it. He'd go straight ahead and publish it. He'd have to. The contents were too concerning to be left unpublished a single moment. If I couldn't get in touch with Adrian immediately my chance of using the memory stick to bargain for my safety, and Natalie's, would be gone. Adrian's people would find Natalie and kill me. Sooner or later they'd track Natalie down and avenge the sick, evil cunt's murder. I'd never see her again.

As a fifth year student writing a doctoral thesis, Ralph had been given a room at University College, where he worked on his research and gave tutorials to junior students.

His room was in the basement of the old college building in Gower Street, below pavement level, his high Victorian ceiling housing the Faculty of Medicine's boilers, heating ducts, dry risers, and ventilation units. I'd visited Ralph there on several occasions. During the day he had lectures. I'd only be really sure to catch him in his room around six o'clock.

The thought of waiting for six hours to see him, with Natalie wandering around London, was intolerable, but I dared not go hunting for him on campus. My face was too familiar from the CCTV, people knew I was his father. It was noon. I had six hours to get through before I could show up at his room. He usually worked there, writing his thesis, after six o'clock, and on into the evening.

I thought of going to the temple. Perhaps Natalie was with Pra. Seeking out Pra, Nok's father, a monk, would be natural, except they'd certainly be watching the temple. I didn't know Yoot's address. I didn't trust Mrs Leepatawat. For a couple of minutes I made up my mind to head for the Caledonian Road. Maybe Hassan had taken her in. But no. No way. The Caledonian Road was a terrible idea.

I drove around all afternoon, listening to a news station on the radio. There were updates on Cyril's death, but no mention of Natalie.

I crossed the river, stopped in a car park in Epping Forest, and tried to get some sleep.

A VW camper van pulled into the space beside me. The driver stared at me as he unpacked his fishing tackle.

I drove around some more. I felt safer on the move.

In Edmonton, a police car cruised past without pulling me over. Frank hadn't sold me out. The Micra's license number wasn't on the police computers. Sam and Mrs. Fairhazel had protected us, too.

I yearned to be back at two three seven Clay Pit Road. Natalie and I had been happy there. If she hadn't bolted, we might have been safe.

It got dark. Every time a newsflash came on the radio, I held my breath. There were further details of Cyril's murder but no updates on 'James Leslie Bright's Thai girlfriend'.

Around six p.m., on the North Circular, the petrol gauge hit empty.

I dared not run out of petrol on the ring road. I turned off the North Circular into a traffic jam in the one-way system around Tottenham Hale Station.

I could ditch the car and take the underground, but I felt too edgy to get on a train without drawing attention to myself.

The service station was big and busy. At the cash desk, the attendant did a double-take. He stood staring at me. Since yesterday afternoon, the CCTV footage from the hotel had been back on the news.

Certain that he was taking down my license number, I made myself walk slowly—not rush—back to the car.

It was half past five. I headed for the West End, against the peak-hour traffic.

I found a place to park, and walked down Gower Street on the college side of the footpath.

The university building took up the entire block. Looking down through the railings, I saw that Ralph's window was lit.

The vestibule was noisy. Bright-eyed young people heading home with rucksacks and briefcases. Porters chatting in their cubbyhole. Lecturers returning armloads of books to the library.

Coming in out of the darkness, the electric light fizzed. I avoided the crowd at the lift, and took the stairs down to the basement.

Ralph's office door was open. He was sitting at his desk.

"Dad!"

I'd forgotten what a frank, open expression my son had. The face I'd carried with me for the last two months had been constricted with anger. Ralph was glad to see me.

"Ralph."

I could hardly speak.

His face clouded.

"Are you alright?"

"Yes. I'm fine... You?" They'd been questioned by the police. Adrian's people had been to the house. Ralph had seen my face on TV, fleeing the hotel. He'd been worried about me. Footsteps passed on the pavement outside, high above our heads. "There's been no...?"

"The police have been hassling us. But Mum didn't know where you were." Ralph tried to sound cool. "Some guys came around."

"I'm sorry I dragged you into this."

Ralph shrugged.

"Into what? We had nothing to tell them."

It wasn't an accusation.

The security man stabbing Cyril. Carla spitting into a tissue. The body lying on the bed. Natalie out on the balcony with string around her neck. I needed to explain it all to him.

"How's Mum?"

"Okay." He said it too quickly, anger jumping in to protect her. "She's alright, on the surface."

"I didn't mean for any of this to happen, Ralph."

"No, I suppose not." Ralph could be sarcastic when he wanted, but there was a kindness in his irony. With his mother's chiselled features and blonde hair, and my height and build, he was an impressive man. "You didn't answer the petition. The divorce has gone through."

"Yes. Of course."

The divorce had hardly crossed my mind in the last couple of months.

"You know the firm went down the pan?" A man of the world. Telling it like it is. Ralph was young, but he had a grip on things. "Rampton Street went belly up. Bernard's set up under a new name."

"Actually, no, I didn't know."

"Jesus, Dad. What's happened? What's the matter with you?!"

I stared out his window, through its frame of ducts and cables, at a tiled wall.

I told him about the Tantric books I'd been studying.

"Yeah. Mum said." I explained about transcendence. It wasn't what I was really here to talk about. Ralph listened patiently. "I'm disappointed in you, Dad. I thought you had more brains than that."

"It's real."

"Yeah? It's not just? You know? That girl?" His irony was swallowed up by something deeper, that I couldn't name. Curiosity? Hatred? Tenderness?

"I love her, Ralph."

He'd watched the news, read the headlines. The sex party. The dead prostitute. Cyril. Natalie's face as I carried her across the footpath. I could hear the words on the tip of his tongue, bursting to fly out at me: 'It's just sex, Dad.' He didn't say them. He was young and passionate. Maybe he even believed me.

I got to my feet.

"I mightn't see you for a while, Ralph. I might be going... abroad. I could be away for a long time..."

The memory stick was in my pocket. So much evil inside two inches of plastic.

I looked into my son's suave, handsome face. Only someone as innocent and intelligent as Ralph could look after such evil and not be touched by it. I put my hand in my pocket.

"I just wanted to see you before I left."

He walked around from behind his desk and locked me in his arms.

"Yeah. Well, you take care, Dad."

I left the memory stick where it was and hugged him back.

It was eight o'clock when I got to Holland Park.

The plane trees lining the footpath formed a nave overarching the road, not cathedral-like so much as dimly secular— what had Jack called it? 'The Church of the New World Order'— their speckled trunks leaning away at a respectful angle from the Victorian mansions.

Adrian's house had its original wrought-iron awning from the footpath, up black-and-white-tiled steps, to a grandiose front door, its panels of scribed glass shielded by arabesque grilles.

There was a stillness behind the glass and iron, a weight in the towering stucco.

My hand hesitated on the bell pull.

I'd been stupid not leaving the copy of the video with someone. A slip of the tongue as I lied, and Adrian would have me killed. He'd find Natalie, and have her killed. There was no way round it. A quiver in my voice, a tremor of my hand as I showed him the memory stick, and both Natalie and I would end up dead.

I pulled the bronze knob.

Chimes echoed deep inside the house.

Footsteps, light and swift, bare feet on marble, hurried downstairs.

The door opened.

"Sawaddee Bee...?" She had two fifty pound notes in her hand. "... Ah...?" She took a step backwards. She was wearing traditional Thai peasant's costume. Blue pyjama trousers ballooned round her legs. A piece of blue silk was wound around her breasts. "... Jim...?" She glanced over her shoulder. Two men were coming towards us from the back of the house. "...Cannot!"

She tried to slam the door.

"Jim!" It was as if marble and cut glass had murmured my name. The greeting came from the top of the stairs. Adrian Whitely stood looking down at us. "Do come up." One of the men pointed a gun at my head. "Natalie, show Jim up, will you?"

I followed her up the stairs, under paintings the size of garage doors—Popes, Duchesses, putti, satyrs—in frames of ornately gilded fungus, the two men ascending after us.

She skipped up ahead of me, her bare feet already at home on the marble treads, her high-arched instep already certain of the smooth bullnoses, the fifty pound notes crumpled in her hand as she mounted.

A Sawaddee Bee Mai takeaway. A quiet night in. She believed in luck. She'd gambled and won.

Adrian waited at the head of the stairs. His expensive suit had the same slightly rumpled look I'd noticed when he came out of White's with Natalie on his arm. For a man with such wealth and position there was something unformed, almost jejune, about his face, something boyish about his double chins.

He showed me into a large sitting room and sat down on a divan. Natalie perched beside him. His men waited at the door.

"What can I do for you, Jim?" If she hadn't been here, I could have stayed strong. If she hadn't been sitting next to him, her peasant pyjamas pressed against his suit trousers, I could have looked him in the eye and toughed it out. I opened my mouth. He smiled. "I'm sorry. I didn't hear you. What was that?"

I didn't know where to begin.

The sitting room took up the whole first floor of the house. It was a 'salon orientale.'

Low divans. Teak thrones not meant for sitting in. Embroidered bolsters. Cloth-of-gold pillows. Lacquer screens. Battles and trysts. Conches and Shiva masks in display cases. A laptop on a marble coffee table. The room was so big, the standing Buddha by the window—fifteen feet of pitted, time-smoothed limestone—didn't look out of place. A Haydn symphony tripped along somewhere in the background.

Sitting on the divan beside him her hand resting on his knee— casually, not bar girl style— Natalie looked as at home as the rest of his collection.

"Jim, I'm not as surprised at your turning up as you might think." Adrian's voice was fastidiously quiet, his lips moue-ing the

words with a studied precision. "Natalie's been telling me what a
hero you are. Getting her out of the hotel with Cyril."

Natalie's eyes skittered away. She'd got a shock when she
opened the door. She hadn't guessed I'd come here.

Adrian nodded at his men lounging at the door.

"You led us quite a dance, Jim. How long has it been? Three
months? It's good of you to drop by."

This wasn't going to work. I was about to die. Not because
Natalie had betrayed me, but because I'd chosen to do what was
wrong over doing what was right. I'd made the wrong choices all
along. I should have gone to the newspapers. Even if Chris
Woodrow wouldn't take the memory stick, I should have given it to
someone, anyone, in the media, even if it was only to the internet
media, some crazy Youtuber, or one of Jack's bloggers. Sooner or
later the evidence on the memory stick might have put vicious
people behind bars, maybe even done some good out on the killing
fields where these people peddled their guns and bombs. I could
have done some good with the memory stick, and all I'd used it for
was to attempt to save myself.

My hand trembled in my pocket, plastic sliding on plastic like
two doomed dice. When Adrian had me searched this men would
find the memory sticks, deduce that they were the only copies, take
them both, and kill me.

"Well, Jim?"

He mouthed a cigarette from a packet. Natalie leaned towards
him and lit it. She made the blatant gesture wholly her own.

She was a gambler. Her eyes betrayed as little as her naked
shoulders, or the smooth hollows above her collarbones, or the
tight swell of her cleavage. When she'd left this morning, she'd
made a gambler's calculation: Adrian was crazy about her—I could
see that right in front of me, with my own eyes— Adrian was
hooked. The weeks he'd been grooming her for the party, Adrian

had fallen for her himself. He'd never have her killed. He'd shield her from the cartel's people. Now that the man in Jack's photo was dead, Adrian might well have even stepped into his shoes. Natalie had taken the plunge and scooped the pot.

"Well?"

I took one of the memory sticks out of my pocket. I didn't know whether it was the original or the copy.

"I found this in your dead friend's jacket." I needed to be forceful, but the words were coming out confused and hesitant. "Do you know what this has on it?"

"Mm."

"SORRY!?"

"No need to shout, Jim. I've a good idea. Yes. I've seen it."

My fingers were slippery. The memory stick slithered about in my palm. Adrian glanced at the two men standing in the doorway.

"I've made a copy..."

"Really?"

He sucked on his cigarette.

"I've left a copy with... someone..."

"'Someone'? Really?"

"... If I don't get in touch with... with my friend... by tomorrow... erm... nine o'clock... they'll take it to the... authorities..."

"Authorities? What authorities is that??" He slipped a cigarette out of his packet, and lit it from his unfinished cigarette. "I thinking you're bluffing." He handed the second cigarette to Natalie. "What do you think, thii rak?"

Natalie shrugged.

"Don know."

She did want to live, after all. 'IS I DO!' was true enough. 'I DON WAN LIVING!' was certainly heartfelt, but living was better than dying, even with the man who'd murdered Cyril and Darya.

The hand with the cigarette hovered in her lap. Her nails
grazed the coarse blue cotton around her waist, touching her scar
through her pants. Over the last few months it had healed. The
disfigurement had turned from a raw welt to a white shadow in her
skin.

"You're a terrible liar, Jim." An arm went around my neck.
My head jerked backwards. I was choking. A hand thrust into my
pocket, found the other memory stick and showed it to Adrian.
"I'm a gambler, too, Jim. I haven't got where I am today by being
scared of taking a risk."

He reached down and plugged the memory stick into the
computer.

Natalie sat up straight. She left her cigarette burning in the
ashtray.

"Cannot."

Her nails scratched the coarse cotton. Her palm rubbed against
the healed-up scar through her pants.

"Cannot what, thii rak?"

"You kill he. You kill I." Her nails picked at the vanished scar
through the cotton. Her eyes were wild. She held onto me with her
eyes as the waters of the Phraya river went over us. *She knew I'd
come. She was ensconced in this luxurious room because she knew I'd
turn up here.* I thrust the thought away. It was impossible. Fear was
putting ridiculous ideas in my head. "Cannot killing."

"He's trying to blackmail me, Natalie. I can't have that."

He clicked to the video on the computer.

"What's the code, Jim?"

A muzzle pressed against my temple.

I gave him the code and he punched it in.

"Cannot."

Natalie's voice sounded fragile, as if she'd suddenly lost
confidence in her English.

"Natalie! Don't be boring."

"You kill he. You kill I."

"Don't be hysterical, honey." He smiled at me. "Too many Thai soaps."

He pressed play.

Grunts. Panting. The Question Time man holding the girl down. Her eyes pleading with the camera.

"I make copy. I give monk."

"EH?!"

He was going to hit her.

Her nails gnawed at the cotton.

"I find in coat. I make copy."

"Natalie. Don't lie to me." He nodded at me, at the gun pressing into my temple. "You see what happens to people who lie to me?"

Dull thuds. The diplomat with the reinforcing rod. Specks of blood dappled the laptop's screen.

"I make copy. I give monk."

"Natalie," Adrian's voice trembled, "You're making me angry."

Her fingers were under her waistband, picking where the scar used to be.

"You kill he. Monk give TV."

For a moment, I thought it was true. She'd gone through the dead man's wallet without telling me, found a laptop in the bungalow—I'd never seen one—and made a copy and given it to Pra.

On the screen, a tamarind tree in a window, in a hot country, the screech of a parrot.

Adrian leant forward and clicked pause. The picture froze at a blur of multi-coloured wings lifting from fringed leaves and spinning tamarinds.

Natalie looked at me.

Adrian's voice turned quiet and fussy.

"You've watched it...okay... what's next?"

"Wah?"

She stiffened. She sat up even straighter, a scared child caught in a lie.

"What comes next, Natalie?" He nodded at the blaze of wings in the tree in a faraway window on the screen. "You said you watched it. You *know*, don't you?"

She stubbed her cigarette out in the large onyx ash tray.

"Know wha?"

"When you copied it. For your monk." He jabbed his finger at the screen. "WHAT COMES NEXT?!"

She looked dazed.

"Only see little bit."

"I don't believe you. You haven't made a copy."

She shut her eyes. She put on a knowing look, the big Buddha woman gazing into space/time. The angel girl studying a piece of wood with ink marks on it. She was as bad a liar as me.

"You."

"EH?!"

"You next."

"Me?" He sneered at her. "You're guessing, thii rak."

Her knowing look grew helpless. The big Buddha woman had been caught telling a lie.

"You do sex."

"Really?! I do sex, do I? Amazing! WHAT ABOUT 'I DO SEX'?!"

"Girl do oral. You cock don't go up." She spoke professionally, without condescension. "Take long time."

Adrian gave a sour pout.

"You could have told me that months ago." He sucked on his cigarette. "Be careful, Natalie. Be very very careful."

She looked at me helplessly.

"You do popper." So that was what the little brown bottle was. Adrian used amyl nitrate. He stared at her hard. "You smell popper."

So that was what the fruity smell was she'd come home with on her skin.

Adrian glanced at the man holding the gun to my head.

The big Buddha woman smiled. She was back in the pub in Marshal Street, gazing through the narrow gaps on either side of her field of vision, where she did her real looking, letting her eyes become mesmerized so she could see with her skin. She saw far more than what was entering her by way of her eyes. She let her mind slip out through her eyes and cover her whole body, her skin seeing everything, making everything vast and equal.

"Smell popper. Do sex okay. Girl happy happy." She stood up. She smiled at me. "Okay, honey. We going."

The muzzle dug into my temple.

Swift calculations skittered across Adrian's eyes. He only half believed her. He didn't believe her at all. He didn't believe in magic either, but we did. We were in love. That was all we cared about. He saw that we were in love and that that was all we cared about. If there was a second copy of the video it was safe with us.

He stared at her with sick longing and dismissed us with a wave of his hand.

We stampeded down the stairs. Natalie didn't wait to collect her things. Her bare feet rang on the marble treads.

We fled down the footpath to the car, bare branches soughing high above us.

The night was freezing. I searched the backseat for a coat for her. Socks. She had to put something on her feet.

"No, honey! No!" She ducked her head, peering up through the windscreen at the shivering branches, searching the speckled boughs for cameras. "Must quick lee!"

I looked back. There was no sign of Adrian's men. No one was following us, but my hands shook on the steering wheel. Something worse than Adrian was coming after us. We tore downhill towards the junction. Something worse than Adrian was catching up with us. Our tyres screamed round the corner as it touched us.

I swung right onto Holland Park Avenue, careening around buses, shooting past dawdlers in the fast lane.

Notting Hill Gate. Bayswater Road. Lancaster Gate.

We were safe. We were free. I was doing ninety heading for the roundabout. No one was following us. There was nothing in the rear view mirror but harmless headlights. I put my foot down.

Marble Arch wavered like a reflection in water. Lit quartz vanished in pinpoints of glitter.

I spun right.

Bare trees illuminated by tall buildings rippled the darkness and dissolved in the rear-view mirror.

Natalie's face flicked in and out of phosphorescence.

I swerved around Hyde Park Corner. A winged goddess rocked in her chariot.

Barbed wire foamed along brick coping. In a backwash of headlights, a man stood pissing against a tree.

Buckingham Palace. Parliament Square. We sped along the embankment. Charing Cross Station. The Savoy. Outside everything.

"Stop! Wan see river!"

I pulled over.

"Here. Put these on."

"Must quick lee! Must quick lee!"

She crossed the road in a pair of socks, my coat flying around her shoulders.

There was a gap in the embankment wall. Some steps led down to the water. We descended till we were shielded by the wall. There was nowhere further to run. We sat down.

The steps were cold. Wind disturbed the dark surface below us. There was a slap and gurgle of water on granite.

Two spears of light, one red-gold, thrown down from the Oxo tower, the other blue-gold, thrown down from a neon installation above the roof of the Hayward Gallery, flexed on the ripples.

On the opposite shore, wind pared pockets of mist and wisps of boiler fumes from the skyline, and, above pulsing city glow, skinned the stars.

"What we gon do?"

"I don't know."

It wasn't Adrian or his gunmen we'd fled. It wasn't the muzzle pressing into my temple. Adrian had believed Natalie enough to let us go. No one was coming after us. We were free.

It was the memory stick we were running from. We were fleeing from what we'd both seen. Finding the memory stick hadn't been a piece of luck at all. The video wasn't a free ticket out of a deadly situation. It never had been. It was the presence of evil. The things on the film were real. The blood that speckled the lens was as real as the granite we sat on. The thud of the rod, the grunts and panting and the crying were as real as the lapping of the water against the embankment wall. We'd soon forget it. We'd already begun putting it behind us. Forgetting was part of the horror. We'd paid for our freedom with the two memory sticks. We were glad that we had nothing to take to the newspapers.

I looked at her.

"Go to Thailand? Stay somewhere up north? With Nok?" I knew she'd had the fantasy too. Looking after her family. Bringing up her child. "The mountains?"

"Can not." Her eyes were bleak as the ruffled water. "Mum Nok's mummy. Not I."

She shivered inside my coat. The peasant trousers were for rich punters in heated rooms, not London on a raw night. The suckling cloth was for sex appeal, not warmth.

She looked at me.

"What you do?"

"Me? I don't know." My company had gone bust. Melissa had divorced me. Islington was finished. "I'll find something."

The wind changed direction. The ripples stood up straight. The neon spears zig-zagged towards each other, till only a patch of black water separated them.

"What about you?"

She shivered.

"Can not working. Don want." She couldn't read or write. Prostitution was the only job she knew. "Don know."

I put my arm around her.

"You saved me."

She shrugged.

"Same you save I. Come hotel with Cyril."

We stared at the water. We'd forget Cyril, too. We were running away from Cyril as surely as if his death was just another clip on the video.

"How did you know I'd come?"

She shrugged.

"Don know. Just know."

"You didn't copy the video, did you?"

She laughed.

"How I do? You find. Not I."

"How did you know what was on it? Adrian? The poppers?"

She smiled.

"I gambling girl. Prostitute woman say lie easy." She pressed against me. "I think Adrian be on video." She leaned her weight into me. "I know how he do sex."

A boat crept past near the other shore.

"But the poppers?"

That was what had saved us.

"I see they in you eye." Her laughter turned bleak. "I big Buddha woman. I number one vics girl. I see same you see."

"Don't laugh."

"Same you see light on river. Come hotel with Cyril."

"It happened. It's real."

It had happened, but then so had the things on the video happened. The magic was real, but the blood on the lens was real, too. Consciousness is the source of the body. There is intelligence at the heart of the pattern, but the World-Bewilderer makes no distinction between good and evil. She Who Is Outside The Universe And Goes Upwards treats suffering and joy the same.

"Look!" She pointed at the spears of light on the water. "Prince! Princess!"

The two filaments—one red-and-gold, the other blue-and-gold—arced towards each other, like two electric eels, failed to connect and fell back into oily blackness.

"Mm."

Prompted by a single mind, we stood.

Late-night headlights rustled along the embankment like autumn leaves in a horizontal flue.

"Let's go."

We turned our backs on the water.

Did you love *She who is Outside the Universe and Goes Upwards*?
Then you should read *The Happiness Wars*[1] by PAUL LYONS!

What was it like to live in a time when abortion was totally illegal,
and not only illegal but taboo?

How does a sunny Aussie family living the zip-a-dee-doo-dah
life in nineteen sixties Sydney deal with a prospect as radical as
abortion, particularly when their snobbish, Nietzsche-reading,
high IQ son falls in love with an underage country girl knocked up
by her uncle?

Happiness is a precious commodity and good people will do
terrible things to preserve it.

---

1. https://books2read.com/u/3JnEBA

2. https://books2read.com/u/3JnEBA

Also by PAUL LYONS

Eddy and the Fiend
The Happiness Wars
Big Des's Thai Angel
She who is Outside the Universe and Goes Upwards

About the Author

I am an australian author. My first novel, 'The Eden Man', Andre Deutsch, London 1987, won an Australian Literature Board New Writers Fellowship and a London Times Book Of The Year Award. The Guardian called it a 'laugh-out-loud' tour de force, 'sure not to be a one hit wonder', a prediction sadly incorrect. 'Natalie, A Kundalini Love Story' is a romance in the field of Buddhist Tantra, published by Life Force Books, California. I've worked in London as a builder and now live in Mae Suai, in Northern Thailand.

9 798223 333562